Raised in a farming family in Northamptonshire, England, **Jack Slater** had a varied career before settling in biomedical science. He has worked in farming, forestry, factories and shops as well as spending five years as a service engineer. Widowed by cancer at 33, he remarried in 2013 in the Channel Islands, where he worked for several months through the summer of 2012. He was forced to retire early from laboratory work by ill-health and now concentrates on writing and interests such as gardening, home-improvement, photography and genealogy. He has been writing since childhood, in both fiction and non-fiction. *Nowhere to Run* is his first crime novel and the first in the series of the DS Peter Gayle mysteries.

Also by Jack Slater

No Place To Hide
No Way Home

Nowhere to Run

JACK SLATER

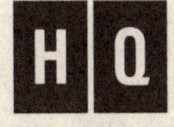

ONE PLACE. MANY STORIES

This novel is entirely a work of fiction. The names, characters and incidents portrayed in it are the work of the author's imagination. Any resemblance to actual persons, living or dead, events or localities is entirely coincidental.

HQ
An imprint of HarperCollins*Publishers* Ltd
1 London Bridge Street
London SE1 9GF

www.harpercollins.co.uk

HarperCollins*Publishers*
Macken House, 39/40 Mayor Street Upper,
Dublin 1 D01 C9W8

This paperback edition 2024

1
First published in Great Britain by
HQ, an imprint of HarperCollins*Publishers* Ltd 2017

Copyright © Julian Slatcher 2017

Julian Slatcher asserts the moral right to be
identified as the author of this work.
A catalogue record for this book is
available from the British Library.

ISBN: 9780008742904

This book contains FSC™ certified paper and other controlled sources
to ensure responsible forest management.

For more information visit: www.harpercollins.co.uk/green

Printed and bound in the UK using 100% renewable electricity
at CPI Group (UK) Ltd

All rights reserved. No part of this publication may be reproduced, stored in a retrieval system, or transmitted, in any form or by any means, electronic, mechanical, photocopying, recording or otherwise, without the prior permission of the publishers.

This book is sold subject to the condition that it shall not, by way of trade or otherwise, be lent, re-sold, hired out or otherwise circulated without the publisher's prior consent in any form of binding or cover other than that in which it is published and without a similar condition including this condition being imposed on the subsequent purchaser.

For Pru – my wife, my best friend, my partner in crime (fiction) and so much more.

Chapter 1

Lauren strained with aching fingers to get purchase on the knot, but all she managed to do was force it tighter around her already sore wrists.

She was breathing hard, heart fluttering in her chest as she struggled to escape. She closed her eyes in concentration. She could feel every strand of the tough, braided nylon. It was rubbing her skin raw, but she had to keep trying. Had to get loose. Had to get away before he came back.

In her ten troubled years she had dealt with all sorts of men, but none like this one. She had heard stories of perverts and child-molesters, had even met a couple, not that she'd known at the time, but this guy – he was more than that. He'd kill her. It was there in his eyes when he looked at her. He'd do what he wanted with her, then . . .

A sob escaped through the gag that was tied across her mouth as her fingers slipped off the rope yet again. She didn't have the strength for this.

*

Pete Gayle stepped into the Exeter CID squad room and a hearty cheer went up. He paused in the doorway, grinning. Glancing around the big, open-plan office, he saw that the noise was being made by a pitifully sparse crew. The place was almost empty, just his own team there, but they were certainly making up in volume what they lacked in numbers.

A bunch of helium balloons shot up over his desk, bright and multicoloured, on strings that held them about halfway to the ceiling. Two of his three DCs stood up, stretching a 'Welcome Back' banner between them.

He stepped forward and took a bow to enthusiastic applause.

'Welcome back, boss.'

'Good to see you, Sarge.' Grey-suited and grey-haired Dick Feeney threw him a salute with his free hand, the bright colours around him emphasising his colourless appearance.

'About time, too.' That was Dave Miles, at the other end of the banner from Dick.

Pete raised his arms. 'Thank you, fans. Thank you very much.' He headed towards them.

Clustered in the far front corner of the big office, his team consisted of Detective Constables Dave Miles, Dick Feeney and Jane Bennett and PCs Ben Myers and Jill Evans.

Dick and Dave pushed the banner onto a couple of pieces of Blu-tack on the wall behind them.

'Nice to be back, boss?' Dave gave him a lopsided grin. Long and lanky, he was dressed in dark trousers and an open-necked white shirt with a waistcoat over it, his dark hair neatly combed.

'I wouldn't know. I haven't even got to my desk yet.'

'It's good to see you, Sarge,' Jill said. Small, slender, dark and immaculate as always, Jill had been a caring but firm PC on the beat and had joined his team two and a half years ago, after impressing him on a case involving a homeless guy whose girlfriend had been raped and murdered. He had looked good for it, with no alibi and a history of drug abuse, but Jill had finally proved that he couldn't have done it and supported him through the process of finding out who had.

He was now off the streets and the gear, and working in a betting shop. Or, he had been, last Pete had heard.

'That's right,' added Ben, the spiky-haired and baby-faced newbie of the team, having moved into the office just over a year ago.

'What did Louise think of the idea?' asked Jane. Shockingly, her red hair, which she had always worn long, had been cut into a stylish bob, parted and swept back at the sides since he last saw her. It was a drastic change, but it suited her.

'She hardly noticed, to be honest,' he admitted. 'She doesn't take much interest in anything, lately.'

Jane's face fell. 'I'm sorry, boss.'

Pete shrugged as he reached his desk and sat down opposite her. 'So, what's the news? What's been happening?'

They sat, the celebratory mood broken.

'Well, today's all about Operation Natterjack,' Dave said. 'Bloody stupid name. Everybody's out, dragging drug dealers, distributors and manufacturers out of their beds and off the streets.'

'Which is why Colin wanted me back in today, to keep you lot under control. Yeah, I know about that,' Pete said. 'What else?'

There was a pause. Then Jane shrugged. 'Not a lot really, boss. We're just hoping for a nice, quiet day. Share a pizza for lunch. Keep the phones manned and wait for the glory boys to trickle back in with all their arrests, which they're going to have to do the paperwork on while we sit back and take the piss.'

He looked from one face to another but no one had anything else to say. 'OK then. A nice, quiet day it is. We hope.'

*

Lauren's cheeks were wet with tears, her chin slick with dribbled saliva. She had pulled and pushed, twisted and wiggled the ends of the finger-thick rope around her wrists, but all she had gained were aching arms and fingers and raw, abraded wrists. She had been trying for what seemed like ages. She was exhausted, no longer caring about how disgusting the gag in her mouth was with the spit and the snot and the tears.

God, she wished she had someone who would come looking for her. Come and rescue her from this bloody middle-of-nowhere barn and the arsehole bastard who'd dumped her here. But there was no one. If she was going to get out of this, it was down to her.

She sucked in a breath and, biting down on the wet gag, set to work once more, pushing through the pain.

Curling her fingers up and around, she touched the knot at her wrists and hooked her short nails into the rough strands. She burrowed one slender finger into the knot then wiggled it around as much as she could. If she could just force the rope back through, then get a hold on it . . . She felt it slip just a tiny bit.

'Yes,' she gasped.

Tension and excitement mingled in her stomach. She felt queasy as she tried again. *Yes, definitely.* She adjusted her grip and tried once more, pulling it straight up and – *yes!* It finally released. She wriggled her wrists and shook her arms. The bindings fell away and her arms slumped to her sides as she fell forward, howling in agony as her shoulders, stuck for so long in one position, dropped free. It was several seconds before she dared to try to lift her arms to untie the gag.

Vision blurred with tears of pain and relief, she could see redness around her wrists, but not how bad they were, as she loosened the gag and spat it out, then reached for the rope at her ankles.

Pulling the knot around to the front, she was glad for the first time of the knee-length white socks they made her wear for school. Quickly, she untied the thin rope and got to her feet. She staggered and put her hand out to the dusty stone wall, waiting a moment until she felt steady. Now she just had to get through those doors and she would be free!

There was no catch or lock on the inside.

She leaned her full weight against the junction of the big, old wooden panels and heaved.

Nothing.

'God! What now?' Her voice sounded strange after being gagged for so long. She felt reluctant to make a lot of noise. Not that she had heard any sign of anyone since the man left, but . . . If she was heard by a friend of his, and caught, then . . .

She flinched as a hiss came from the rafters, above and to her right, all the way at the end of the barn. She looked up into the darkness under the roof tiles. Saw a pair of eyes staring down at her. Then another pair.

'What are you looking at?' she muttered to the two young owls.

Their parents had it easy. They came in and out of the barn through a hole in the corner of the roof. She had watched them numerous times. She, on the other hand, had to get through these bloody doors.

Chapter 2

Pete heard the door open behind him. He finished pouring his coffee, put the jug back on the coffee maker and turned to see who had come into the small kitchen.

'Jane.'

'Hey, boss.'

'So, come on. What weren't you telling me earlier? What's been going on while I've been gone?' He took a sip of his coffee and moved aside so she could get some for herself.

'Well . . . there hasn't been much, really. Just the usual odds and sods. Burglaries . . . We cracked that string that we were working on when . . . well, you know. A hundred and eighty-seven, it ended up at. All down to one bloke. Derek Atkins. He's due in court in a couple of months.

'There was an illegal licence plate deal going on, down on the Marsh Barton industrial estate. We closed that down a few weeks back. They were making them and selling them for cash, without documentation, to all and sundry. Mainly crooks wanting falsies for getaway cars. Major coup, that was. The blokes doing it kept records of who they sold to, stupid sods. We got loads of leads out of that, for all over the place. Here, Dorset, Avon and Somerset, West Mids, Thames Valley, even the Met. I don't know how many cases got solved out of that one bust. Anyway, they're the highlights, I suppose.

'Currently, DS Phillips is on a job out at the airport, in conjunction with Transport Police and Customs and Excise. A smuggling ring. They're hoping to make some arrests on Wednesday, I think. And DS Hancock has got something else going on, on the industrial estate. A series of break-ins. Tools and equipment nicked and safes and cash boxes raided. I don't know all the details, but I don't think they've got much yet. What about you? How are you doing?'

Pete pursed his lips. He'd known Jane since they were in uniform together, eight or nine years ago. She'd been the first recruit to his team when he'd got his sergeant's stripes, closely followed by Dave, and he knew full well when she was prevaricating. 'Never mind me. What's been happening about Tommy?'

Jane sighed. 'Boss, you know how it works. You've got to stay out of that. If you don't, anything we find can be compromised.'

'I don't need lectures, Jane. I need facts. I'm his dad. I need to know what's happening and Simon's told me sweet FA over the last month or more.'

Jane grimaced. 'As far as I know, there's been nothing to tell. He hasn't got anywhere.'

'Well, why the hell not?' Pete set his coffee down before he spilt it. 'Surely, a missing kid – and a copper's kid at that – takes priority over a smuggling ring that the Transport guys should be handling on their own, anyway?'

'Of course. But they've got nothing new to work on. They've run down all the leads they had. It's like he's just disappeared off the face of the earth, from what I can gather. And I have been keeping up with things on the quiet.'

Pete sighed, reaching out to put a hand on her shoulder. 'Sorry, Jane. I'm just—'

'Frustrated to hell and back, I expect,' she cut in. 'We've been helping where we can, but it's Simon's case, so . . .' She shrugged. 'How's Louise coping?'

Pete pursed his lips. 'Not so good. If anything, she's been getting worse, not better, the past few weeks. And I can't seem to help. If I try, all she does is snap my head off, so . . . I just leave her to it as much as I can. I don't like to, but . . .' He shrugged.

'Must be tough on you, too, though, eh?'

'Yeah, well. It's supposed to be, isn't it? It was me that wasn't there to pick him up.'

'Oh, come on. It wasn't your fault.'

He felt a swell of bitter guilt. 'If I'd been there when I was supposed to be, it wouldn't have happened, would it?'

'Yes, but it wasn't like you forgot or didn't bother, was it? You were busy. Saving my arse, as it happened.'

Pete smiled, knowing what Dave Miles would have said to that, as persistently politically incorrect as he was. It was true; he had been working – caught up in an arrest with Jane and a couple of PCs. An arrest that had gone horribly wrong until he managed, somehow, to rescue the situation.

They'd gone to bring in a shopkeeper who had been using the cover of furniture imports to bring in cannabis from Thailand. A job that had, ultimately, been a contributing factor leading towards today's Operation Natterjack. But when they got there, the guy wasn't where they expected him to be. Instead, he was in the back room, unpacking a delivery. When Jane went in through the back door, a PC in tow, while Pete went in the front with the other uniform, the bloke had seen her badge and panicked. The Stanley knife in his hand had become a weapon. He'd grabbed her, threatening to cut her throat. It had taken Pete twenty minutes to talk him down.

Twenty minutes that made him late getting away at the end of his shift.

'What, so now it's your fault, is it?' he asked with a smile.

Jane's green eyes flashed. 'No. If anyone's to blame its Ranjit bloody Seekun, the bastard who held a knife to my throat. Or whoever actually took Tommy.'

'Mmm.' Pete picked up his coffee and took a sip. 'Ugh. This is bloody cold already.'

*

The doors at the back of the barn had straw bales stacked along in front of them, a double row then a single, like a line of seats in one of those old Roman places. Lauren imagined a row of men sitting there, watching her as she lay in the straw, and a shiver ran through her. Suddenly, it seemed to get darker and the temperature dropped. Then the noise started. An intense rattling on the roof above her. She wondered what the hell it was, then she heard a rustling from outside as well. Hail, she realised. But hail or not, she had to get out of here. She jumped up onto the bales, heaving at the doors behind, throwing all her weight into it.

The doors barely moved, but, as she pushed, she saw light down behind the bales.

A gap.

She jumped down, heaved on the bale in front of her and shrieked as she fell back, the bale coming away far more easily than she had expected. She got up, pulled another one away, then another. Behind them, the ancient wood had rotted away and a sheet of corrugated iron had been fixed over it, on the outside.

And metal could bend.

'Yes!' Lauren was breathing hard, but the excitement of possible escape kept her going. The rattle of hailstones on the roof continued as she sat down, put her feet against the metal and pushed.

*

By five o'clock, the squad room was back to full capacity and as noisy as Pete remembered it, with the incoming officers chatting and joking about the arrests they had made that morning. They had begun to drift in from mid-afternoon. Teams brought in the men and women they had arrested during the morning raids, processed them into custody and interviewed them, then came upstairs to type up their notes and reports. Even with an extra man on the custody desk, it was a slow process. Officers were frustrated and short-tempered by the time they got to the squad room, but when they came in and saw Pete at his desk, they each came over and welcomed him back, asked how he was doing, expressed their sympathy or asked after his wife and daughter.

Leaning back in his chair, his day almost over, Pete heard a phone ring among the hubbub and looked up to see whose it was. DS Mark Bridgman picked up his phone and held a hand up to the two men who were chatting next to his desk. Pete watched as he spoke briefly into the phone, then put it down and stood up, heading for the door to the DI's office at the far end of the squad room.

He knocked and went in. Emerged a minute later and returned to his desk.

'So, what do you reckon, boss?' Dave Miles asked.

Pete spun his chair back around.

Dave was looking at him with a half-smile. 'Looks like gardening season's over, so are you back for good, or what? Do you reckon you'll be able to stand the pace?'

'Well, if today's anything to go by, I reckon I'll cope.' *We'll see how Louise dealt with it when I get home*, he thought.

The door at the far end of the room opened and both DI Colin Underhill and DCI Adam Silverstone entered the room.

Hello. Something's up.

He hoped they were not going to make a meal out of welcoming him back. He'd had plenty of that through the afternoon. He didn't need the official version, especially from Silverstone. He sat up straighter in his chair as Underhill raised his hands for quiet.

Silverstone stepped up beside the older man. In his immaculate uniform, he looked exactly what he was – a career desk-jockey who'd barely know one end of a baton from the other and had certainly never felt the greasy collar of a drug-pusher or a burglar. Yet, he'd come into the force with degrees in professional policing and criminology, and was slated for swift promotion into the upper echelons. Hence his nickname among the lower ranks. The contrast between the two men was almost laughable. Colin was the bigger man in every sense apart from rank. An inch taller, a good four stones heavier, fifteen years older and hugely more experienced, he was a man-manager, not a pen-pusher. He'd walked the beat, come up through the ranks and he looked every inch of it in his slightly rumpled tweed jacket and cord trousers.

'Right,' said Silverstone. 'What's everyone doing at the moment? I need to know what cases each DS has on their desk, as of now, excluding this morning's haul. Mark?'

Bridgman looked up and set his pen down. 'We've got the city centre muggings and the break-ins down on the Marsh Barton industrial estate, sir. We're at a crucial stage with the muggings.'

The DCI nodded. 'Simon?'

Phillips glanced at Pete. 'Tommy and the Jane Doe, sir. And the airport job.'

'Jim?'

'We're leading on the drugs, sir. All this morning's stuff, plus trying to track down where it's coming from.'

'Right. OK. I think, Simon, you ought to have this new one. A missing girl. Thirteen years old. Rosie Whitlock. Dropped off at school this morning and never went in. Parents are Alistair and Jessica. Live in the St Leonard's area of the city. Mark's got the details.'

Pete spun around to face his team. 'What are we? Invisible?' He pushed himself up out of his chair as Dave shrugged.

'Maybe he thinks it's too soon for you, boss,' Jane suggested.

'I'm here, aren't I?'

*

With a sinking heart, Lauren peered through the gap she'd created at the blackened forest of stinging nettle stems beyond. But, she only had two choices – stay or go. And if she stayed . . . She didn't even want to think about what would happen to her. She grabbed a couple of big handfuls of loose straw, pushed it out through the gap in front of her, then started to wriggle through, arms in front of her face, hoping that the sleeves of her cardigan might offer some protection from the burning stings.

Metal scraped the back of her head and she ducked lower. She felt the dull edge dig into her shoulders. There was no going backward now, even if she wanted to. It was forward or nothing. As long as she didn't get stuck . . .

'Oh, God.' A vision filled her mind of her stuck half-in and half-out of the barn, wedged under this bloody door when the man came back and found her. Caught hold of her legs and . . . Throat clogged with terror, she scrambled forward. The old stems crackled like fire as they snapped and broke, adding to the noise of the hail. Then, between her panting breaths, she thought she heard something else.

She stopped moving. Held her breath, straining to hear.

'No, no, no.'

An engine.

He was coming.

She pulled herself forward. The corrugated iron pressed down on her backside. Her thighs. Then she was rolling out and free, curling into a ball to protect herself from the nettles, barely registering the miracle that she had yet to be stung. Her bare legs felt suddenly chilled. Goosebumps rose on her skin. She got up, pressing herself against the stone wall and looking around for the first time.

The hail was still coming down hard, thick enough that she could not see clearly through it. The nettles were bending and swaying beneath it – nettles that stretched away, dense black and brown, in front and to the right, all the way to a dense thorn hedge, beyond which lay open fields. To her left, there was a gap at the side of the barn, a barbed-wire fence and woodland, dark and inviting.

The van sounded terrifyingly close. She began to edge along the side of the old stone wall, reaching out with her left foot to press down the nettles, breaking the stems before moving over them. The engine stopped.

Oh, God. Her breathing got shallow and fast as terror gripped her.

He was here. She moved faster. At least the noise of the storm would mean he couldn't hear her.

The side door of the van slid open and she stepped forward, pushing through the wet stems rather than pressing them down. She would just have to suffer the consequences for the next couple of days.

But she was amazed to find that she wasn't stung.

She heard the door roll shut.

Nearly there. Just another metre to the end of the barn and about three more across the gap beyond. She ran and leapt for the fence and the sweet freedom of the dark and sheltering woods.

Chapter 3

Pete stalked up the length of the room as the two senior officers turned back into Colin's office.

The door had not quite closed behind them when his open hand hit it hard. Silverstone was halfway through the interconnecting door to his own office when the loud slap behind him made him stop and turn.

'A word. Sir,' Pete said stiffly.

The DCI's eyebrow rose. 'DS Gayle?'

Pete ignored Colin for now. He was standing behind his desk, out of the direct line between him and Silverstone. 'That case should have come to me and my team. You know it and I know it.'

'This is your first day back, Peter. And it's a missing girl.'

'So? I haven't got anything else on the board and if it's a missing girl, it's not likely to be related to Tom, is it? Paedos' 101. Basic training. Ninety-eight per cent of the time, they go for boys *or* girls. Not both.'

Silverstone stepped forward and let the door close behind him. 'That may be, but I still feel it's too close and too soon, Peter. I want the parents to know that the person handling this is on it one hundred per cent. No distractions.'

'Right. So, you give it to a guy who's already got a full caseload.

That makes sense. Sir. And what progress has DS Phillips made on the Jane Doe or my son?'

Silverstone sighed heavily. 'This is not about DS Phillips, Peter. Can you honestly tell me that you're ready to cope with something like this? Whether it's a boy or a girl? Because I don't know that you are, and I'm not going to risk the safety of a thirteen-year-old girl to prove a point.'

Not going to risk the safety of your promotion, more like, Pete thought. 'If I wasn't ready, I wouldn't be standing here. And I've got a damn good team behind me, so, even if you doubt me, there's no reason to doubt them.'

'It's not that I doubt you, Peter. Your abilities as a detective are well established. I simply don't want to put you in a position where you might become overwhelmed, for personal reasons – the similarities between this case and your own, albeit this one's a girl.'

DI Underhill sat down at last and Silverstone turned to him. 'Help me out here, Colin. What do you think? Honestly?'

'Honestly?'

Pete looked at him. Honesty was the last thing the DCI wanted from his deputy right now. What he wanted was support.

'I can see both sides here, sir,' the older man said. 'I mean, I can understand why you'd show Pete some consideration, in the circumstances, but I can also understand how it might leave him feeling frustrated. Not trusted. And how it will look to the rest of the guys out there.' He nodded towards the squad room.

Silverstone's eyebrows pinched closer together. 'And how is that, Detective Inspector?'

'Well, like you're hedging your bets, sir, possibly to the detriment of the case. And the girl.'

'I see.'

'What it comes down to, sir, is who's able to give the case most commitment at this moment in time. And I have to admit, Pete's right. If he's back with us fully and completely, it's him.'

Silverstone turned to face Pete. 'And are you, Detective Sergeant? Back with us fully and completely?'

'Yes, sir.'

The DCI sighed noisily. 'Very well. But I want you to share the case with DS Phillips. That way, if it does get too much, you can hand it over without any break in continuity. And it may tie in with what he's already working on, which was why I chose him to begin with.'

Pete drew a long, slow breath. What was he – some bloody rookie on his first job? He'd been a detective since before this jumped-up twat got to bloody secondary school. He didn't need his hand holding. He let the air out through his nose. 'Sir.' He turned away, grabbed the door handle and went back through to the squad room before he had a chance to let himself down.

'Simon.'

The younger detective looked up. Tall, but a couple of stones overweight, with curly brown hair and a baby face, he had been a DS just over two years and Pete still struggled to take him seriously in the role.

'Hi, Pete.'

'I'm taking that new case off your hands. The missing girl. DCI's had a change of heart.'

'You sure?'

'Don't you bloody start.'

'I mean that he's got a heart to change.'

Pete smiled. 'No, but he's changed something. What have you got?'

Simon handed him a sheet of paper. 'Just what you heard a few minutes ago. And the parents' address and phone number.'

'Apparently I've got to keep you in the loop. Might be a connection to your Jane Doe. What's that about?'

'She was found ten days ago in the river, down by Powderham Deer Park. About ten, eleven years old. Sexually assaulted, strangled and naked. We're still trying to find out who she was.'

'Shit.' Pete let his eyes close for a second as he absorbed that information. *Still trying to ID her and still trying to find Tommy. Some detective you are*, he thought. 'All right. We'll have to keep an open mind on a possible link then.'

'Yup.'

Pete went back to his desk and sat down. He put the report sheet on his desk, picked up the phone and, taking a deep breath, started dialling.

The phone was picked up almost before it had rung. 'Alistair Whitlock.'

'Mr Whitlock, this is DS Peter Gayle. I've just been handed your daughter's case and I'd like to come and talk to you about it – and your wife, if she's there?'

'She is.'

'Perfect.' He glanced at the address. 'We'll be there in a few minutes, OK?'

'Thank you.'

He put the phone down and stood up. 'Jane, you're with me.'

'Boss?'

'Interview time. The Whitlocks.' He headed for the door.

'Wh—We've got that now?'

'Yes. Come on, chop-chop.' He paused long enough to hold the door for her, then hurried on down the stairs, feet clattering on the polished concrete.

They were moving along the back corridor, towards the car park behind the police station, before she caught up with him. 'How did you swing this then?'

'By being open and honest. You didn't mention the Jane Doe earlier, when I asked you what had been going on. None of you did.'

'Yeah, well... We thought it might be a bit close to home, boss.'

He hit the release button by the back door and pushed through. The late afternoon air struck him with a chill that had not been there this morning. An after-effect of the hail storm they'd seen earlier, he guessed. 'You're driving.' He followed her across the car park towards her car. 'My son is missing, Jane. What we're talking about now is a murdered girl. How would that be close to home?'

'One paedo case, another potential one. We were trying to do you a favour, that's all.' She stopped at the side of her bright green Vauxhall Nova and pressed the button on the remote. The car beeped and the locks snapped open. They climbed in.

'If there's something to know, I want to know it, Jane. I'll hear things eventually. If they're sensitive, then maybe I'd be better hearing them from one of you, rather than some plod I barely know. Did you think of that?'

She sighed. 'No, boss. Sorry.' She slipped the car into gear and back out of her space. 'Where are we going?'

*

Lauren charged headlong through the green twilight of the woods, the hail a distant clatter on the leaves far above. Down here, it was almost dry, the ground firm beneath her flying feet. She did not look back or sideways, just concentrated on what was in front of her. Running, chest heaving, jumping over brambles and ferns, darting around trees, kicking through low-growing weeds, she went as fast as her exhausted legs would carry her. She had no idea how far these woods stretched, what they held or what lay beyond. She just knew she had to run, to get as far away from that barn as she could, to have any hope of escaping the man she was sure was behind her.

Chasing her.

She had heard the twang of the barbed wire as he jumped over it, the crashing of heavy footsteps through the undergrowth. He had shouted once.

'Hey! Come back here!'

But since then, nothing.

The noise she was making, combined with the rattle of the

hail on the leaves above her, covered any more distant sounds. But she knew he was still coming. He had to be. There was no way he'd have given up.

She hit a narrow trail, barely visible on the ground, and turned onto it. It was too narrow to be man-made – must have been an animal of some sort – but it had to be going somewhere and it was away from the barn, which was all she cared about for now.

She ran on.

The trail wove around trees and bramble thickets and weird little prickly bushes that she'd never seen before. She began to see light through the trees ahead. The edge of the wood? A pool? A road?

Her legs were getting wobbly and weak. Her chest and throat felt raw. It was hard to suck enough air into her burning lungs, but she had to keep going.

The brightness spread across her field of view. It had to be the edge of the woods. She had no idea what that meant but, whatever it was, she would deal with it when she got there. She just had to get there. Get away from the man behind her.

The trail was helping – it made the running easier – but she didn't know how much longer she could go on. She tripped on a root, staggered, exhausted, put out a hand to a narrow tree trunk for balance and pressed on. She couldn't stop. Not now. She glimpsed a grey sky between the leaves up ahead. Noticed that the rattle of hail had stopped. The storm was over. Then, lower down, she could see the bright green of leaves in sunshine. A hedge, maybe? A road?

She caught the glint of wire. A fence. The trail led right up to it and through into the long grass beyond. A huge, rough-textured oak tree stood just to the right, its bark green with algae.

She ran up to the fence, panting hoarsely and bent to climb through.

Then screamed as an arm darted around her waist and snatched her off her feet.

'Come here!'

Chapter 4

Traffic was queueing into the city on Heavitree Road, so Jane turned left out of the station.

'You look a damn sight better than you did last time I saw you,' she said as she changed up through the gears.

July, Pete recalled. Annie's tenth birthday. Jane and Dave had called round to give her a little something from the team and to let him and Louise know the latest on Tommy's case. Not that there had been much news to pass on. 'Yeah, well. I hadn't been sleeping too well for a few weeks by then.' He'd lain awake for hour after hour every night, getting up two or three times a night. Sometimes he would stand in Annie's doorway and just watch her sleep. Other times, he would wander the house, check the doors and windows or go to his office and sit at the computer, trying whatever he could think of in a search for clues – anything that would tell him where Tommy might have gone.

'It showed. You looked like you'd done five rounds with Frank Bruno.'

Pete grunted. 'Thanks. Back to my normal, handsome self now, am I?'

She slowed, indicating right. Gave him a brief laugh. 'Don't know about that, but you certainly look a bit more normal than you did then.'

'That's all right then. Wouldn't want to frighten the punters.'

She made the turn into a side street lined on both sides with parked cars and accelerated again.

'So, come on. What's the latest on Tommy?'

She glanced at him, meeting his gaze for an instant before returning her eyes to the road ahead. Sighed. 'There's nothing to tell. It's like he vanished into thin air.'

'Except people don't. He went somewhere, somehow.'

She took a left turn, working her way through the back streets towards the home of the Whitlocks. 'Well, yeah. But, how are we supposed to find out where and how if he wasn't seen?'

Pete sighed. This was not a discussion to be had with Jane. It wasn't her problem. It was Simon Phillips'. But, one thing he was certain of – there was no way the Whitlocks were going to suffer months of the same agony that he and Louise had. Not if he could help it. Whatever it took, he would find their daughter.

'Here we go.' Jane turned at another junction and drove slowly until she spotted the right number on a gatepost.

'Blimey, they ain't poor, are they?'

The house was set in its own neatly manicured grounds behind a high, thick hedge.

Jane turned in through high wooden gates that already stood open and parked in front of the double-width garage.

'You never been round this way before?' Pete asked as they stepped out and made their way to the front door.

'Don't get too much crime up here, do we? And you know me. I come from the other side of the river.'

Pete laughed. 'Well, that's closer than me. Only money round Okehampton is the old kind. Manor houses and the like.' He reached for the bell-push, but hadn't touched it when the door opened to reveal a man in shirtsleeves and smart trousers.

'Detective?'

'DS Peter Gayle. And this is DC Bennett.'

'Come in. My wife's through there.' He stood back and indicated a door to the right of the big hallway.

They went into a large, bright sitting room where Mrs Whitlock sat on one of three cream sofas, a barely touched cup and saucer on the coffee table in front of her. In her thirties, blonde hair held back from her face in a chignon, Pete could see that she was a woman of natural style and beauty, despite the haunted look she wore now.

Her husband followed them in and sat beside her, taking her hand. 'Please, have a seat. These are the detectives, Jess.'

She glanced up, clearly in shock.

Pete took the sofa at right angles to theirs. 'Pete Gayle. This is Jane Bennett. We just need to establish the facts of the situation, then we'll get out of your hair.'

'Please. Ask us anything,' Alistair said. 'Just . . . find her, Sergeant.'

Pete took out his notebook and saw Jane doing the same. 'That's what we're here for. Now, we only have what you told my colleague on the phone, so . . . We need to build as full a picture as we can.'

'Why? Surely, it's not Rosie's fault she's gone? What can we tell you that'll help find whoever took her?'

'If she's been abducted, rather than gone off on her own . . .'

'Of course she hasn't gone off on her own,' Whitlock snapped over him. 'She has no reason to. She's perfectly happy at home. And at school.'

Pete raised his hands. 'As I was saying, if that's the case, then whoever took her would have probably at least seen her before. It may well be someone she knows or someone you do. Or, if it was random, then one of you may have seen something out of the ordinary. Perhaps an unusual vehicle on the road out there.' He waved towards the street. 'Someone hanging around when you picked her up from school or in town. Anything.'

Whitlock squeezed his eyes shut and tilted his head back for a moment. 'I'm sorry. Where should we start?'

'We'll need a picture of her. As recent as possible. Mrs Whitlock, you took her to school this morning. Is that usual?'

She looked up, a dazed look in her hazel eyes, took her hand back from Alistair and clasped them in her lap. 'We share the job. Sometimes I do it, sometimes Alistair does.'

'All right. Which way did you go? As much detail as you can, please.'

She shook her head slightly. 'The same way as always. Left at the end of the road, bear right then turn right by the junior school. It's really not that far. We only drive her because she's never up in time to walk.'

'Did you see anything out of the ordinary along the way?'

'No.' She shook her head. 'Nothing. It was just an ordinary morning.'

'No one following you, perhaps?' Pete pushed. 'An unusual vehicle parked nearby when you got there? An accident or roadworks?'

'No, there was nothing. As I said, just a normal morning. I dropped Rosie barely a hundred yards from the school gates. There were mothers and kids everywhere, just like always. I pulled away and . . .' Her face crumpled and she covered it with her hands as she burst into tears. Her husband put an arm around her shoulders and held her.

Pete recalled Louise's similar reaction in this same situation, just a few months ago, and his own seething need to stop talking and get out there, searching for his child. Emotion swelled like a lump in his chest. 'I'm . . .' He coughed and cleared his throat. 'I'm sorry, Mrs Whitlock. But this is very necessary. You didn't see anyone you knew when you got there? Stop for a chat, maybe?'

She took a deep, shuddering breath and shook her head. 'As I said, I dropped her off, pulled away and went on to work.'

As she took out a tissue and dabbed at her eyes, Pete turned to her husband. 'And if you take Rosie to school, you go the same way?'

'Yes.'

'At the same time?'

'Of course.'

'And when you realised she was missing, you phoned her friends?'

'Yes. That was my first thought. Maybe she'd gone home with one of them. She doesn't have any evening activities on a Tuesday. But they said they hadn't seen her all day.' His voice seemed to clog. He swallowed.

Instinctively, Pete was inclined to believe the couple. They gave every appearance of being genuine and honest and, having been in this same situation himself, just a few months ago . . . Or was it that that made him feel this way? He was going to have to work hard to maintain his objectivity on this one. 'Evening activities?'

'She swims at county level. Loves tennis, too.'

He nodded. 'We'll need a list of her friends. Has she got a boyfriend?'

Jessica looked horrified while Alistair shook his head. 'Not that I'm aware of.'

'Mrs Whitlock?' Pete pushed.

'No. Good Lord, she's only thirteen.' She looked about to crumble again, but held herself together somehow.

'Of course. But, kids these days – you never know, do you? We also need to know about anywhere she goes regularly. Like for the tennis and swimming. Anywhere she goes with friends. Or with you or other family members.'

Alistair shook his head like a man confused by what was happening around him. 'She goes into town with her friends, like all teenage girls, and she has school and her sports. That's it, apart from the occasional party or sleepover and the usual family stuff.'

Pete nodded. 'If you could make us a list of her friends, with their contact details, and where she goes to swim and play tennis, then, sir.'

'Right.' He got up and stepped out of the room.

'Does she have a favourite place, Mrs Whitlock? Somewhere she might feel safe?'

'What? Why?' She looked confused.

Pete shrugged. 'We have to allow for every possibility.'

Alistair came back into the room, a small beige address book and a notepad and pen in his hands. 'What's this?'

'I was asking if there's anywhere Rosie might consider special. A safe haven. Favourite place. Anything like that.'

Alistair shook his head. 'We've never . . . Why would she need a place like that?'

'You'd be amazed at what goes on in kids' heads,' Jane said. 'She doesn't have any history of depression or anything like that, does she? Mood swings beyond what you'd expect from a teenage girl?'

'No. Certainly not.' Mrs Whitlock's eyes grew wide with outrage.

Alistair sat down and took her hand again. 'She's just a normal teenager.'

'What about school?' Pete asked, thinking of his son, Tommy. 'Is everything OK there? No undue pressure? Exams coming up?'

Jessica shook her head.

'Has she been bullied at all? At school or perhaps online?' Jane asked. 'On social media and so on.'

'She's not into that kind of thing,' Alistair said. 'She uses her mobile a fair amount, texting and chatting with her friends, but that's all as far as I know. And she's not bullied. She's very popular, by all accounts.'

'We'll need her computer, tablet, whatever, just to make sure,' Pete said. He'd still never seen Tommy's again after all this time, he remembered suddenly. He'd have to ask Simon about that. 'I expect she had her mobile with her?'

'Yes,' Jessica said softly. 'But it's switched off. Goes straight to voicemail. That was the first thing we tried when I came home.'

'OK. We'll need the number then, and the service provider. I take it it's all right for us to check the call log?'

'Of course.'

'And you, sir. You were already home?'

'Yes. I worked from home today. I'm a lawyer. Look, is anyone actually out there searching for Rosie, Sergeant?'

Pete paused, writing in his notebook, then looked up again. 'As soon as we have somewhere to search, we'll be going over it with a fine-tooth comb, sir. But we need all the information we can get in order to get to that stage. What other relatives are there?'

They glanced at each other and he spoke again. 'We both still have our parents. I have a brother, Jason . . .'

Pete noticed a faint grimace cross the woman's face.

'. . . Jess has a sister, Penny. Penny Child. She's divorced, but she's kept her husband's name.'

'So, she's single now?'

'No,' said Jessica. 'She's got a boyfriend. Michael Gibbons. They've been together – what?' She glanced at her husband. 'Two years or so? But what's this got to do with anything? None of the family would have—'

'And that's it?' Pete broke in.

'Family-wise, yes.'

'Right. We'll need a list of contacts – family, friends and colleagues – even if they don't know Rosie.'

Alistair frowned. 'Why?'

'For elimination and for cross-reference. People forget things, don't notice them, *do* notice them. You'd be surprised. Tell you what, you've got your little book there. While you do that for us, would it be OK if you made us all a drink, Mrs Whitlock? Jane can give you a hand.'

'OK,' she said, looking a little surprised by the request. 'I'm sorry. I should have offered before. It's just . . .'

'We understand.' He nodded to Jane to go with her, then waited until Jessica had led the way out of the room. 'Jane.' He got up and went to the door, stuck his head through and said quietly, 'Ask her about her brother-in-law. And if the girl's all right around her father, as well as anyone else you can think of. Grandfathers, friends.'

'Right, boss.'

'What was that about?' Alistair asked as Pete returned to his seat.

'Oh, just something I remembered at the last minute. How are you doing?' He glanced down at the notebook on the coffee table in front of the other man.

'Coming along.'

'So, you're a lawyer. What kind of law do you practice?'

'Corporate, Sergeant. Company takeovers, property purchases and sales, staff disputes, that sort of thing.'

'Big money involved at times then.'

'Yes. But it's the client's, not ours.'

'Nevertheless.' He glanced around the room. 'You're obviously not on the breadline.'

'*And*, Sergeant?'

'Well, one of the things we have to consider in these circumstances is the possibility of kidnapping. For ransom.'

'What?' He stopped writing as he stared at Pete in shock. 'I'm just a West Country lawyer, not some big City banker. Why on earth would that kind of thing affect me?'

Pete shrugged. 'You never know, sir.' In his own case, Simon had looked not just at ransom, but at the influence someone might want Pete to bring to any of the cases that were being worked at the time. 'You haven't received a demand of any kind?'

'Certainly not.'

'If you do, you will tell us?'

'Of course.'

'Only, very often, these things include a proviso that you

mustn't contact the police. It's never a good idea to go along with it. It's aimed at isolating you, making you more vulnerable, that's all.'

'As I said, Sergeant, we've heard nothing from anyone. And, if we do, we'll be sure to inform you.'

Pete nodded.

Alistair leaned back in his seat. 'Anyway, why are you – a sergeant – handling this? I thought an inspector would have come out.'

'That's the TV and the movies, sir. In the real world, especially these days, with all the cutbacks, there's usually only one DI in a station, if that. And he or she's in a more supervisory, management-type role than an active investigative one. They allocate cases, oversee progress and chip in if we ask them to.'

'I see.' He resumed writing, resting the pad on his raised knee. 'So, you were at home all day?'

'Yes.'

'And you didn't hear anything from the school, asking why Rosie hadn't turned up, anything like that?'

'No, they . . .' He sat forward again. 'It's not like your average comprehensive, Sergeant. They assume the students have some level of responsibility. They allow them a day for sickness before chasing them up.'

Pete grimaced. He'd never heard of a school treating its students like that before. Maybe a college or university, but not a senior school. 'OK. We spoke about her mobile and so on. Do we have your permission to check on your landline and Internet provider, too?'

'Of course. Anything that'll help find Rosie, though how they might is beyond me.'

'The more information we have, the better.' Hopefully, the records would allow him to verify Alistair's whereabouts for at least part of the day without needing to ask him directly at this stage. That could come later, if it proved necessary – statistically, the majority of missing kids were missing because of something a parent or close relative had done, but, at the same time, he knew how distressing that kind of suspicion could be. He remembered answering these same questions five months ago, from Simon Phillips. How he'd seethed to get out there, do something – anything – towards finding Tommy, instead of wasting time, answering damn fool questions.

Jane opened the door and held it for Mrs Whitlock to come through with a tray, which she put on the coffee table.

'Great. Just what we need,' Pete said, as she handed him a cup and saucer.

'Thanks, Jess. There we are, Sergeant. Rosie's mobile number is at the top. Our home line. Then you have my parents', Jessica's, my brother's, her sister's, Rosie's school. Her best friend is Becky Sanderson. We spoke to her earlier. You've got the numbers there for our tennis club, King's, plus Northbrook swimming pool, which she uses at this time of year because the outdoor one at Topsham is closed, my office and Jessica's school. The other ones are just friends of ours. Purely social. From uni and so on.'

'Excellent. Thank you. That should speed things up considerably.' He took a sip of his tea. 'So, she uses Topsham pool when it's open?'

'Yes.'

Tommy had enjoyed swimming, too, but he had never bothered with the open-air pool. Had preferred to stick to the indoor one in the city – where he'd been waiting for Pete to pick him up on the evening when he'd . . . Pete sucked air in through his teeth, breaking the chain of thought. 'One thing I would say. I don't know how – it baffles me, even after all these years – but it never takes the press long to get hold of things like this. My strong advice, for now, would be not to say anything to them. Just in case. As soon as we've established there's no reason not to keep things quiet, we'll probably call a press conference ourselves and involve you both in that, if you're up to it. It keeps things under control a bit, that way. Less intrusive, at least to start with.'

'Why wouldn't we want to talk to the press? Jessica asked. 'I'd have thought . . .'

'In case she was kidnapped,' Alistair said before Pete could reply. 'What?'

'It's unlikely,' Pete said gently. 'But if she was, and the press are already involved, that might not be a good thing.'

'Oh my God! I hadn't even thought of that. You mean, if it gets out they might . . .?'

Pete held up his free hand. 'As I say, it's only a faint possibility. It's just one of the things we have to consider at this stage.'

Clearly, the missing girl was desperately loved. Pete felt the old determination building inside him. He wasn't going to allow these people to go through what he and Louise were going through. He would do his level best to bring their daughter back alive and well, whatever the odds.

'God, this is unbelievable. It's just so awful!' She looked as if she was going to break down again.

'I'm sorry. I know how you feel, Mrs Whitlock, and—'

'Don't be so bloody patronising,' Alistair snapped. 'How the hell can you possibly know how we feel?'

'Sir, I . . .'

'Has your daughter ever gone missing, Sergeant?'

Pete felt himself go pale, a wave of coldness sweeping through him.

'DS Gayle lost his son in similar circumstances, just a few months ago, sir,' Jane said stiffly. 'So he knows exactly how it feels. I don't, but he does.'

'That'll do, Jane,' Pete said softly.

'I'm sorry. I didn't know.'

'Yes, well . . . As DS Gayle was saying, we'll do all we can to find your daughter and bring her back safe.'

*

Lauren woke in complete darkness, snuggled tight against the warm body of another person. For a brief moment she felt safe and cosseted. Then the smell of the hay brought her back to reality with a jerk. Who was this other person? Another girl. She smelled feminine. Lauren could feel her long hair, a skirt and bare legs against her own. Where had she come from? She tried to ask, but there was a gag in her mouth. She moved to free it but her hands were tied behind her with something thin and hard. Shifting in the hay, she found her ankles were bound too. Shit, they really meant business now.

'Iss OK.'

The other girl tried to say more, but was clearly also gagged.

'Uh-huh.' Lauren swallowed, but it went the wrong way and she began to choke and cough. She heard the other girl trying to say something through her gag, but couldn't make it out. Then she moved in the darkness. Lauren felt hands brush against her clothes. Her choking was getting more urgent as she fought for breath. The other girl's hands fumbled blindly, moving from her cardigan to her blouse to the knee-length sock that was tied across her face as a gag. She felt the gag being pulled away and stiffened her neck, pulling back to help. The knotted cloth snapped free and she was coughing and gasping.

Finally, with a clear airway, the coughing fit ended, leaving her panting for breath.

'Thanks,' she gasped. 'That nearly killed me. Roll over, I'll get yours.'

Lauren felt the girl roll away, heard the rustle of movement, then felt hair against her face. The girl's body pressed warm against hers before moving downward as Lauren went the other way until her head bumped painfully into the wall.

'Ouch. You'll have to go further. I've hit the wall,' she said.

'Uh-huh.'

Lauren rolled over and got to her knees. Felt around with her bound hands. 'Where are you?' The sharp ends of the hay dug into her shins, but she ignored them as she searched awkwardly. She touched wool, then cotton. Skin, firm over bone, then the softness of a cheek. Cloth. A sock. She grunted and fumbled along the tightly stretched material, towards the girl's mouth. Her finger brushed a lip and the girl grunted something. Lauren got a hold of the material and pulled. She felt the other girl pulling back, the material stretching. Lauren's fingers ached with the strain, but she kept pulling, straining to get the gag free. Then her fingers gave way. She cried out as sock snapped back into place and the other girl moaned in frustration.

'Sorry.'

They tried again. The girl opened her mouth as wide as she could, tilting her head and working her jaw to try to get it free. Lauren felt the gag catch briefly on the girl's front teeth, but then it was out.

'There.' Lauren heard the snap of the girl's teeth closing, then the draw of breath. 'No use yelling,' she said. 'Nobody will hear.'

The other girl moaned and rolled onto her back. 'Where are we? What's happening?'

Chapter 5

Pete waited until they were in the car and Jane had turned out of the Whitlocks' drive.

'So, what did you get from her?'

'You were right. She doesn't like her brother-in-law. He's way too familiar for her taste – with her and with Rosie – but she's not aware of any signs of actual abuse, from him or from anyone else. And, as a teacher, she should know what to look for.'

'Yes, but is she being honest? With us or with herself?'

Jane shrugged. 'I suppose she could be in denial because it's easier that way.'

'Regardless of what she says, we've got to check everyone out for ourselves. Friends, family, colleagues, the lot. I'd better phone Lou. Tell her I'm going to be late.'

'You already are, boss. You should have been home forty minutes ago.'

'Shit.' He pulled his mobile from his pocket, called up his home phone and hit 'dial'.

'Hello?'

'Lou? It's me. Sorry, love, I'm running a bit late. We had a case come in about twenty minutes before I was due to knock off. The kind of thing I can't just leave to the morning.'

'Why's it got to be yours?'

'Everybody else has got a full caseload. I'm just back, so mine's empty. Simple as that.' He shot Jane a glance that told her to keep her raised eyebrow to herself.

He heard Louise sigh on the other end of the phone. 'All right.'

'I'll bring fish and chips, how's that?'

'We'll see you when we see you then.'

'I shan't be too late.' He ended the call and looked across at Jane.

'None of my business, boss.' She shrugged.

'That's right. But, no, I'm not deliberately trying to stay away from home. This does need sorting. And she wouldn't understand that, in the circumstances, so I just tried to make both our lives easier, all right?'

'So, where do we start?'

'We need to speak to this Becky Sanderson and do background checks on the people Alistair Whitlock's given us. Also, we need to check Jessica's route from home to the school for CCTV cameras, get the call log on Rosie's phone and see if we can get into her laptop. Then we see who we can get hold of and go from there.'

*

'We're in a barn in the middle of bloody nowhere. And what's going on is some sicko bastard and his sidekick have snatched us and put us here, to play with as they feel like.'

'But . . .' The girl paused. 'You mean . . .'

'Yeah. Bloody paedos.' Lauren shuddered. 'Perverts.'

'What's your name?' The girl was well spoken, almost posh sounding.

'Lauren Carter. What's yours?'

'Rosie. Rosie Whitlock. How old are you?'

'Ten last month. You?'

'Thirteen.'

'Well, thanks again for getting that bloody gag out of my

mouth. I bloody near choked on it.' She felt the damp material hanging around her neck like a cowboy's bandana.

'That's all right. Thanks for helping with mine.'

'So, what now?'

'What do you mean?'

'Well, we've got to get out of here, haven't we? I mean, for one thing, they're not going to like it that we've got our gags off. Plus, if we stay put, they're going to . . . Well, you know what they're going to do.'

'Oh God!'

'Yeah, where's *he* when you need him?'

*

Pete handed Rosie Whitlock's laptop to Dave Miles.

'Here, see if you can get into that, will you?' He sat down at his desk. 'Jane, you get hold of Becky Sanderson. Find out what she's got to say about Rosie. Is Colin still in?' He directed the question to Dave.

'No, he's gone off home.'

'What about Fast-track Phil?'

'In his office.'

'He would be, wouldn't he? OK, I'll go and have a word.' He got up and headed for Adam Silverstone's office, going via the corridor, rather than through the DI's office. He knocked sharply on the door.

'Come.'

He stepped in. Silverstone was behind his desk, a file open in front of him. 'Ah, Peter. What have we got?'

He closed the file as Pete shut the door and stood opposite him.

'A thirteen-year-old girl, the mother a junior school teacher, father a corporate lawyer, disappeared from outside her school. Bearing in mind their address in St Leonard's and the school she goes to, which is Risingbrook, we have to at least consider the possibility of a kidnap, although there's been no contact as yet, according to the parents.'

'And you believe them?'

'Yes, sir.'

'So, we need to get a team in there for the night and perhaps tomorrow. Phone taps on landline and mobiles so that we can trace any callers.'

'Yes, sir.'

'I take it you've got their permission for all that?'

'Sir.' Pete nodded.

'I'll get on to HQ and set it up then. Perhaps Jane can go with the team, to introduce them. I'll also get on to the press office, get them to hold off until we've established a few of the facts. And you're following up other leads, I take it?'

'Friends and family. Local paedophiles. Possible contacts on her mobile and computer. Considering the time of day, there's only so much we can do immediately, of course. But, come morning, we can look for possible witnesses and so on. Go down to the school and interview parents, teachers and pupils.'

'Quite. Carry on then, Peter. And let me know if you need more manpower. As I said, we have to give this top priority.'

'Sir.'

Silverstone was lifting his phone as Pete turned to leave.

Back at his desk, he saw that Dave was working on Rosie's laptop. 'Any joy yet, Dave?'

'Not yet. I got on to her mobile phone provider, though, got her call log. Nothing out of the ordinary on it. No calls from unusual numbers. And I had it pinged to get its location, but it's not just off, it's completely dead.'

So, the battery and/or SIM card had been removed. Someone wasn't stupid, Pete thought. If this was an abduction, that was not a good sign. And how many thirteen-year-olds knew that you had to take the battery out of a phone to prevent it giving away its location, even if it was turned off? 'I don't like that. Not at all. I'll get onto the PND and see what I can find out about the people on Alistair's list.' He fired up his computer and logged in to the Police National Database. With Alistair Whitlock's list at his elbow, he began to search.

First Jason Whitlock then Michael Gibbons came up clean. No criminal record or known associations on either. He looked up. 'Jane, have you got the names of Becky Sanderson's parents there?'

She put a hand over her phone. 'Neil and Geraldine.' She returned her attention to the person on the other end of the line. 'Sorry about that. You were saying . . .?'

Pete typed Neil Sanderson into the computer. The screen flashed up.

'Hello.'

'Thank you,' Jane said into the phone and hung up. 'What you got, boss?'

'Neil Sanderson. No criminal record. Regular CRB checks. Looks like he's into judo. And, it says here, he's a known associate of one of Jim's customers, downstairs in the holding cells. One Stephen Lockwood. Priors for drug possession and distribution and living off immoral earnings.'

'Ooh. A pimp and a pusher. Maybe we'd best go and have a word?'

'I'll call down first, see who actually brought him in. Don't want to go stepping on toes as soon as I get my foot back in the door, do I?'

Jane laughed.

'What, you going soft in your old age, boss?' Dave asked, looking up from Rosie's laptop.

'I suppose you've never heard of old age and treachery, Dave.'

'What?'

'It always beats youth and skill.' Jane grinned. 'Not that you've got that much youth on your side.'

'Oi!' He hit a key on the laptop and sat back abruptly in his chair. 'Gotcha. I've got into this thing though.'

'Well, she didn't keep a paper diary,' Pete said. 'So, if there's going to be anything to indicate she was unhappy at home or at school, it should be on there. What did Becky Sanderson have to say?'

'She's not aware of anything wrong in Rosie's life, boss. No bullying, cyber or otherwise. Apparently, she's quite the girl to be seen with. A leader, not a follower. Not a bad girl though. Good grades, into sports, friendly. An all-round nice kid. She just didn't turn up at school today. No phone call, no text, no nothing. And it's not something she's done before. Not her style at all. She's too conscientious.'

'Boyfriends?'

'Not that Becky's aware of. And you saw her parents' reaction to the idea.'

The phone on Pete's desk rang and he picked it up. 'DS Gayle.'

'This is DS Parker from Middlemoor. Communications. I gather you need a phone tap set up?'

'Ah. Yes. Possible kidnap. Seems unlikely, but we've got to cover all bases. The address is in St Leonard's. My DC's been there. She can go with you and give you the intro, if you pick her up from here.'

'Right. We'll be there in twenty.'

He put the phone down and Jane was looking at him, eyebrows raised. 'Nice of you to volunteer me, boss.'

'I didn't. Fast-track did. I just forgot to tell you. It shouldn't take long if you go in your car. Just lead them round there, introduce them, then you can scoot off.'

'What about all this?' She indicated the paperwork on her desk, her notebook, computer and phone.

'There's only so much we can do tonight,' he said. 'I'll stay and carry on. What about you, Dave?'

'I'm all right. I can stop as long as it needs.'

'Right. Between the two of us, what we can do at this time of day won't take too long.'

'OK. Thanks, then, boss.' She got up, picked up her coat and bag and headed for the door. 'Goodnight.'

''Night, Red,' Dave called, closing Rosie's computer down and setting it aside. 'So, what else do we need to do, boss?'

'Well, when you're done with that thing, there's the parents' alibis to check, you could carry on down this list of contacts or see who we've got in the area in the way of known paedophiles and check on them.'

'Right. Lovely.'

'Meantime, I'll see about Stephen Lockwood.' He slid the list across to Dave, picked up the phone and dialled an internal number.

'Custody desk. Sergeant James.'

'Bob. Pete Gayle. You've got a guest down there, Stephen Lockwood. Who was his AO?'

'Hello, Pete. How you doing? Hold on, I'll find out for you.'

Pete waited, hearing the tapping of a keyboard behind James' heavy breathing. 'Here we are. The man himself. Jim Hancock. Why? What's up?'

'Oh, I might have a connection with another case. I'll talk to you later.'

'Cheers, Pete.'

He ended the call and dialled again.

'DS Hancock.'

'Jim, it's Pete.'

'Hello. You still in the office?'

'Yeah. Looking into this missing girl. Thing is, I've got a crossover between that case and one of your arrestees from this morning. A Stephen Lockwood. He's a known associate of the father of my victim's best friend. Do you mind if I have a word with him? Not as a suspect or anything, just a possible witness.'

'He'll want something in return, mate. I'd bet on it.'

'If so, what can I offer him?'

Jim sucked in air. 'He's a prime player, Pete. He's going down this time, so the cupboard's bare unless he can give us his international connections as well as what you want.'

'Oh, well. I'll have a go anyway, if that's all right.'

'Sure. Go for it. Just don't hold out too much hope, eh?'

'Fair enough. See you tomorrow.'

He put the phone down again and got up from his desk. 'Right, I'm off to the dungeons.'

Dave looked up from his screen. 'There's nothing on her laptop to indicate anything amiss.'

'OK. That was quick.'

'We aim to please, boss.'

Pete headed for the door, the squad room almost empty now, with the day shift nearly all gone.

Downstairs, he signed into the custody suite and let the fat, wheezing middle-aged sergeant lead him along the narrow corridor between the cells. He stopped at one about a third of the way along on the left, shot the steel shutter on the hatch and peered in, then inserted the key and turned it. 'There you go.'

'Thanks, Bob.'

Pete stepped in and the door clanged shut behind him. 'Hello, Stephen. DS Gayle.'

Lockwood was in his mid-thirties with long, straggly brown hair and skin that looked like it had needed a wash since soap was invented. He stared blankly up at Pete from the built-in bed at the back of the cell, where he slouched indolently.

'What do you want?'

'I gather you're a pal of Neil Sanderson's.' Pete leaned against the wall, just inside the door and folded his arms.

'Don't know him.'

'Yes, you do. I'm not involved in the drugs thing. His daughter's a friend of a girl who's gone missing. I want to know if he'd be involved in something like that. As far as you know.'

'What? Kiddy-fiddling? I don't know nothing about that.'

Pete sighed. 'I didn't say you did, did I? I want to know if Neil Sanderson might, that's all.'

'Then why don't you ask him?'

'Because I don't like being lied to, Stevie. And if he was involved, that's what he'd do, isn't it? Lie to me.'

Lockwood laughed. 'You're in the wrong job, ain't you? If you don't like being lied to.'

'I don't like it. Doesn't mean I can't see it when it happens. Or that I won't do something about it.'

'Well, screw you, piggy. I ain't telling you anything. And that's no lie.'

'So, you'd rather see a paedophile get away with it, than talk to me?'

'What of it?'

'Makes you an accessory after the fact, that's what, Stevie. And kiddy-fiddling, as you call it, gets you a whole lot more downtime than pushing a few pills. Whether or not I let it be known that's what you're in for, in Her Majesty's hotel up the road, is another matter.'

Lockwood looked considerably paler all of a sudden. 'You wouldn't.'

Pete raised an eyebrow, his gaze locked on the other man's, and waited.

Lockwood swallowed and wiped a hand over his face. 'Look, I know he likes them young, but I don't know nothing about nothing like that. Why don't you ask his missus? His kid? They'd know, wouldn't they?'

Pete watched him carefully for a long second. 'All right. Thank you, Stephen. And how do you know Sanderson?'

'Judo. I used to do a bit.' He sat up straighter, staring at Pete.

Pete smiled and pushed himself off the wall. He tapped on the door. The key turned and it swung open. 'Thanks, Bob.'

'You get what you need?' The uniformed man swung the door shut with a clang and locked it.

'Mm. Not that it got me any further forward.'

Chapter 6

By the time Pete turned into the street where he lived, barely a mile from the station, the smell of fish and chips that permeated the car had gone from appetising to nauseating as he worried about the problems this case could throw up. Its similarities to their own were bound to cause trouble at home. It would be a reminder, if nothing else. But there was nothing he could do about that. The girl needed him – and needed him to be on top of his game. To find her before the sick bastard who'd taken her – if that was what had happened – went one step further and killed her like the Jane Doe they had discussed earlier.

His mind conjured an image of a forlorn-looking body, naked and filthy, lying in the mud at the side of the river, like so much discarded rubbish. A young life snuffed out, as if it meant nothing. He shook his head. He could not afford to think like that. He had to be positive. He had to expect and plan to find Rosie Whitlock alive and soon. For her sake as well as his own.

He turned into his drive and got out of the car, warm paper package in hand. The front door opened before he reached it.

'Daddy! Good day?' Annie grinned up at him in jeans and T-shirt, a glittery pink elephant covering most of her slim chest.

Pride swelled like a physical lump in his throat and he wrapped his free arm around her, lifted her up and kissed the top of her head. Her long brown hair smelled mildly of shampoo. He took a long breath and set her down again. 'Hello, Button. You smell nice. It didn't go to plan, I can tell you that. I was hoping for a nice, easy slide back into things, but instead I went and picked up a big case. Here, take these into the kitchen, will you?' He handed her the food and shut the door against the chill of the night.

'OK.' She took the package and skipped away.

'Hi, Lou,' he called, as he slipped off his shoes and jacket, but there was no response.

He went through. She was sitting in her usual place on the sofa, dressed in jogging bottoms and a sweatshirt, her dark, greasy hair tied back in a ponytail. The TV was playing some kind of game show, the sound barely audible.

'How you doing?'

She didn't take her eyes off the TV. 'OK.'

'What you been up to?'

'Nothing.' Her voice was dull, uninterested. She'd been like this, or worse, for months now, ever since the first flush of frantic panic faded a few days after Tommy's disappearance. It was like she'd suffered an emotional overload that had used up everything inside her and she had been unable to replenish it.

He kept trying. Anything to get a response. 'Heard from anyone?'

She shook her head.

'Thought you might have gone out,' he said. 'Gone shopping or something.'

'What for?'

'To get out of these four walls. Get a bit of sunshine. See some people, other than me and Annie.'

'See a bloody doctor, you mean,' she said sourly.

'I didn't, but it couldn't hurt, if you feel ready.'

'I don't.'

'Tea's ready,' Annie called from the kitchen.

Pete let out a long breath. He was finding it harder and harder to cope with the expressionless monotony of her depression. But what could he do? If Louise didn't want to see a doctor, a grief counsellor or a psychiatrist, he couldn't force her to. He'd made the suggestion more than once and she'd steadfastly refused. *'I don't need a grief counsellor. Tommy's not dead,'* was her standard answer. Or, *'Our son's missing, for God's sake. What do you expect?'*

'Thanks, Button,' he called. 'Hold on, I'll fetch it through.'

Annie had plated up the food and poured three glasses – two of shandy and one lemonade. Pete reached out and drew her into a hug. 'You're a wonderful daughter, you know that?'

'I know.' She gave him an impish smile.

Pete laughed and ruffled her hair.

'*Dad*,' she complained, swiping her fingers through it to settle it.

'Come on, let's eat.' He picked up two of the plates and carried them through to the dining table in the conservatory while Annie carried her own, then he came back for the drinks. 'Lou,' he said as brought them through.

She got up, turned off the TV and came through to sit with them. Which was an improvement on a couple of weeks ago, he thought. Then, she would have eaten on the sofa, staring at the TV and barely noticing what was on her plate.

'You done your homework?'

'Yep. Didn't have much. Just a bit of maths and some geography.'

Her two favourite subjects. 'Good girl. I'm going to have to go back in for a couple of hours, so you'll need to get yourself to bed, all right?'

'Why?'

'What do you have to go back for?' Louise asked.

'I need to get things organised for the morning. We need a search team and canvassers out first thing, and I've got people to call to arrange interviews.'

Louise grunted and shoved another chip in her mouth, chewing silently.

Pete glanced at Annie, picking apart her fish, and suddenly pictured the photos of Rosie Whitlock that he'd seen in the sitting room of her home. How would she be coping right now, wherever she was? How would Annie cope in the same situation? Would she panic? Would she lose it and get completely stressed out? Or would she deal with it as capably as she seemed to be dealing with Louise's condition and the disappearance of her brother?

She had been as distraught as Pete and Louise when it happened, of course – crying night and day, demanding answers – but she had grown up a lot in the following weeks. As Louise spiralled downwards, withdrawing into herself, Annie had stepped up. Taken on the role of mother in the household.

He didn't know what he would have done without her, if he was honest. But the thought of her going through what Rosie Whitlock must be enduring right now, clogged his throat with horror.

'Dad?'

He blinked. Cleared his throat. 'Sorry, Button. What was that?'

'Are you all right?'

'Yeah, of course. Don't worry about me.' He forked up a piece of fish, unsure how long he had been lost in his awful thoughts. 'What was it you said?'

'Nothing. Just, you looked . . . I don't know. Like you'd seen a ghost or something.'

Pete smiled. 'Nothing that exciting, love. I was just thinking, that's all. These chips are good tonight, aren't they?'

'Yeah. Did you go somewhere different?'

'Same place, but there's different people in there. They looked Greek or something.'

'What, the old guy's retired, has he?'

'Must have. I didn't ask. Maybe I'll find out later. See what the gossip is in the station.' He glanced at Louise, but she didn't respond. Simply chewed stoically, her gaze turned inward, barely aware of her surroundings or the people in them. 'I shan't be too late back, anyway. Just do what's needed and come home. No sense getting overtired. Nobody does their best that way, and we need to be on top of our game on this one.'

'Bad, is it?'

'As bad as it gets. But nothing for you to worry about.'

'*Dad.* I'm ten years old. I'll be able to get married in another six.'

Pete almost spat out his fish. 'No, you won't, young lady. Not without mine and your mother's permission. Not until you're eighteen, at least, and not then if you've got any sense.'

'Why? You and Mum are all right.'

'We didn't get married until much later than that. When we were old enough to know what we wanted out of life and who we were. Getting married as young as that never lasts. You're still growing up. Anyway, what's the rush? You've got your whole life ahead of you. And you haven't even got a boyfriend yet, have you?'

'*No*,' she said heavily. 'But that's not the point.'

Pete's eyebrows went up. 'Oh. And here I was thinking that was the whole point.'

'See, you just don't understand, do you?'

'Honestly . . . not a clue.' He grinned and reached out to tousle her hair. 'I just know that I love you and I want you to be happy.'

She ducked away. 'Well, so do I. That's why I need to plan ahead. To be aware of my options.'

Pete suppressed a laugh. 'Oh, yes? And who's been putting ideas like that in your head, eh? You got a life coach started working at that school of yours? If so, send them round here. I need some lessons of that sort.'

'What's a life coach?'

'Someone who gets paid enormous amounts of money for talking a mixture of common sense and pointless rubbish.'

'Sounds like a good job. Easier than yours.'

'Too right. I'll tell you what – give it a couple of years, then look into it. See if your careers teacher can point you in the right direction.' He swallowed the last of his chips. 'But in the meantime, you make sure you're in bed and asleep before I get home tonight, all right?'

'Yes, Dad.'

'Good girl.' He stood up, briefly touched her cheek then rested a hand on Louise's shoulder and kissed her forehead. 'See you in a bit.'

*

Pete paused, shocked, in the doorway of the squad room. His whole team were at their desks, working quietly and, across from them, a whiteboard had been set up with photos of Rosie, her parents and the basic details of everyone they knew of who was linked to the case, all in Dick Feeney's neat hand.

Dick looked up from his computer. With his cheeks darkened by a day's stubble, he looked every inch his nickname of Grey Man. But this was the kind of commitment and work ethic that should have seen Tommy found, months ago. And, Pete was sure, would have, if the same team were on it. He just wished they could have been.

'How's the missus?'

'Pissed off at me for coming back in, but she'll get over it. What's going on?'

'We've just been doing a few background searches. Seeing if there's anyone linked to the family with a record,' Jane told him.

'And?'

'Nothing yet, apart from your man, Sanderson.'

'What did you find on known local paedophiles, Dave?'

'There's three on the register. I've got the details here.' He held up a piece of paper.

Pete nodded. 'We'll need to visit them. Get their alibis, if they have any. Also, talk to the neighbours and the people who live around the school gates. But, before that, we need to make certain of the parents' alibis. Ben, if you've got a minute, you could do that. Call the head of the school where the mother works and one of the partners of the father's firm. Meantime, I'll take Jill and see if we can knock the mother's sister up. Jane, you and Dick see if you can get hold of Alistair's brother, Michael. Dave, when you've finished what you're doing, take Ben and follow up on the registered paedophiles. Verify whatever alibis you can.'

'Bearing in mind who and what they are, have we got to be gentle with them?' Dave asked.

'Until you can put one of them in the frame, Dave, they're as innocent as you are, as far as this case goes.'

'If they were innocent, boss, we wouldn't be looking at them,' Jane pointed out.

'You know what I mean. Anyway, I thought you were going home?'

She shrugged.

'Well, thanks for coming back. All of you. Come on, Jill. And don't forget your brolly; it's pissing down out there.'

'Bugger, we thought you were just sweating from the stairs, boss,' Dick said, as Jill rose from behind her desk.

Pete ignored him. 'If we're done by nine, I'll pop back in here. Otherwise, I'll see you all in the morning.' He held the door for the slim, dark-haired constable.

'Thanks, boss.' She finished shrugging into her heavy coat and started down the stairs ahead of him. 'So, where are we going?'

'Exmouth. They live down near the front, just up from the river mouth.'

'Very nice.'

'Hmm. Especially for a bar manager and a social worker.'

'Jane was saying the mother reckons he's a bit too touchy-feely.'

'Yes. So, you take his missus and I'll have a word with him, assuming they're in.'

'Right, boss.'

Pete pushed open the back door and let her through, then ran for the car, the rain now turned to sleet again and coming down hard.

Chapter 7

'Susan Whitlock?'

'Yes.'

'DS Peter Gayle. This is PC Evans. Jill. Can we come in?'

'Of course.' She stepped back. 'This is about Rosie, yes?'

'That's right.'

'Jason's in the bath, I'm afraid,' the willowy brunette said as she led them into the wide hallway. 'Jason,' she called. 'The police are here, darling.'

'I'll be down shortly.'

Pete heard the faint slosh of water from upstairs.

'That's all right,' he said to Susan. 'We can wait.'

'Would you like something to drink in the meantime? Tea? Coffee?'

'Tea would be excellent. Thanks.'

'So, have you started the search yet?' she asked.

'We'll get going on that in the morning. No sense stumbling about in the dark, destroying evidence.'

'Oh.' She paused, unsure whether to lead them into the kitchen or the sitting room. 'I thought . . . Well, that little boy in Scotland, they were out looking straight away, weren't they? And that little girl in Wales, a year or so before.'

'Different circumstances.' Pete raised a hand towards the kitchen and she led them through.

'How do you mean?'

'Well, Rosie's older, for one thing. She's not likely to have run off or got lost. And her family situation – Alistair's job, for instance – brings other possibilities. Talking of which, there are no issues that you're aware of, are there? People they've had a problem with? No one who would want to hurt them?'

'No.' She flicked the kettle on and set about making drinks.

'What can you tell us about Rosie herself? How does she get on with her dad? With Jason? With you and her mum?'

'Oh, she's fine. She hasn't got to the rebellious stage yet. Wait a minute . . .' She looked up from what she was doing. 'What do you mean – how does she get on with Al and Jason? You don't think . . .?'

'We don't think anything yet. We're gathering information and we have to look at all possibilities, however unlikely or unsavoury, if only to eliminate them.'

'Well, you can eliminate that for a start. Al would never . . . And Jason – he's very tactile, very huggy, but that's just his way. There's nothing sexual about it. Trust me – I'm his wife.'

Pete heard heavy footsteps coming quickly down the stairs.

'What do you mean by that?' Jill asked.

'Nothing. Just . . . We have a normal sex life, he's not a pervert, that's all.'

'Who, me?' Jason Whitlock asked from the doorway. 'Why are we discussing my sexual proclivities, may I ask?'

'For elimination purposes,' Pete told him.

'Ah. Well, that's all right then. I think. Elimination from what, exactly?'

'From the possibility that you were involved in what happened to Rosie,' his wife told him.

'Of course I wasn't! Al said it happened this morning, around eight-fifteen, yes? Well, at eight-fifteen I was at work. I had a call to make, to California. I left here about seven thirty.'

'And can anyone verify that?'

'I don't know. I often see George, next door, on the way out. Didn't notice him this morning, though. And there wouldn't be anyone else at Stone's at that time of day unless there was a delivery scheduled.'

Pete grunted. Bars were not known for being overpopulated at eight in the morning but he would still have to verify Jason's story. 'We'll need details of who you called and when.' He would also check on what car Jason drove and see if it could be spotted on CCTV or if it had been seen near the bar that morning. 'Is there anyone either of you can think of that might have been involved in Rosie's abduction?'

'No.' Jason glanced at his wife, who shook her head. 'Al's not the type to make enemies like that. And Jess is a primary school teacher, for God's sake. Who's she going to piss off enough to make them abduct her daughter?'

'You don't have children?' Jill asked.

Pete glanced at her as the couple both said, 'No.'

'Then, could this be a revenge attack one step removed? Has either of you "pissed anyone off enough" for them to abduct your niece?'

She focused on Jason as she asked the question, but it was Susan who said firmly, 'No! Certainly not.'

Pete picked up on this. 'Jason? No disgruntled creditors, people you've let down or annoyed enough for them to want payback?'

Jason shook his head. 'Not that I can think of.'

'Well, if you do think of anything, let me know right away, yes? We don't know where Rosie is or what she's going through, so the sooner we can find her, the better.'

'Of course.'

'And I'll need the details of that call you were making this morning.' Pete turned over the page of his notebook and handed it over, with his pen.

*

Pete watched Annie running towards her friends at the bus stop and felt suddenly reluctant to let them out of his sight. Danger was stalking these streets. Tommy was gone, so was Rosie Whitlock and there was the Jane Doe, down by the river. The thought of losing Annie too was more than he could bear. He watched as she merged into the cluster of uniformed girls and boys on the grass behind the shelter, waiting until he could no longer see her in the crowd, then drew a long, shuddering breath and turned away. Much as he would have liked to, he couldn't stay here until the bus came.

As understandable as it was for a father to want to protect his little girl, it wouldn't be good for her, or for him. Or for Rosie Whitlock.

By the time he got to Risingbrook School, the rest of the team were already on-site and the road, which would be near deserted in another hour, was beginning to get busy. He pulled up behind a patrol car and climbed out. Jane was across the road, talking to a mother who had just sent her daughter into the school with a couple of others. She waved to him without pausing in her conversation. He crossed towards her and waited a few feet away until the woman stepped away and Jane turned towards him.

'How's it going?'

'Still quiet, yet. And early. Another ten minutes to when Rosie was dropped off.'

An Audi saloon turned into the top of the road as a BMW pulled up across from them. Pete crossed the road. A woman in her early thirties, long blonde hair hanging loose over her shoulders, looked up as he approached.

Pete flashed his badge. 'DS Gayle. Can I have a moment of your time, please?'

'What's this about?'

'A young girl went missing here yesterday morning. We're checking to see if anyone saw anything unusual or out of place.'

'Missing? You mean she was abducted?'

'We're not sure at this point.'

'Well, I don't think I saw anything unusual here yesterday. It was just a normal morning. Sarah?'

'Nor me. I met Angie and Richard at the gates and we went in together. You saw us.'

'That's right.'

'Richard said later that he hadn't seen Rosie all day. Is that who's gone missing?'

'Rosie?' Pete countered, seeking confirmation.

'Rosie Whitlock.'

Pete pursed his lips. This was going to be all over the school by lunchtime, whether he announced it or not. 'Yes, I'm afraid it is.'

'Oh my God! I take history and maths with her.' The young girl's eyes went wide. 'What happened?'

'We don't know yet, but myself and another officer will be coming into school later to speak to everyone.'

'Can I go in now?'

Pete nodded.

'Yes, but be careful,' the mother said. 'I'll pick you up later, as usual. Don't come out of the gates until you see me, all right?'

'Yes, Mum.'

'Love you.'

'You too.' The girl leaned over the seat to give her mother a quick peck on the cheek, then climbed out and ran across the road, her satchel clutched to her chest.

'You were here at the same time yesterday?' Pete asked.

'Yes.' The woman checked her watch. 'Pretty much spot-on. I drop Sarah off on my way to work.'

'I see. And where's that, Mrs . . .?'

'Taylor. Jeanette. I work in Exmouth, at Diehl and Slaughter, solicitors.'

'Oh, you're a lawyer?'

'No, no,' she laughed. 'I'm the receptionist.'

'Ah. And you didn't, perhaps, see a girl in school uniform walking away from the school yesterday morning?'

She shook her head. 'No.'

'OK. Well, thanks for your time, Mrs Taylor.' He stepped back as she pulled away. Turning around, he saw Jane's Audi moving away, too, the two cars purring off in opposite directions. Up and down the street, other officers, some in uniform, others not, were approaching vehicles as they stopped or pulling over those that looked to be driving straight past. He saw Dick Feeney, in his customary grey suit, flag down a black VW Golf and lean down to the passenger window as Dave Miles straightened up from a bright blue Porsche and waved it on.

Five months ago, these same things would have been happening outside the swimming pool. Cars and pedestrians being stopped. Questioned. Asked if they'd seen anything relevant to the disappearance of a young boy. Signs would have been put up, asking any witnesses who hadn't been questioned to come forward. The difference was that another crew had been handling that case. Pete and his team had been specifically excluded, in accordance with standard protocol.

And the other difference, he thought, was that they would find Rosie Whitlock. Her parents would not go through the protracted hell that he, Lou and Annie were suffering. He would not allow it.

Chapter 8

'Right, what have we got then?'

Pete stood by the whiteboard that Dick had set up the night before and surveyed the team, as the last uniformed PC closed the door behind him. None of them looked pleased with themselves or glad to be here. 'Dave, what did the street search turn up?'

'Bugger all, basically, apart from the remains of a mobile phone that may or may not have been the victim's. It was smashed to bits. Looked like it had been chucked out of a moving vehicle and run over by an artic. But we've sent the bits to the tech boys, to see if they can do anything with them. Other than that, we combed the street from the junction down to the corner, both sides. There were one or two little bits and pieces. The odd fag end and so on, but nothing that could be from the victim and nothing that says, "Kidnapper was here." We'll get what we did find off to forensics, but unless he smokes or chews gum – and there were only two bits of that fresh enough to be relevant – I don't think it'll get us anywhere. Certainly not before we've got him in custody some other way.'

Pete nodded. 'Thanks, all of you, for trying anyway. As far as the school itself, an initial search turned up nothing, but we've got a full team going in there to do the job properly, in . . .' he checked his watch '… about an hour. Other than that, the only thing that came up was a young lad who seems to have had something of a crush on Rosie, from a distance. Richie Young. The consensus among the other kids seems to be that he's a bit weird, a bit of a loner, but essentially harmless. Follows her around at a distance. He's not in school today, though. His mother phoned in this morning. He's off sick.'

'Could be a coincidence, boss,'

'Could be, but you know me, Jane. I don't like 'em. So I'll follow up on him when we're done here. Anybody got anything to add on the school before we move on?'

Heads were shaken in a silence that Pete allowed to stretch for a few seconds.

'Right. We need to check with the school – and with the one Rosie's mum works at – that all the staff have current CRB checks in place. No one's there that shouldn't be. Make sure they've all got solid alibis for yesterday morning. Any that haven't, we'll need to interview. The rest of us need to carry on with last night's interviews. Track down those we weren't able to get in touch with and check on the alibis of those we spoke to. Dick and Jill, if you want to start checking alibis, grab a couple of uniforms to help out. Jane, you can get a list together of all the people we still need to interview and get started on that with Ben. Usual drill – neighbours, close family and friends first, then widen the net. Colleagues, friends of friends, schoolmates and the parents of, and don't forget the folks that live around Risingbrook itself. Right. Anything else?' He gazed around the assembled team. They looked determined, ready to go. 'No? Let's get to it then. And anybody who finds her by lunch gets a pint on me.'

A ripple of cynical laughter went around the room and Pete gave it a few seconds before holding up his hands. 'Rosie's been missing for twenty-six hours now, so it's time to pull our fingers out and get a wiggle on. And the press moratorium has been lifted, as of five minutes ago. I spoke to our beloved leader and he's got that in hand.'

'I bet he has,' Feeney said dryly.

'We might as well make what use of him we can. Now, come on. Let's try to find this girl before any harm comes to her.' Pete stepped away from the whiteboard, as those who were seated stood up, and everyone moved off to get on with their assigned tasks. 'Sophie,' he called.

One of the PCs who was on the way to the door stopped and looked around.

'I need you with me, OK?'

Her eyes widened in surprise. 'Yes, Sarge.' She stepped out of the group. 'What are we doing?'

'Having a talk to the Young boy. Best to have two of us there.' Pete often found that a female presence helped in such situations. It tended to keep things calmer. Plus, there was the different perspective that they brought to an interview. They tended to see things differently – and see different things – to men, which could be useful. It was one of the reasons he worked so well with Jane. 'We need to find out if young Richie Young is as innocent as he ought to be, or if his mum's covering for him.'

*

Richie Young's dark hair was lank, and longer than Pete would have expected to be allowed at a school like Risingbrook. Its central parting was failing miserably, so that it hung down like a ragged curtain in front of his too-bright eyes and pale, shiny face as he sat sullenly against far too many pillows in a bed that smelled stale and unwelcoming. His thin chest was heaving, as if he'd just run all the way from school. His mother sat on the corner of the bed, her hand firmly on his knee, as if to prevent it from bouncing in front of the two police officers.

Pete pulled the chair out from under the desk and turned it

around. With a jolt, he noticed a maths textbook on the desk that was the same one Tommy had been using. Then, on a shelf beside the desk, what looked like a brass coin. He recognised it as a token from an amusement arcade. There were several in Tommy's room too, from time he'd spent in the place down Fore Street.

Pete had been shocked when he realised that his son was gambling. He remembered wondering what else the boy got up to that he didn't know about. Did this lad and his son know each other? He leaned forward in the chair, fighting the urge to ask. *Come on, Pete. Stick to the subject.*

He shared a glance with Sophie, who was standing by the door, arms folded as if guarding it. 'So,' he said. 'Do you know of anyone that Rosie's been receiving unwanted attention from? Anyone she's having problems with?'

'No.'

'And you would know, right? You being a close friend of hers?'

'Are you taking the . . .' he glanced at his mother '... mick?'

'Why would you think that?'

'You must have got my name from school, so you must have talked to the other kids.'

'And?'

'No, I don't know of anyone she's having problems with. She's popular. She's not bitchy or stuck-up like some of them. She includes people, you know?'

People like you, Pete thought. *Outsiders.* He nodded. 'And you're sure you didn't see anything unusual, anything out of place when you got to school yesterday? Or hear anything, maybe?'

'No. If I had, I'd say, alright?' For a moment, he looked like he wanted to continue, but then he clammed up once more, his arms folded across his thin chest.

'Well, that just leaves me wondering one thing, Richie. What aren't you telling me?'

'Nothing.'

Pete couldn't read Richie's expression through his hair, but his mother straightened in her seat, about to object, then held her silence as a tiny doubt took hold in her mind. She'd seen it, too. The question was, was it relevant? Did he want to push the kid now, in front of his mother, or keep him as a potential witness for later?

'Who did you see when you got there? Give me some names.'

The boy's lip curled. 'I don't . . . There was Matt Andrews and a couple of his friends. Holly Gregson. Tess Carver.' He shrugged. 'That's about it.'

Pete wrote the names down. He would check with them later. He stood up, putting away his notepad and pen. 'Well, if you think of anything, or remember anything that might be relevant, you call me, right?' He took out a card, but the boy had retreated into himself. Pete turned the chair back around and put the card on the desk. 'My number's there. Any time.' He nodded to the mother. 'Thank you, Mrs Young. Sorry to have troubled you.'

*

'What d'you reckon, Sarge?'

Pete started the engine and glanced across at Sophie. 'I reckon he knows more than he's letting on. Maybe it's because his mother was there, maybe more than that. But she saw it too, so maybe she'll have a go at him now that we've gone. Meantime, we'll check with the kids he mentioned, see if they corroborate his arrival time.'

Pete's phone rang in his pocket. He fished it out and handed it to her. 'Here, answer that, would you? Stick it on speaker.'

'Hello? DS Gayle's phone. Hold on, I'm putting you on speaker.'

A tinny voice came from the little speaker. 'Hey, boss. Wanted to check something with you.'

'What's that, Dave?'

'I've just been visiting with one of our local sex offenders, a Barry Enstone. He claims to have an alibi, provided by his girlfriend. Only he doesn't want us to speak to her until he's had a chance to tell her about his past, which he hasn't done yet. I don't think he's involved, so am I all right to just check up on her indirectly and leave him be until tomorrow?'

'You're sure about him, are you?'

'As sure as I can be.'

Pete drew a breath. 'All right. If the girlfriend pans out, then move on.'

'OK. Cheers, boss.' There was a click and the connection was cut.

Sophie handed him back the phone. 'Another one bites the dust?'

'We can't always drop on the right guy first time out the door.'

'No, but once in a while would be nice, wouldn't it? Especially when we're on the clock, like we are with this case.'

Chapter 9

'Bloody weather.' Sophie knocked the rain off her hat and replaced it neatly on her head as the lift carried them up to Neil Sanderson's workplace.

'Yes. Which is another reason why we need to find Rosie as quickly as we can.' Pete looked up at the row of numbers above the lift doors. Number two lit briefly as they passed that floor. 'We don't know where she is, or, if someone's taken her, what conditions she's being held in. *If* she's still being held.'

'Yeah, but . . . statistically, they reckon we should have another twenty-four hours before . . .' Her voice trailed off.

'That's what the stats say.' *But we all know what they say about stats*, he thought, but kept to himself.

The lift stopped with a *ping*. The doors slid open and they stepped out. Pete showed his badge to the receptionist. Molyneux and Richards was picked out in large, silver lettering on the wall behind her. 'We'd like to speak to one of the owners, if possible.'

'Mr Richards is in. I'll tell him you're here.'

'Thank you.'

She picked up the phone and dialled. 'Mr Richards, there are two police officers here. Can you speak to them?' She nodded.

'OK.' Putting the phone down, she looked up at Pete. 'He'll be out in a second.'

Moments later a tall, well-built man in his fifties came through the door to her left, his brown eyes direct as he shook Pete's hand. 'Brian Richards. How can I help?'

'DS Gayle. This is PC Clewes.' Pete glanced at the girl on the front desk. 'If we could perhaps go through to your office?'

'Yes, sure.' He led the way through a large, open-plan workroom where Pete counted nine staff at a mixture of desks and drawing tables. His office was one of two half-glassed enclosures at the far side. He stepped in and offered them chairs. 'Now . . .'

'We're looking into the disappearance of a young girl,' Pete said. 'Her best friend is the daughter of one of your employees, Neil Sanderson. As a known associate, we need to eliminate him from the inquiry, so I was hoping to ask you about him.'

'OK.'

'How well do you know him?'

'Not well, in the sense of spending time together outside the office, but I've known him as a colleague for . . . seven years now, I think.'

'Is there anyone here he spends time with outside the workplace?'

'He's big mates with Tony.'

'We'll need a word with Tony then, if that's OK. But, before that, is there anything you might want to tell us about either of them? Anything you might be aware of that's in any way irregular?'

'What, you mean . . .? No. They're just two regular guys, as far as I'm aware. They've both always been the height of professionalism at work. Both very good at their jobs. There's never been any hint of anything inappropriate with either of them.'

'OK. We haven't spoken to Mr Sanderson yet. We're just compiling backgrounds and alibis for now. But if you could point him out?' Pete turned in his chair.

'There, second from the right.'

'Dark-haired guy with the blue and yellow check shirt?'

'That's right.'

'And his mate – Tony?'

'Sitting across from him.'

'Right. Well, we don't want to disrupt your day any more than we have to. Is there somewhere we could have a word with Tony?'

'We have a conference room. Grand title for an office not much bigger than mine, really, but it has a table and a projector with a screen for talking to clients and so on. It's next door.'

'That would be perfect.'

'Right.' He stood up and went to the door. 'Tony. Have you got a minute?'

The man looked up, then stood and came towards them. As he stepped into the small office, Richards said, 'Tony Stillwell, DS Gayle and PC Clewes. They'd like a word if that's OK. I said you could use the conference room.'

Pete stood up and held out his hand. 'Nothing to worry about, sir. We just need to ask you a few questions about a friend of yours, that's all.'

Stillwell's handshake was tentative. 'OK.'

Sophie moved to replace her chair in the corner.

'Don't worry about that, I'll get them,' Richards told her. 'If you want to take them through, Tony . . .'

'Uh . . . Yes, sure.' He led the way back through the studio to the reception and past the receptionist's desk to the door at the other side of it. 'Here we are.'

There was a table big enough to seat ten people. A projector on it was aimed towards a screen on the far wall. Stillwell went around to the far side and took a seat, the windows behind him. 'So, what's this about?'

'A young girl went missing yesterday,' Pete told him. 'Her best friend is the daughter of a friend of yours, Neil Sanderson, so we need to ask you about him.'

Stillwell relaxed visibly. 'OK. No problem.'

Pete saw Sophie readying her notebook from the corner of his eye. 'First, as a matter of protocol, where were you yesterday morning, between eight and nine o'clock?'

'Me? I was on the way here, I suppose. At least part of that time. I leave home around eight-fifteen, get here about ten to nine, as a rule.'

'And that was the case yesterday?'

'Yes.'

'Can anyone verify that?'

'Yes, I suppose. I thought you wanted to ask about Neil?'

'We do, but we have to establish reliability. Who can verify where you were? Do you drive in with someone?'

'No. My wife saw me off from home. Bridget out there saw me arrive. What do you mean, "reliability"?'

'And was Mr Sanderson here when you arrived?'

'Uh . . . No, in fact, he was late yesterday. He didn't get here until just after nine thirty. Said he'd had a flat tyre.'

Pete glanced at Sophie, who was writing swiftly.

'I see. And how well do you know Mr Sanderson?'

'Pretty well, I guess. We hang out together sometimes. Go to the pub on a Friday night, or bowling. Play five-a-side. The odd barbie.'

'You know his family, then?'

'Yes. We were over there on Sunday.'

'We?'

'My wife and I.'

'I see. Who was there, apart from you and your wife?'

'Neil, Geraldine, Becky, her friend Rosie and her parents, Alistair and Jess. Then there was another couple, Derek and Polly Howe, and their daughter Karen. I think she's at school with Becky and Rosie. They were off on their own most of the time, of course – the three girls, I mean. And Jerry and Linda Bateman.'

Alistair had included the Howe family on his list, but Pete didn't recall the Batemans. He wrote the name down, followed by the note: 'Party Sunday'. 'How do the Whitlocks know the Batemans?'

'I think Jerry and Alistair were at school together or something. It goes back a lot of years, anyway.'

'And Neil and Alistair?'

'Uni, I think.'

'OK. And you just know Neil through work, yes?'

'Yes. We met when I started here five years ago.'

'And you share a number of interests.'

'Yes. Look, what's this all about?'

Pete drew a breath. 'How's Neil around Becky and Rosie?'

'What? Fine. What is this?'

'The girl who went missing is Rosie Whitlock, Mr Stillwell. You've confirmed that Mr Sanderson wasn't at work at the time. We need to make sure he's not involved in her disappearance. We're looking at all known associates of hers and her parents. It's standard procedure. So I'll ask again. Have you ever noticed Neil take anything other than a normal interest in Becky or Rosie, or the girls to have any reluctance or excessive keenness to be around him?'

'No. He has a perfectly normal father–daughter relationship with Becky, as far as I'm aware. Why would you ask these things?'

'As I said, Mr Stillwell, elimination. OK. I think we've taken up enough of your time for now. Sophie, do you want to go with Mr Stillwell and send Mr Sanderson in here?'

He had planned to leave talking to Sanderson until later, when he'd had a chance to corroborate his alibi, but Stillwell's comments had blown that out of the window. With Sanderson having no alibi, it was essential to talk to him now.

'OK, Sarge.' She snapped her notebook closed as Stillwell stood up and headed for the door.

'And Sophie?'

'Sarge?'

'When you've sent him here, have a word with Richards. Get

any password that might be needed and have a quick shufti through Sanderson's computer, all right?'

'Is that legal?' asked Stillwell.

'It is, if we've got your boss's permission,' Pete told him.

As they left the room Pete moved around to the far side of the table then made a few notes while he waited for Sanderson to come through.

He had just finished writing when the door opened and he looked up to see the tall, slim architect enter and close the door behind him.

'You wanted to see me?'

'That's right. Take a seat.' Pete waited for Sanderson to sit opposite him.

The sun had come out and Sanderson squinted slightly against the brightness, although the window was facing west and it was still not yet noon. 'We're looking into the disappearance of Rosie Whitlock. We understand you know her.'

'Yes, of course.'

'Where were you between eight-fifteen and eight-forty yesterday morning?'

'Uh . . . On my way here. I was late getting in because I had a flat tyre. Why?'

'Where exactly did you get this flat?'

'Between Marsh Green and the airport. We live at West Hill.'

'So, a minor road with very little traffic.'

'That's the idea. Better for getting here in the rush hour.'

'Did anyone see you while you were dealing with your flat tyre?'

'As you said, it's a minor road with not a lot of traffic. So, no, I don't think so.'

Pete pursed his lips. 'Anybody see you leave your house?'

'Why? Am I a suspect here?'

'Everybody who knows Rosie is a suspect until we eliminate them. Did anyone see you leave home?'

'No. My wife leaves before I do.'

'So you have no one to corroborate your whereabouts from – what time did your wife leave the house?'

'Eight.'

'From eight o'clock to nine thirty-ish, when you arrived here, then?'

'I suppose. But that doesn't mean I had anything to do with whatever happened to Rosie. What did happen, anyway? Alistair couldn't tell me much last night when he rang.'

'What's your relationship like with her? I understand she's your daughter's best friend.'

'What's my . . .? Wait a minute. What is this? It sounds like you're accusing me of being some sort of paedophile.'

His answers were all perfectly reasonable but, with the victim being his daughter's best friend, he had been just a bit too offhand until the last question. Pete decided to push him a bit, now the opportunity had arisen. 'Not at all. But she is a pretty girl. And they grow up fast, don't they? Look sixteen when they're thirteen, given half a chance. And the fashions these days . . .'

Something flickered in Sanderson's eyes then he frowned sharply. 'You must have me confused with someone else, Sergeant. I'm certainly not attracted to my daughter's friends.' He rubbed at his cheek. 'I'm a married man. A happily married one, in fact. Ask my wife.'

Pete nodded. *We will*, he thought. *And your daughter, if needs be.* 'OK,' he said.

The door opened and Sophie entered. She gave him a slight shake of the head. Nothing untoward on Sanderson's computer. Not that Pete had expected anything on a work machine, but you never knew. Sanderson watched her move around the table and sit down next to Pete. Pete could see the question in his eyes. 'Right then,' he said. 'I understand my colleague spoke to you yesterday evening, asking for your permission to check your daughter's computer, her emails and so forth, to see if there's anything in there that might point towards any problems Rosie might have been having.'

'Yes, and I gave it.'

'Your wife just works mornings, yes?'

'Yes, but . . .' He shrugged and straightened his collar. 'If it's all the same to you, I'd like to be there when you check. I'm not really comfortable with strangers being in my house when I'm not.'

Pete grimaced. 'Have you got a number for your wife?'

'Of course.' Sanderson reeled off the number and Pete wrote it down then clicked his pen shut and stood up.

'OK. Thank you for your time, Mr Sanderson. We must crack on now. Time is of the essence in cases like this. Come on, Sophie.' He ushered her quickly out of the room and towards the lifts.

Once the doors had closed behind them, she turned to him with a frown. 'What was that all about? You were out of there like a cat with a banger up its arse.'

'He's got no alibi for the time in question, he had plenty of time to get to Risingbrook and snatch the girl. And there was something not right about his reaction when I mentioned girls her age and the way they dress. So, I want to talk to his wife before he can and get her to let us in and check out both the daughter's computer and his. What time is it?'

'Ten to eleven.'

'So, if she finishes at twelve thirty – give her an hour to get home – we've got a couple of hours to get there and be ready for her.'

Chapter 10

'How's it going?'

Jane watched him rub some of the rain out of his hair. 'I've been to Alistair's office, spoken to his colleagues and run their names, as well as those of all their recent clients. I got confirmation from him while I was there that the phone we found in bits outside the school was Rosie's. I also checked his computer. Nothing. So I went back over to their place, spoke to several neighbours to see if they've seen or heard anything out of the ordinary lately.'

The phone on Pete's desk began to ring.

'They haven't. Of course, they weren't all in.'

Pete held up his hand for her to pause and picked up the phone. 'DS Gayle.'

'Hey, boss. It's Dave.'

'What can I do for you?'

'Just calling in to let you know what we're up to. I've got Mick Douglas with me. We're with one of the blokes you asked me to follow up on. A Kevin Haynes. He claims to know nothing, but he's got no alibi, so we're just popping round to his place to see if we can establish where he was yesterday morning.'

Pete glanced at the board, where Dave had added three names

under the heading RSOs –registered sex offenders. Kevin Haynes was the second of them. 'OK. Anything else to report?'

'Not a lot. We've checked on Enstone's supposed girlfriend. Colleagues confirm she's got a bloke who matches his description. Been going out for four or five months. They don't know where she was night before last and into the morning though.'

'OK. Carry on with this other one then. See what you find.'

'Will do.'

Pete put down the phone and looked up at Jane. 'Where were we?'

'They're still searching the school grounds. Nothing yet. I spoke to the officer in charge about ten minutes ago. He reckons they'll be there until around four. Only other thing to report is the CCTV just came in. There isn't much. You want me to check through it?'

'If you get a chance. If not, give it to Ben. I'll take Sophie with me again. We've got to visit Neil Sanderson's place. Check his daughter's computer and so on. The wife's going to be there in a little while. I want to catch her before Neil has a chance to talk to her. We tried her mobile – it's switched off.' He stood up and lifted his jacket off the back of his chair. 'Let me know if anything comes up.'

'Will do.'

Pete tilted his head at Sophie Clewes, who was waiting tentatively by the door. She stood up straighter. 'You and me again, kid. Let's go.'

*

Sophie checked her watch. 'We're early. She won't be here for another ten minutes at least.'

'Better to be on the doorstep when she gets here than knocking on it just after. She can't ignore us that way.' *And her husband can't call her before we get to her*, he thought but didn't say. He swung the car into the drive of the big, expensive-looking house and parked well over to the left, so that Geraldine Sanderson could get past if she wanted to put her car in the garage. 'Come on. That porch will keep us dry.'

They ran through the fine, icy rain and into the open-fronted porch. Pete rang the bell. Waited. Rang it again. 'You've got a hat on, PC Clewes. Pop round and check the windows and the back door, would you? I'll stay here.'

'What for, Sarge?'

'Just to see what you can see. You never know – she might be back already and ignoring us. And you might spot where Mr Sanderson keeps his computer while you're at it.'

'Yes, Sarge.'

'Off you go. Don't get too wet. Don't want to drip on the carpet when we get inside, eh?'

'No, Sarge.'

She ran to the nearest window, peered in through cupped hands then moved on. She was still around the back of the house when Geraldine Sanderson's dark red SEAT hatchback pulled into the drive. Pete saw the front of the car dip as she braked, seeing the unexpected car in the driveway.

'Constable,' he called.

Sanderson drove up to the garage doors, switched off the engine and climbed out of the car. Pete saw her eyes shift to the left and her expression change as Sophie appeared around the corner of the house behind him, feet crunching on the gravel pathway, her uniform giving away the identity of the strange presence at the front of the house. The woman pulled her long coat up over her head and ran for the porch.

Pete showed her his warrant card. 'Mrs Sanderson? I'm Detective Sergeant Gayle. This is PC Clewes.'

She was small with large, liquid-brown eyes. She was dressed conservatively but smartly, and her hair was pulled back into a clip.

'Detective. I take it this is about Rosie?' She took her keys from her handbag and stepped past him.

'Yes. We'd like a quick word if we may. And I believe you're aware that your husband gave us permission to check the computers in the house and Becky's phone, if it's here. See if we can find anything that would indicate Rosie was having problems with anyone. You know how girls confide in each other.'

'Come in. Yes, of course . . . As you say . . .'

'Do you know of anything in that way? Anything that Rosie might have said, perhaps, or Becky, to suggest there was anything out of the ordinary going on in her life?'

'No. No, she's always been such a happy girl. Well adjusted, friendly . . .' Her gaze finally met his as she shrugged off her coat. 'No, I can't think of anything, Detective.'

He nodded. 'Well, if it's OK with you, perhaps we can start with the main computer of the house then?'

'Of course.'

Pete glanced at Sophie. There was their permission. Anything they found now was covered. Emails, Twitter, Facebook, photos, he could check it all. Geraldine opened a door almost opposite them.

'This was supposed to be a dining room, but we never used it. The sitting room and kitchen are both big enough to double up, so it's our joint office,' she said as she led them in.

There were two desks – one under the window that looked out over a plain grass back garden, the other against the wall to their right. Both held laptops. Bookshelves covered the walls between them. The desk at the window was cluttered with papers and books, the one to their right neat and orderly. On a small table behind the door was a combined printer and scanner, a shelf underneath holding paper and inks.

'This one's mine. The other one's Neil's.' She stepped across to the right and opened her laptop, switching it on. While it powered up, she crossed to the other desk and opened the second computer. She logged on to both machines and stepped back. 'Help yourselves. Would you like some tea? Coffee?'

'No, thanks. We don't want to put you to any trouble, Mrs

Sanderson. What we could do with is passwords and so forth. Emails, Facebook, Twitter, that kind of thing.'

'Oh, I only use email. Neil uses Facebook a bit, but not Twitter. Here.' She crossed to her desk, drew a notepad out of one of the drawers and wrote on a clean page then handed it to Pete.

'Thank you. We'll give you a shout when we're done, if that's OK.'

She hesitated then reached for the door. 'I'll be in the kitchen or the lounge if you want me.'

'Thanks.' Pete moved across towards the window, as she stepped out and closed the door behind her.

'Nice of her to give us permission.' Sophie grinned.

Pete put on a strong Irish accent. 'It's the way I tell 'em.'

She laughed as they took their seats and settled down to work.

Pete started with the My Photos file. There was not much in it. A few holiday snaps from the last couple of years, filed by date. He opened My Documents and found folders for work, home, sport, music and videos. The music and video folders were empty. Sport contained a fixtures list for Bristol Rovers football club and another for the local five-a-side team that Tony Stillwell had mentioned. It also contained a diary spreadsheet titled 'Squash', and another for 'Judo'.

'Busy bloke,' he muttered as he closed the folder and opened the one titled 'Home'. Five sub-folders popped up: Bills, DVDs, Phonebook, Appointments and Banking. Pete opened DVDs and found a list of titles with actors and genres. Movies ranging from *Harry Potter* to *The Exorcist* to *Die Hard*. Nothing out of the ordinary. He closed it and tried the other folders. Again, all was boringly ordinary, though why anyone would want to keep a telephone list on their computer, rather than on paper by the phone, Pete couldn't imagine – and why two diaries, one for sports fixtures and the other for doctor, dentist and other routine appointments? Again, he didn't understand, but clearly Sanderson liked to keep the different sides of his life separate.

He wondered what Simon Phillips had made of his own home computer when he'd done this same thing, five months ago. He had taken Louise out for half a day while Simon and his team checked their house and devices. It was easier that way. The only problem was that it left him not knowing what they'd found, if anything.

He closed the folder and clicked on Work. Behind him, Sophie sighed.

'Nothing on here, Sarge.'

'I'm nearly done.' He scanned down a list of files, most of them either Word files or JPEGs with some PDF files mixed in. The titles all suggested architectural subjects apart from one. 'Ah-hah.'

'What you got?'

'His CV. Might tell us something we don't know.' Pete double-clicked on it as Sophie scooted across on her chair to look over his shoulder. The file opened and he scanned down it. Education in Exeter. University in Bristol – a degree in architecture. Then a job in Bath for two years, followed by the move back to Exeter. 'Didn't know he'd worked in Bath,' Pete said. 'Might be worth checking out. Make a note of the details, would you, and get on to the locals up there. See if they've got anything tied to him or any cases similar to what we've got here with Rosie.'

'Right.' She wrote down the details and pushed herself back across to the other desk, so that she could work without disturbing him further.

Pete saw nothing else of interest, so closed the file and moved on. He checked a few JPEGs, finding architectural drawings and a couple of photographs – one of a cardboard and plywood mock-up, the others of actual buildings. He scrolled back to the top of the folder. There were two sub-folders, one labelled 'Inspiration', the other, 'Models'. He opened the first and found a whole lot of JPEGs. He clicked View and selected Thumbnails. A whole series of pictures opened up, of buildings both ancient and modern. Ignoring Sophie's quiet voice as she spoke into her phone, he scrolled down the page, confirming that all the files were of similar subjects, then closed the folder and opened the other one.

'Whoah. That's definitely not what I expected.'

'What's that, Sarge?'

He glanced over his shoulder. Sophie was holding one hand over the mouthpiece of her phone as she stared past him at the screen.

'What I expected was lots of cardboard and plywood models of buildings. What I've got instead is lots of young girls. And I mean *young* girls. Including . . .' He opened one of the files. 'Thought so. That's Becky.' He clicked the Next button. 'And Rosie.'

'Sorry,' Sophie said into the phone. 'We just found something significant. We're looking into a case that appears to involve a Neil Sanderson. He worked in Bath from 2010 to 2012 at an architect's studio in Argyll Street: Matthews and Roebuck. We wondered if you guys had had any cause to look at him, or any unexplained disappearances of young girls during those years? Say, between the ages of nine and thirteen? OK. Can you make it soon? We're trying to eliminate him from a child abduction. Thanks.' She hung up. 'They'll call me back.'

'Right. We need to check Becky's laptop or whatever. I want her phone checked, as well, ASAP.' He got up and crossed to the door. 'Mrs Sanderson?'

*

'These are all selfies or ones they've taken of each other,' Sophie said, leaning back in her chair.

'How do you know that?'

They were in Becky Sanderson's bedroom, the door closed. Pete was sitting on the bed while Sophie took the single chair and swiped through Becky's tablet, not bothering with the detachable keyboard.

'Apart from the obvious ones, where they're in front of a mirror with a camera phone in their hand, you can tell by the camera angles, the expressions on their faces. They're having a laugh, a bit of fun. The nearest they're expecting to get to anyone else seeing these, is if they email them to a boyfriend or something.'

'Then how come they're on the machine downstairs?'

'I expect Mr Sanderson found them and copied them, same as you did, Sarge.'

'And has she sent them to anyone? Check her email.' He handed over the sheet of paper Gail Sanderson had provided with a list of passwords.

'OK.' Sophie closed the picture folder and opened Google Chrome. 'Let's see . . .'

There was perhaps ten or twelve years between himself and PC Clewes, Pete thought, but it was like they'd been brought up in different worlds. Sophie appeared to be clued in to all the social media and modern technology, whereas he just stood by on the periphery, an outsider looking in. Much as he had been in recent years with Tommy's life. Where had he gone wrong? What had happened to put that distance between them?

He blinked as the realisation dawned.

This. Police work. That's what happened. He'd spent too much time on the job and not enough at home. Emotion welled up inside him. God, how he wished he'd done things differently, arranged his priorities differently.

If they could get Tommy back alive, then he would put that right in future, he promised himself. Work would come second to family, not the other way around. And, even if Tommy didn't come back . . .

Sophie opened up Becky Sanderson's email account and clicked on the Sent Mail box. Scanning down, she checked for emails with attachments, then looked at who they had been sent to. 'Several to Rosie.' She opened one and, sure enough, there were half a dozen pictures of Rosie herself, in underwear, topless and nude. She closed the email. 'I thought you checked her laptop, Sarge?'

'We did. She must have deleted them. Or these have gone to an account that's not on the laptop. One she just uses on her phone, perhaps, or . . . *Stupid sod.*'

'Who is? Why?'

'Me. I never thought to ask if she's got one of those Kindle things. She could have an account set up on that, couldn't she?'

'Depending which model it is, yes.'

'I'll have to check on that. Don't let me forget.'

'Right, Sarge.' She turned back to the screen. Scrolled down a bit further. 'Hello.'

'What?'

'One here to our little buddy, Richie Young.' She opened it up. A line of three photos appeared, of Rosie in her school uniform. In the first, she was blowing a kiss at the camera, fully dressed. In the second, she was peeling off her blouse and in the third, she was in her bra, squeezing her breasts together provocatively. 'She's teasing him.'

'You think? We didn't find these on his computer, did we? So did he delete them, or has he saved them on something else? Not his phone – we checked it.'

'He could have stored them online and then deleted them off his computer, though. We wouldn't pick them up on the hard drive if he's defragged it since.'

'Where would he put them online, though? And how do we find them? And link them back to him?'

'Depends where he put them, I suppose. Could be Facebook or a Twitter feed, maybe a photo storage site like Dropbox, Photobucket or Flickr – there's loads of them.'

'Could we pick up on a subscription to something like that?'

'Maybe. A lot of them are free though. And again, he doesn't need to have set it up on his own computer. He could have done that from school even.' She closed the email and scanned down further, looking for other possibilities. She found one with some holiday photos, then there was a long gap before another attachment showed. She opened it up. 'Ooh. Here we go. This one's to a Chris Mellor.'

Again, several pictures had been sent. Sophie clicked on the first. 'That's Becky.' She scanned through the set. 'In fact, all of them are Becky. Must be a boyfriend. This is ... seven months ago.'

'Another name to check out then.' Pete made a note. 'This is getting more complicated, not less.'

'The modern age, Sarge. Information technology.'

Pete grunted sourly. 'For every silver lining, there's a big, ugly cloud.'

Chapter 11

'Jane. What do you know that I don't?' Pete crossed to the whiteboard and wrote Chris Mellor's name next to Richie Young's. Underneath, he wrote, '? Boyfriend of Becky Sanderson'.

'Not a lot, sadly. The search of the school grounds finished half an hour ago. Turned up nothing of any use. A couple of dodgy roll-ups behind the sports hall, that was about all. I've been through the CCTV. There isn't much. Nothing from outside the school itself. No cameras on that road. It's mostly residential, so no need. There is one on the main road, about six hundred metres east of the junction, looking towards it and on down to the roundabout, but that's all.'

'Anything of interest?' He crossed to his chair, hung up his jacket and sat down.

'A silver Peugeot estate car came out of the end of the road about the right time, turned left and then right at the roundabout. I picked him up on the cameras outside here and the old hospital site, then he turned off just past the golf course and I lost him. The relevance being, it's the same make and model as Dave's mate, Kevin Haynes, drives, which he claims is off the road at the moment. While he was at home yesterday morning. Alone, he says.'

'Don't let Dave hear you calling Kevin Haynes a mate of his.'

Jane laughed. 'Anyway, with all those sightings, you'd think I'd have got a registration plate, but no such luck. He was in front of a Transit-type van when he came out by the school. Then, at the roundabout, the sun was just at the wrong angle – it shone straight onto it, flared it out to white. And you know the camera out here's not aimed right. Nor is the one up the road. It's aimed to pick up vehicles going in and out of there, same as ours is.'

'So we've got no proof of whether it's him or not.'

'No, but it's highly suggestive, isn't it? Right place, right time, right kind of bloke.'

'Mm-hm. Worth another interview at least. And checking on his car. Meantime, we've "borrowed" Neil Sanderson's laptop. There are some highly suggestive photos on it.' He held up the laptop, in its plastic evidence bag. 'Nothing illegal, as such, but they certainly look dodgy in the circumstances. We took a copy of the relevant folder, just in case, but it could do with going through, to see if there's anything more on it. And we need another word with Becky. Preferably at school, to keep her parents out of it. And we need to know what's on her phone. If there are any pictures on it that she hasn't downloaded to her tablet.'

'OK . . .'

'Her and Rosie seem to have been making a game of taking selfies in less than the usual degree of attire.'

'I see. And they're what Neil's got on his laptop, are they?'

'Those and others that he's taken. Opportunistic rather than posed by the look of them. Some while the girls were asleep.'

'Which puts him nicely in the frame.'

'Yes. And Richie Young's got some pictures that he shouldn't have, too, of Rosie. And we need to talk to Chris Mellor.' He waved a hand towards the whiteboard. 'He's another student at Risingbrook. Might be a boyfriend of Becky's.'

'Bloody hell. You have been busy.'

'Trouble is, it hasn't brought us any closer to Rosie. Where's Dave? Have you heard from him?'

'He's on his way. Didn't get anywhere with Haynes, but he did tell me they went back to where Barry Enstone's girlfriend works and interviewed several people, including her. She confirmed she was with Enstone at the time Rosie was taken, so that puts him in the clear.'

'One down then. At least that's a start, I suppose.' He took out his phone and dialled. It was picked up on the second ring. 'Dave? Where are you?'

'Just pulling into the car park, boss. You in the office?'

'Yes.'

'Be with you in two then.'

'No, you won't. Sorry, mate. I need you to go out again.' He saw Sophie come into the squad room with two coffee mugs. 'We've had a few developments. I need you to go see Richie Young. Be a bit heavier with him than I was. We know he's got some pictures of Rosie somewhere. Laptop, phone, Kindle, Cloud account – I don't know, but he's got them. We've seen the transmission from Becky Sanderson's tablet. I want to know everything he's got like that, where he got them from (if not all from Becky), and when. His mum knows that he wasn't telling us everything this morning, so hopefully she's had a word with him in the meantime. And while you're doing that, I'm going to see your man, Haynes.' He took one of the steaming mugs from Sophie, sniffed it and took a sip. Standard cop-shop coffee. He grimaced. 'It seems he might have lied to you. A car very like his was spotted coming away from Risingbrook at about the time of the abduction. We haven't got a plate, but it wants checking, at least.'

'You sure you don't want me to go see him again, boss?'

'No. Let's leave you as the sympathetic one for now. And me with Richie Young, eh?'

'Righto.'

Pete rang off. He got up and went to the whiteboard, where he took a red marker and drew a thick line through Barry Enstone's name.

'Sarge,' said Sophie. 'I heard back from Bath while I was getting the coffees. They've got nothing on Sanderson and just one relevant case while he was there – an eight-year-old girl who went missing after her evening judo lesson.'

Pete paused, a wave of cold rushing down his spine. 'Our Mr Sanderson's into judo.'

She nodded, eyes widening. 'Teaches it, doesn't he?'

'I think we need another chat with him. Here, in the station, after we've seen Kevin Haynes. Jane, I need you to find out what you can on this Chris Mellor, then go and see him. Again, he's got pictures. The ones we know of are of Becky, but you never know. And even if that is the case, it doesn't mean he doesn't have a fancy for Rosie, too. Or that he hasn't passed them on to anyone.'

'OK.'

'One of these buggers knows something. They've got to.'

Chapter 12

The wipers thumped monotonously, barely clearing the windscreen. The rain had started in earnest while they were in the station; not too heavy, but the drops were large and relentless, shining silvery in the headlights.

It was evenings like this when Tommy had most enjoyed his favourite movie, *Twister*, when he was younger – the weather outside adding to the atmosphere as the characters battled each other and the elements. When Pete had got home from work at a reasonable time, they would huddle up together and he would let Tommy put the DVD into the machine and press the Start button.

Pete didn't know how many times they'd watched that film. He glanced at the clock on the dashboard: 17:01.

Sophie grimaced. 'So, if Sanderson's been spying on the girls, does he get caught, do you think? Have to keep Rosie quiet? Maybe an accident happens in the process? Or are we looking at more than that? Has he actually been abusing one or both of them?'

'We can't know the answer to that unless Becky talks. And she hasn't yet, despite the opportunities we've given her.' Pete flicked on the indicator and slowed for the junction. Headlights dazzled through the rain-smeared windscreen.

'No, but I don't suppose we've asked the question directly, have we? I mean, you wouldn't, would you, unless there was a bloody good reason to? Not about her own dad.'

Pete made the turn. 'Just up here on the left, apparently. Number twenty-seven.'

'That one's fifteen. Nineteen.'

Pete's phone began to ring. He fished it out and handed it to Sophie.

'DS Gayle's phone, PC Clewes speaking.' She paused. Pete could hear a male voice through the tiny speaker as he pulled into a space on the opposite side of the road from Haynes' house.

'One moment, sir. I think you need to be speaking to DS Gayle.'

Pete switched off the lights, the windscreen wipers and the engine. The rain seemed to drum louder on the roof of the car as he took the phone back from Sophie.

'Gayle speaking.'

'Where the hell do you get off, taking my computer away, Sergeant? Or even being in my house in the first place? I specifically told you I wanted to be here when you came round. You had no right to go snooping in my personal property. The permission I gave was specifically for Becky's stuff, not mine.'

'We had your wife's permission, Mr Sanderson. And, as for you wanting to be there, I made no promise on that. There's a young girl missing, in imminent danger. We don't have time to wait on people's usual timetable.'

'Well, this is a bloody disgrace. I'm going to get on to my lawyer. I don't know what powers you think you have, but that was a blatant invasion of privacy. There's no way it was legal. Whatever you might think you've found will be inadmissible. You don't have a leg to stand on, Sergeant.'

'What we found on your computer is directly related to what's on your daughter's, so I think you'll find we've got more than enough legs to stand on, Mr Sanderson. We can extend our enquiries to your judo club, too, if it proves necessary. Now, if you don't mind, I've got work to do.' Pete snapped the phone shut, not giving him the opportunity to reply. 'Right. Where are we looking?'

'That one's nineteen, so twenty-seven should be four doors up. The one with the black door, I reckon. He sounded a bit pissed off.'

'Did, didn't he? Come on then. Let's go see if we can spread the joy a bit further. I really should get myself a bloody hat.' He pushed the door open and stepped out into the rain, pulling his coat up over his head as he ran around the car. He clicked the remote locking device as he ran across the road.

Haynes' gate was open. They ran up the path, Sophie in the lead. Pete dropped his coat back into place as they stepped under the porch. He pressed the doorbell. The chime sounded distantly in the house, but there was no response. He waited a few seconds and tried again.

'Looks like he's not in, Sarge. What do you reckon? Should we wait a bit or come back?'

'What's the time?'

She checked her watch. 'Nearly five-fifteen.'

'He might not have finished work yet.'

'Where does he work?'

'The tyre place on Freemont Street.'

'We could go there.'

Pete grimaced. 'Dave went to see him there. I'd rather catch him at home. Put him off his guard.'

'Yes, but at least we'd see if he was still there. We could pop back here and catch up with him after.'

He shrugged, took out his phone and dialled Dave Miles. 'Dave,' he said as soon as the DC picked up, 'have you got a picture of Kevin Haynes?'

'Not with me. There's one on his record sheet though. Where are you?'

'Outside his house. He's not here.'

'So why don't you call Jane in the squad room? She can forward one to your phone.'

'Jane's not in the squad room. I sent her out. But, good idea. I'll call in and get whoever's there to do it.' He hung up and redialled. 'Hello, Ben. Can you call up the record sheet for Kevin Haynes and send his picture to my phone?'

'Yes, Sarge. I'll get on it now.'

'Thanks.' He hung up again. 'Hold tight,' he said to Sophie. 'Might as well wait in the dry.'

Moments later, his phone pinged. He checked the incoming message window and found a picture of a plump man with a jowly face and stringy blond hair. 'Here we go.' He showed the image to Sophie as a set of headlights swept along the almost dark street.

She grunted softly. 'Didn't get where he is on his looks, did he?'

'He's not exactly handsome. But, now we know what he looks like, I can go into his workplace and see if he's there.'

'Time to get wet again then.'

A white van slowed on the street in front of them. Its indicator began blinking bright orange in the low light.

'Hold on, Sophie. We may have been premature.'

Sure enough, the van turned into the drive and stopped. The lights were switched off, then the engine. Pete breathed a sigh of relief. He wasn't going to do a runner, having seen them. A man emerged from the far side of the vehicle and slammed the door, his hair slicked down by the rain.

'Evening, Mr Haynes. DS Gayle. This is PC Clewes. We need a word.'

'What do you want?' Haynes' hoarse voice was flat and hostile as he pushed past, key in hand.

'You weren't entirely honest with my DC earlier. In fact, I could go so far as to say you lied to him.'

Haynes turned to face him. 'No, I didn't. What about?'

'Your car, Mr Haynes. We've got CCTV of it leaving the scene outside Risingbrook School at the time when our victim was taken.'

'Bollocks. You can't have.' He looked from Pete to Sophie and back again.

'Would you prefer to do this inside, Mr Haynes? Where the neighbours can't hear?'

Haynes swallowed. He looked ready to tell them to get lost, but abruptly turned, pushed the door open and stepped inside, leaving them to follow. He turned left into a sitting room, flicked on a light to show an old, worn chintzy three-piece suite, a small 1930s display cabinet with a collection of antique cameras and a large flat-screen TV with satellite and DVD player underneath. He sat heavily in one of the chairs.

Pete took the near end of the sofa, leaned his elbow on the arm so that he was closer still. 'So . . . What have you got to tell us, Mr Haynes?'

'Nothing. I wasn't there and nor was my car.'

Pete pressed his lips together as Sophie stepped in and took the other armchair. 'I've already said, we've got CCTV. A silver Peugeot estate car, exactly the same as yours, is clearly visible turning left out of the end of Downton Road less than two minutes after Rosie was dropped off by her mother. We've got you, Kevin. The evidence is there, in living colour, ready to be played to the jury on a screen a damn sight bigger than that one you've got in the corner there.'

'And I'm telling you, you're seeing things. It's not me. It's not my car. Have you got the registration? You haven't, have you? So, you've got nothing. A coincidence, at most, if this isn't complete bullshit.' He sat back in his chair, appearing to relax.

'Let me explain something, Kevin. What we've got is a known paedophile, whose car we can show was on the scene of a child abduction. Whether or not you can see the registration, do you honestly think a jury's going to accept that as a coincidence?' He shook his head. 'Not in a million years, matey.'

'All right. How many silver Peugeot estates do you reckon there are in Devon? Or even in Exeter? They ain't rare. And mine don't go at the moment, so it can't have been there. You can take it in and have your mechanics check it out, if you like. They'll tell you.' He laughed. 'They might even get it going again for me in the process. Save me the expense.'

Pete nodded. 'Set that up, would you, PC Clewes?'

'Sarge.' She stood up and stepped into the hallway to make the call.

Pete waited, watching Haynes for any reaction, any faltering or nervousness. There was nothing. Sophie returned, the call finished. 'They'll be round in ten minutes with a tow truck.'

'And it's where, right now?' Pete asked Haynes.

'In the garage.' He jerked a thumb towards the garage at the side of the house.

'Best move the van, then, eh? Let them get at it.'

He grunted, stood up and headed for the door.

Pete's gaze went to Sophie as Haynes stepped past her. She shrugged. Either he'd do a runner when he got in the van or they were on the wrong track. They followed him outside and watched as he climbed into the van and backed it out of the driveway, heading slowly up the street until he found a parking space. He pulled in. The lights were switched off, the engine went quiet, the door slammed and Haynes trudged back towards them through the rain.

'Might not be him, then, Sarge,' Sophie said quietly.

'Either that or he's a damn good poker player.'

'Which is one thing paedos are known for, it has to be said. Bluffing and bullshitting their way into people's confidence.'

'Hm.'

Haynes came up the drive, water running off his hair and soaking his jacket.

'We'll wait for the tow truck, see the car loaded,' Pete said.

'Meantime, I'll go get a camera and take pictures of it. Not that I don't trust the police or anything.'

'We're not interested in a stitch-up, Kevin. We just want to find Rosie Whitlock. Preferably alive and well.'

'I hope you do,' said Haynes. 'And not only because she'll

exonerate me.' He went inside, emerging moments later with a camera. He said nothing as he stepped past them and went into the garage. The flash started firing while Pete and Sophie stood under the porch, waiting.

'So, what do you reckon, Sarge?'

'At this moment, I reckon he's telling the truth. But we'll wait and see.' Pete stuffed his hands into his pockets and hunched his shoulders against the autumn chill.

He stared out into the rain. *Where are you, Rosie Whitlock?*

His mind conjured an image of another occasion when he'd been staring out at the rain, this time from the warmth of his own living room, his arm around the slim shoulders of his son. Tommy had been no more than four, and had wanted desperately to go out and play football in the garden with his dad. Pete had just concluded a major case, which had been taking up his every waking hour for weeks, so this was his first opportunity to spend time with the boy for at least that long. And to a four-year-old, weeks were almost endless. He'd looked down at Tommy's glum little face and not been able to stop himself from laughing.

'It's not the end of the world, son,' he'd said. 'We'll have loads of chances to play outside when the weather's better.'

God, how he wished now that he'd made more of those chances. He squeezed his eyes shut and tried to swallow the lump that had formed in his throat.

His phone rang in his pocket and he took a deep breath, letting it out slowly as he pulled himself together before answering it. 'DS Gayle?'

'Sergeant. It's Alistair Whitlock. It's been twenty-four hours since we spoke. Is there any news?'

Pete grimaced. He knew exactly what Whitlock was going through and the last thing he wanted was to treat the man in the same way as Simon had treated him, back in May, but at this stage . . . 'Sir, we're pursuing a number of lines of inquiry. I'm on one right now, in fact. But there's nothing definite to tell you as yet. As soon as there is, I'll be in touch, believe me. But right now, I've got nothing to tell you, apart from the fact that we're doing everything that can be done.'

'You've got nothing? How can you have nothing after a whole day, for God's sake?'

With their alibis – and his instincts – confirmed, he felt nothing but sympathy for the Whitlocks, along with his natural determination to find their daughter. If it was up to him, he'd tear the city apart looking for her, but he was a police officer. He couldn't ignore the rules. 'I didn't say we've got nothing, sir. What I said was, I've got nothing to tell you. There's a process that we have to go through and we're doing that as swiftly as possible.'

'But you're still no closer to finding Rosie at the end of the day. Am I right?'

'Actually, no. You're not right, sir. We've taken some significant steps towards finding your daughter. We do know what we're doing and I will be in touch as soon as there's anything to tell you.'

A powerful engine sounded from the end of the road and he looked up to see a tow truck coming towards them, a police car with its lights flashing behind.

'Now, I don't want to be rude, sir, but there's a lot to do in as little time as possible so, unless you've got anything you want to tell me . . .'

'No, you're right, Sergeant. I just wanted to know what's going on, that's all.'

'Trust me, you will, as soon as there's anything I can tell you without compromising the case.'

'Thank you.'

Pete ended the call as the tow truck pulled up at the end of the drive and Haynes emerged from the garage, the camera now on its strap around his neck. He drew a long, deep breath and let it out through his mouth.

*

'Mrs Sanderson. Is your husband at home?'

Pete stood on the doorstep of the Sandersons' house in West Hill. It had stopped raining just after they left Exeter and the temperature was already dropping under a clearing night sky.

She stared at him coldly. 'He is. What do you want, Detective?'

'To find Rosie Whitlock, preferably alive and unharmed. The chances of which are decreasing every minute that goes by. But, for the present, I need to talk to your husband.'

'What about?'

'A number of things. Among them, certain pictures we found on his computer, which were the reason we took it with us earlier. Also, the disappearance of a young girl, Alison Stretton, in Bath, in 2011, as she was walking home from her evening judo lesson.'

'What's that got to do with anything?'

'That's yet to be determined. Your husband teaches judo, isn't that right?'

'Yes, but . . . I remember that case. The girl lived on the other side of the city. There was no connection to Neil. There couldn't have been.'

'Oh? Why's that?'

'Because the night she disappeared, he wasn't teaching. He was at home with Becky and me. I remember the announcement on the news. We remarked on the similarity with Becky's age and the fact that the girl did judo.'

'I see.' He turned to Sophie and spoke quietly. 'Check with Bath, will you? See when the announcement went out, in relation to when the girl went missing?'

She nodded and turned away to make the call.

'So, that being the case, Mrs Sanderson, it still leaves us with the pictures on his computer to explain.'

'What pictures?'

'I really think I'd be better discussing that with your husband.'

She sighed heavily. 'Very well. You'd better come in.' She stepped back to allow them entry.

He heard Sophie, behind him, saying, 'OK. Thanks for that.' Her phone snapped shut and she moved closer. 'Avon and Somerset confirmed that the news didn't go out until the day *after* Alison Stretton went missing. So Mr Sanderson's alibi falls kind of flat.'

The horror dawned slowly on Geraldine Sanderson's face. 'Oh God,' she moaned.

They stepped inside and she led them through to the lounge. 'Do you want to speak to Becky? I'll call her down.'

'That won't be necessary just now, thanks.' Much as Pete needed to talk to Becky, he didn't want to do it when either of her parents could intimidate her into silence or lying. Better to wait until morning and catch her on neutral ground. Have a teacher or a school nurse present, a social worker maybe. 'We just need a quick word with your husband, then we'll be on our way.'

'Oh. Yes. Of course.' She went to the door. 'Neil,' she called. 'The police are here. They want to talk to you.'

'I'll be there in a sec.'

She came and sat back down. 'So, what are these pictures that you want to discuss with my husband?'

'Nothing illegal, but they might be relevant to the case.'

'Relevant? How?'

'As I said, that's—'

The door opened and Sanderson stalked in. 'Gayle. What do you want now? What the hell happened to a man's home being his castle?'

'Mr Sanderson, your wife wants to know about the discoveries we made on your computer, earlier. I've left it to you to explain them to her. In the meantime, I'd like to discuss them with you, if that's all right?'

'If you must.' He sat down heavily in the free armchair. 'Do you want to go and get a coffee or something, love?'

She got up. 'Oh, I'm sorry. I didn't offer you anything, Detective. Constable. Would you . . . ?'

'We're fine, thanks, Mrs Sanderson,' Pete told her.

'Right. I'll . . . be in the kitchen, then. Neil?'

He shook his head. 'This won't take long.'

He waited until she had left the room, the door clicking softly shut behind her, then sat back, arms spread wide on the sides of the chair. 'All right. Ask me.'

'Or maybe you should just tell us, Mr Sanderson. Why have you got nude pictures of your daughter and her best friend on your computer?'

He coloured. 'I . . . I got them off Becky's computer. I was checking up on her one day and found them. I copied them so that I could have it out with her about them, the next day, in my office rather than her room. You know how kids will lie about stuff and it's easy enough to wipe them so there's no evidence.'

'And did you? Have it out with her about them?'

'Yes. She said they were just messing around. I suppose, at that age, kids are just becoming aware of . . . Anyway, I told her to be careful. Not to send them over the Internet or email, or anything. They could be misused. And to get rid of them, as I thought I had from mine.'

'She didn't, though, did she? Get rid of them. And nor did you.'

'I thought she'd done as I told her. That that was an end of it.'

'So, what about the ones that weren't taken with a phone camera? The ones where the girls were asleep? I'm thinking you took those yourself, Mr Sanderson. With a camera that the girls wouldn't have had access to.'

'Of course they would. It's in the hall cupboard. They could have borrowed it at any time. If one was asleep, the other could have borrowed it, to take a picture or two, then downloaded them and wiped them off the camera.'

'But why take the risk? If they had their phones to use instead?'

'Well, that's obvious, Sergeant. The SLR is a lot more sensitive in low light. I expect they didn't want to wake each other up in the process.'

'I see. Then maybe you've got an explanation for the ones

in which they're both asleep? And the ones we found on your machine that feature other girls?'

'What? Well . . . I don't . . .' He sat forward, elbows on his knees, focusing on Pete as if Sophie wasn't even there. 'There's nothing illegal on there, Sergeant. They're all perfectly innocent.'

'The subjects are, yes. Perfectly innocent underage girls. Who happen to be naked or nearly so.'

Chapter 13

Pete was almost asleep when the phone rang, loud in the darkness. He snatched it up before it woke Louise, whose breathing was already in the steady rhythm of slumber. Rolling away from her, he put the receiver to his ear. 'Gayle.'

'Sergeant. PC Steele. You need to get down here ASAP. We've found a body.'

'What kind of body? And where's here?'

'A young girl. Around ten or eleven years old. Long, blonde hair, no identification, in the river at the top of St James' Weir. A late-night dog-walker spotted her. He's here, waiting on your arrival, sir.'

'Late night? What bloody time is it?'

'Eleven-oh-three, sir.'

'OK. I'm on the way.' *Christ, an hour and a half*, he thought. That's all it was since he'd got home, too late and too tired to eat. He'd sat for an awkward half-hour with Louise, who barely spoke, before coming to bed. He put the phone down and climbed out of bed.

Louise moaned as he sat up. 'What is it?'

'A young girl's been found at St James' Weir. Dead. Could be our victim.' He stood up and reached for the clothes he had taken off just a short time ago.

'Oh God. What time is it?'

'Just after eleven. Go back to sleep, love. I won't be any longer than I have to.'

She turned over as he stood up and began to dress by the dim light of the street lights. After quickly finger-combing his hair, he picked up his watch and went down the stairs. He'd never gained any benefit from coffee in these situations, so he went straight out, climbed into the car and kept the revs down as much as possible as he backed out and drove away. First stop, the all-night minimart just up from the fish and chip shop on Heavitree Road, where he picked up a Mars bar and a Red Bull. He had finished both, and was fully awake, before he reached the turn down towards the riverside park.

Lights sparkled on the water through the trees, the park stretching away in darkness towards the playing fields and the main road and street lights beyond. Paved paths, like pale ribbons, separated mown grass and council flower beds of a style that had gone out of fashion in the 1960s. As he pulled up by the tall iron gates, he could see a group of people standing around in the far corner, where the main flow of the river was interrupted by a low weir, a side channel cutting off along the edge of the park. Torches made lines and pools of light around them. His breath misted in the crisp air as he headed down towards them.

*

'Shit.'

Pete stared down at the body caught at the top of the weir. The PC was right – she was young. Nine, ten, maybe. About the same age as Annie. He thought back to that morning, when he had left her at the bus stop, the thoughts and feelings he'd had then, and his breathing stopped. He coughed and shook his head, fighting to stay focused on the here and now.

The girl's long blonde hair swirled in the fast-flowing water.

One foot was caught in the bushes at the side of the river, her slender arms swinging in the stream. She must have been newly dead when she went in. Rigor mortis had not yet stiffened her limbs. She was nude, her pale skin almost translucent.

He looked up at the uniformed sergeant. 'Who the hell is she? Because she's not Rosie Whitlock.'

'I . . . I don't know, sir.'

Anger and fear flared in Pete's mind. 'What in God's name's going on here? Did we even know there was another girl missing?'

The sergeant shook his head, clearly at a loss.

'Pete.' The call came from behind him. He turned. Coming towards him at an easy, long-legged stroll, was a tall man in a mackintosh and trilby hat. Bundled up against the chill, he looked almost normal weight, but his face was still cadaverously thin. Pete recognised John Carter, the coroner's officer.

'John. You look like you're putting on weight.'

'Need to. Bloody cold, these winter nights.' He pushed gloved hands into his coat pockets.

'Winter? It's not even November yet, only just autumn. Global warming, I suppose.'

'*Warming*? How the hell can you even speak that word while your breath looks like steam in front of your face and your knackers have shrunk to raisins and gone into hiding?' He shivered.

'So, what have they told you, to drag you out at this time of night?'

'Aren't you supposed to be the bloke in charge here?'

Pete looked around. 'In theory, yes, but this isn't the victim I was expecting.'

'I know nothing, mate. Just a dead girl in the river. The forensics guys are behind me, though.' He jerked a thumb over his shoulder. 'They were just unpacking when I started down here.'

Pete glanced towards the road and saw three pale figures in white disposable overalls, carrying several aluminium cases each, still only halfway across the park.

'I hope to God we don't have to rely on DNA to figure out who she is.'

'Suppose I ought to have a look, now that I'm here.' Carter stepped forward. Stopping at the water's edge, he stared at the body for a long moment then looked up at Pete. 'I'd hope she's on the missing persons database. Girl her age.'

'Yeah. Along with how many thousands of others?'

Carter shook his head. 'Outside my purview, mate.'

'Makes you wonder what the bloody hell's going on round here. The girl over the river, the other week. Rosie Whitlock missing. Now this one.' Despite himself, Silverstone's words came back to him. Was Tommy another victim? He didn't fit the known profile, but . . . He shuddered. 'How many more are there?'

'The one in Powderham is the first that we know of.'

'Maybe, but if this girl's not been dead long, is Rosie still alive?'

'Perhaps one was a replacement for the other.'

'But this girl looks like she was killed after Rosie was taken.'

'Could be he's like a chain-smoker. Lights another before he puts the first one out.'

The forensics team arrived, led by a stocky man with a soft belly bulging under his thin white overalls. He nodded to Carter and turned to shake hands with Pete. 'Harold Pointer. Are you the officer in charge?'

'Seems so. DS Pete Gayle.'

'What have we got?'

'Down there, behind me. A girl, maybe nine or ten years old, nude, caught in the bushes at the edge of the river, probably because of the slower flow at the top of the weir. Looks fresh to me. Don't know if she was dumped here or further upstream, but the position suggests the latter.'

'And I don't suppose we've a chance of proving the former, with all the boots that have been plodding about down here since she was found.'

'Unlikely, I'd agree.'

'Right then. We'd better get to it. The pathologist is on the way. He'll be here in about five minutes.' He turned to his team, began to give crisp, practised orders.

'Suppose I'd best have a word with the witness,' Pete said to Carter. 'Then I'll see who I can shake up at the station and get the misper search underway.'

'Best of British, mate.' Carter took off a glove and offered a large, bony hand. Pete shook it firmly and turned towards the man standing at the edge of the park, with a golden retriever and a young constable.

He was in his mid-sixties, Pete guessed, dressed in pale corduroy trousers and walking boots, a sweatshirt under a waxed jacket and a woollen hat. His jaw was grizzled with a day's growth of grey stubble. His gaze, when he looked up at Pete from petting the dog, was dull.

'Mr Scottsdale?'

'Yes.'

'I'm DS Gayle. I understand you found the body down there?'

'Yes. Well, Nell did. She wouldn't leave it alone, so I went to see what she was so interested in.'

'What time was this?'

'Don't know exactly. Don't wear a watch. No need, since I retired. But we usually come out around ten, for about forty minutes, so probably around twenty past.'

'And you called it in right away?'

'Yes. Wife makes me carry a mobile when I'm out on my own. In case of emergencies.' He rubbed the dog's ears. 'Like this, I suppose.'

'Thank her for us, would you? Did you notice anything else out of the ordinary tonight? Unusual activity on the road at the top of the park maybe? Footprints near the body? Anyone running, that wasn't a regular jogger?'

He was shaking his head, his right hand worrying at the dog's ears and the top of its head. 'No, nothing like that. It was just a regular evening until . . . until Nell found her.'

'And how long were you in the park before you found her?'

'Oh, about fifteen minutes or so, I suppose.'

'OK. Thank you. If you leave your contact details with the constable, we'll let you get on home.' He shook the man's hand and went back down to the river. The body had been lifted from the water and was lying on a plastic sheet. A small, wiry man in his fifties, his greying hair trimmed to little more than stubble, was bending over it, a large leather case open beside him. Pete recognised Dr Tony Chambers.

'Evening, Doc.'

He glanced up. 'DS Gayle. Nice to see you back in the saddle.'

'I'd say it's nice to be here, but . . . hardly, in the circumstances.'

'Quite.'

'So, what can you tell me?'

'Probably nothing you haven't already gleaned for yourself. Time of death is complicated by the water temperature. I'll have to check back at the mortuary. But only a matter of hours. And she's probably been in the water for most of that time so, given the location, I'd suggest she went in somewhere else. And she was put in, she didn't jump. Neither did she drown. They're hardly visible yet – we'll be able to see more detail in a day or two – but there are bruises on the neck consistent with strangulation.'

'All right. Thanks, Doc. I'll have to get a search organised upstream for the dump site then.' He glanced at his watch. It was a little after eleven thirty. 'Meantime, we need to find out who she was. Don't suppose you can help with that, can you?'

'Sadly not, I'm afraid. Not unless she's in the system already, at her tender age.'

'Worth a check, I suppose, but she's not very old.'

'Nine, ten, at a guess.'

'So we should know that she's missing, for Christ's sake.' He brought out his phone and held it up. 'You mind?'

'Go ahead.'

Pete snapped a couple of close-ups of the girl's face.

'I'll have the autopsy done by midday, if you want to pop round. First on the table, as it's a child.'

'OK. See you later.' He headed off up the hill. This bloody case was getting more complicated, not less. And he didn't have time for complications, if he was going to find Rosie alive and well.

With his phone in hand, he checked the contact details the old man had given him and dialled with his thumb. It was picked up on the second ring.

'Hello?' A nervous-sounding female voice made it sound like a question.

'Mrs Scottsdale?'

'Yes.'

'I'm DS Gayle, from Heavitree Road CID. I was wondering if I could talk to your husband.'

'Oh, he's out with the dog. I've been expecting him home for half an hour or so. I don't know where he's got to.'

'What time did he leave?'

'The usual time. About ten.'

'OK, well, not to worry. I'll call him in the morning.' He hung up. He'd have liked to tell her the old man was fine and would be home in a few minutes, but it would only complicate things if he now went back on his previous subterfuge. And she would only have to worry a few minutes more. At least he had confirmed that the old man had nothing to do with the body, other than finding it.

*

Angry and dismayed that he did not know anything about the dead girl, Pete went straight to the station. The desk sergeant looked up from the magazine he was reading. 'What the hell are you doing here, at this time of night? Haven't you got a home to go to?'

'Yes, and a nice warm bed. But it looks like I've got a new

bloody case to go with the missing girl I caught yesterday.' Pete checked his watch. 'Yes, it still was yesterday. Just.'

'What, this dead one? She's not yours, is she?'

'She is now. But she's not Rosie Whitlock.'

'Shit. Do we know who she is then?'

'That's why I'm here at this time of night. To start trying to find out.'

The big man shook his head. 'It's a wicked bloody world, isn't it?'

'Too damn right.' Pete tapped the combination into the door lock and headed upstairs.

The squad room was in darkness. He flicked just one of the four light switches on and crossed to his desk. Left his coat on as he sat down and switched on the computer. Opening the Missing Persons Bureau website, he typed in the dead girl's details, as best he could guess them. No results. That, sadly, could not be right. He removed the date last seen and hit the search button again. Thirty-two cases came back.

Pete sighed and settled in to scroll through them. Most could be eliminated immediately – they were way too long ago. Of the five remaining, three were in Yorkshire and one in London. The fifth looked possible though. He took out his phone, navigated to one of the pictures he had taken of the dead girl and held it up beside the computer monitor. She looked very similar. He cursed his stupidity for not checking the dead girl's eye colour. After closing the picture on his phone, he found the pathologist's number and dialled.

'Hi, Doc. Pete Gayle. Sorry, I forgot to check. Do you have the dead girl's eye colour?'

'Slipping, Peter?'

'Second day back and all that, I suppose. Plus, I'm knackered.'

'And a lot on your mind, I expect.' The doctor sighed. 'I was really sorry to hear about young Thomas. But back to the matter in hand. Yes, the girl has blue eyes.'

'OK. Thanks. I think I might have an ID.'

'You haven't entirely lost your touch then.'

Pete gave a short laugh. 'We'll see. 'Night, Doc.'

He looked at the computer screen, at the bright and sassy-looking little girl with blonde pigtails that stared back at him. Lauren Carter. Age – he checked the data beside the photo – would be ten now. Last seen six weeks ago, at the children's home where she resided in Barnstaple, north Devon. This was the third time she had absconded from there, which appeared to follow a trend from her previous foster carers – hence her presence in the home. She'd been in the system since the age of six, when her single mother died of an overdose of class A drugs.

'Poor kid. Never had a chance, did you?' he said softly. 'Well, if that is you we found tonight, it's too late to help you now, but we will get the bastard who killed you. I promise you that.'

*

Pete downloaded the photos of the dead girl from his phone and printed them out, along with the missing persons file on Lauren Carter. He stuck them to the board and wrote underneath, 'Our victim? Confirm'.

He was just reaching for the power button on his computer when the phone on his desk rang. He hesitated for an instant. Should he answer it at this time of night?

He sighed and picked up the receiver. 'DS Gayle.'

'Sergeant. You're the man leading the Rosie Whitlock inquiry that I read about in the evening paper?'

'That's right.'

'This is the A & E sister at the Royal Devon and Exeter. I'm afraid there's been another attack.'

Chapter 14

Pete checked his watch. It was after midnight, but there was no choice in the matter. He picked up the phone and dialled.

'Yes?' Jane's voice was groggy, full of sleep.

'Sorry, but I need you at the hospital, ASAP.'

That woke her up. 'Huh? Why? Has she been found?'

'No. There's been another attack. I just got the call from the A & E sister. This time the girl survived. The perp brought her to the RDE and just let her go, or so it seems. She walked in under her own steam. Barely dressed, but OK apart from the rape and the trauma of what she went through.'

'So, she can give us a description?'

'Don't know. Like I said, I just got the call myself. And I thought any questioning would be better coming from you, in the circumstances.'

'Right. I'll meet you there. Where are you?'

'Squad room.'

'At – getting on for 1 a.m.? What the hell for?'

'That's another story. And one we will discuss, but not now.'

'I see.' Her tone said she didn't, but he let it go.

'See you there. I'll have a word with the nurse or doctor while I wait for you.'

'OK. Shan't be long.'

Pete left the incident room and headed down the stairs. The sergeant at the front desk was waiting for him to pass.

'Something promising, I hope?'

'Potentially. We've got a survivor,' Pete told him. 'On my way to get the details now.'

'Good. Hope she can give you a description. Preferably with a name and address to go with it, eh?'

Pete laughed. 'That ain't my kind of luck – not lately, at least.'

'That can change.'

Pete pulled his coat tighter around him as he stepped out into the freezing night. *I bloody hope so*, he thought. *For Rosie Whitlock's sake.*

He had parked the Mondeo out front, with no reason not to at this time of night. He hopped in and swung the car out of the space and down towards the road. After driving quickly to the hospital on clear roads, he parked in one of the few spaces outside A & E. A man was standing to one side of the entrance doors, smoking. In his late twenties, at a guess, in dark jeans and a leather jacket.

Inside, the reception desk was staffed by a young woman with blonde hair in a short ponytail. He showed her his badge. 'DS Pete Gayle.'

'Ah. You'll be here for the girl who came in earlier. Molly Danvers.'

'I wasn't told her name, but if you're talking about the rape victim, yes.'

She hesitated briefly. 'I don't . . .'

He held his hands up. 'I don't want to talk to her. Not at the moment, anyway. I've got a female colleague on the way for that. I'd like to speak to the person who treated her if possible. Or the sister who called it in.'

'Ah.' Her relief was obvious. 'In that case, let me give them a call, yes?' She picked up the phone and dialled an extension.

'Sister? The policeman you called about Molly Danvers? DS . . .' Pete held up his badge again. 'Gayle. He's at the front desk. He'd like to see you.' A brief pause. 'OK, thanks.' She put the phone down. 'She's on the way.'

'Thank you.'

Pete looked around. It was remarkably quiet. No rush of trauma victims, no moaning or wailing. It was almost restful. He guessed it was the time of night. Chairs lined the far wall, which was covered in medical posters. To the left of the reception desk was a large rack of leaflets about various illnesses and issues, from heart disease to getting the pill without your parents' permission. Pete was wondering about the ethics of that, when he heard the clip of heels on the polished floor and turned to see the sister coming around the corner towards him.

She was small and stocky, with a brisk step and confident, enquiring eyes in a face that could never achieve stern, he thought. 'Detective Sergeant Gayle?'

He shook her hand and was surprised by the quick, firm grip. 'Pete.'

'I'm Veronica Martyn. This is a terrible business.' She shook her head. 'The poor girl was in an awful state. Simply awful. Would you like to come and talk in my office?'

'Yes. Thanks.' He turned to the receptionist. 'My colleague, DC Bennett will be here shortly. Direct her to us, would you, please?'

'Of course.'

He followed the sister around the corner and along a corridor. She turned off to the right, into a wide waiting room with several doors off it and a handful of people sitting, waiting. At the far side, another corridor led off. She turned in at the second door on the left.

Her office was small but neat and tidy. Two chairs stood on the near side of the desk, a larger, more comfortable one on the far side, the window behind looking out onto a small garden space hemmed in by buildings.

'Please, have a seat.'

Pete sat and took out his notebook and pen. 'So, what can you tell me about the girl? Molly Danvers, was it?'

'Yes. She came running into Reception not half an hour ago, wearing just a school skirt, hands taped together, screaming that a man had attacked her and was chasing her. As we calmed her down, it transpired that she had been abducted from quite close to her home, outside the city, raped, then brought here, where she escaped from her abductor in the car park. I called you and then her parents. They're on the way.'

'How old is she?' Pete asked.

'Fourteen.'

He nodded. 'A brave girl. Did she say anything about the man who did it? What he looked like? What he was driving?'

'She gave us no description of him, but she did say that he was driving a white van. I imagine a Transit or something, from what she said.'

Pete nodded. 'Is there any CCTV coverage of the car park here?'

'There should be. Sadly, it's not operational at the moment. It broke down last week. Should have been fixed by now, but apparently the part that's required has to come from Germany.'

Pete grimaced. 'Did she say anything else that might be useful? When was she abducted?'

'This afternoon, on her way home from school. She wasn't more specific.'

'And injuries? Were there any, apart from those caused by the rape itself?'

'Her wrists were quite sore from the tape. We treated and bandaged them. It's too early for any bruising to show, of course, but she has no broken bones, knife wounds, anything like that, no.'

'OK. It's just that the more you can tell me, the less my colleague has to ask her at this stage. Less stress for her – you know.'

'Of course. That's . . . very understanding of you, Detective.'

'I've got a daughter of my own,' Pete said. 'Ten years old. I'm just aware of how I'd want her to be treated in a case like this, heaven forbid.'

'Yes, quite. We didn't question her too closely for the same reasons. We thought that best left to yourselves. We just let her say what she wanted to.'

There was a knock at the door and Jane came in.

'Ah. DC Jane Bennett, this is Sister Veronica Martyn.'

Jane shook hands with the sister and took the vacant chair.

'So, we've got a fourteen-year old victim, abducted from near her home, outside the city, by a man in a white Transit-type van, bound, raped, but not beaten significantly. Sounds like he might have been planning to drop her off here, but she escaped from him in the car park and ran in on her own. Parents are on the way,' Pete summed up. 'So there was no mention of a gun, a knife, a Taser – anything like that?' he asked the sister.

'No. Nothing. She was quite distraught, of course, but that's all I can think of to tell you, Detective.'

'Well, thank you. You've been very helpful.'

'Can I talk to her?' Jane asked.

'We haven't sedated her so, as long as she's willing, yes.'

'The sooner we can get all the information she might have, the easier it'll be to catch the man that did this.'

'Of course.'

They stood. 'Call me when you're done,' Pete said to Jane.

'Will do.'

He thanked the sister again and headed back towards the front of the hospital while the two women went in the opposite direction. He nodded to the nurse on the front desk and walked outside. Maybe the guy smoking near the doors had seen something. But he was gone. Pete returned to the reception desk.

'When I came in there was a bloke outside here, smoking. Mid-twenties, maybe. Dark hair. Leather jacket. Any idea who he was?'

'Um . . . None of . . . Oh, maybe that reporter guy. We had a girl come in earlier. She'd been knocked off her bike somewhere in the city. Broken arm and some cuts and bruises. I don't know how he heard about it.'

'Do you know which paper he was with?'

'*E & E*, I think.'

'Thanks.'

*

Pete hurried back to the squad room. If a reporter had seen the girl go into the hospital, it would be all over the papers in the morning. Combine that with the story on Rosie Whitlock, and you were guaranteed to have either a panic or a bloody witch-hunt for paedophiles on your hands by lunchtime. He needed to get across this now. There was no time for going back to bed.

On the other hand, if a reporter had seen the girl going in there, why hadn't he called it in? Arrogant sod thought the information highway had one-way signs on it, probably. Well, he'd see about that. He'd have the little bugger in here for the rest of the damn night, if needs be.

He pictured the man standing under the light near the hospital doors, drawing on his cigarette like some kind of latter-day James Dean. And above his head, the globe of a CCTV camera that wasn't working and hadn't been for over a week.

Was that coincidence? Or was it deliberate? White van. Maintenance. Of course, anyone working at the hospital would have had a CRB check done. But all that meant was they hadn't been caught yet, and you could say that about the majority of paedophiles.

He threw his coat over the back of his chair and picked up the phone. Dialled Jane's number for the second time that night.

'Jane, it's me. Are you still at the hospital?'

'Yes.'

'Find out who the maintenance guy is, who should have fixed

the CCTV, will you? Any details they're willing to give. Stress the circumstances if need be.'

'OK. Is that it?'

'Yes. Talk to you later.'

'Right, boss.'

She hung up and he reached into his desk for a notebook, flipped through it until he found the number for the Exeter *Express & Echo*. He used the landline, on the basis that police numbers would not come up on caller ID, whereas his mobile might be recognised. Tucking the handset under his ear, he fetched out his current notebook and opened it to a fresh page. He had not had time to click out the tip of his pen when the call was answered.

'News desk. Angela Jennings.'

'Got you on the night shift now, have they?'

'Who is this?'

'Police. CID. Who did you have at the RDE tonight? Young lad, mid-twenties or so.'

'Now, that would be telling, wouldn't it? Why do you want to know?'

'I want to know because he failed to report an incident that he witnessed while he was there.'

'Well, if you know that, you don't need him to report it, do you?'

Pete felt the flare of anger and fought to keep his voice calm. 'I'm investigating the disappearance of one young girl and the rape of another. So I'm not in the mood for games. I want his name and number. Anything short of that will be seen as obstruction. And press privileges will not cover it.'

'So, you're suggesting that the two events are linked? The disappearance and the attack tonight?'

'I'm not suggesting anything. I'm not telling you anything. And I won't be telling you anything unless you stop fannying about and give me what I need.'

'OK. Hold on a minute. I need to get to my office and look it up.'

'If you hear the sound of blue lights in the next couple of minutes, it'll be because I was holding on too long.'

'All right, all right. Just a minute.' She put him on hold. He waited, drumming his fingers on the desk, for what seemed like far too long until, at last, she was back. 'Who am I talking to? Specifically?'

'DS Pete Gayle.'

'Ah. I wondered if it might be. I covered your son's case.'

'I remember.' His mind pictured a woman in her late thirties with long, dark hair and strong features. 'Have you got what I asked for?'

'Yes. But I was wondering . . . this girl who was attacked tonight? What can you . . .'

'At this moment, I can tell you nothing. It's an ongoing investigation. The name and number?'

'You really don't play nice, do you?'

'It's late and I haven't got time for games.'

'Well, it's Lee Birch you want. I'll give you his mobile number.' She read it out.

'And his address?'

She read that off too. Pete recognised it as being on the hill, on the far side of the river. 'Thank you,' he said and hung up. He dialled zero for the front desk. When it was picked up, he said, 'It's Pete Gayle, upstairs. You might get the *E & E* ringing up in the next few minutes. Block them, alright?'

'My pleasure.'

Pete grinned. 'Thought it might be. Cheers.' He killed the call and dialled Lee Birch's number. It rang and rang. Pete began to wonder if the little bugger was going to pick up or ignore it, but finally, it was connected.

'Lee Birch, Exeter *Express & Echo*.'

'Mr Birch. Detective Sergeant Gayle, Devon and Cornwall Police. I saw you earlier this evening, outside the hospital.'

'Uh . . . Yes, I was there.'

'So you saw the young girl that ran in there, barely dressed.'
'Yes, but I . . .'
'Was just about to phone us? Yeah. Believe it or not, I've heard it before,' Pete interrupted.

'Yeah, well . . . I couldn't add anything to what you'd already have from the girl and the hospital CCTV, so why waste your time?'

'OK.' Pete let up just slightly. 'So, what exactly did you see?'

'The girl ran in from the far side of the car park. Then, as I was watching her, I heard an engine. I turned round and this van was peeling out of there. Big, white job. Might have been a Nissan or a Toyota. Something like that.'

'And did it have anything distinguishing on it? A logo? A name? A phone number?'

'No, just plain white.'

'Did you see the driver?'

'Only a flash: just enough to tell there was one.'

'The number plate?'

'The van was at the far side of a bunch of cars. I only saw the top half of it.'

The door opened and Pete glanced up.

'Well, thank you for your assistance, Mr Birch.' He hung up. 'Jane, what are you doing here?'

'It's as easy to come in as phone you. Especially as you've been on the phone for ages.'

'So, what have you got?'

'The girl was dropped off – and attacked – in a white van. Like the one Kevin Haynes drives on occasion, while his car's in dock.'

'OK. But we eliminated him from Rosie's abduction. He was elsewhere.'

'I know, but . . .' She paused. 'There was something about a white van.' She snapped her fingers. 'I know what it was. The CCTV from near the school. It was a white van that was blocking the view of the Peugeot that we thought might be Haynes'.'

He aimed his pen at her, gun-like. 'Spot on. Have we got a number for it?'

'Not yet. We were concentrating on the Peugeot.'

'What about the hospital maintenance guy? What did you find on him?'

'Name, address, phone number, CRB reference. And the fact that he doesn't drive. He rides a bike to work.'

'He might have the use of a car though. Or a van. Parents, girlfriend, sibling – you never know. We'll need to check in the morning. And see if he lives alone, where his parents live and so on.'

'Easier to go talk to him. I'll do that on the way in.'

'OK. Did the girl give you anything in the way of a description of her attacker?'

'Scruffy blond hair, chubby face. She's going to do a composite in the morning.'

'Sounds like Haynes.'

'Yeah, but like you said, he didn't take Rosie Whitlock.'

'Doesn't mean he didn't do this one.'

'Shit, you think we've got two on the go now?'

Pete sighed. 'It's the last thing I want to think, but we've got to accept the possibility.'

'We going to knock him up then? Have a word?'

'Not until we've got the composite. We need something firm to knock him off his game. You know what these blokes can be like. Glib as a bloody estate agent on double commission.'

'In which case, I reckon it's bedtime – again.'

Pete grimaced. 'Yeah.'

He just hoped he could get back and into bed without waking Louise.

Chapter 15

Pete gently pushed the front door closed and slipped his coat off. He hung it over the end of the bannister and headed upstairs, carefully stepping over the second stair, which always creaked loudly. There was no way he could make it upstairs completely silently, but he hoped he wouldn't wake Louise. After all, it was a perfectly normal noise. It happened whenever anyone went up and down the stairs.

Without putting the light on, he undressed and climbed into his pyjamas, which he had left on the chair when he dressed.

He slipped under the duvet, closed his eyes and let out a soft sigh. Louise's breathing had not changed.

'Was it her?'

Pete's eyes snapped open. 'Sorry. I thought you were asleep. No, it was another girl – one that I didn't even know was missing.'

'What, so you're the missing kid specialist now? The one to call every time a kid turns up missing or dead?'

He sighed. *Here it comes.* 'No. It was a young blonde girl with no identification. The officer on the scene thought it might be Rosie Whitlock, but it wasn't. She was too young. More like our Annie's age.'

'So, what took you so long? You don't normally spend that

long at a scene. Nowhere near. Was *she* there? Jane? Detective Constable Bennett?'

'No.'

'But you called her, didn't you? Commiserating with each other, were you? Holding each other's hands through the difficult process of discovery?' Her voice had got louder as her tone grew more bitter.

'Keep it down, will you?' He turned to face her, pushing himself up on one elbow.

'What? Don't want to disturb the neighbours?' She sat up against the headboard. 'Don't worry – I'm sure they're used to my little outbursts by now. They can understand a grieving, neurotic woman's need to vent. Especially when her husband would rather be at work than at home with her.'

'I wasn't thinking of the neighbours. I was thinking of Annie. She—'

'Annie understands perfectly well that her dad would rather spend time with a pretty redhead at work than with her mother.'

Pete sat up quickly. 'What the hell are you on about? What have you been telling her? And what's Jane got to do with anything?' *Shit.* He slumped as soon as the words left his mouth. The last thing he needed was to encourage her.

'You're screwing her, aren't you? Jane bloody Bennett? You must be. All I ever hear about when you're at work is "Jane did this . . .", "Jane said that . . ." And you couldn't wait to get back there to her, could you?'

Here we go again, he thought. Accusations and arguments like this, based on her own lack of self-confidence rather than anything he'd actually done, had become an increasingly frequent feature of her self-destructive depression over the past several weeks. At least partly, he thought they might be some sort of twisted way of gaining reassurance from him, but that made them no less difficult and traumatic to deal with. Especially as, before Tommy went missing, she had been so strong-minded.

'I've been here, with you, for the last five months. I went back because they needed me to cover while they did all these simultaneous drug raids. You know that. But, when this case came in, I couldn't pass it up. It wouldn't have been fair to rest of the guys or the victim. And it's not a five-minute job. There is no easy answer. And, in the meantime, the victim's out there, somewhere, going through Christ knows what, probably at the hands of a pervert who seems to be killing his victims when he gets bored with them. Like this one tonight. Murdered and dumped naked in the river at roughly the same age as our Annie. Who I didn't want you waking up because she's got school in the morning and she needs her sleep.'

'So, what took so bloody long then, if you're so bloody innocent?'

'Another attack. Another girl. But this one survived, so we had to go and see what we could find out about what happened to her, who'd attacked her.'

'So, I was right. You did call her.'

'What the hell is wrong with you? I am not screwing Jane Bennett. I never have. The thought has never crossed my mind. Or hers, I'd imagine. We're both married. I've never been unfaithful to you and I don't suppose for a minute that she has, to Robbie.'

'Yeah, right. And I'm just supposed to take your word for that, am I? Trust you, like a good little wifey? All the time you spend with her. The amount you talk about her, it's like there's nobody else in the bloody station. Or if there is, they're just background.'

How the hell could he get through to her? To break this cycle of baseless suspicion? He drew a breath. 'Jane is to me what I was to Colin Underhill, a few years ago. A student and an assistant. And a friendly ear, now and then, I suppose, but certainly nothing more than that. Yes, of course, her being female makes a difference at times. Like tonight, with this new victim. *I* couldn't very well go and talk to her, could I? The last thing a young girl who's just been attacked and raped needs to see is another man, especially one in authority. So I sent Jane, as a sympathetic ear, in the hope of getting some kind of a lead from her.'

'And did you? Get a lead?'

'Potentially, yes. We've got a couple of things to follow up on in the morning. And the girl's agreed to do a composite.'

'So, then this'll all be over?'

'We hope so, yes.'

She gave a long, shuddering sigh. 'I'm sorry.'

'What? What for?' He would never get used to these sudden switches.

Her eyes shone as she gazed back at him in the dim light. 'Being such a pain. Such a useless bloody wife. I know you don't deserve all the shit I give you. I just can't help it sometimes.' She choked back a sob.

Pete drew a breath. 'I haven't dealt with the situation perfectly either. I know that. I just cope in different ways to you, that's all. When you've gone through what we have, it brings out the differences between people. It's bound to. And, I suppose, in the heat of the moment, those differences can be hard to cope with.'

'Yes, but, if you love each other, you ought to be able to help each other through, hadn't you? I mean, we seem to be pulling in different directions, not the same one. And I don't blame you for that. It's just . . . I don't know how to carry on anymore. What there is to carry on for. We made a son, to carry on for us after we're gone, and now he's gone before us. What was the point of it all? What are we doing here?'

Oh, Jesus. Now she was getting maudlin. How was he supposed to cope with this? 'What we're doing here is raising Annie,' he said. 'If nothing else, we've got her and we need to be here for her. She's lost a brother, the same as we've lost a son. We're supposed to help her through that.' *Not the other way around*, he couldn't help thinking.

'Well, thanks for pointing that out,' she sniped, her mood switching abruptly again. 'That makes me feel so much better.'

Shit. 'I didn't mean it as a dig. Just . . . I don't know. My poor way of saying I can't do it all on my own. I need your help sometimes.'

'Oh, just sometimes, is it? Mostly, you can manage on your own, eh?'

'That's not what I said, or what I meant. If you're going to twist everything around, there's no point in me saying any more, is there?'

'Oh, here we go. Silent treatment again now?'

'Jesus! You're just arguing for the sake of arguing now.'

'At least it makes me feel something! Even if it is just anger, it's better than constant nothingness.'

The door burst open and Annie rushed in, in her Winnie-the-Pooh nightie. 'Mum! Don't argue. Please.' She ran to her mother's side and threw her arms around her neck. 'I don't like it when you argue.' She sobbed into her mother's shoulder.

Louise's arms went around her. 'I'm sorry, love. It's all right, really. I didn't mean to upset you. I have a job dealing with things at the moment, that's all. And sometimes I just lose my rag, for no good reason. It's nothing to worry about.'

Pete sighed. He worried about it and had for months now, but what could he do? He silently thanked Annie for coming to his rescue. Reaching across, he stroked her back. He honestly didn't know how he'd have got through the past few months without her.

Chapter 16

Pete headed straight for Colin Underhill's office when he arrived in the morning, bursting in without bothering to knock. He slammed the thin door behind him. 'What the fuck's going on in this place, Colin?'

Colin looked up from the documents he was reading. 'Meaning?'

'Another dead girl was found last night, down by St James' Weir. I didn't even know there was another one missing until she was found. I feel like I'm operating in a bloody vacuum here. Nobody's willing to tell me anything in case it hurts my feelings, yet I'm supposed to somehow know everything that's been going on while I was off. I'm not bloody psychic.'

Colin folded his hands together on his desk and sat back. 'Then maybe you'd better start again from the beginning and try making some sense this time. A girl was found down by the weir . . .'

'Blonde. Roughly ten years old. Naked and recently dead. Her picture's on the board, with a possible ID that I found last night. I was called because the responding officer thought it might be Rosie Whitlock, but it wasn't. And I hadn't been told of any other missing girls, apart from the one who was found over at Powderham the other week – and that was only because I overheard something and asked a direct question of Jane Bennett. I do not need treating with kid gloves, Colin. I wish you'd tell the team that, so they can get over the idea ASAP.'

'OK. Well, I wasn't aware of any other missing girls either, so you can climb down off that horse for a start. Which means, you need to follow up on that possible ID. Get on to the Missing Persons Bureau and the National Crime Database and get it confirmed.'

Pete felt as if the wind had been knocked out of him. 'OK then. But in the meantime, can you have a word with the team, anyway? Tell them to put the bloody cotton wool away. If it comes from you as well as me . . .'

'OK. How's it going, otherwise?'

'We've got Rosie Whitlock missing, another girl snatched from outside her home and raped last night, and this new one dead in the river.'

'I know about the one who turned up at the RDE. How come you caught it?'

'I was here, so Barry put the call through.'

Colin grunted. 'You going to cope with all three?'

Pete sighed. 'Not you as well? If they're not related, I hate to think what's going on in this city. So, yes, I'll cope.'

'OK then. But don't go assuming anything. Including a link —much as we might hope there's one.' Colin picked up the papers from his desk. 'Anything else?'

'No, that's it.' Pete reached for the door handle.

'Right then. Let me know if you need anything. You've seen the vultures gathered out the front?'

'Yeah.' You could hardly miss the huge TV lorries, film crews clustered around cameras on big tripods, soundmen holding booms with grey, woolly microphones. He had seen Sky News, ITN and the BBC in front of the station.

'There's two more crews at the RDE, plus another one or two down by the river, apparently. So best behaviour, all right? The whole team. I'll leave you to tell them that.'

No doubt the national newspapers would be hovering around somewhere close at hand, too. Pete had enough to deal with, without the added pressure of working under that kind of spotlight, but there was no way of avoiding it in this day and age.

He reached for the door.

'Gently, this time,' Colin said, looking up from his paperwork.

Pete closed the door and returned to his desk. 'Dave, have you got this morning's *E & E*?'

'Yeah. Here you go.' He folded the paper in half and tossed it over.

A stock photo of the Royal Devon and Exeter hospital filled the prime spot on the front page, with a smaller night shot of the place inset in one corner and a report under the banner headline, 'Another girl attacked in Exeter'. Pete scanned the sensationalist article with Lee Birch's byline. The bare facts of the girl's arrival at the hospital, the reason behind it and her condition at the time were interspersed with a lot of hyperbole about the safety of Exeter's streets and its young people and the lack of activity on the part of the police.

'Cantankerous little bastard,' Pete muttered, as he flipped open the newspaper. The story that Birch had been at the hospital to cover had been relegated to page three, in deference to the much more sensational cover story. 'Councillor accused in hit-and-run'. He read on. 'A 57-year-old city councillor was last night charged with leaving the scene of an accident after witnesses saw his BMW 7 Series hit 15-year-old Rebecca Davenport, who was riding her bicycle on Western Way, and fail to stop. Rebecca was knocked off her bicycle, and narrowly missed by another vehicle travelling behind the councillor. She was wearing a hi-visibility jacket and reflective strips on her cycle helmet and her bicycle was displaying both front and rear lights. She was admitted to the Royal Devon and Exeter Hospital with a broken arm, cuts and bruises. The councillor was unavailable for comment, but a police spokesman confirmed that his BMW had sustained damage. The councillor himself has been charged with driving without due care and attention, leaving the scene of an accident and driving while under the influence of alcohol. He is due to be bailed today.'

Pete closed the paper and tossed it back to Dave.

'Jane told us about the girl who was attacked last night,' Dave said. 'White van again. Could be the same guy as took Rosie Whitlock.'

'We hope.' Pete checked his watch. 'The artist should be with her any time now, to try for a photofit.'

*

'All right. Here it is.'

Pete stuck the new photofit image up on the board. 'Fresh from the artist.'

'That's Kevin Haynes,' Dave said straight away. 'Got to be.'

'Yep. Who wants to come with me to pick the bugger up?'

Every hand in the room shot up instantly.

'Preferably someone who's not going to kick his balls up into his throat in the process,' Pete qualified. 'We need to make a case that's going to stick like superglue. Plus, we've got the press camping in the car park, watching our every move.'

All hands stayed up.

'OK. Dave, you interviewed him the first time. It's your shout. Sophie, will you get DCI Silverstone to sign off on the warrant?'

She nodded and Dave Miles was out of his chair in an instant, to a chorus of boos from the others.

'We'll need forensics to go over his van and his house, too,' Pete told Sophie.

'OK, Sarge.'

'Jane, while we're out, I need you to get started on the dead girl's identity. I came up with the possible on the board there last night, but it needs confirming. You know the drill – the Missing Persons Bureau and Missing People databases, then get onto HQ, up the road, Avon and Somerset and the Dorset forces, make sure they haven't got anything outstanding.'

'Right. Will do.'

There was a general bustle of movement as Pete headed for the door.

'Hold on, I've got some Swarfega somewhere, to cut through the grease. Make sure he doesn't slip through your fingers again, Dave,' someone called.

'Gently does it, mate. Not.'

'Best check your handcuffs before you go. Make sure he can't slip out of them.'

Dave turned to face the room. 'Trust me, he won't be slipping anywhere. Except maybe on a wet patch, so he lands on his face somewhere nice and hard.'

'There'll be none of that,' Pete said. 'The last thing we need is for him to have any excuse to get out of here, once we've got him.'

'Yes, boss.'

*

'We've got you, Kevin. There's no point in bullshit and fairy stories.' Pete leaned back in his chair in Interview Room One. 'The only way you can help yourself is by telling us everything.'

Dave was sitting forward, pen poised over his notebook while the video camera and digital voice recorder whirred away softly. Haynes, sitting opposite them, was sweating now.

'Forensics are going over your house right now, and the van. Plus, we've got witnesses. The girl herself, and someone who saw you leaving the hospital after you dropped her off. And that's significant, you know – the fact that you took her there. It'll count in your favour. But you need to talk to us. The more you tell us, the better off you'll be when it comes to sentencing.'

'And the more likely you are to survive your sentence,' Dave added coldly. 'You know how things get leaked from government departments and so on. Happens all the time. A careless word. A document left out by accident when someone's desperate for a pee. And then the other cons get to know what you're in for and . . . Game over. A quick shiv in the shower or behind the washing machines, and you're bleeding your life away.'

'You're threatening me,' Haynes whined.

Dave shook his head. 'Just pointing out the facts of life.'

'But it doesn't have to be that way.' Keeping his voice level, Pete stifled the disgust and burning rage he'd felt for months now against anyone who took an unnatural interest in kids. He had to try to play the good cop here. To show empathy. Get the guy onside. Get him talking. 'You tell us everything – not just the one you let go, but the others too. The girl you took the other morning, the one we found last night down by the old Priory and any others that we don't know about yet. Because, trust me, we will find out. Forensics will see to that. It's bloody amazing what they can come up with, these days. The tiniest little thing, they can get a DNA profile off it and get an ID just like that.'

Haynes' expression had been changing as Pete spoke, his frown deepening, the look of horror in his eyes intensifying. Then it shifted the other way.

'But you won't find anything from any other girls,' he said. 'Because there isn't anything. I didn't do any others.'

'Just the one you took to the RDE,' Dave clarified.

'Yes. And that was your bloody fault. Pressuring me. Hounding me for no good reason. I'd been clean. I hadn't even gone near an underage girl. Hadn't even wanted to since I came out. But you had to start on me, didn't you? Just because I had a record. No evidence against me, but I'd done it once, never mind how long ago, so it had to be me. Well, it wasn't. I didn't have nothing to do with that girl the other day. And I've never even been down by the Priory.'

Dave leaned forward again, arms flat on the table as his gaze locked on Haynes. 'You don't need to have been there, Kevin, and you know it. You dumped her in further upstream, didn't you? Let her float downriver, hoping she'd end up in the sea. Well, she didn't, see. She ended up in the reeds, at the top of the weir there. So we found her, and it won't matter that she's been in the water, because if we can't get DNA off her skin, we can still get it from inside her.'

Haynes' eyes widened. 'I bloody hope so, because then it'll clear me. I haven't killed anybody. You know my record. You know I've never killed anyone.'

'Not before, no,' Dave insisted. 'But it's been a while, hasn't it? Like you say, you've been a good boy now for – what? Three years, is it? Must have been building up something rotten – the frustration. The need. It gets that intense, it's easy to make a mistake, isn't it? Press a bit too hard when you're holding her down. Squeeze a bit too tight when you're trying to shut her up.'

Pete leaned forward. 'What Dave's trying to say, Kevin, is that murder isn't necessarily what we'll be looking at here. If it was an accident, then manslaughter might well be an option. But you've got to come clean with us. We can't help you if you don't help us. That's the way it works.'

'But I didn't kill anyone! I'm telling you – that one last night's the only girl I've touched since I came out of prison. And I wouldn't have done that, if it wasn't for—'

'The pressure we put you under,' Dave finished for him. 'Yeah, you've said already.'

'All right. Give us a minute,' Pete said. 'Dave . . .' He stood up and reached for the door handle.

Dave followed him out and closed the door behind them. 'What do you reckon, boss?'

'He's coughed to Molly Danvers, not that he had much option. But the others – he knows forensics will pick up any trace of them in his house or the van, so why wouldn't he admit to them, too, if he took them?'

'Murder's a damn sight bigger than abduction or child sex offences.'

'Yes, but manslaughter? He could be out in four or five years.'

Dave nodded. 'We'll need to check that he hasn't got any other property anywhere. And make sure the forensics guys go over his car. We don't know how long it's been out of commission.'

'Do that, would you? I'll go back in there and see if I can ease anything more out of him.'

Chapter 17

Pete leaned forward, elbows on the table. He desperately wanted to pick the little shit up and shake the truth out of him, but he couldn't let it show. He had to push the urge down. Force it into a cupboard at the back of his mind and lock the door on it, so that he could maintain the sympathetic edifice he'd created in an attempt to get Haynes onside. 'See, Kevin, I'm a simple kind of bloke. I see two and two, I add them together and they always make four. I don't know any other way to do it. So, I've got your van – the one you drive, anyway – on CCTV not two hundred yards from the scene of an abduction, right at the time it occurred. Then I've got you picking Molly Danvers up in that self-same van, not thirty-six hours later. And she identifies you. So, what am I supposed to think, eh? Add them or multiply them, two and two make four. That's it.' He sat back, hands spread wide in the air.

'Except you've read the signs wrong. I've got a great big minus sign called an alibi, remember? And you take two from two, what does that leave you? Sweet bugger all. Which is what you've got on me, and what you'll get from that van, as far as any girl other than Molly Danvers. Because I didn't take any girl other than her.'

'So, you're telling me there's two of you operating at the same time in a little town like this, and that's just a coincidence?'

'I wasn't bloody *operating*, as you call it, until your boy pushed me so hard he drove me to it. I wasn't even planning anything when I went out. I just went for a drive. To calm myself down. It wasn't premeditated, what I did. It just happened on the spur of the moment. The stress . . .' He paused at a sharp knock on the door.

Pete turned as the door opened and Dave Miles stuck his head in. 'Sorry, boss. It's important.' He jerked his head in a beckoning motion.

Pete glanced at Haynes. 'I'll be back in a minute.' Then he stood up and joined Dave in the corridor, closing the door behind him.

'What's up?'

'It's Louise, boss. She just phoned. She sounded bloody awful. Desperate, like.'

A wave of cold fear swept through Pete's body. 'What did she say?'

'All she actually *said* was she needs to speak to you. But, it was after she said it. There was this wail, like a wounded animal, then she just cut the phone off and now she won't answer it. It just rings.'

'Shit. Put matey here in a cell. We've got him for Molly Danvers, if not the others. I'll go see what's up.'

'Do we think he did the others, though?'

Pete grimaced. 'I don't think so, no. Either way, we need physical evidence. Plus, there's his alibi to crack for Rosie Whitlock's abduction. Get on to that while I'm out, eh?'

'OK. But, if he didn't take Rosie and the others . . .'

'There's somebody else still out there who did.'

Pete walked swiftly away towards the custody desk and the back door of the station. It took all his self-control not to run until he got outside. Then he let himself go. He charged across the car park, jumped into the Mondeo and rammed the key into the slot, gunning the engine and slipping the clutch. He was sorely tempted to hit the lights and sirens, but somehow resisted.

What the hell had happened? There was no way that Louise would make a call like that unless it was something serious. But what?

He imagined the desperate cry that Dave had described and his stomach twisted. The thought that his wife had made that sound . . . What had prompted such a horrific response? Louise was not the type to be melodramatic. She would blow up at him sometimes, but much more often she was simply quiet and withdrawn, so something awful must have happened.

The traffic was light at this time of day, so he put his foot down hard until he turned off the Heavitree Road into the estate. The kids were at school, so shouldn't be running around on the streets, but nevertheless, he moderated his speed as he pushed the Ford through the slalom of parked cars that cluttered the narrower streets.

Finally, he pulled into his driveway, jumped out of the car and ran to the front door, barging into the house. 'Louise?'

'In here.' Her tear-filled voice came from the sitting room. He rushed through. She was curled on the sofa, a blanket pulled protectively over her. She sat up as he entered, her face wet with tears.

'What is it? What's happened?'

'Pete.' She sobbed as she threw herself into his arms. 'Oh, God, I'm sorry. It was awful. She practically accused you of being either bent or incompetent.'

'Who did? When?'

'Some bloody reporter.' Her voice was muffled against his shoulder. 'She came knocking on the door. I thought, the way she spoke, she must be one of your lot. But then I opened it and she started on, wanting to know what I thought about you working on a missing kid case when you hadn't even found our Tommy. Like it was your fault or something.' She was still sobbing as she spoke. 'I put her right. Told her the way it was and then told her to bugger off and not come back, but what if she's just the first? Now that you've got a dead one too, what if the press come round here in force? I mean, it'll be on the news, won't it? So the nationals will get in on it and drag up Tommy again. They'll be camping on the drive all over again.'

Pete held her tight as she cried into his shoulder. His mind slipped back to the early summer, when more or less exactly what she described had happened. The fact that the missing boy's father was a copper had been played up by the press. Expectations had been high. The clamour for interviews with both of them had been relentless. They had been followed when taking Annie to school, as they'd had to, to prevent the reporters mobbing her.

That had been the start of Louise's decline. She had quickly taken to staying indoors. Had withdrawn first from society, then from him and Annie.

'Who was she, this reporter?' he asked when her sobs eased a little.

'I don't know. Ellie something.' She paused. 'Turner. That was it. Ellie Turner. She said it like it should mean something to me. That's why I thought she must be in the job. I wouldn't have opened the door otherwise.'

'They'll try all sorts of tricks to get to speak to you. Did she say who she was working for? What paper, who her boss was – anything like that?'

'No. She spouted her bullshit, I put her right, then I slammed the door on her. But then I was terrified she'd just be the first, that they'd all turn up here, like last time.' Her arms tightened around him as her cries intensified again.

'Well, there's no sign of anyone out there now. And, if they do turn up, you just have to ignore them and call me.'

She drew a long, ragged breath. 'I'm sorry, Pete.'

'What for?'

'I haven't been much use over the past few months, have I? To you or Annie. It just got so . . . I couldn't cope. It got too much, too quick and I couldn't handle it. So, I'm sorry. But I told that reporter bitch that, regardless of what she might think, you were the best person for the job of finding that girl. And you are. I know I gave you grief over it, but I didn't mean it. You know that, don't you?'

She looked up at him imploringly.

Pete nodded. *But, are you right?* he thought. *Am I the best man for the job? Could someone else see things more clearly? Find the evidence more quickly? Stand a better chance of getting to Rosie before . . .?*

He looked into her tear-filled eyes, and his heart melted. He pulled her close again, wrapping his arms around her. 'I know, love. Don't worry. I love you and so does Annie. We just want you to get through all this and get better in your own time, that's all. What comes in between doesn't matter. As long as we're together and safe, nothing else matters, all right?'

'Oh, God!' She burst into tears again and Pete held her as she cried and cried.

*

'Hey, boss. How's Louise?' Jane asked, as Pete sat down opposite her.

'She's OK now, thanks.'

'What was the problem?'

'The press.' He sat down, picked up his pen and opened the file on Kevin Haynes, effectively closing the conversation.

'So, what do you reckon the odds are of it being a coincidence that Rosie Whitlock and Molly Danvers go to the same school?'

'What?' He looked up sharply.

Jane grinned. 'Got you there, didn't I? It's true, though. They're a year apart, so they probably don't know each other, but they both go to Risingbrook.'

'When did you find that out?'

'About twenty minutes ago. I spoke to her parents.'

'Listen up, everybody.' Simon Phillips' voice cut across the room as he stood up from his desk. 'Thanks, Kate.' He nodded to one of his PCs. 'We've finally got an ID on the girl found on the riverbank at Powderham Deer Park. She was Amanda Kernick, from Fishponds in Bristol, age nine at the time she went missing, on or about 7 July this year.'

Cheers and applause rang across the squad room, until Dave Miles asked the two obvious questions. 'How the hell did she get all the way down here then? And how come it's taken until now to identify her?'

'To take your second question first, Dave, she was the single child of a single-parent family. They'd only moved to the area a couple of weeks before. The mother was killed in a hit-and-run and Amanda disappeared at the same time, so the neighbours just thought they'd moved away again. The schools were closed for the summer and the mother was estranged from her family, so nobody missed the girl until the schools opened again and she didn't turn up. Then it took a few weeks to figure out that she wasn't where she should be, and wasn't anywhere else either.'

'Jesus, that's just sad,' Jane said. 'Poor kid.'

'As for your first question – your guess is as good as mine at this stage. We don't know if she had family down this way and came down under her own steam or if she was snatched immediately – by whoever killed the mother, perhaps – and brought here against her will.'

'In which case, whoever brought her down here has links to the Bristol area,' Dave pointed out. 'Do we know anyone?'

'Are we talking about a ring then?' Sophie asked. 'Because theses blokes tend to know each other, or at least know of each other, right?'

'Not necessarily an organised ring,' Pete said. 'But you're right – they do tend to at least be aware of each other, if only to share and exchange images and sometimes even victims.'

'And we've got one of them downstairs,' Dave pointed out.

Pete nodded. 'True. I'll go and have a word. You want to come, Si?'

'Too bloody right, I do.'

'So, what have you got on this bloke? Haynes, isn't it?' Phillips asked as they went down the stairs.

'He abducted a young girl last night, raped her, then had a pang of conscience and took her to the RDE. He's admitted the attack, but claims it's the only one he's done since he got out of prison, three years ago.'

'And you believe him?'

'I'm inclined to, yes. Forensics are working on it, but we've got no evidence that he's involved in the other attacks.' Pete pushed open the door to the custody suite and approached the high-fronted desk. 'Bob. We're here to see Kevin Haynes again.'

The big man stepped out from behind the desk. 'You'd better offer him a drink then. He'll be parched, all the talking he's doing this morning.'

'I could use a coffee myself. You, Si?'

'No, I'm OK.'

They reached the correct cell and Bob opened it up. 'Wakey-wakey, Kevin. You want a drink?'

Haynes was sprawled on the built-in bunk at the back of the cell, the thin, grey police-issue blanket wrapped around him like a shawl. 'Please. Tea would be great.'

'One tea, one coffee on the way. Interview One's free.'

'Righto. Thanks, Bob. Come on, sunshine,' Pete said. 'We need to talk some more.'

'What now?' Haynes stood reluctantly. 'I've told you everything I can.'

'Not about this, you haven't,' Phillips said.

Pete led the way to the small interview room opposite the custody desk. He flipped the slider on the door to 'Occupied' and led them in. When they were all seated, he pressed the large red Record button on the machine to his left. 'All right.' He checked his watch and quoted the date and time. 'Present in the room are myself, DS Peter Gayle, DS Simon Phillips and Kevin Haynes. Kevin has been read his rights and is fully aware of them, isn't that right, Kevin?'

Haynes grunted. 'Do I need a solicitor here?'

'That's up to you, Kevin. As I said, we're not here to talk about what you were arrested for. But, for the benefit of the tape, can you confirm that you're aware of your rights?'

'Yes.'

'Right, then, if you're happy as we are . . . Simon, you want to kick off?'

Phillips sat forward in his chair, forearms on the desk. 'Mr Haynes, I'm not accusing you of anything here. I'm aware of why you're currently in custody and I want to ask you about a different case. I'm simply seeking any pertinent information you might have, is that clear?'

'Yes.'

'OK. So, eleven days ago, a body was found on the edge of the River Exe, at Powderham Deer Park. It was the body of a young girl. She was naked and had been sexually abused. We've since discovered that she was nine-year-old Amanda Kernick of Fishponds, Bristol. She was abducted at around the same time as her mother was killed in a hit-and-run incident by an unknown vehicle. Do you know anything about these events? Have you heard anything on the grapevine, as it were?'

Haynes' eyes had widened in horror. 'No. No way. I don't get involved in stuff like that.'

'Yet, you attacked a girl yourself, not twenty-four hours ago.'

'That was a one-off. I told him.' He nodded at Pete. 'I'm not part of that scene. I keep to myself. I know these rings exist, but that's all I know about them.'

There was a knock at the door and Bob came in with two steaming plastic cups. He put one down in front of Pete and one in front of Haynes. 'Drinks, gents.'

'Thanks, Bob.' For the benefit of the recording, Pete added, 'Sergeant Robert James has just brought drinks for myself and Mr Haynes, and has now left the room.' He focused on Haynes as he picked up his drink and took a sip. Putting the cup down again, he held the other man's gaze. 'So, you're saying that you never heard even a whisper of a girl being brought down from Bristol for reasons of sexual exploitation, this summer?'

'That's right.'

'But, if you had to speculate, is there anyone you know of that might have been involved in something like that? Anyone you'd immediately think, *I bet that was him*?'

'You're asking me to grass somebody up on pure guesswork.'

'We're asking you to suggest a starting point for an investigation,' Simon said stiffly.

Haynes shook his head. 'I don't know. Like I said, I never got in with that kind of crowd. And, anyway, they use handles, never real names.' He shrugged. 'Sorry. I can't help you.'

'Or is it that you won't?' Simon asked. 'In which case, you'd be acting as an accessory after the fact in at least one murder.'

'Hey, I told you,' Haynes protested, 'I don't know anything, all right? If I did, I'd tell you. I'm in enough shit already, thanks very much. I don't need more.'

'You say they use handles. Even one of those'd be a starting point,' Pete said. 'A web address. Whatever you can remember. These are killers we're talking about here, Kevin.'

'Yeah, and I've never had anything to do with them. Never wanted to. I just know, in principle, how they operate, that's all. You can check my computer, whatever you want. You won't find any connection between me and that sort of thing.'

'We already are checking your computer, Kevin,' Simon told him. 'We'll be checking every connection you've ever made on the Internet.'

'Hah. You'll be lucky. I've only had that computer just over a year.' Haynes sat back, grinning.

'Maybe, but your IP address hasn't changed,' Phillips argued. 'That can tell us just the same, going back to when it was first set up.'

Haynes looked sceptical, then less sure.

'So, you've got no knowledge, direct or otherwise, of anyone who might be involved in these abductions, Kevin?' Pete broke in.

'That's what I've been saying all along.'

'All right,' Pete said. 'I think we're done for now then.'

Phillips looked at him. 'Really?'

Pete nodded. 'Bob can take him back to his cell. Interview terminated at—' he checked his watch '—eleven twenty-three a.m.' He stood, picked up his drink and led Simon out of the room

As soon as the door clicked shut behind them, Phillips rounded on him. 'What the hell was that about? We'd hardly got started.'

'We've already checked his computer and searched his house. There's no evidence that he's been involved in anything until he took Molly Danvers. I don't think he can tell us anything.'

'You didn't give him a bloody chance!'

Pete felt the pressure swell in his head. 'Don't even think about telling me how to do my job,' he snarled. 'Not until you can tell me where my son is.' He stalked away, leaving Phillips to follow when he was ready.

'Take our friend in there back to his cell, would you, Bob?' he asked, as he passed the desk.

'Right you are.'

Pete headed up the stairs, Simon's footsteps heavy behind him. As they entered the incident room, an expectant hush fell over the assembled officers. Pete looked around. Almost all faces were focused on him, watching and waiting. He drew a deep, calming breath and shook his head, a soft moan of disappointment passing across the room in response.

'No good?' asked Dave.

'He doesn't know anything.'

From across the room behind him, he heard Simon Phillips

saying, 'Waste of bloody time. If it had been me, I'd have beaten the damn truth out of the little perv.'

Pete stiffened, but held himself in check. This wasn't the time or the place. He reached for the forensic report on top of his desk. He flipped it open, and had barely read the title, when his phone rang. He picked it up. 'Gayle.'

'Detective Sergeant Gayle?'

'Speaking.'

'This is DC Andrew Tibbetts of the technical office, HQ. I've finally finished assessing the emails, Twitter and Facebook accounts on Rosie Whitlock's computer. She also had Instagram and Photobucket accounts, you know.'

'No, I didn't know.'

'Well . . . nothing remarkable in them. I'll email you the results, of course, but I thought I'd better call first. There are several contacts among her emails and on Facebook from one Thomas Gayle. Isn't that your son's name?'

Chapter 18

Pete heard the question as if from a distance through the echoing hollowness that had descended over his senses. *'Isn't that your son's name?'*

'It is.'

'Then perhaps you should check the details. I expect you know his email and social network accounts inside out by now, with all that's happened.'

'Yes. I'll do that.'

Tommy. Tommy knew Rosie Whitlock. My God.

Why didn't he remember her name from five months ago?

He hadn't been directly involved in Tommy's case, of course, but surely Phillips would have asked about anyone and everyone in his contacts list?

He put the phone down as if in a dream. It took him several seconds to register Jane's voice.

'Boss? Boss? Are you all right?'

He blinked. 'What? Yes, I'm fine.'

'Well, you don't look it. You're as white as a sheet.'

He drew a long, deep breath. 'I'll be fine. Don't worry about it, Jane.'

'What was the phone call?'

'The IT guys. They've cracked Rosie's email and social network accounts. They're emailing me the details.'

'So, what's so awful about that?'

'Nothing, Jane. Let it lie, will you?'

She stared at him for a moment, then put her head down, concentrating on what she had been doing.

Pete felt bad about snapping at her, but he couldn't tell anyone what he had just learned. Not yet. It could get him pulled off the case, and that was the last thing he wanted. He was too far in to give it up now. And Rosie Whitlock could ill afford the delays involved in bringing another team up to speed. If he had to step aside, he'd have to, but he wasn't going to if he could help it.

Especially not for Simon Phillips, he couldn't help thinking.

He logged into his email and, sure enough, there was one from the IT department, Devon and Cornwall Police Headquarters, Middlemoor. He opened it. At the bottom of the summary page were links that would get him into the relevant email listing, Twitter page and Facebook account.

He soon found what Tibbetts had been talking about. Several emails had been exchanged, over a period of more than a year, between Rosie and an address that he recognised instantly as his son's.

But Tommy hadn't gone to Risingbrook School. He had attended the local comprehensive, so how did he know Rosie? He had certainly never mentioned her.

He chose one of the emails at random and opened it.

Hi Rosie,

Cool session on Friday. And after!! Best ever. So smooth.

Do it again this week?

T.

Friday? What did Tommy do on a Friday? Pete tried to think, but it was not as if he was regularly home in the evenings to take that much notice of what the kids were doing in their spare time. Or what Louise was doing, as long as they were looked after . . .

Shit, he really hadn't been much of a dad, had he? Or a husband, come to that. Far too absorbed in the job to . . . *No*, he thought. It wasn't that he didn't care. It was just that there was always something important to be done. Some urgent case to deal with; a criminal to get off the streets before other potential victims were harmed.

'Sarge? What's up?'

He blinked at the sound of Jane's voice. Looked up over his computer screen and saw her staring at him again, a look of concern on her face. 'What's up is that we're back to square one,' he said, hitting a key to minimise the email on his screen. 'Haynes took Molly Danvers. No doubt on that. But I don't believe he took Rosie Whitlock and I'm pretty certain he didn't kill either of the other two. I don't think he's got anything to give us on who did either. Dave, what did you make of him?'

'He's a loner. He doesn't mix any more than he has to.'

'So he wouldn't be part of a ring.'

Dave shook his head. 'He'd be too nervous for a start. Wouldn't want to take the risk.'

Pete nodded. 'That's my feeling, too. So, like I said, we're back to square one.'

'Not quite square one,' Jane said.

'Why?'

'We've got the white van, which we didn't have before.'

'Have you got any idea how many white vans there are in Exeter, never mind in south Devon?' Dave asked.

'Hundreds. At least. But surely it's worth re-canvassing? Checking if anyone saw it – maybe noticed it being out of context and remembers a partial plate or a distinctive logo or mark of some kind?'

'Alright,' Pete said. 'Any other news? What about Neil Sanderson? Anything back on him?'

Jane held up a hand, thumb down, and imitated a game-show wrong answer claxon. '*Ee-eeeh*. The pictures he's got, while definitely dodgy, aren't actually illegal. The girls weren't involved in any kind of sexual act or portrayed in a sexualising manner. And it looks like he was caught twice on camera on the way to work that morning – passing the Airparks entrance, and that big antiques warehouse a little way along from it.'

'It was definitely him?'

She shrugged. 'No actual registration because of the angle in both cases, but it was the same make and model with a male driver of his size, build and general description.'

Pete nodded. 'OK. So, Simon's got Amanda Kernick. We concentrate on the others – Rosie and the girl in the weir. We need to confirm her ID ASAP.'

Dave Miles' phone rang and he picked it up. 'DC Miles, CID. Yes. OK, great. Thanks. What have you got?' He listened for a few moments then thanked the caller again and put the phone down. 'That was forensics. They recognised the urgency of the situation and put a rush on Kevin Haynes' place and the van.'

'And?'

'Nothing in his house. Not even any porn. And the only trace in the van came back to Molly Danvers.'

Pete pursed his lips. 'As he said.'

'Yep.'

Pete's phone rang before he had a chance to say any more. He picked it up. 'DS Gayle, CID.'

'Peter, it's Tony Chambers.'

'Hello, Doc. What do you know that you didn't last night?'

'The victim at St James' Weir is, as we estimated at the scene, nine or ten years old. Difficult to be more precise. Generally well nourished, though not in the past few days. She died of strangulation a little over twenty-four hours ago. Your perpetrator has smallish hands. There was no penetrative sex around the time of death, as far as I can tell, but she was not a virgin. No trace evidence of course, after immersion in the river for several hours.'

'Any way of telling how long she'd been in the river?'

'Not precisely. Hours, rather than days, but I'm afraid I can't narrow that down for you.'

'And the sex – can you tell if it was consensual or not? Or how recent?'

'With her age and size, there was some physical damage, but... well, there are variables to consider, of course, but I'd say it could have been more severe. And, as for timescale, we're talking about the last week or so. Ten days, at the most.'

'What – for the first time?'

'Yes.'

'OK, Doc. Thanks.'

He put the phone down.

'Well?' Jane demanded. 'What'd he have to say?'

'The girl was strangled some time yesterday morning, then tossed in the river. And she'd been a virgin until a week or ten days ago.'

'So, she was abducted, raped and killed when he was done with her.'

No one needed to say that Rosie Whitlock was probably going through exactly the same now, while they sat here without any real leads.

Rosie Whitlock, who had clearly been a friend of his son's.

Jane's computer pinged and she focused on the screen as she began typing. Pete closed the email he had been looking at, then took a thumb drive from his desk and plugged it in. When the computer had opened it, he dragged the information from IT onto it, then slipped it into his pocket as Jane looked up from her screen.

'I've got her.'

'Well, do tell.'

'You were right, boss. She's Lauren Carter, ten years old, from Barnstaple.'

'How did you confirm it?'

'She's in the system. Shoplifting. Forensics took her prints before Doc Chambers took her to the mortuary and ran them through the system. She's resident in a children's home there. Was. She's been in and out of care since she was six and this isn't the first time she's gone missing. Hence the lack of a report, I suppose.'

Pete grunted. 'Anything else on her?'

'Not as yet. I'll get on to it now.'

'Good. We need to know how she got down here for a start. Known associates. If she's gone off before, then where to and how?'

'OK. I expect you want to get on to the kids' home?'

'Yes,' he said heavily.

She scribbled quickly on a Post-it and handed it across. 'Here are the details.'

'Thanks.' He stuck the little yellow note to the top corner of his screen, picked up the phone and dialled.

'Sunnyside. Can I help?' asked a bright female voice.

'This is Detective Sergeant Peter Gayle, Exeter CID. I'd like to speak to the person in charge there, please.'

'That would be me. Catherine Hammond. How can I help, Detective?'

'Does the name Lauren Carter mean anything to you?'

There was the slightest hesitation. 'Yes, of course. She's one of our clients.'

'Then maybe you can tell me where she's been for the past ten days, and who with?'

This time the hesitation was more marked. 'Um . . . I'm not sure that I can discuss that sort of thing over the phone like this.'

'Then look up Exeter police station and call me back. But do it soon, Ms Hammond. Ask for me by name and they'll put you through. Detective Sergeant Gayle. All right?'

'Yes. Yes, I'll do it now.'

There was a click and the line went dead. 'Well, that put the wind up her,' he said. 'Now we'll see if she's true to her word.'

He sat back and waited. Jane picked up her phone. Dave was concentrating on the screen in front of him as he typed something into the keyboard. Seconds passed. Then Pete's phone rang. He picked it up. 'DS Gayle.'

'Mike on the front desk. I've got a Catherine Hammond on the line for you.'

'Good. Put her through, thanks.' There was a click. 'DS Gayle speaking.'

'Detective Gayle. Thank you for your patience, but I'm sure you understand the needs of confidentiality in my circumstances.'

'Of course. You were going to tell me about Lauren Carter.'

'Yes, well, I'm afraid I can't tell you much about the last few days. She absconded, you see. Not for the first time. So we were waiting to hear that she'd been picked up somewhere by your colleagues. I gather, from your call, that she has been?'

'She's been found here in Exeter,' Pete said. 'She's been missing before, you say?'

'Back in March of this year, we got a call out of the blue from Thames Valley police. Two off-duty officers had observed her trying to catch a ride in a lorry from Chieveley Services on the M4. They picked her up and took her to the local station, at Newbury.'

'But you didn't report her missing, Ms Hammond.'

'No, well . . . we thought she'd be picked up shortly anyway, so why trouble you until it was necessary? You've found her in Exeter this time?'

'Yes. What can you tell me about how she might have got down here?'

'Nothing, really. In the past she's simply hitched lifts to where she wanted to go, but I can't imagine why she'd have headed in your direction. What does she have to say for herself?'

'She doesn't, Ms Hammond. And she won't. I'm afraid she's been killed.' He heard her gasp but ignored it. 'Her body was found in the early hours of this morning. She'd been raped and strangled.'

'Oh my God. That's awful.'

'So, you see, we need to determine both how she got here and why she would have come here. Do you know of anyone she associated with, in or out of the home, who she might have talked to, confided in? Friends, family, staff members? Anyone who might have helped her or anywhere that would have been a starting point for her journey?'

'I'm sorry. I can't believe this.'

'Well, I'm afraid it's true, Ms Hammond. And we believe that whoever killed her has abducted another girl, so we need to find all the information we can as quickly as possible. Lauren lived with you for how long?'

'Uh . . . since June of last year.'

'Over a year then. So there must be something you can tell me about her.'

'Well . . . she tended to keep herself to herself. She was very self-reliant. Didn't make friends easily. She was quite a dominant personality.'

'Was this before or after her mother died?'

'A few weeks after. She'd been in foster care, but ran away after the funeral. The foster parents couldn't cope with her.'

'Did you or any of your staff spend any time with her, one to one? Try to get through to her?'

'Well, we tried, of course, but . . . she really didn't want to know and we have twenty-seven other children here. It's not like we have the time to deal with someone like Lauren, Detective. Like she was then.'

'So, no friends and no authority figure to turn to. What about family, other than her dead mother?'

'We were led to believe there was no one. Her mother had long since been disowned by her parents, so there was no contact there. Hadn't been since before Lauren was born, or so we understand. We don't have an address for them or anything. I seem to remember they were in London, but I'm not even certain of that much and there's nothing in her records about them. Lauren's father was unknown and her mother had no siblings that we're aware of.'

'I'll need the contact details for her previous home. The foster family.'

'I can get that for you. Hold on a moment.' There was a clunk as she put the phone down then a series of faint noises before a scrape and a rustle of paper. 'Detective?'

'I'm here.'

'A couple in Bideford. Michael and Mary Hall.' She read out the address and phone number. 'I . . . I still can't believe this. It's just too awful for words.'

'And the worst part is, we might have had a chance of preventing it, if we'd known she was missing. Thank you for help, Ms Hammond.' Pete put the phone down and sat back with a sigh. What the hell was the point in a system that was run by people who just couldn't be bothered? *'We just didn't have time for someone like her.' Well, you should have sent her to someone who did then*, he thought, *instead of just ignoring her. Then, maybe, she'd still be alive.*

He shook his head, disgusted by the pointless waste. But there wasn't time to dwell. He picked up the phone again, not sure if he would have better luck with the previous foster parents or would end the call even more depressed and disgusted than he was already.

He was part-way through dialling the number when DCI Silverstone's voice rang out across the squad room. 'DS Gayle. My office. Now, please.'

Chapter 19

Pete closed the door behind him with butterflies swirling in his stomach. How had the DCI got on to him so bloody quickly? Had IT informed him of the connection to Tommy? They must have: it was the only way. He stood to attention on legs that felt like rubber. 'Sir?'

'Why have I got the press demanding to know if we've got our man on the Rosie Whitlock case? Apparently, they not only have a picture of him being brought in, they also have his name and address.'

A heady mixture of emotions swept through Pete's mind. 'What? H—' He stopped as realisation dawned. 'Lee bloody Birch from the *Express & Echo*. He was out the front when we brought Haynes in. I spoke to him afterwards at the front desk. He said he'd seen us. He didn't mention that he'd got a bloody picture. Must have combed through their files, I suppose, to get the name. Little shit.'

'"Little shit" is not the way we need to be referring to members of the press, Detective Sergeant. We need them onside. Which brings me to another bone of contention. They seem to have got hold of the fact that you're heading the inquiry and the wisdom of that is being questioned, given your recent history.'

'My recent history, as you call it, has nothing to do with this inquiry, sir. I thought we'd established that.'

'That'll depend on results, Peter. And you haven't answered the question. Have we got our man?'

'Not for Rosie Whitlock, no. Nor for Amanda Kernick or Lauren Carter.'

Silverstone frowned.

'The Jane Doe at Powderham Deer Park and the dead girl at the weir this morning. What he is guilty of – what we have evidence against him on – is the abduction and rape of Molly Danvers, using his employer's company van.'

'So there's another bastard out there, abducting and killing young girls?'

'That's right.'

'And where are we on finding him?'

'Right now, sir, about where we were twenty-four hours ago.'

'You've got nothing?'

'We're closing in, sir. We've eliminated several likely suspects, including Kevin Haynes. We've got more canvassing to do. And we're waiting for forensics on Lauren Carter. I was just about to call her previous foster parents, to see if they could be of any help.'

'Well, let's see if we can stay at least one step ahead of the press, yes?'

'Sir.'

'On you go then.'

Instinctively, Pete put a hand to the thumb drive in his pocket as he returned to the squad room. It was safe and secure there, thank God, until he could examine its contents in some degree of privacy.

He sat down at his desk.

'What was that all about, boss?' Dave asked.

'Apparently, the press has got hold of the fact that we've got Kevin Haynes in custody. They want to know if he's our man.'

'Bloody hell, that didn't take long,' Jane said.

'Little bugger from the *E & E* was out front when we brought him in. Got a snap of him in the back of the car, apparently.'

'Pressure's on then,' Dave said dryly.

'The pressure was on from the get-go, Dave. One, I had to fight for this case in the first place. And two, Rosie Whitlock is out there somewhere, in danger for her life.'

Dave looked away and concentrated on whatever he was doing.

'So,' Pete said, picking up his phone. 'I was about to make a phone call. Jane, when you've finished what you're doing, why don't you go see if you can knock up any more of the residents around Risingbrook, as you suggested it?'

'OK.'

'Take Dick or Ben with you. And when you've finished with the residents, go into the school and have a word with young Chris Mellor, eh? Find out what he knows, if anything. He's got those pictures of Becky. That should give you some leverage.'

'Right, boss.'

'Dave, when you've finished what you're doing, I need you to follow up on the research you did before into the local paedophiles. I know there's only three convicted ones, but there have to be others, that haven't been caught yet, or, at least, convicted. Check into ongoing or outstanding cases, non-confirmed suspects, anything like that. Maybe Enstone or the other guy, whatever his name is, can give us a lead. They might well know something about someone. You don't go from nothing to murder in one step, unless it's a panic reaction, and then someone would notice a change in behaviour afterwards. Also, the maintenance guy at the hospital – we need to check on him thoroughly.'

'That's what I'm doing now.'

'And?'

'Nothing yet. Gimme another twenty minutes, I should have it finished. Should we get Fast-track Phil to have a word with the press? Put an appeal out for anyone who's been acting strangely in the last day or so?'

'Good idea. I'll do that. Then I'm going to see if I can nail down where Lauren went into the river.'

*

Pete saw the tree from some way off, with the bright yellow Mini parked beneath it, a strange trailer attached to the back. Beyond it, he could make out the roof of the pub that the little car belonged to and, just this side of it, the narrow junction of a side road on the left. He was travelling north up the A396, a few miles out of Exeter, approaching the little village of Up Exe. As he got closer to the junction, he could see that the trailer on the back of the Mini was made from the front end of another Mini, also painted yellow, and it held a large decorative well with the name of the pub prominently displayed.

He had been here a couple of times with Louise and the kids. He remembered sitting in the garden at the back after a huge meal, feeling stuffed and satisfied while Annie and Tommy raced around, laughing and shouting, scrambling over the slide and the climbing frame as they chased each other happily. He'd looked at Louise, sitting next to him, and thought he was living the perfect life.

And now, Tommy was gone and Louise had barely been out of the house in months. Jesus! *Where are you, Tommy?*

And what the hell was Simon Phillips doing to find him?

He slowed and made the turn into a lane that was barely wide enough for two cars to pass. The tarmac was pitted, the edges cracked and broken from lack of maintenance. A couple of hundred yards down, a farm-shop notice pointed across to a double-width gateway. As he changed up through the gears, his phone rang abruptly. He slowed the car and pulled out the phone.

'Hold on a sec.' He dumped the phone on the passenger seat and flicked on his indicator.

The car dipped and splashed as he turned into the puddled and potholed car park of a farm shop in a big green metal barn. He stopped and picked up the phone.

'DS Gayle.'

'Boss, it's Jane. Nothing useful on Downton Road, but there's one house we still haven't managed to catch anyone in yet. I've had a word with Chris Mellor though. Seems he split up with Becky a couple of weeks ago. Or at least, she did with him. She accused him of letting his mates see her pictures, which he denies vigorously and, I must admit, convincingly.'

'So, why did she accuse him?'

'She reckoned that people saw the photos and made fun of her and the only place they could have seen them was on his phone.'

'What about on Rosie's phone? There were some of her in the computer, too. Maybe they shared them?'

'Possible. We're never going to know, though, the state her phone's in.'

'True.'

'Maybe someone nicked Chris' phone and then put it back. They're not allowed to have them in class.'

'But he'd keep it in his locker, wouldn't he? Especially if he knew things like that were on it.'

'You'd think. So . . .'

'Look into it a bit further. Find out exactly who saw them and what they've got to say about it.'

'OK. How are you getting on?'

'I've figured out how far Lauren's body could have travelled in the time she was in the water – a maximum distance, at least. Now, I'm trying to find where she might have been dumped in, within that range.'

'Good luck with that.'

'Actually, there's only about half a dozen possible sites. If I can find the right one, it might give us a lead. A witness, a tyre track, some forensic evidence.'

'We'll see you later then.'

'Yes.' He ended the call and started the engine. Turning left out of the entrance, he headed downhill, towards the river.

Chapter 20

'What the hell are you trying to pull?'

Pete frowned as Barry Enstone shouted down the phone at him. He caught movement in the corner of his eye as Dick Feeney looked up, hearing Enstone's voice on the phone from six feet away.

'You couldn't pin anything on me, so you set the bloody press on me, is that it?'

Pete had completed his search for dump sites and returned to the station half an hour ago. 'You'd better tell me what you're talking about, Mr Enstone.'

'I've just got home from an early shift and there's a bunch of bloody reporters outside my house, wanting to know if I'm involved in the Rosie Whitlock abduction or the bodies in the river. I didn't even know there *were* two bodies in the bloody river.'

'I'm surprised there's any left to be at your place, Mr Enstone. Most of them were parked outside the station here, a little while ago. But, whatever they've got, it hasn't come from me or from anyone else on my team. I can guarantee it.'

'Yeah, right. Even if it wasn't you, there's that Miles bugger and the other one that was with him. I could tell they had it in for me from the off. Especially the one in uniform.'

'Mr Enstone, they both know better than to pull a trick like you're suggesting. If I found out about it, they'd be out on their ears and they know it.'

'Bollocks. They'd get a promotion, I bet. This is harassment, this is. And I haven't bloody done anything. Christ, they're knocking on the damn door now! I can't take this.'

'Have you told your girlfriend about your past yet, Mr Enstone?'

'I was going to do it tonight, when she gets home, but with this lot out the front, it's going to be too bloody late, isn't it? She'll find out from them, and then where does that leave me? In the bloody shit, that's where.'

'I'll have someone come round and get rid of them for you, when I've got a minute.'

'When you've got a minute? When's that? Next bloody Tuesday? I need these leeches gone, I'm telling you.'

'Don't worry, Mr Enstone. We'll get on to it.'

'Well, make it soon, yeah? Please.'

'All right. I'll have a word.'

Pete ended the call and headed for the door.

He found DCI Silverstone going through some papers. 'DS Gayle. What can I do for you?'

'I've just had a phone call, sir. From Barry Enstone. He's one of the three local men currently on the sex offenders register. We interviewed him yesterday and cleared him of any involvement in the current cases, but it seems like the press have got hold of his name and address from somewhere. They're camped out in front of his house, asking if he had anything to do with Rosie Whitlock's disappearance. And we both know they're not inclined to ask nicely or take no for an answer. One of them was round at my place, earlier. Louise was in a right state by the time they finished.'

Silverstone's lips were pursed. His gaze had lost focus. 'Yes. Well. I suppose he's done his time. He ought to be able to get on with his life unmolested. But, on the other hand, the press is free to come and go as they please. There's not a lot we can do about it.'

'They might be free to come and go as they please, but slander and harassment aren't included in that. Especially when we've already established his alibi.' It was much simpler not to go into the finer detail that they hadn't actually talked to the person providing the alibi yet, he thought.

'True. True. But what are we supposed to do about it?'

'Well, the only thing we can do is go and talk to them. Tell them that we're on the case and we've already established that he's not involved. We're narrowing down our suspect list and he's no longer on it.'

'And we're sure about that?'

'Yes, sir. He's not involved.'

Silverstone sighed and flopped the folder closed in front of him. 'All right. I suppose, if anyone's going to have the authority to make them move on, it'll be me.'

'That's true.'

'Mmm.' Silverstone tried to sound reluctant, but Pete knew he was already seeing his mug in the papers yet again, declaring his authority and the competency of his team. He stood up.

'I'll leave it with you, then, shall I, sir?'

'What? Yes. I'll need his address, of course.'

'Send it to your phone, shall I?'

'Perfect.'

As Pete returned to his desk, he saw Dave Miles watching him and gave him an OK sign with a circled thumb and forefinger. Dave grinned and dropped his head, at least pretending to concentrate on what he was doing.

'So, how are we doing then?' Pete asked as he dropped back into his seat.

'I spoke to Enstone and the other guy on the register – Jeremy Tyler – and got nothing. They both say they've been out of the scene since they got sent down, so they don't know anything of any use. And the blokes at HQ couldn't do any better. I just spoke to them while you were in with FTP. I've still got to get on to CEOP in London, see if they've got anything popping in this area.'

CEOP, Pete knew instantly, was the Child Exploitation and Online Protection command of the National Crime Agency, a centralised specialist unit devoted to dealing with cases of child sexual abuse, both on-line and in the real world.

'Do that. I'm going to have a word with Forensics and get them to check a couple of the sites I went to earlier.'

'Did you find anything useful, boss?' Jane asked.

'Well, there are only two places with the necessary access in a remote enough location that our man might have risked it. I couldn't see any sign of activity at either, but you never know: the boffins might come up with something.'

'I hope so. I told you I spoke to Chris Mellor, didn't I?'

Pete nodded.

'I also took the opportunity to talk to Becky again, while I was there, with the school nurse present as a responsible adult.'

'And?'

'She confirmed what Mellor said about the pictures and splitting up with him. Reckons they couldn't have come from anywhere but his phone. Rosie didn't have them. I pointed out that someone might have borrowed his phone without his knowledge, but I don't think it helped. It did let me ask about the pictures, though. I asked if her dad knew about them and if he'd ever taken any of her like that, but she reckoned he didn't and he hadn't. He was just a normal dad. She said, "I'd just die if he saw them. It would be so embarrassing." I didn't like to tell her that we knew he already had those and more.'

Which he claimed to have talked to her about, Pete thought. 'So, you reckon there's nothing to the idea of her dad being involved?'

'I don't know that I'd go that far, but I'm pretty sure he's not been abusing her.'

'Hmm. He might have been abusing her friend though. Mind

you, if that were the case, Rosie would have stopped going round there, wouldn't she?'

'Depends what he threatened her with, I suppose. Or promised her. She's a good kid. Kind. Helpful, by all accounts. If he threatened her friend or her family, she might well put up with what he was doing to protect them.'

'Yes, but he's got an alibi for when she was taken.'

'Bit of a shaky one, though, eh? I mean, just because it's the same make and model of car, male driver about his size, doesn't mean it was actually him. And if he travels that route every day, he'd know if another, similar vehicle travelled it as well.'

'Possibly. But how do we find evidence, one way or the other?'

She shook her head. 'Dunno, boss. I leave the clever stuff to you.'

*

'Boss, that was CEOP in London.' Dick put down his phone, grimaced and shook his head. 'They've got nothing in this area.'

'Well, it was worth a try.' Pete's phone rang and he picked it up. 'DS Gayle speaking.'

'This is all your bloody fault! You've screwed everything up. Everything!'

'Barry?' The man sounded distraught. As if he had been crying and could start again at any second. 'What are you talking about? I acted as soon as I spoke to you. My DCI was coming round in person.'

'Well, he was too bloody late, wasn't he? It's finished. Ruined. She knows and so will the neighbours in the morning. And the blokes at work. I won't have any work by lunchtime, you wait and see. They'll find an excuse to get rid of me. What's the bloody use, eh? It's all ruined.' He slammed the phone down.

'Shit.' Pete put the phone down and reached for his notebook, flipped it open, searching for Enstone's number.

'What's up with Enstone?' Dave asked.

'Apparently, our beloved leader's bedside manner needs further refinement,' Pete said dryly. He found the number, picked up the phone again and dialled. It rang and rang, but the man clearly wasn't going to answer. Pete let it ring until the automatic voice cut in: *'The number you have dialled is not available. Please try again later.'*

Well, if he wasn't going to answer, there was more than enough else to do. He put the phone down. He would leave it a while. Maybe Enstone would calm down a bit in the meantime.

Jane stood up and took her coat from the back of her chair. 'I'm off to the airport,' she said. 'Airparks reckoned they'd have the extra CCTV footage ready for half past five and I don't want to get caught in the traffic both ways.'

'What about the antique place?' Pete asked.

'They won't have theirs ready until tomorrow sometime. But I thought at least I could get a start on the Airparks stuff. Might not need the other lot.'

'Fair enough.'

Jane headed for the door and Pete noticed Dave Miles staring at him. 'What is it, Dave?'

'I was thinking, boss. Like you said before, you don't go from looking at dirty pictures on the computer to murder in a single step, unless it's a mistake or a panic reaction. And you don't get two of those in three weeks. So this guy must have been doing stuff for a while that we'd surely have picked up on. Unless he's just moved into the area, and then there'd be a record of him wherever he moved from.'

'Right. So, we need to check the national database for offenders that match this guy's MO, then see which, if any, of them have been planning to move down here.'

Dave nodded.

'You've just given yourself a bloody big job, then, Dave.'

Dave looked horrified. 'There'll be bloody dozens of them.'

'Make an overall list, then we'll get some extra manpower on it, divide it up and check with the relevant police forces and parole offices. But we need to get a move on. There's no telling what Rosie's going through right now. Or how long we've got until she follows Lauren Carter and Amanda Kernick into the Exe.'

Chapter 21

'Hello.'

Louise looked up as he entered the sitting room. She was dressed in fresh sweatpants and a T-shirt, and had washed her hair.

Her expression did not change as her brown eyes slid across his and away to the TV, a game show playing with the sound turned down. 'So, this is it, then, eh? Straight back into the twelve- and fourteen-hour days. Whatever happened to easing back in gently?'

Shit. Already? he thought. 'Two young girls are dead and another one's missing, that's what happened,' he said, trying to sound reasonable, rather than irritated. 'We need to find the bastard who's doing it before any more have to die. *Then* I can ease back on the hours. Don't you think I want to? You think I like being away from you and—' he stopped himself before he could say *the kids* '—you and Annie all this time? I'd much rather be here, believe it or not.'

She sighed. 'I know. It's just . . . why's it got to be you? Why can't someone else be doing this? Jim or Mark or Simon? Or Colin Underhill? They're all as qualified as you are, as capable as you are, or supposed to be. Why do you have to take on a job like this, right off the bat?'

'Because this isn't the only case that's going on right now. That's why they needed me back, remember.'

'It never is, though, is it? Never will be.'

He shook his head. 'Police and nurses – two professions that will always be needed and there'll never be enough of.'

She smiled and he caught a glimpse of the old Louise – the Louise from before Tommy went missing. 'I'm sorry. I shouldn't be carrying on like this. I know you're doing your best. And that you did your best over Tommy. With the rules as they are, and a self-centred prick like Silverstone in charge, there was nothing more you could have done without putting your job on the line. I just can't help it sometimes. It gets all bottled up inside me – all the hurt and anger and grief and God-knows-what-else – and it has to come out somehow or I'd just explode. And there you are, in the way of it, like a bloke standing too close to a ladder when the window cleaner drops his bucket.'

He sat and reached for her hand. 'I've spent too much time at work for way too long. I know that. I get caught up in the chase. Once we get this bloke, I will ease back though. I promise. I'll try to be a better husband. A better dad. To be here when I'm needed, instead of out on a case – like I should have been the night Tommy was taken. If I'd been there when I was supposed to be, instead of twenty minutes late . . .' His throat clogged and his head dropped forward as the guilt overwhelmed him.

He felt Louise put her other hand over his. 'It wasn't your fault, Pete. You can't say that.'

I can think it though. And know it's true. His jaw clenched as he fought the emotions welling up inside him. He couldn't break down now. He had to stay in control. Stay strong for Louise, for Annie and for Rosie Whitlock. He was no use to any of them in a blubbering mess. He had to find Rosie and get her back to her parents. Knowing, as he did, what they were going through, he could not let them down. Even while he knew he needed to be at home with Annie and Louise more, he still had to find Rosie.

*

'Well, I've got the list.' Dave waved a wad of paper nearly half an inch thick in the air, as Pete walked back into the squad room little more than an hour after he'd left.

'Give me half and we'll make a start.'

'OK. You asked for it.' Dave slipped a fingernail into the top corner of the stack and lifted off a section. 'Here you go.'

Pete leaned over and took it from him. He was halfway back into his seat when his phone rang. He dumped the papers on his desk and picked it up. 'DS Gayle, CID.'

'Sergeant, it's Jessica Whitlock.' Her voice was thin and hollow, like she was operating on autopilot.

'Mrs Whitlock, I spoke to your husband last night. We're doing all we can, believe me. I wish there was more I could tell you.'

She let go a long sigh. 'That's not why I phoned, Detective. There's someone . . . someone you don't know about who has a connection with us. With me. A man I've been seeing. Damon Albright. He lives in Exmouth. I'm certain he has nothing to do with what's happened to Rosie, but you wanted to know all the facts, relevant or not, so I'm telling you.'

Pete blew the air slowly out of his lungs. 'Thank you, Mrs Whitlock.'

She put the phone down before he could say any more.

He slumped back in his chair.

'What's up, boss?'

Pete lifted his eyes to return Dick's quizzical gaze. 'That was Jessica Whitlock,' he said. 'With the wonderful news of another potential suspect.'

'How come?'

'It seems she's been having an affair. And, reading between the lines, I reckon hubby Alistair's just found out about it.'

'Ouch. That's not good.'

'Not for her, no. Or for us. It's another person we've got to check out.'

'And another motive for Alistair to be involved,' said Dave. 'Retribution, if he found out before and only just admitted it.'

Pete frowned. 'How does that work?'

'Well, if Rosie isn't his . . . I mean, how long has this affair been going on? And is it her first? Maybe it's a case of kill the daughter first, then do the mother in after she's suffered a bit.'

'If you're going down that road, it's much more likely that the boyfriend did it, to get the wife away from the husband, isn't it? Or maybe even the affair with the mother was simply a ruse to get access to the daughter.'

Dave shrugged. 'So, who is the boyfriend?'

'Damon Albright of Exmouth.'

'Right. I'll give him a quick google, see what comes up.'

'You do that. I'll look in the phone book.'

'I love it when you go all old school on me.' Dave grinned.

'Get on with it.' Pete reached into the bottom drawer of his desk for the phone book and opened it. He flipped pages until he got close, then scanned down with a finger.

'Here he is,' Dave piped up.

Pete glanced up. 'All right, smart-arse. What does it say?'

'Got a Facebook page and an entry from the *Daily News*, three years ago. He had a hardware store in Exmouth. Sold it to one of the chains for a pretty packet.' He grunted. 'Looks like his lawyers at the time were Alistair Whitlock's firm.'

'There's your connection then.' Pete glanced back down at where his finger had stopped on the page. 'And here's his current address and phone number.'

'We going to check him out first, or get on with this lot?' Dave asked, indicating the stack of papers he had printed earlier.

'Do a quick search on him in the National Crime Database for a start, see what comes up.'

'OK.' He concentrated on his keyboard again as Pete lifted across the printout he had accepted earlier and began to scan through it. It comprised every child sex case in the UK for the past seven years. Hence the thick wad of paper. But he quickly began to find ones where the offender was still in prison or deceased or otherwise unsuitable. He picked up a pen and began to cross them out. He had just turned to the fourth page when Dave said, 'Nothing. He's clean, as far as I can tell.'

'All right, you carry on with this stuff and I'll go and see him. Best see if he's home first, I suppose.' He reached for the phone but hadn't quite got there when Jane spoke.

'Boss, I've been thinking, while I've been going through this stuff.'

'There you go again,' Dave said, shaking his head. 'Multitasking, for Christ's sake. No wonder us men have to keep you under the thumb.'

'Are you finished?' she asked.

'Don't mind me. The floor's yours.' He gave her a mock bow.

Jane turned back to Pete. 'Whoever this perp is, what if he's a loner, like Kevin Haynes? Works alone. No Internet. No ring.'

'Then no one would have a clue about him unless he's been seen around the parks and playgrounds, taking photos or using binoculars. Anything more perverted than that, we'd have heard about.'

'Which means more canvassing,' Ben said. 'All the parks, playgrounds, swimming pools, schools – everywhere in the city that you could observe kids without causing a fuss.'

Dave gave a long, low whistle. 'That's a lot of man hours. More than this, by a long shot.'

'But both jobs need doing,' Pete said. 'And so does the elimination of Neil Sanderson and Damon Albright. The latter being my next job.' He picked up the phone at last and dialled.

*

'Mr Albright. Thank you for seeing me.'

'Not at all. Come in.' He stepped back from the large front door, allowing Pete to enter.

The dark-haired man was a good six feet tall, clean-cut but casually dressed. The way he held himself showed a physical confidence and a degree of fitness that suited his late-forties age but certainly not his retired status. A former shopkeeper – he must use a gym, Pete thought.

The house was grand in an understated way. Antique furniture that suited its surroundings.

'This way.' Albright showed him into a sitting room that was comfortable and stylish at the same time. Like it had been designed, rather than accumulated over the years.

'Very nice,' he said.

'Thank you.' Albright inclined his head slightly. 'I like it. Can I get you something? Tea? Coffee?'

'No, I'm fine, thanks.'

They sat opposite one another, across a square coffee table with a large glass panel in its centre. 'So, how can I help?'

Pete leaned forward, elbows on his knees. Albright was lounging, relaxed and at ease. 'Well, I'm here about Rosie Whitlock, Mr Albright. Or, more particularly, about her mother, Jessica. Your relationship with her.'

'Ah.'

'Yes?' Pete prompted.

'We were hoping to keep that quiet. Save any hassle for Jessica at home, you know?'

Pete nodded. 'But, now we've established the fact of it, how long has it been going on?'

'A little under three years. It's tailed off a little, of late. I haven't seen her more than twice in the past three or four months and one of those occasions was this afternoon.'

'So, things have cooled between you?'

'No, no. Nothing like that. It's just that – and I fully understand why, of course – Jessica wanted to prioritise her family.'

'At the expense of your relationship.'

Albright shrugged. 'I suppose, if you want to think of it that way.'

'And was that the way you thought of it, Mr Albright?'

'No. I fully supported her. I *do* fully support her in the need to maintain a stable family environment for Rosie to grow up in. She's just come into her teens. These are vital years for her.'

'That's very understanding of you. Do you know Rosie then?'

'No, I've never met her. I know Alistair. He did some work for me, some time ago. In fact, he introduced me to Jessica – not that we started seeing each other straight away. That wasn't until some months later.'

'And lately, as you haven't been seeing as much of her, is there anyone else in your life?'

'No, not right now.'

'But before?'

'I've had a few girlfriends. Even a fiancée once. We split up about six months before I sold the shop.'

'So, she was the most recent, before Jessica Whitlock?'

'Yes. I was with her for four years.'

'Would you mind giving me her contact details?'

'Whatever for?'

'Standard procedure, Mr Albright. We can't just take people's word on things. They have to be corroborated.'

Albright's lips tightened briefly, then relaxed. 'OK. I haven't been in touch with her for nearly four years, so the information might be out of date . . .'

'That's OK. If you wouldn't mind.'

He got up and went out to the hall. Moments later he was back with a flip-up personal phone directory. He ran the plastic slider down and opened it. 'Here you go.' He handed it across. 'Monica Devlin.'

Pete brought out his notebook and made a note of the address and phone number. 'Thank you. Now, if I can just ask . . . where were you between eight and nine in the morning, the day before yesterday?'

'Uh . . . Here.'

'Alone?'

'Yes, I'm afraid so.'

'OK. Were you perhaps doing anything that would confirm that? Surfing the Internet, perhaps? Phoning or texting someone?'

'No. I usually have breakfast around 7.30, watch a bit of morning TV to get the gist of the news, then spend an hour in the gym.'

'Here in the house, or do you use a public gym?'

'I have my own. It's small and basic, but it has everything I need to keep reasonably in shape.'

'I see. And what about *this* morning?'

'Today, you mean?'

'Yes.'

'Ah, well, that I can help you with. I went to see my brother in Paignton. Got there about a quarter to ten. I stopped off at the garage just beyond Topsham about 9.15. And, before that, I was in town, getting a birthday card. I dare say there's CCTV in the High Street. Probably in the car park, too, I expect.'

'OK. Well, I think that about covers it for now, Mr Albright. Thank you.' Pete stood up and put away his notebook and pen. 'I expect I should warn you – I believe Alistair Whitlock now knows about your affair.'

'Ah. What makes you think so?'

'The way Mrs Whitlock spoke when she told me about it earlier.'

'I see. Well, thanks for the heads-up, Sergeant.' Albright put out a hand. His grip was firm and dry.

*

It was fully dark by the time Pete made it back into the city. He'd tried twice during the drive to reach Barry Enstone without success. As the man lived not far from the station, he'd decided to call round rather than try again. When he got there, the street was lined along both sides with parked cars. He saw that the lights were on in Enstone's sitting room. Reaching the end of the road, he had still found nowhere to park so, with little other choice, he turned around and drove back down to double-park and leave the hazard lights flashing.

He rang the doorbell and stood waiting in the porch. The place was neat and well maintained. Perhaps the orderliness of prison life had crossed over into Enstone's civilian existence.

A shame timeliness hasn't, he thought and rang the bell again, knocking loudly to back it up. After several seconds, there was still no movement from within. He crossed to the sitting room window. Peering in through the nets, he could see the whole room – including the back of Barry Enstone's head, slumped back in the armchair that was facing away from the window.

'Wake up, you dozy sod,' Pete muttered and banged on the window with his knuckles, expecting Enstone to jump up, disturbed from a nap. But there was still no reaction. Pete frowned. That was not natural. Something was wrong. He went back to the front door, tried it, but it was locked, so he went around to the back of the house, down the narrow, gated passage at the side. The passage opened out on to a long, narrow garden, lit only by the nearly full moon and stars. A window was high in the wall at his side. Beyond it was the half-glazed back door. Pete tried it. It opened silently. He stepped into the small kitchen.

'Barry,' he called.

No answer.

He went through into the hall. Into the brightly lit sitting room. Enstone was slumped in his chair, mouth open. A glass tumbler was on the small table beside him with a bottle of cheap whiskey and . . .

'Shit,' Pete muttered, as he saw the pill bottle behind the whisky. He stepped forward quickly. Touched Enstone's shoulder. 'Barry. Come on, wake up.'

But Enstone simply slumped to the side. Pete felt for a pulse in his neck.

'Oh, bollocks.'

Chapter 22

'999. Which emergency service do you require?'

'This is DS Gayle, Exeter CID. I need an ambulance and the pathologist to this address. I have a dead body here. White male, late thirties. Overdose of alcohol and prescription medication, by the look of it.'

'Thank you, sir. Can I take the address and your badge number, please?'

Pete gave the information and ended the call, then called the station. 'Jane,' he said when it was picked up. 'I'm at Barry Enstone's place. He's dead. Looks like suicide.'

'Bugger. Does that mean he's our man and couldn't stand the guilt, or that he wasn't, but couldn't take the pressure, do you think?'

'I don't know, but we need to find out sharpish. Get forensics over here, will you? And I want you and Ben to search the place. Also, get Dave to text me the girlfriend's details. Once the blue lights get here, I'll go see what she can tell us. And we need to know if he had access to a vehicle.'

'He hasn't got one registered to him, we know that. And there won't be one with his job.'

'Again, I'll check with the girlfriend. He's got no living relatives, has he?'

'No, we checked on that when he first came up.'

'OK, so we need to talk to his colleagues and his parole officer, find out about his friends, associates, club memberships and so on.'

'Right, boss.'

Pete ended the call and went out to move his car further up the street, allowing access for the ambulance and other vehicles that would be on the way.

Damn it, this was all he needed. Now, they had to rule Enstone in or out of the inquiry definitively and fast, because if he was guilty and working alone then Rosie had to be found before she starved to death.

His mind conjured an image of Rosie, bound and gagged in some dark and dank hiding place, waiting in vain for her captor to come and feed her. Getting weaker and thinner, her mouth working behind the gag as thirst grew into a desperate need. The fight going slowly out of her, as dehydration shut down her body and her mind until, finally, she lost consciousness and died there, alone and undiscovered.

Where was she?

Where would Enstone have stashed her if, indeed, he'd taken her?

He went back into the house, headed for the kitchen to lock the back door, but stopped himself just in time. He had compromised the scene more than enough already. Enstone's death looked for all the world like a suicide, but it was like the guy in that Steven Seagal movie said – assumption was the mother of all fuck-ups. And the last thing he needed right now was to screw anything up.

He went back to the front door. As he reached it, his phone buzzed with an incoming text. He stepped outside and stood on the porch. The text was from Dave: a simple name and address. Karen Upton, the address just a few streets away from his own. He closed the phone and was returning it to his pocket when it buzzed again in his hand. Another text, this one from Jane, more conversational and complete. *'Enstone worked at Old Mill.*

Parole officer Heather Styles.' A phone number followed, but Pete recognised it as an office number. She would not be there now. No one would. He would have to wait until morning to talk to her.

But not Enstone's boss.

The Old Mill. A cold shiver ran down Pete's spine as he pictured the big pub and carvery on Cowley Bridge Road. And, more importantly, on the side of the river, on the northern outskirts of the city. Upstream from where the bodies of both Amanda Kernick and Lauren Carter had been found. If that wasn't opportunity, Pete didn't know what was. Damn it, he had driven past the place earlier, in his search for possible dump sites for the two bodies. Was Jane right? Was he their man after all, and his suicide a matter of guilt?

He looked up at the flash of blue lights from the end of the street. A police car was coming towards him. Then, as he watched, an ambulance turned in behind it, followed by the black Honda Civic of the pathologist, Dr Chambers.

The three vehicles pulled up, one behind the other, effectively blocking the street. As John Carter unfolded his lanky frame from the police car, the door of one of the houses across the street opened and a head came out, then pulled back in and the door was firmly shut.

Pete heard another engine from the far end of the street and glanced that way to see a large white van approaching, a small logo on the side, near the back end. Forensics.

He stepped aside for the coroner's officer. 'John.'

'You it, then?'

'So far. I expect there's some uniforms on the way.'

'This is getting to be a habit, you and me.'

'I know. We'll have to stop it. You know what the station's like for gossip.'

'So, what have we got this time?'

'The house owner, Barry Enstone. Conviction eight years ago for possession and distribution of indecent images of minors.

Nine years, served five. Looks like suicide. Called me earlier today, in a state, saying he thought we'd set him up – or, more specifically, I had – with the press, because we couldn't pin anything on him for Rosie Whitlock's disappearance. Evening, Doc.' The pathologist stopped beside Carter. He was dressed in a black suit and tie. 'Been somewhere nice?'

'I was at the golf club. Hence why it didn't take me long to get here.'

'Ah. Sorry to spoil your dinner.' Pete turned back to Carter. 'I called him back, couldn't get an answer, so I thought I'd pop round on the way back from interviewing another potential suspect. Saw him through the nets, went round and found the back door unlocked, so I went in to check on him.'

'Hold on a moment, please,' Chambers said to the ambulance crew, who had come up the path with a stretcher. Then to Pete, 'So, you checked for vital signs?'

'Yes. He's dead. Looks like an overdose. Pills and booze. But that may be what it's meant to look like. As I said, the back door was unlocked. And it seems out of character, despite the circumstances.'

The forensics team arrived, in white bodysuits and overshoes, hoods up and masks hanging around their necks for now, carrying two shiny aluminium equipment cases each. Harold Pointer also held a stack of metal stepping squares. 'Evening, Sergeant. Doctor. Constable. What are we looking for here?'

'Apparent suicide, so evidence to corroborate or deny that,' Chambers told him, then bent to set his leather case on the ground at his feet. It would be a few minutes before he could gain access.

'You'll find my prints on the back door, the front door and I touched the deceased to confirm death,' Pete told Harold. 'I haven't been anywhere else in the house. Left that to you lot. Back door was unlocked, front wasn't.'

'So, you opened the front door.'

'Yes.'

'Righto. In we go.' He pulled his mask up over his nose and mouth and stepped forward, setting the first of his square metal steps down just inside the threshold.

'Suspect in your case?' asked the pathologist, tucking his hands into the pockets of his suit jacket.

'Yes.'

'Mm. You'll need full access to this place as soon as possible, then, to search for evidence.'

'Yeah.'

'Good luck with that, with Harry on the case,' said Carter. 'He won't miss anything, but he doesn't rush.'

'I'll have a word, see if he can expedite things as much as possible,' the doctor offered. 'Perhaps he can clear a room at a time and allow you access to it.'

Pete nodded. 'That would be helpful. Where the hell have my uniforms got to?' He pulled out his mobile phone and dialled. 'Jane, chase up the bloody uniforms, would you? Then get round here as quick as you can.'

'We were just leaving, boss.'

'OK.' He cancelled the call and put the phone away.

'Was he a good suspect?' Carter asked.

'Not until a few minutes ago, when I found out where he worked. We just had to eliminate him, that was all.'

'So, how did the press get on to him?'

'Don't know,' Pete shrugged. 'Not from my team, that's for sure. I suppose they must have checked the sex offenders register.'

'Can they do that?'

'Legally? No. Practically? Of course they can.'

'So, anyone else on that register is at risk of the same treatment.'

'Yes, if they haven't already had it.'

Harold Pointer stuck his head out the front door. 'Ready when you are, Doctor.'

'Thanks, Harold.' He picked up his bag and went inside.

Pete glanced up at the distant flash of blue lights. A patrol car was coming up the street. 'At last.'

'Reinforcements?' Carter suggested.

'The bloody uniforms, I hope. Then I can at least get back do doing some detective work.'

'And what does Louise think about that? You getting back to work, I mean.'

Pete drew in a deep breath. 'She's not overly happy about it, but one of us has to earn a crust.'

The car pulled up a short way down the street and Pete stepped down from the porch and went to meet the three uniformed constables who climbed out. 'Right, I need crime scene tape around the property, front and back, then I need a man on the front gate and one on the back door until forensics have finished. No one but myself and my team, when they arrive, in or out without my permission until the doc and the forensics guys are finished, OK?'

'Right, Sarge.'

Another car was pulling up behind theirs. Pete recognised Jane's bright green Vauxhall. As she stepped out, the tall, boyish figure of Ben Myers unfolded from the other side. Pete joined them on the pavement.

'This is getting to be a right traffic jam, isn't it, boss?' Jane observed.

Pete glanced back at the vehicles filling the street. 'Best get some more uniforms at either end of the street, I suppose; get it cordoned off until we can clear it. Why the hell didn't we know before that he worked at the Old Mill?'

'Didn't come up, I suppose. Dave interviewed him at home, didn't he? And then we were concentrating on his alibi, which was his girlfriend.'

'Yeah, I need to go and talk to her. Doc Chambers is inside with the forensics team. He said he'd get them to clear a room at a time so we could search it. I want everything examined, down to the fluff under the wardrobes. If there's anything to find here, I want it found, OK? I'll see what Karen Upton has to say for herself, then I'll be back to help.'

'OK.'

Pete walked with them as far as the gate, then waved to John Carter and went on to his car, while Jane and Ben headed up the path.

Using the back streets, it took him just a few minutes to reach the address that Dave had texted him. He pulled up outside a neat 1960s semi, one of a row of similar houses, each with its own drive and garage. Most had at least one car outside. This one had a nearly new Fiat 500 on the drive.

There was no doorbell so Pete knocked sharply on the frosted glass. Moments later, a shadow moved beyond it and the door was opened just a few inches by a small, pretty woman in her late thirties, her blonde hair cut in a neat bob.

'Yes?'

Pete showed her his warrant card. 'Sorry to bother you. DS Gayle, CID. Miss Upton?'

She seemed to relax slightly. 'Yes.'

'Can I have a word, please? It won't take long.'

'What about? Barry?'

'Yes.'

'I've said all I want to say about him, thank you.' She went to shut the door.

Pete raised a hand quickly. 'It's not entirely about that, I'm afraid.'

She paused. 'Then what is it?'

He gave a small gesture. 'Do you mind? As I say, it won't take long.'

She pursed her lips briefly. 'All right.' She stepped back and allowed him to enter.

The wide, square hallway was tastefully decorated. Four doors led off, three of them closed. The fourth, in front of him, opened into the lounge. A dark leather sofa stood against the wall that he could see and, beyond it, a small bookcase. She led him through and waved him to a seat at right angles to the sofa, which she perched on, hands between her knees.

'So, what's this about?'

'I'm investigating the death of a young girl and the disappearance of another. You may have read about it or seen it on the news.'

She grimaced. 'Yes. I never imagined Barry would be involved in anything like that.' She shivered. 'It's creepy.'

'Yes. I know you've spoken to my colleagues, but before we go any further, I need to confirm your whereabouts on the mornings of yesterday and the day before, around eight o'clock to nine.'

'I've already told your DCI Silverstone, I was at Barry's place. With him. I've stayed there every night this week.' She shivered again. 'To think . . .'

'Then, I have some bad news for you, I'm afraid.'

'What?'

'I've just come from Barry Enstone's house. I'm afraid he's dead, Miss Upton. He died this evening.'

'Oh God. How?'

'At this stage, it looks like an overdose, but that's to be confirmed.'

'My God, that's awful.'

'Miss Upton, you seem to have spent a reasonable amount of time at his house. Was there anywhere in the property that you were . . . discouraged from going into? An office, a workroom, spare bedroom, anything like that?'

She frowned. 'No.'

'There was nowhere you didn't go?'

'No . . . Well, the loft, I suppose. But you wouldn't, would you?'

Pete inclined his head. 'And did Barry spend much time up there, that you know of?'

'A bit. He was looking for something. A document he wanted to show me from amongst his mother's things.'

'But he didn't find it?'

'No, not . . . No, he didn't. Why?'

'And you didn't ever hear anything unusual from up there?'

'Only him moving boxes around. Why? What are you thinking – that he was holding one of those girls up there all the time we were . . . God, no. He couldn't have.' She stared at him, wide-eyed. 'Could he?'

Pete shrugged. 'At this stage, I really don't know. Do you know if he had a computer?'

'Yes. In the spare room. He didn't use it much. Emails and eBay, I think that was about all. It's quite old.'

'Did he have a password on it?'

'Yes. He changed it recently to my name and birthday. Karen253. Twenty-fifth of March.'

'OK. And was he in any clubs or associations that you know of? Maybe a supporters' club, a darts team – anything like that.'

She shook her head. 'Not that I'm aware of, no.'

'So his emails were . . .?'

'I don't know.' She shrugged. 'Mostly junk, like most people's, I suppose.'

'You say you stayed there all this week. As the house is now a crime scene, we'll need you to pop into the station at some point and provide DNA and fingerprints for elimination.'

'OK.'

He nodded. 'And one last thing. I'm not trying to be offensive, but . . . I take it you were having sex with Mr Enstone? How . . . how was he as a lover?'

She shifted awkwardly on the sofa, clearly embarrassed. 'He was . . . not skilled, but he was kind, considerate, gentle . . . He wanted to please me. You can't really think he was doing these things, attacking these young girls, while we were . . .' She shivered. 'God! I can't believe that. I just can't.'

He stood up. 'Thank you, Miss Upton. Sorry to have troubled you and for your loss.' He stepped into the hall, turned back with his hand on the door handle. 'If there's anything else you think of, don't hesitate to call us, OK?'

'Of course.'

Pete nodded and let himself out. Glancing back from the end of her drive, he saw that she was still standing in the doorway. He waved briefly, but her only response was a brief grimace that he guessed was meant to be a smile.

*

'Found anything?'

Pete stepped into the spare bedroom. The forensic team were working in the kitchen and the main bedroom, white-suited figures going quietly about their business, just the rustle of their thin overalls to show that they were actually real, not some weird type of spectral apparition. Jane was sitting in front of a cheap, wood-effect workstation with an old tower-style desktop computer. The screen in front of her flickered and shifted, showing a photograph of a golden autumn lane overlaid with a variety of icons.

'Just got in here,' she said. 'Harry's next door. Reckons this room's clean. Like, very clean.'

'Mm-hmm.'

'Yeah. So, now we've got access to the computer, let's see what's on it.' She clicked a couple of keys and a small screen came up with a series of little brown folder icons. She clicked on the first one. Several Word documents showed up, along with a sub-folder. She opened that, to reveal yet more Word documents and a few saved web pages. She tried one of these. It appeared to be a news item, downloaded from a newspaper website. She closed it and tried another. A similar article opened up. She navigated to another folder and opened it. More Word files. Another folder gave the same result.

'Hang on,' Pete said. 'You can save pictures in Word documents.'

'True.' Jane clicked back and opened one of the files. A letter appeared, addressed to a judge at the county appeal court. 'OK. Don't see the point of that, but still . . .' She closed it, scanned down the page and tried another one. Another letter opened up, this one to his solicitor. 'Has Harry finished in the sitting room, do you know?' Pete asked.

'No idea, boss. I daren't ask.'

Pete turned to the door. 'Harold,' he called.

'In here, Sergeant.'

Pete stepped out on to the narrow landing. 'Have you finished in the sitting room?'

'Yes. We did that first, to allow Doctor Chambers access to the body.'

Pete stepped up to the doorway of the main bedroom, in which Harold was working. 'Did you find anything of interest in there?'

'Forensically, no. A few books that probably wouldn't get published nowadays, but nothing too untoward.'

'OK. Thanks.' He headed downstairs, leaving Jane to the computer and Ben Myers to search the loft, the ladder of which was pulled down just a few feet from the doorway into the spare room.

He was less than a third of the way down the stairs when Ben called out. 'Hey, boss. I've got something up here.'

Pete turned on the stairs. 'What?'

'You'd better come up and have a look.'

'Really?'

'When you've done that, you'll want to come and have a look at this, too, boss,' Jane said from the spare room.

'Jeez! One at a time, folks.' He grabbed the side of the metal ladder and started up into the roof space. As his head emerged into the loft, he saw that it was fully lined, floored and carpeted, with a Velux window looking out to the rear. Ben was standing over an old-fashioned trunk, its lid thrown back to reveal a stack of papers and magazines.

'What you got, Ben?' He stepped up into the sloping, roofed space.

'These.' He handed over a sheaf of papers and Pete glanced down at them. Not papers, he saw. Photographs. The thin, cheap paper had fooled him from a distance.

He began to flick through. 'Christ. So much for not being into this kind of thing anymore.' The photographs were of girls ranging in age from around eight or nine upwards. None of them were family snaps. He flicked through several then looked up at Ben, who was watching him carefully. 'How many have we got here?'

'Dunno. Hundreds, by the look of it. There's a few magazines and books in between, to stabilise the stacks, I suppose. But mostly, it's pictures in here.'

Pete looked into the trunk. About three feet by one and a half, it was roughly half full of stacks of papers and books. *Hundreds? More like thousands.* He sighed. 'This whole lot's going to need taking back to the station, cataloguing and putting into evidence.'

'Shit.'

'Yeah. Not going to be light, is it? We'll have to use evidence boxes. Come down and see if you can lay your hands on some while I see what Jane's got.'

'I haven't finished searching this place yet.'

'OK. Do that, then see about the evidence boxes.' He stepped down onto the ladder and began to descend. 'Nice work, Ben.'

Ben grunted. 'Thanks.'

Pete grinned and continued down the ladder. 'What you got, Jane?' he asked as he went back into the spare room.

'Found what we're looking for,' she said. 'Filed under "Journey planners".'

She looked up at him as she clicked an icon and an image opened up. Disgust mingled with horror as Pete looked at the image on the screen.

'Yeah, all right,' he said. 'That'll do. What else?'

'A whole folder full. Here you go.' She ran the caster-footed chair to one side, leaving him room to stand at the computer. Pete reached for the mouse and reluctantly lined it up and double-clicked. Another image came up, almost as sick as the first one. The girl must have been no more than nine, the man with her probably in his late fifties or more – his face was blurred out, but you could tell by his hair colour, and not just that on his head. He was as naked as she was and evidently far happier to be there. He clicked on the Next button and went rapidly through several pictures until he stopped at one. 'This is one of those that Ben's got upstairs, in print form.'

'Maybe he prints them out, but keeps them on here too,' Jane suggested.

'Mm.' Pete moved on, flicking through several more pictures. He saw another that he recognised from the prints upstairs. Then another. 'Looks like you're right. There's more here. But, do these files have any data on them as to where they came from?'

'They're just picture files, rather than web pages, so I don't know, boss. I know they would if he'd taken them, but, as downloads off the Internet, they'd just have the file size and download date, as far as I know. Dave would probably know if there's more, but I'm not as up on this stuff as he is.'

'Another little something to take away with us then.'

'Yeah. And London didn't have anything on file from down here.'

Pete grunted. 'Lot of use they are, then, eh?'

'And what's "Journey planners" got to do with anything? Does that suggest he goes somewhere to be involved in this kind of stuff, do you think?'

'Or it's just a title to put off a casual searcher. Shut it off and get it ready to take away,' Pete told her and turned away. 'Harold! How you doing?'

Harold stepped out of the main bedroom. 'Almost done. Lots of forensic material, but I was expecting that in here, of course. What I wasn't expecting was this.'

'What?' Pete stuck his head into the room to see Harold holding up a small suitcase, filled with neatly folded clothes. But not male clothes, he saw. And not adult sizes either.

'Jesus! Swab them for DNA, Harold. And compare it to every unsolved case in the database that involves a young girl. Including, and especially, Lauren Carter and Amanda Kernick.'

Chapter 23

Jane adjusted the position of the small trolley that Barry Enstone's computer was standing on at the side of her desk. 'Right. I don't know if this is the kind of stuff I need to be looking at before I go home to my bed, but here goes.' She pressed the power button. The fan began to whir and the screen lit up. The bright gold colours of the sunlit autumn scene that he used as his home page seemed completely incongruous, knowing what was concealed behind it.

'We're going to have to go through all the pictures on there, see who's on the missing persons database or the national crime database and look for anything recognisable in the backgrounds,' Pete said.

'That's going to be a bloody big job, with that amount of pictures to go through.'

'I know. While you start on it, I'm going to see if I can find out how Enstone got to work and back. Like we said earlier, whoever took Rosie had the use of a vehicle and we've got nothing to suggest he had one.'

He picked up his jacket from the back of his chair and headed out once more.

*

The Old Mill was a large, sprawling building with a car park at its north side, set between the main road and the river. The suspension footbridge that stretched across the two arms of the river at this point extended from just beyond the car park, its intricate and strangely decorative framework lit by spotlights now that darkness had set in. The car park was almost full. Pete found a space at the back, overlooking the river. As he climbed out of the car, the smell of roast dinners wafted warmly towards him, in stark contrast to the cold, shadowy trees and swift-flowing water in front of him. He headed inside.

The bar was not crowded yet. That would come later in the evening. But the restaurant area was busy, the noise of numerous conversations like a physical buffer as he stepped inside. A pretty blonde girl in her early twenties was serving at the bar. She finished taking the money for a round of drinks, gave the buyer his change and turned to Pete. 'What can I get you?'

'I need to talk to the manager.' Pete showed her his warrant card.

'Oh, right. One moment, sir.' She left the back bar and headed towards the restaurant area, to his left. Seconds later, she came back. A woman in her late thirties, with dark hair pulled back from a face that was handsome rather than beautiful, broke away from behind the girl to approach Pete.

'Can I help?' she asked.

'I hope so. DS Peter Gayle. I need to ask about one of your employees, Barry Enstone.'

'He's not in today, I'm afraid. Why? He's all right, is he?'

'Actually, no. You are . . .?'

'Carrie Evans.'

'Miss Evans, I'm sorry to have to tell you this, but Barry Enstone died.'

'My God! He was only in here last night. What happened?'

'We're not sure yet, but it looks like it might have been suicide.'

'Jesus. Poor guy.'

'You say he wasn't in today. Why not?'

'He was due to work Sunday.' She shook her head. 'My God.'

'Do you know of anyone he had a problem with, who might have wanted to harm him?'

'No. He was always quiet, mild, got on with his job and everyone he dealt with. I can't believe this.' She looked around as if searching for somewhere to sit.

'Do you have an office we could use?'

'Uh, yes, of course.' She led him through the bar and into the corridor that led towards the toilets. At the far end, a door was marked 'Private'. She unlocked it and showed him into a small office. 'Take a seat.' She indicated a chair in the corner as she moved around to the far side of the cluttered desk and sat down. 'I still can't get my head around this. He was just a nice, quiet bloke. Conscientious, pleasant. Didn't have any enemies that I know of. Wouldn't have it in him to make any, as far as I could tell. So . . . You say he died, but are you suggesting he was killed?' She shook her head slowly.

'We're not sure yet. How did he get around? Get to work and back?' Pete asked. 'He doesn't appear to have had a car.'

'He used the bus sometimes. Other than that, I don't know.'

Pete nodded. 'You never saw him on a bike or anything?'

She gave a short laugh. 'I wouldn't fancy biking up that hill, would you?'

Pete shrugged. 'People do.'

'No, I never saw him with a bike. I don't know exactly where he lived,' she said, as if she'd only just realised it. 'Sad, isn't it? You work with someone for what? Two, three years. And you never really get to know them, do you?'

'Happens to a lot of us, I suppose. Is there anyone here who might have known him better than you?'

She grimaced. 'Derek might, I suppose. Give it a few minutes to let the rush die down and we'll go and have a word.'

Pete raised his eyebrows in a silent question.

'He's the carvery chef tonight. If there was someone else who could take over from him, I'd pull him off, but . . .' She shrugged. 'Won't be long, anyway. There's always a lull after about 6.45.'

Pete looked at his watch and was shocked to see the time was after half past six. 'I didn't realise it was that late,' he said. 'I'll have to give the wife a quick ring.'

'Tell her to come over,' she suggested. 'Save cooking.'

'I would, but she won't come out on a Thursday,' he said. Any excuse to keep things professional. He stood up and lifted his phone from his pocket. 'I'll just step outside.'

'Sure.'

Pete stood in the corridor, the door closed at his side as he made the call. As usual, Annie answered it.

'Hello, Button,' he said. 'It's Dad. Sorry, I clean forgot the time. I'm out talking to a witness. You and Mum go ahead and eat, all right? I'll grab something out for tonight. I'll tuck you in when I get home.'

'You promise?' She knew that meant he would be back before she should be asleep.

'I promise.'

'All right,' she said with a mock sigh. 'I suppose I'll let you off this once. But don't make a habit of it.'

'Aye, aye, Captain.'

'See you later, Dad. Love you.'

'And I love you, Button.' He felt a swell of emotion in his chest as he said it. 'You'll never know how much.'

He ended the call and returned to the office. Carrie Evans looked up from a ledger she had been going through. 'Any excuse for a minute to check on things,' she said, closing the maroon-bound book.

'Good to get the chance, I expect. Must be a busy place.'

'It is. Pretty much non-stop from noon to ten thirty. Eleven thirty on music nights.' She checked her watch. 'Shall we go see how it's going out there? See if we can grab Derek yet?'

'Good idea.'

Pete held the door for her and led the way back towards the bar. He heard the key turning in the lock behind him, then her heels clicking as she hurried to catch up. Looking across as they stepped into the bar, he could see that the queue at the carvery was gone.

'Looks like we're in luck,' she said. 'I'll introduce you and let you get on with it, if that's OK.'

'Perfect.'

The chef was in his early twenties, wiry with dark, spiky hair, a stud in his nostril and a line of stubble along his jaw, but his gaze was open and friendly.

'Derek, this is Detective Sergeant Gayle,' she said. 'Derek Smith.'

Derek wiped his hand on his apron and extended it across the carving counter. His grip was firm and dry. 'What can I do for you?'

'I need to ask you about Barry Enstone. I gather you worked with him, knew him a bit?'

'Yeah, I . . . Wait a minute. What's with "worked" and "knew"? Has something happened to Barry?'

'Yes, I'm afraid it has. You were friends?'

'Yeah, I suppose. What's happened?'

'There's no good way of telling you. I'm afraid Barry's dead, Derek.'

'Jesus! How? When?'

'This evening. We're not certain about the how yet. We're still investigating. One of the things I need to ask you is, do you know how he got to work and back?'

'Not really. I gave him a lift a couple of times, but other than that, no, I don't. Why?'

'You don't know if he ever had access to a vehicle of any kind?'

Derek shook his head. 'No.'

'OK. And do you know any of his other friends or associates? Anywhere he hung out, any hobbies or interests he might have had?'

'Not really. I know he had some mates in Bristol, but I never met them. And I got the impression he might have got himself a girlfriend recently. A customer from here.'

'Yes? You don't know any names?'

'No. Sorry.'

Pete saw an older couple approaching the counter. 'OK. Thanks for your time.'

*

Pete stood by the car, looking out at the white-painted suspension bridge, and phoned Jane Bennett's number in the squad room.

'Jane,' he said when she picked up. 'Are Jill and Ben back in yet?'

'Yes.'

'What did they learn?'

'Not much. They confirmed that he was engaged to Monica Devlin, as she was then, and that he was a misogynist arsehole at the time, but she couldn't tell them much more than that.'

'OK. Send one of them to meet me back at Enstone's place, will you? The other one can help you until you've had enough. Have you found anything yet?'

'A couple of faces match missing persons files. One from Bristol, the other from Taunton.'

'Bristol again? I was told that Enstone had friends there. No details, unfortunately.'

'Interesting.'

'Yeah. One of the things I'm going to need to search for at his house, is an address book or phone list. You could check his email account with that in mind.'

'Already did. There's nothing untoward in it at all.'

'Well, if he did have friends that far away, he had to contact them somehow. Try his history. See if he had another email account. Hotmail or something, maybe.'

'OK. But you need to remember, boss – I've got a home to

go to, but you've got a wife and kid, too. They need to see you sometimes.'

A car pulled in behind him. He heard the engine cut out, doors slam and happy voices: male, female and a couple of kids. He resisted the temptation to turn and look.

'I know, Jane. But what can I do, eh? Split myself in two? This isn't just about surviving relatives and public safety. There's a live victim we're trying to save.'

'I'm just saying, boss.'

'Yeah, all right. Send Jill or Ben round there, OK? I'm on the way.'

'Will do.'

He ended the call with his gaze locked on the shadowy tree-covered island in the middle of the river. Bare branches rose up to entangle the far end of the bridge, darkness reaching out to claim the bright, modern structure and draw it back from the spotlights into the night. He climbed into the car, slammed the door and started the engine, his mind once more conjuring an image of a young girl with Rosie Whitlock's face, lying in the dark somewhere, bound and gagged, terrified and alone.

Chapter 24

'Jane, it's Pete. We've finished at Enstone's. One bus ticket that his boss has confirmed he used for work and one telephone/address book. No bike and no driving licence. You've got Ben helping you, right?'

'Yes,' she said cautiously.

'Not any more. We need a full, deep background on Barry Enstone. Right down to the roots. Family ties, where he grew up, friends and associates, former girlfriends, where they live now and where they lived when he was with them, everywhere he's ever lived, every piece of property he owns. I want to know everywhere he could possibly think of going. The bus ticket and lack of a driving licence suggest he's not our man, but we need to be sure. Any more progress, your end?'

'We've identified a few more of the girls on Enstone's computer and one of the blokes.'

'Oh, yes?'

'Known paedophile from Swindon. He's currently residing at Her Majesty's pleasure in Northumberland.'

'From Swindon? Sounds like this might be bigger than we thought.'

'It's a bloody lot of work, I know that.'

'Then we need to find a way to prioritise, because Rosie has to stay as our main focus.'

*

Pete's stomach growled as they trudged up the stairs to the squad room.

'Blimey, boss. Anybody would think you were hungry. They probably heard that down the takeaway.'

Pete's mind offered an image of the succulent meats on the carving counter at the Mill on the Exe. 'I can think of something I wouldn't mind getting my teeth into.' He pushed open the squad room door and almost did a double-take then stepped forward before Jill could bump into him from behind. 'Jeez.'

All the lights were on and his full team were there, diligently concentrating on computer screens, printouts or files. He also saw Sophie Clewes and three other uniformed constables, two of whom he recognised from Barry Enstone's place, earlier in the evening.

Jane looked up from her screen, her hands pausing over the keyboard. 'Hey, boss. What are you doing here? I thought you were going home.'

A few other people looked up when she spoke, but most just concentrated on what they were doing.

'Never mind what I'm doing here,' he said, heading for his desk. 'I'm leading this inquiry, remember? The question is, what are you lot doing here at this time of day?'

Jane spread her hands in a gesture that encompassed the whole room. 'Volunteers, boss. There's a bloody lot to do and not much time to do it in, so . . .'

'Well, in that case, what have you got?' He hung his coat over the back of his chair and went around the desks to stand beside her.

'OK, all the photos are Internet downloads rather than originals. He's not the photographer. Which is not to say he doesn't know the photographer, but . . .' She shrugged. 'They almost all appear of a type, a style, which suggests a single photographer or a small group of them. There are more than thirty different girls. I've managed to identify half a dozen so far, from the Missing Persons database and the National Criminal Database. They all come from different places: Bristol, Bath, Swindon, Oxford, Taunton and Minehead, so far. And still just one of the blokes. The one I told you about, from Swindon. Steven Arnold Southam, aged forty-nine.'

'SAS? That's for real?'

'Yep. He's currently in Morpeth, Northumberland, in the first of a four-year term for gross indecency with a minor.'

'So, we may have stumbled onto a major ring. But does it get us any closer to Rosie?'

'Not yet, boss. But if Barry wasn't the only member in Exeter, then it could do. We just need to ID some of the other blokes in the pictures. That's what Sophie's working on.'

Pete looked up. Sophie Clewes was sitting with her back to him, at the desk of one of Simon Phillips' guys. He could see that she was running a facial recognition program. As he watched, the screen in front of her brightened and filled with two photographs, side by side. Even from this distance, Pete could tell that they were of the same man.

She turned to face them. 'Got another one.'

The gentle noises of a working team stopped, silence descending heavily until Sophie declared, 'Adrian Chandler, fifty-one, from Bristol. He's done two terms for child sex offences, currently on parole after the second one. Got out a year ago.'

And there was the Bristol connection again. As well, Pete thought, as the Bath one with Neil Sanderson. 'Nice one, Sophie. What else are we doing?' He turned back towards his crew.

'I've got CCTV from the BP garage on the Exmouth road, the morning Rosie disappeared,' said Dave. 'One sighting on it of a car that may be Albright's. It's at the time he suggested, but there isn't a clear view of the number plate, so I can't confirm it. I'm just looking at the stuff from the entrance of the Royal Marines Training Centre, up the road from there, and I've got a request in for the footage from the roundabout outside the Fire and Rescue place. That should be coming through shortly. They work twenty-four hours there. Then there's the M5 Deepway Junction, the A38/A380 junction at Bickham and a couple of cameras in Paignton to check. One of them's bound to give us what we need, if he's telling the truth.'

'But how soon are you likely to get them?'

'Some will come in tonight. Most of the traffic cam stuff will have to wait for morning.'

Pete's phone rang in his pocket. He took it out and checked it. His home number showed on the screen. 'Hang on,' he said and headed for the door. Out in the corridor he lifted it to his ear.

'Dad.' Annie's voice came accusingly over the airwaves. 'Are you coming home tonight, or what?'

'Hello, Button. Yes, of course I am. I've just been caught up in stuff at work, that's all. You know how it gets, especially on a case like this. There's never enough hours in the day or hands and eyes to cover everything.'

'I know, but I'm missing you. And so's Mum, although she won't say so. Have you even eaten?'

'Don't you start. I get enough of that from your mum.'

'Don't change the subject, Dad. Have you?'

'No, young lady, I haven't yet. I haven't had time. I hope you have, though?' He glanced at his watch and grunted in shock. It was after nine. 'God, it's nearly your bedtime. I hadn't realised.'

'I cooked Chinese for Mum and me.'

'And have you done your homework?'

'Yes.'

'Good girl. I'll be home in a bit. And I miss you too. And your mum. Give her a kiss for me, will you?'

'*Dad.*'

Pete laughed. 'I'll tuck you in when I get home, all right?'

'OK. But don't be too late, or I'll be asleep.'

'Yes, Mother.'

She giggled. 'Just do as you're told then.'

'See you soon, Button. Goodnight.'

'I'm not saying goodnight until you get home. That's incentive.'

'Ooh. Big words for a small person.'

'I could quote you some more, but the longer you're on the phone, the later you'll get here. Bye.'

'Bye, love.' He put away the phone and headed back into the squad room.

Jane looked up from her screen as he reached his desk. 'Go home, boss. We've got this covered. And they need you.'

'So does Rosie Whitlock.'

'If we get anything, I'll ring you myself. Promise.'

Pete was torn. He really ought to be here, doing something useful. But, as Jane said, Louise and Annie needed him at home too. And he was all too aware of the little, plastic thumb drive nestled in his pocket, waiting to show him exactly how well his son knew Rosie Whitlock.

They were missing something. They had to be. Something obvious. He stood with his hands on the back of his chair, head bowed, thinking. Every vehicle that came out of the end of that road during the few minutes around the time of the abduction had been identified, bar two: the silver Peugeot and the white van that had shielded its number from the camera up the road.

The woman in the VW Touran that the white van had pulled out in front of, had been identified and interviewed. She'd had little to say about the van or its occupants. It was just another white van. Two occupants, both male, one with a hoodie, the other wearing a beanie hat. The one in the passenger seat had struck her as small, but that and the fact that he was white was really all she could say about him. She wasn't sure about the driver. She hadn't noticed anything about him at all.

All they'd found tonight seemed to point away from Barry Enstone, although it did suggest that he may well have known the perpetrator, whether or not he knew he was guilty of this particular crime.

He looked up at Jane, who was busy pretending not to be watching him. 'We need a detailed list of Enstone's associates. One of them knows who's doing this. Or is the person doing it. And we need something on those two vehicles – the Peugeot estate and the white van. Give me the address you haven't contacted yet on Downton Road. I'll go there in the morning, see if I can see anyone.'

Jane took out her notebook but kept it defensively closed. 'Are you going home now, or what?'

'Anybody would think you were trying to get rid of me. What have you got to hide?'

'How am I supposed to wrap your Chrissy present when you're sat there in front of me, eh?'

'Oh, you've got me something? You shouldn't have.'

'Don't worry, I haven't. But neither will Louise and Annie if you don't remind them occasionally that you still exist.'

196

Chapter 25

The house was in near darkness, just the upstairs landing light and a table lamp in the lounge shining dimly into the hall. He could see the bluish glow of the TV as he hung up his jacket. Louise was curled up on the sofa, her eyes glued to the set. He glanced at it and recognised one of those modern light-hearted American cop shows.

'Hello, love. Sorry I'm so late. There was another death today.'

'Another one?' She looked up from the screen. 'Jesus, how many's that now?'

'This was an adult. Male. He was a suspect in the others, but I don't think it was him. Looks like he might have topped himself.'

'Was he the one on the news earlier?'

'Might have been. There were a bunch of reporters outside his house at one stage. Silverstone went round there in person to move them on.'

Her eyes widened. 'What? He came out of the station during working hours?'

'There was a bunch of press there.'

'Ah. Right. Sounded like the bloke deserved whatever he got though. He was a convicted perv.'

'We're supposed to think of them as being ill these days,' he said with a smile.

'They're certainly sick. It's not necessarily the same thing.'

He nodded. 'Where's Annie?'

'She went up ten minutes ago. Just after she phoned you.'

'Yeah. As I said – I'm sorry she had to. Once this case is over...'

'There'll be another,' she said dully.

'There already is, but it'll be a nine-to-five type one.'

She looked up at him again, frowning.

'Came out of tonight's death. Looks like he was involved in a huge paedophile ring.'

'And you found it, so it'll be yours to investigate?'

'If we can keep it. But, like I say, that sort of thing is a nine-to-five job. It's not like an abduction or a murder where we need to catch the culprit quick. It's more of a paperchase.'

The frown had faded, but she still said nothing. Pete could guess what she was thinking. There were still victims. Maybe even ones that needed to be rescued. And, of course, she was right, but until they found out about them, they could only track the perpetrators and build cases against them. 'I'll go see Annie,' he said.

Upstairs, he found her door ajar, her light switched off. When he pushed the door gently and stepped in, he saw that she was curled up on her side, facing him. Her eyes gleamed in the light from the landing. 'Hi, Dad. Caught the bad guys yet?'

'Not yet, Button. Between you and Jane Bennett, I had to give up for tonight.'

His stomach growled and her eyes widened. 'Did you leave me any of that Chinese you cooked?' he asked.

'Nope. I ate it *all* up. Every last morsel.' She grinned up at him.

'So, now I've got to go hungry all night? I'll starve down to a skeleton.'

She sat up and he saw that she was wearing her favourite Winnie-the-Pooh nightie. 'Don't be silly. It takes longer than one night to starve. And there's some in the microwave.'

He hugged her tight. 'God, I love you. Thanks, Button. I don't know what I'd do without you.'

'Starve?' she suggested.

'Noo. I'd live on fish and chips and get as fat as a barrel.' He gave her a squeeze then stepped back.

'What about Mum?'

'She'd probably starve.' He ruffled her hair. 'No, I'd get her fish and chips, too, and we'd both end up like Rab C. Nesbitt.'

'Who's he?'

'Sorry, you're too young. It was a Scottish comedy from years ago, designed for people a lot older than you.'

'So, it had a lot of swearing in it?'

'Is that a comment on adult comedy or the Scots?'

She screwed up her face, pretending to think. 'Probably both.'

Pete laughed. 'You're probably right. Now, go to sleep and I'll see you in the morning, eh?'

'OK.' She settled back beneath the covers, pulling them up around her chin.

'Goodnight, Button. Sleep tight.' He brushed her fringe back and kissed her brow.

''Night, Dad.'

Pete paused in the doorway, looking back at her. *God, if anything ever happened to her . . .*

He drew a long, ragged breath. He didn't think he could survive that, too.

He pulled the door closed, leaning for a moment on the jamb while he got his emotions under control, before heading back downstairs, taking the laptop computer from the spare room with him.

Louise was still glued to the TV. 'I'm going to have my tea,' he told her. 'Do you want anything?'

She shook her head, not looking up.

Pete went through to the kitchen. Checking the contents of the microwave, he switched it on, then sat down at the small table and booted up the laptop. The computer was ready first, so he stuck the thumb drive into the slot and let it load up while he took the plate from the microwave and a fork from the drawer.

When he sat down again, he saw that the file from the drive was loaded and ready, so he opened it, removed the drive and tucked it back into his pocket before taking a forkful of food and starting to read.

The file consisted of a series of emails, but he saw that they were written more like texts. Short, abbreviated phrasing with little in the way of greetings or idle chatter, using the addresses to identify themselves. The first one was dated almost two years ago.

Last night was great. Same again next week?

I'll be there.

Pete smiled. Ambiguous. Clever girl. He scrolled down. More brief, innocent messages followed, not frequent, but enough to maintain contact and prove a friendship. Then a cartoon head, smoking a cigarette showed on the screen. He stopped and checked. Tommy had sent it to Rosie. Underneath was the message: *Sorry. Should have warned you. But it's really relaxing when you get used to it.*

Tommy was smoking? When was this? He checked the date. It was a month after his twelfth birthday. Bloody hell. Pete hadn't been aware of that at all. And for it to be 'really relaxing', what had he been smoking? Clearly, he had tried to introduce Rosie to it and it hadn't worked out.

She had replied: *I'll take your word.*

In other words, *I won't be trying it again.* Good for her, Pete thought and took another forkful of rice and veg before scrolling down further. Six weeks later, Tommy had written, *Hope you've got time after. Got something nice for your b'day.* And a couple of days after that, she had sent back: *Wow! That felt good. Thank you.*

Pete frowned and stabbed a king prawn. What had they done for her twelfth birthday that felt so good? Surely, he hadn't . . .? *They* hadn't . . .? No. She was a sensible girl. She'd know better than to start that, at that age. And Tommy: Pete didn't think he'd be that stupid either. But then, there was clearly a lot he didn't know about his son.

He chewed absently, wishing the boy was here so he could ask him. Talk to him. There was so much that they'd missed out on over the years . . .

He scrolled down further.

Nothing else incriminating came up for several months. Just innocent chit-chat until Tommy sent a simple, *What u doing?* Pete took a forkful of rice and scrolled down. He nearly spat the food out when a picture came up of a naked backside. Below it was the message: *What's it look like?* Then another picture, this one of Rosie's face, very close to the camera, her lips puckered in an exaggerated kiss. Tommy replied: *Peachy. Where r u?* Rosie's response: *My bff's outside town.* Tommy sent back: *Shame. I'd v come over.* To which Rosie responded: *Bet u wd.* She ended the exchange with another picture, this one full length, taken from behind. Her hair was swirling, as was her short skirt, her legs tight together in a parody of a ballet pose. A parody because, once more, her backside was bare.

Pete swallowed. Her bff's. Becky Sanderson's. And this was a picture he hadn't seen before, so who had taken it – Becky or her dad?

He suddenly didn't feel hungry any more. His stomach swirled, but he had to eat. He scrolled down a little further, just to get rid of the image from the screen, then ignored the computer while he reluctantly finished his meal. He poured himself a glass of water from the filter jug and sat back down to carry on.

He hadn't got far when he came across the next naked parody picture. This one was of Tommy, from the rear, doing a muscleman pose despite his small stature and slim build. *Just call me Arnie*, said the message underneath. *You Arnie, me Jane*, had come the reply. So, while Becky was sexting with Chris Mellor and Richie Young, Rosie had been doing the same with Tommy.

Yet, her parents knew nothing about it. How could that be?

Pete shook his head. He had known just as little about his own son. The answer was easy. The kids didn't want their parents to know everything about them and what they got up to. And, on the other side of the coin, was what he was doing right here and now, in his own kitchen.

Working.

He sucked in a breath through his teeth. Was this why Tommy was gone? Had he run off because his parents were too busy to spend time with him?

God, what an awful thought!

But this was different. This was something he had to do at home, out of sight of the rest of the team, and especially DCI Silverstone. Even Colin Underhill, come to that, because if any of them saw this stuff, he'd be off the case as quick as a mouse-click. And where would that leave Rosie Whitlock? *Right back at square one, that's where*, he thought. If only for her sake, he couldn't let that happen.

He looked back at the screen, but he'd seen enough for now. The proof was there of a connection between Tommy and Rosie. They knew each other. Well. But whether it meant anything for the case – for either case – was another question entirely. And perhaps a more important one was, why was this the first he knew of it? How had Simon not picked up on this stuff? Or had he, and not mentioned it?

He closed the computer down, washed his plate and fork and went through to the sitting room.

Louise had not moved and she didn't now as he sat beside her and took her hand. 'You know I love you, don't you?' he asked quietly.

'Yes,' she said, not taking her eyes from the TV screen. Then, after a moment, she blinked and looked at him. 'I . . . I don't feel anything. Not love, not anger, not . . . anything. It's like I'm dead inside.' A tear squeezed slowly from the corner of her eye. 'What's wrong with me?'

*

Jane clicked on to the next image and the next. Close-up followed close-up. A crotch shot. A hand on a buttock, fingers squeezing. A young face screwed up in anguish. Then a wider shot. She leaned forward, peering at the screen, head twisted at an awkward angle as she studied the picture, trying to make out detail, to make a decision. The photographer had inadvertently caught himself in a mirror at the edge of the shot, part of his face showing over the top of the camera. She tried zooming in, but lost detail so zoomed back out again. Finally, she sat back. 'Dave. Here, have a look at this, will you? Tell me what you think.'

She pushed herself to one side and he scooted over on his chair, grabbing the edge of the desk to stop himself. He stared at the screen for a long moment. Then she saw the corner of his mouth begin to lift. At last, he looked at her and he was smiling.

'I think,' he said, 'that looks very much like Neil Sanderson. Have you got any more of him?'

'Don't know yet. I've only just found that one.'

'Then, keep looking, my lovely, because I reckon you've got him.' He pushed himself back from her desk, allowing her room.

'I bloody hope so,' she said, saving the shot into a sub-file of potentially useful ones and clicking onto the next image. And the next.

Back at his own desk, Dave carried on with what he was doing as she continued to check through the images, searching for something to identify the subjects or their locations. Then she stopped again. She could not see the subject's face. It was hidden by a fall of long, dark hair. But she recognised the duvet cover and the nightie. She had seen them earlier. She looked across at Dave again. 'I'm no expert, with only personal experience to go on,' she said. 'but how individual do you reckon the veining pattern is in someone's skin?'

'I'd imagine it's fairly unique. Why? What have you got now?'

'Someone trying to be artistic and dropping themselves in the crap while they're at it, if I'm right.'

Dave scooted over again, far enough to see her screen. He laughed. 'Good luck putting together a line-up.'

'You going to volunteer, are you?'

'You wish.'

'Actually . . . no.' She shuddered.

Dave shook his head, still chuckling as he went back to his desk and Jane looked back at the screen. At the bottom of the shot, a hand gripped the shaft of an erect penis, its veins blue against the pale skin as the owner stared at the semi-naked, apparently sleeping young girl in front of him.

She saved the picture into her sub-file and moved on. A closer shot of the same girl. Definitely Becky Sanderson. Then another. She had moved, giving a different view of her lower body. In the next one, she had moved again and his left hand was on her, his wedding ring gleaming in the low light that appeared to be coming from the doorway behind him. Jane's breathing stopped as she moved on once more, dreading what she might be about to see. 'Oh, Jesus.' She saved the image to the same sub-file as the others. 'You sick bastard.'

The next one was completely different. Taken in daylight, it was a shower scene, the head of the subject cut off by the angle and proximity of the camera. It was followed by several more similar ones, then another change of subject. A girl of about the same age, but with straight, pale blonde hair replaced Becky. Jane let out her pent-up breath. 'No luck,' she said. 'Just that one, though it's among several of his daughter.'

'What about the frame details? Do they show a link?'

'They follow one another, yes.'

'Good enough for me.'

Jane sighed. 'I'm knackered. We can tell the boss about this in the morning. Go and arrest the sick bugger then. It's not like he's going anywhere.'

'Knocking off time then?'

'I reckon.' She glanced at her watch. It was after ten. 'I need my beauty sleep.'

He stared at her, examining her face in minute detail, then nodded. 'Yep. I can see a wrinkle coming, just there.'

Jane looked quickly around for something to throw at him, but there was nothing to hand. 'You keep on like that, matey, you'll need to wear your motorbike helmet indoors or I'll box your bloody ears for you.'

Chapter 26

Pete took a small bottle of Coke from the fridge and turned to pick up a Mars bar from the shelves behind him, then headed for the counter at the back of the little shop. Newspapers and magazines were racked all along one side of the long, narrow space. As he passed the local newspapers, he could not help glancing at the huge, glaring headline on the *Exeter Daily News*: POLICE STUMPED.

He stopped and looked closer. His eyes narrowed when he saw the byline for Ellie Turner. The thoughtless bitch who had come to his house, trying to get an interview from Louise. He picked up the paper and read on.

> Terror stalks the streets of Exeter
> while a killer roams free.
>
> Police are tonight no closer to finding abducted schoolgirl Rosie Whitlock, 13, who they suspect was taken by the same man who killed two other young girls, 9-year-old Amanda Kernick of Fishponds, Bristol and Lauren Carter, 10, of Barnstaple, both found in the River Exe in the past few weeks.

> With two men discounted, despite being on the sex offenders register, they are as baffled now as they were when Rosie was first reported missing on Tuesday evening. Parents in the city are living in fear. Jaqueline Armitage of St Leonard's, a mother of two school-age girls, said today, 'I've half a mind to keep my girls at home, out of harm's way, until they catch this pervert.'

'Jesus,' Pete muttered. The bloody woman had no conscience at all. Bloody journalists. He stopped reading and took the paper with him to the counter. After quickly paying for his purchases, he went back out to the car, dumped the paper and his afternoon snack on the passenger seat and started the engine.

Reversing out of the little parking area in front of the shop, just a couple of streets from his home, he turned right at the end of the road, away from Heavitree Road and the station, and worked his way through the estate towards the school. The roads around it were crowded, cars parked in every available spot, legal and otherwise, as mothers dropped their little darlings off for the day. He drove slowly along the packed street and turned into the school, parking beside what he recognised as Jessica Whitlock's Range Rover. Climbing out of the car, he checked his watch. 8.40 a.m. Plenty of time to have a quick word with her before she headed for class. He headed in, ID in hand. A staff member was standing just inside the wide glass doors, keeping an eye on the throng of children who were flowing like a living multicoloured river into the building. Pete stepped across and showed her his badge.

'DS Gayle, Exeter CID. I'm looking for the staffroom.'

'Uh . . . Perhaps I should fetch the headmistress?' The woman was small, plump and fiftyish, wearing a dark, floral dress that matched her dyed hair.

Pete smiled. 'She's probably already there, at this time of day, isn't she?'

The woman nodded. 'I expect so, yes. Especially this morning.'

Pete raised an eyebrow.

'With Jessica – Mrs Whitlock – coming back to work today,' the woman explained. 'I must say, that was unexpected, but she said she needed to be doing something, so . . .'

'Ah. Of course.'

'I expect you're . . .'

'Yes, exactly. Which way is it?'

She pointed down the corridor. 'All the way to the end, turn left and it's the second on the left.'

'Thank you.' Pete headed down the corridor, through the seething, noisy throng.

Stepping into the staffroom was like entering a haven of peace. Men and women sat and stood around, chatting quietly, most with cups or mugs in hand. Pete couldn't see Jessica Whitlock, but most of the people in the room were in a loose huddle near the centre. He stepped forward.

Jessica was seated at the centre of the group, two other women at either side of her. The one to her right, who looked like she should have retired long ago, was holding Jessica's hand in both of hers. Pete caught snatches of questions being asked and support being offered.

'. . . any news yet?'

'If there's anything we can do . . .'

'We all ought to be out there, searching.'

Jessica looked up at that one, from a male colleague. She spotted Pete through the crowd. Their eyes met and she hesitated. He stepped forward between two men.

'Mrs Whitlock. Could I have a word?'

He sensed eyes on him from all around as Jessica surged to her feet.

'Have you found her?'

He shook his head. 'No. I'm sorry. I just need to ask you a couple of questions that might help us do that.'

'Shouldn't you be out searching, instead of here, bothering Jessica?'

Pete looked to his left. The question had come from a blond man of medium height whose mean features were pulled into an aggressive frown. 'The circumstances of this case don't suggest that a search of the type you mean would be of any help.'

'I thought in any case like this, a search was the first thing to be done.'

'Then I can only imagine you haven't been involved in many cases like this, Mr . . . ?'

'It's OK, Malcolm,' Jessica said. 'Leave it.'

'I'm here to gather information that could help bring Rosie Whitlock home,' Pete told him.

'How? Jessica didn't take her, did you?' He turned towards her as he added the question.

Pete had had enough of the man. He too turned to Jessica. 'Mrs Whitlock, is there somewhere quieter that we could have a brief word?'

'Don't worry, Jess,' Malcolm said. 'We're with you all the way. Aren't we, guys?'

Her eyes went from him, to Pete, to the woman sitting at her left, and back to Pete.

'You can use my office, if you like,' the woman said. 'I'm Angela Webster, head of the school.'

He nodded. 'Thank you, Mrs Webster.' He offered Jessica a hand, which she took, looking semi-dazed as she rose from her seat. Her hand was cold and dry. Pete released it and made a path through the crowd of teachers. He opened the door for her and let her lead the way back towards the front of the school.

At the foyer, she headed left and went along a short corridor with three doors leading off it, opposite an outer wall of full-height glass. The first door was marked 'Head'. She went in and stood, at a loss, in the small but tidy office.

Pete indicated the chair behind the desk. 'Do you want to take a seat, Mrs Whitlock?'

She complied, moving automatically. Pete leaned against the floor-to-ceiling bookcase that ran the length of one side of the room and waited for her to look up at him.

'I want to ask again if Rosie has, or has had, a boyfriend as far as you know?'

She frowned. 'No. I said before. She spends most of her free time with Becky.'

'And what about Becky? Is she into boys?'

'What . . .?' She shook her head quickly. 'I don't know, Sergeant. What's this got to do with Rosie's abduction? You think she's run off with a boy? I can assure you, she's far too sensible for that.'

'No, it's just . . .' He couldn't tell her the truth. That the boy he was thinking of was his own son. But, clearly, she didn't know of the connection between them. 'Boyfriends sometimes know things that no one else does. Secrets. Habits. Favourite places.'

'Well, I'm quite sure she doesn't have one, so . . .'

Pete saw the time on the big wall clock across the room. 'OK. And, talking of boyfriends . . .'

She blushed. 'I'm sorry, Sergeant. I couldn't very well tell you in front of Alistair, could I?'

Pete tilted his head. 'So, do I take it that Alistair found out about him last night?'

'Yes.'

'And you're sure of that?'

'What?'

'That he didn't know before.'

'Yes, quite sure. If he'd known before, he'd have . . . Well, he didn't. I could tell.'

'And Mr Albright. Has he ever said or done anything that would make you think he's jealous of your husband's position in your life?'

'No. He's known the situation from day one. In fact, Alistair introduced us, so . . .'

'Has he ever met Rosie?'

'No.'

'Or seen a photo of her?'

'What? What is this? You suspect Damon now?'

'We don't suspect him, Mrs Whitlock, but we do have to eliminate him.'

'Well, you can certainly do that, Sergeant. He's never had anything to do with Rosie. He's never had a reason to. The whole point of being with him was to . . . It sounds awful when you put it into words, but it was to escape for a while. To have time just for me, away from the family and work and everything else.'

All of which confirmed the impression he'd got from Albright himself. They'd still have to confirm his alibi, but at least it made him less of a priority in the meantime. 'OK. I'd best let you get along to class then. Thank you, Mrs Whitlock.'

*

Jane hesitated as the phone on her desk rang abruptly. She clicked the Next button on her computer. The image on the screen changed and she picked up the phone.

'Bennett, CID.'

'Got a visitor for you, DC Bennett. A David Green.'

'Who's he?'

'Says he's from the Antique Barn. Is that the one out by the airport?'

'Ah. Yes. I'll be down in a sec.' She put the phone down, grimaced and pressed the power button on the bottom of the screen to switch it off. There was no need to inflict filth like that on anyone else, first thing in the morning.

At the bottom of the stairs, she hit the button and went through, turning towards the public area at the front of the station.

A man was standing back from the desk. In his forties, he was dressed in dark cords, brogues and a dark green waxed jacket, his brown hair neatly trimmed.

He heard the door and turned towards her. His features were broad – large like the rest of him – but open and friendly.

'DC Bennett?' He extended a hand which swamped Jane's when she shook it, but was gentle at the same time as firm. 'David Green of the Antiques Barn. I got into work this morning and there was a note on my desk that said you wanted some CCTV footage. I saw the news last night, when I got back, so when I saw the note I put two and two together and thought I'd best bring it in as soon as poss.' He took a CD case from his coat pocket and handed it to her.

'Thank you. Thank you very much, Mr Green. That's very good of you. You've been away?'

'A few days in France. Not that good at the lingo, but I know enough to be able to haggle. Brought some bits back for the shop.'

'I see. Well, thanks for this.' She held up the CD case. 'I'm hoping it'll either confirm or deny an alibi.'

He nodded. 'The camera's on a pole across the road from our entrance, so it's got a good view of vehicles coming and going, but it also gets everything going up and down the road. The idea is to get number plates of everything coming in and out, in case they need to be traced. I've given you everything from the morning you asked about, from six to ten. I hope that's OK.'

'Perfect. Thanks again.'

'I hope it helps.' They shook hands again and Jane hurried back up to her desk.

Dave had arrived while she was downstairs. She nearly barged into him as he drew himself a cup of water from the dispenser just inside the door. 'Whoah,' he said. 'Blimey, you're keen.'

Jane waggled the CD case at him and went back to her desk. She switched the screen back on, closed the file of photographs from Enstone's computer, put the CD into the drive and nudged it closed. Dave had come across to stand behind her, water in hand.

'What you got?'

The drive whirred as the CD loaded. 'Footage from the Antiques Barn, out by the airport. Bloke just brought it in.'

'Good of him.'

'Yeah.'

The file finished loading and the screen came up with a single brown envelope icon. Jane double-clicked the folder, as the door opened and Pete walked in.

'Morning, boss,' she called and was surprised when he did not respond. He crossed quickly to his desk, slapped the paper down on the surface and tossed the bottle and the chocolate bar into the bottom drawer. Taking off his jacket, he hung it on the back of his chair and sat down.

'Jane. Dave. What are you looking so pleased about?'

'Two things,' Dave told him, as Jane wondered what the hell had got him so riled up at this time of the morning. 'One, we think we've got Neil Sanderson in the pictures on Barry Enstone's computer. And two, the footage from the antique place out by the airport's come in. Jane's just loading it up.'

'You've got Sanderson?' Pete was out of his chair again and coming around the desk. 'Doing what?'

'The five-knuckle shuffle while he's looking at his daughter's crotch,' Dave said bluntly.

'Jesus!'

The video was loaded and ready to play, but Jane minimised it to the bottom of the screen and opened up the sub-file of pictures she had saved from Enstone's files. 'Here you go.'

Pete stood at her shoulder, one hand resting on the back of her chair as she double-clicked on the first thumbnail. When the image came up full-size, she started a slide-show of the images in the folder and leaned back in her chair.

'Shit,' Pete said. 'We've got him with that. And these weren't on his machine.'

'No, they weren't,' Jane realised.

'So, did we miss something? Has he got another computer or a separate storage device? An external hard drive or something?'

She nodded. 'Could be. They've got a hell of a lot smaller, even in the last twelve months. You could easily hide one somewhere.'

'Then, I suggest we go and find it.' Pete stepped back from her chair. 'Jill, when DCI Silverstone gets in, get him to organise a warrant. Home and office. Jane, you found this stuff, so you're with me. Dave, while we're out, see what shows up on that CCTV footage, will you? The more we've got to throw at him, the better.'

'Right, boss.'

*

There were double yellow lines the full length of the road outside the offices of Molyneux and Richards, and the other side of the road was filled with cars, parked nose-to-tail.

'Damn. What's the time?' Pete asked.

Jane checked. '8.53 a.m.'

'He might not be in yet. We don't want to stand out, in case he sees us and does a runner.'

'Too late. There he is, look.'

Sanderson was walking down the far side of the street, about forty yards away. 'Got him. He doesn't know you, does he?'

'No.'

Pete checked the mirror and stopped the car. 'I'm dropping you off for work, then, OK? I'll drive up a bit further and come at him from behind.'

'Right.' Jane quickly unclipped her seat belt and stepped out of the car. 'Thanks, hun. See you later.' She tapped the roof before running across the road as Pete pulled away. She started up the hill towards Sanderson, head down as if in concentration, hands pushed deep into her coat pockets.

Glancing up, she saw the silver car pull over several yards beyond Sanderson. The hazard lights began to blink as Pete climbed out, checked the road and ran across, starting down towards her.

Sanderson was between them now, just five paces from her and completely oblivious.

She saw Pete stepping it out, closing the gap as swiftly as he could without drawing attention.

Six feet.

Pete was still too far away to intervene, but there was no more time. She stepped across into Sanderson's path. 'Sorry.'

He sidestepped and she went with him. Smiled an apology. He went the other way. 'You're Neil Sanderson, aren't you?' she said.

Pete was ten feet away.

'Yes. Sorry, do I know you?'

'No.' She pulled her hands out of her pockets, her badge in one of them. 'I'm DC Bennett and you're under arrest for the possession and distribution of indecent images of children.' She grabbed his wrist and twisted, turning him around to face Pete as she slapped the cuffs on.

*

'Duck now or forever be famous,' Pete said, as he neared the police station, the road outside it crowded with lorries, vans and cars.

'What?' Sanderson whined.

'Press conference,' Jane told him.

'Oh my God!' He fell sideways across the back seat, covering his head with his arms just as Pete swung the car into the station entrance and gunned the engine, shooting up the slope so that a couple of stragglers at the back of the crowd had to leap out of his way.

Pete heard several curses, but ignored them as he drove quickly up the side of the building and around the back. He swung the car into a space. 'Everybody out, quick as you like.' After stepping out, he opened Sanderson's door, took the man's arm and the three of them headed quickly towards the rear of the building, where he swiped them in and they headed for the custody suite.

'While you book him in, can I borrow the phone?' Pete asked.

'Sure.' The sergeant pushed it towards him.

Pete turned it around on the desk, picked up the receiver and dialled the squad room.

'DC Miles, CID.'

'Did Jill get that warrant before his lordship went for his media fix?'

'Yes. Where are you?'

'Downstairs, booking Sanderson in. I'll come up and fetch it.'

'Uh, there's a problem there, boss.'

Pete went very still as a sense of dread settled over him. 'What kind of problem?'

'Well, it looks like Sanderson's not our man. Not for Rosie Whitlock.'

'I'm coming up.' He slammed the phone down and turned to Jane. 'You can deal with this, can't you? I'll be upstairs.'

''Course. What's up?'

'Don't know yet.' Pete was already jabbing the release code into the door lock. He pushed through and ran up the stairs. At the first floor, he slammed into the now full squad room and marched towards Dave Miles' desk.

'What is it?'

Dave pointed at Jane's computer, on the desk next to his. 'The CCTV from the antique place.' He reached over and nudged the computer mouse to reawaken the screen. 'Sanderson was five miles away when Rosie was taken. It wasn't him.'

Pete sat down heavily in Jane's chair. A still image faced him on the screen.

'I took a screen-shot from the CCTV footage and reduced the windscreen glare in Photoshop. You can see it's him behind the wheel.'

Along with the registration plate on the front of the vehicle, Pete saw. 'Shit.'

He checked the date stamp in the bottom corner of the screen. 'You've confirmed that's right, I suppose?'

'It matches the timing on the Airparks camera and they have to keep theirs right because of meeting flights and so on.'

'Bugger it,' Pete said again. 'I liked him for this.'

'Me, too, boss. We've definitely got him on the child porn thing, though.'

'Yeah. What you got there?' Pete could see he had more CCTV footage up on his own computer.

'This is the stuff I was waiting for last night from the A38–A380 junction. I'm just about to run it. I've checked the stuff from outside the Fire Service training centre. There was a vehicle that might have been Albright's going past there at the time he claims he would have, but you can't see the registration plates. This looks like it might be more useful.'

The camera angle was high, the camera clearly set up on an overpass, but the vehicles were coming directly towards them as they watched. Zooming in should give them a number plate.

Dave pressed Play and the cars, vans and lorries began to stream past beneath their viewpoint. They watched for a few seconds until Dave said, 'There,' and reached for the keyboard.

'No, it's a Freelander.'

Dave relaxed and they watched some more.

'That's one.'

Dave hit Pause and zoomed in until they could make out the number plate. 'Not him.'

'Keep going.'

He pressed Play again. The dark Range Rover passed out of frame and was almost immediately replaced by another, travelling close behind a Toyota with a caravan in tow.

'Bugger, we're not going to . . .' Dave fell silent as the Range Rover pulled out to overtake. 'Yes, my beauty.' He waited until it reached the sweet spot in the frame and hit Pause again. Zoomed in. 'Gotcha.' He glanced up at Pete. 'That's him.'

Pete sighed heavily. 'And if we confirm that Enstone's out of the frame now as well, that leaves us right back at square bloody one.'

'Except with two paedophiles arrested and another one dead,' Dave reminded him.

'Yeah, but what good does that do for Rosie Whitlock?'

Chapter 27

'Check the bus cameras anyway, to make sure,' Pete said, picking up the red marker from underneath the whiteboard. He drew a heavy line through Damon Albright's name on the suspect list at the left side of the board, then another through Neil Sanderson's. 'And keep going through those pictures. They might throw up something,' he said, as he capped the pen and put it down. He looked around, spotted PC Clewes talking to Jill. 'Sophie, are you busy?'

'No, Sarge.'

'You're with me then. Come on.' He led the way back down to the custody desk.

It was deserted.

Looking through the long, narrow window in the door leading to the cells, he saw Sanderson stepping into a cell. He tapped on the wire-reinforced glass and Jane and the sergeant both looked up. They locked Sanderson in the cell, before coming back down the corridor.

Pete held up the piece of paper in his hand. 'Jane, you and Sophie go and search Sanderson's house. I'll serve this on him and see what he's got to say for himself.'

'OK.'

He turned to the custody officer. 'Brian, have you got an interview room free?'

'Of course. Number one OK?'

'Perfect.'

'Right, you go get ready in there. I'll bring him along.'

'Keys were in his possessions,' Jane said. 'Shall we use them?'

Pete nodded and headed for the interview room. Inside, he checked the recording equipment, lifted the warrant from his inside pocket and flattened it on the desk. Moments later, there was a knock, the door opened and Brian showed Neil Sanderson in.

'Take a seat, Mr Sanderson.' Pete indicated the chair on the far side of the table.

Sanderson sat down. 'What the devil am I here for?' he demanded. 'I've done nothing wrong.'

Pete started the recording equipment. 'Well, that's where we have a difference of opinion, Mr Sanderson. See, my colleagues and I were going through the computer files of the late Barry Enstone last night. Did you know him, by the way?'

'No. Who is he?' Sanderson maintained the belligerent tone.

'He was a convicted paedophile, on the sex offenders register. Died yesterday evening, unexpectedly. Evidently, he was not abiding by the conditions of his parole. He was finding and downloading images of child pornography from the Internet. And some of those images were of your daughter, Mr Sanderson. Images that we didn't see on your computer yesterday. Hence, the need for this.' He turned the paper towards Sanderson and pushed it forward.

'What's this?'

Sanderson glanced down and read the heading, his eyes widened and he looked up. 'You can't do that. There's no one there at the moment. My wife's at work.'

'There doesn't need to be anyone there, Mr Sanderson. If there was, we'd have them wait outside or in a specific room that we'd already searched.'

'I want my solicitor here, right now.'

'You're probably going to need him, but it makes no difference to this warrant.'

Sanderson fought to maintain his front of anger, but he was beaten and he knew it. 'Alright. My keys are in the bag with the rest of my possessions, out there.' He nodded towards the booking-in desk.

Pete placed his forearms on the table between them, concentrating on the man in front of him. 'You know what my colleagues are going to find in your house, don't you?'

He saw the flicker of truth in Sanderson's eyes. Of recognition and fear. 'I don't know what you're talking about.'

'I'm talking about a spare laptop, a remote hard drive, a collection of thumb drives or CDs. Wherever it is that you store all those pictures you don't want your wife to know about. What baffles me, is why you left some of that stuff on your computer, where it could easily be found.'

Sanderson said nothing.

Pete let the silence drag for a moment. He was just about to say something when there was a knock on the door. 'Come in,' he called.

Dave Miles opened the door, a laptop computer in his free hand. 'As requested, Sergeant,' he said formally.

'Thank you, DC Miles.'

Pete took the laptop from him and set it on the table. He opened it up and pressed the power button. The screen came up almost immediately.

'In the file, labelled "Supplementary folder",' Dave told him.

Pete clicked into the relevant folder. 'Thanks, Dave.'

Pete waited while Dave left the room. Heavy-handed was not the way to play someone like Sanderson. You needed to appeal to his mind, not his physical fear. 'When we're faced with a huge amount of data, and not all of it is relevant, we find it handy to pull out what we need into a supplementary folder,' he said. 'In this case, we've got these.' He turned the laptop around so they could both see it. 'That is Becky, isn't it?'

Sanderson stared fixedly at him.

'Look at the screen, Mr Sanderson. That is your daughter, isn't it? Is she really asleep there, or are these pictures posed?'

Sanderson held himself rigid in the chair. His eyes flicked across to the screen and back without reaction.

Pete pressed the right arrow key. 'And this one, Mr Sanderson, who's that in the bottom of the frame?'

A frown flashed briefly across Sanderson's features and he looked again. Pete saw his jaw tighten.

'You know, the veining in a person's skin is unique. Like a fingerprint or an iris scan.' He tapped the right arrow again. 'Also, I recognise that ring.'

Sanderson couldn't help himself. He looked again. And swallowed heavily.

'It's amongst your possessions out there, isn't it? Along with your keys. So, did Becky know about these pictures being taken?'

'No,' he said hoarsely. He cleared his throat. 'She was asleep.'

Pete leaned forward in his chair, leaving the screen as it was. 'And did you take similar ones of Rosie when she stayed over? We're still searching through Enstone's computer.'

'No.'

'Funny thing is, that computer's also given us a link back to your old stomping ground – Bath,' Pete told him. 'Do you know David Grover?'

Again, a frown flashed across Sanderson's face, leaving his expression very slightly altered.

'David Grover is another known paedophile,' Pete said, hammering the point home. 'Another man who exchanged images with Barry Enstone, like you did. Do you suppose, when my colleagues in Bath visit his home, they're going to find images of Becky there? And possibly of the girl who was killed a few years back, when you were living there? And when my officers find your storage device, as they certainly will, are there going to be links to him on there? Maybe even pictures of Alison Stretton?'

Sanderson stayed silent, but Pete could see the fear worming its way into his mind.

'I'm fully aware of the things that go on in some of these images and films. I don't have you pegged for that kind of thing, Neil, but there is a thing called guilt by association. And another called aiding and abetting after the fact. Which means, if you've got these pictures, if you've even seen them and not reported it, you're as guilty of what happened in them as the blokes who did it. Whether it's the girl in Bath or Rosie Whitlock, if you've got pictures of her, taken after her abduction, we can charge you as an accessory in that abduction and in whatever happens after it. You think about that, and think through what's on that storage device or spare computer back at home, Neil.' Pete sat back once more, arms folded. 'Then think about whether you want to talk to me and make some sort of deal, or whether you want to take the full brunt of the law.' He sat and waited for what he'd said to sink in and have its effect on Sanderson.

There was obviously a whole range of degrees of paedophilia, a whole range of men who indulged in it and of reactions they might have to a given situation. However, Pete knew the one thing could be relied on amongst almost all of them, and that was narcissism. The overriding need to look after themselves and their own interests. And everyone knew what happened to paedophiles in prison.

'What is it that you want to tell me, before I find it out for myself, Neil?'

Sanderson looked at him. 'I don't know anything about Rosie's abduction. I don't know who did it or why or where they took her. And nor do I know anything about what happened to Alison Stretton.'

'But?' Pete prompted.

Sanderson paused. Then he sighed. 'Alright. I can give you links to the picture sources. Some of them, at least.'

Pete inclined his head. 'Thank you.'

Chapter 28

Pete parked just short of the entrance to Risingbrook School and cut the engine. The houses across the road were detached 1920s mock-Tudor, behind low brick walls surmounted by high hedges. Their entrances were paired in the same way that semi-detached properties would be. The pair he approached had wooden field-type gates and a low brick wall between them. He checked the numbers. The one he wanted was on the right. He entered, closing the gate behind him and approached the small porch. After ringing the bell, he stood back to wait.

'Hello? Can I help?'

The voice came from his left. He looked across and saw a man in his fifties, dressed in a waxed jacket and flat cap, emerging from the garage next door.

'I'm DS Gayle, from Heavitree Road CID.' He showed the man his warrant card.

'You're looking for Ron? I'm afraid he's away at the moment.'

'Any idea when he's due back?'

The man shook his head. 'Sorry. He's always flitting off somewhere or other. Work stuff, you know?'

Pete nodded. 'I take it my colleagues have already spoken to you about what happened out here on Tuesday morning?'

'That girl? Yes. Awful business. I didn't see anything. I'm not usually here in the mornings.'

'Oh?'

'I generally go to my daughter's. Look after the dog, you know? She works mornings at the cathedral, so I'm away from here about half past seven as a rule, to miss the school run. Bloody chaos, that is. She's got a day off today. Her birthday. So I'll be going round later, for a change.'

'I see. Well, thanks for your help.'

'He's not often away over the weekend, Ron, so he might be back later today or in the morning.'

'Great. If you see him, can you get him to give me a call?'

'Yes, of course. DS Gayle, was it?'

'That's right. I'll put my card through his door, but if you could give him a nudge too, that would be great.'

'No problem.'

Pete took a card, wrote on the back of it: 'Please call me ASAP. Any time.' He pushed it through the letterbox then headed back to the car with a wave to the neighbour. 'Thanks again, Mr . . .?'

'Taylor. Bill Taylor.'

'Mr Taylor. Bye now.' Pete stepped out onto the pavement and closed the gate behind him.

Back in the car, he called the squad room and got Dave Miles. 'Dave. What's new?'

'Two new victims identified from Enstone's computer files. You remember the Harvey girls, about eighteen months ago?'

'From up north somewhere . . . Manchester, was it?'

'Oldham.'

'That's it. What – they're on there?'

'Yep. Both of them. And we've got more pictures of our man from Swindon. Plus, I've got the footage from the bus company. It clearly shows Barry getting on the bus when and where we were expecting.'

'Which corroborates his alibi.'

'Yep.'

'Well, keep looking, Dave. I'm going to the Sandersons', to help Jane and Sophie.'

'Right, boss.'

'You and Jane did the canvassing of the houses round Risingbrook School between you, right?'

'Yes.'

'Which of you spoke to Bill Taylor – lives opposite the entrance?'

'I did. Why?'

'Just wanted to confirm he's not in the frame, while I'm here.'

'No. He was . . .' Pete heard the rustling of paper over the line. 'At his daughter's. She confirmed his arrival there at ten to eight.'

'OK. I was just talking to him. Chasing up on his next-door neighbour who hasn't been spoken to yet.'

'There was nobody in when I was there.'

'He's away. Due back today or tomorrow. I left a card.'

Dave laughed. 'Yeah, me too.'

'We'll see if he calls either of us, then. See you later.' Pete ended the call and started the engine. As he passed the gate, he stared at the brick-red school across the wide expanse of mown grass. Three days, he thought. Three days and we've got exactly nowhere.

*

'How are you doing?'

'Nothing yet.' Jane stepped back to allow Pete to come into the Sanderson house. 'We're still looking, but I've got to be honest, boss, we're running out of places to look.'

Pete closed the door behind him. 'All right, let's apply a bit of logic. He's got these files that, presumably, he doesn't want the wife or the daughter to know about. He wants to keep them safe and hidden, but he wants access to them. So, if there's no extra computer or tablet in the house – and if there was, I'm guessing you'd have found it by now – they must be on a storage device of some kind in easy reach of the computers we know about, yes?'

'Yes. We've searched the office, the main bedroom, and we're in the spare room now.'

'And nothing.'

'That's right.'

Pete ran his bottom lip across his teeth, barely aware that he was doing it. 'OK, let's see.' He went into the family office and stood in the middle of the room, looking around. Shelves of books and files. Two desks and chairs. A filing cabinet. Framed pictures on the walls. 'You've checked in the box-files?'

'Yep.'

'And all the books are actually books?'

'Yep. We've had all of them down.'

'The filing cabinet. Hanging files?'

'Yes. We've checked in all of them too.'

'And under them? In the bottom of the drawers?'

'Yep.'

'What about *under* the bottoms of the drawers? And those in the desks? Anything stuck to the undersides?'

'Nothing. We thought of that too. And in the bedroom, in his bedside cabinet, the dresser and the chest of drawers. And, of course, we checked all the contents of the desk drawers and cupboards.'

Pete nodded, still looking around the room. Where else was there?

He sat at Sanderson's desk, ran his fingers along the back of the combined printer and scanner. Nothing. A CD stacker stood in the corner, full of what appeared to be computer program CDs. He pointed at it and sent an enquiring look Jane's way.

'Yes, we checked them all. They are what they look like.'

He tilted his head in a shrug and turned back to the desk. If it wasn't a separate computer, it had to be here. But where?

He sighed. Then, looking down, he noticed something. He

pulled the central drawer of the desk part-way out and reached in with both hands, ignoring the contents as he felt along the underside of the desktop. There was a space about a centimetre deep that had, necessarily, to be clear of any of the drawer contents. A bit of Blu-tack, Velcro or double-sided tape and you had a prime place to stick a thumb drive or a CD.

But his fingers reached the edges of the drawer without finding anything.

He looked up at Jane, who nodded slowly.

'Check the filing cabinet.'

As she moved to obey, he closed the drawer in front of him and opened the smaller one to the side of it. Reaching in, he felt across the underside of the desktop again.

'Here,' Jane said. 'Nice one, boss.'

She lifted out a small, flat object, not much larger than a business card case and turned it in her hand. 'Blimey. This little bugger holds a full terabyte.' She handed it to him. He saw a small, round hole for the power cable and a USB port. 'Where are the power adapters?'

'Second drawer.'

Pete opened it and was met with a tangle of adapters and cables, a card reader and various other bits and pieces. He checked the little drive for a manufacturer's name. Eventually, he found it in tiny print along the edge. Samsung. He began to search the drawer and found it almost at once. 'Here we go.'

He scooted across to the other desk, where Geraldine Sanderson's computer sat undisturbed. Powering it up, he plugged in the drive and connected it to the computer. The computer whirred for a moment, then the box came up in the centre of the screen: 'Removable drive E'.

He opened it up.

'Enter password'.

'Shit.'

Pete looked over his shoulder. 'Yeah. We'll have to take it back to the station, see if he'll give us the password or if we'll have to get the tech boys at Middlemoor on to it.'

'I wonder if it's the only one.'

'I should hope so, if it's a whole terabyte.'

*

A small stack of files waited on Pete's desk when he got back to the office. He dropped his coat over the back of his chair and sat down. Two beige ones from Forensics – damn, they had pulled out all the stops – and one blue one from the pathologist.

He flipped open the blue one.

He was greeted with a close-up photograph of a young girl's face, eyes closed, her skin pale and slightly greenish in death. He began to read: 'Autopsy of Caucasian female identified as Lauren Carter, age ten years and two months. Orphan. Last known residence, Sunnyside Children's Home, Barnstaple, Devon.'

Pete sighed. *The summary of a young life, wasted*, he thought and read on. There was no more preamble. The report plunged straight into the pathologist's findings. As they'd thought at the scene, she had been strangled then dumped in the water. She had been dehydrated before death and she had not eaten for at least two days, probably longer. There were marks on her wrists and ankles consistent with having been bound with a narrow, hard restraint of some kind – measurements were given – and further marks across her face that suggested she had been gagged, as well as the post-mortem abrasions probably caused by going over one or more of the weirs upstream from where she was found.

So, bound, gagged, raped and starved, Pete summed up in his mind. *Then killed and dumped like so much discarded rubbish.* Jesus, he wanted the bastard who had done this!

He closed the folder, put it aside and opened the first of the Forensics files. 'Forensic Examination of the home of Barry Enstone, esq., deceased.' The address was given underneath. Pete glanced up at the board and saw that someone had already crossed his name off the suspect list there. Which left it completely empty now. He sighed heavily.

The file confirmed that Enstone's girlfriend had stayed at his house on more than one occasion recently and that no one else had been in there, other than the police presence they already knew about. So Enstone was a looker, not a toucher, these days, as far as his paedophilic proclivities were concerned.

Pete opened the last file. The crime scene at the park where Lauren Carter had been found. He skimmed through it and read the summary at the end. Basically, nothing. Footprints, but they all appeared to be from the guy who had found her or the attending police and pathologist. No clothing or fibres. No cigarette butts. No damaged vegetation to indicate where she went into the water. She'd fetched up there after being dumped into the river somewhere else. And there was still nothing from the possible dump sites he had given them to check. A bigger job, of course, and one that they probably wanted to treat as a single job and produce a single report on, he guessed. Not that that helped him in the meantime.

He picked up the phone and dialled.

'G4S Forensics. How can I help?'

'This is DS Gayle, Exeter CID. Can I talk to the duty lab manager, please?'

'One moment. I'll put you through.'

There was a click, a couple of notes of music, then another ringing tone. 'Forensics. How can I help?'

'Is that the duty lab manager?'

'Colin Mason, yes.'

'DS Gayle, Heavitree Road CID. I wanted to thank you for getting these reports over to me so quickly – Barry Enstone and the Lauren Carter case. And I was wondering if you could give me any idea on the progress of the other job I gave you. The possible body-dump sites, north of the city.'

'Ah, DS Gayle. Yes, you've certainly been keeping us busy the last few days. The sites you're talking about . . . I think we've almost finished processing everything from them. Just a couple of bits left to finish off, so . . . later today sometime, I'd imagine. I can't promise, of course.'

'No, of course. But anything you can give me would help.'

'All right. Hold on, I'll check.'

The phone clunked onto a desk and Pete heard footsteps. After a pause, they returned; there was the scrape of the handset being picked up. 'DS Gayle?'

'I'm here.'

'As I thought, we've got a few bits and pieces to finish off. Tyre treads to identify from one site, a few odds and sods from the other. Shouldn't take too long.'

'Tyre treads, you say? What kind of tyre treads?'

'Something large enough to fit a panel van, but we've yet to determine make and model.'

'Excellent. Which site was this?'

'Uh . . . I'm not familiar with the area, but it's listed as "Bridge, Upton Pyne Hill off A377, Devon".'

'Perfect. Thanks for that.' Pete ended the call and put down the phone.

'Crediton Road,' he announced to no one in particular.

'What about it?' asked Jane.

'Forensics aren't quite finished yet, but it looks like that's where Lauren Carter went in the river.'

'So, he's holding them somewhere in that direction. We hope.'

'Or, if not, he knows the area round Newton St Cyres.' He stood up. 'Right, I'll go down and have a word with Sanderson.'

Downstairs, at the custody desk, he leaned on the high counter and asked, 'Have you got an interview room free for me, Brian?'

The custody sergeant nodded. 'Interview One again?'

'Suits me. Can I have Neil Sanderson in there?'

'OK.' Brian grabbed a set of keys and came out from behind the counter.

Pete settled himself in the interview room, relaxing back in the chair. He didn't move when the door opened to admit Sanderson.

'Neil. Take a seat.' He waved at the chair on the other side of the table. 'We'll continue from where we left off, so you're still under caution, OK?'

'Should I have my lawyer here?'

Pete shrugged. 'You tell me. It's your decision. While you make it though . . .' He took his hand from his pocket and put Sanderson's hard drive on the table between them, lifting his hand away to reveal what it was. 'Maybe you'd like to tell me the password for this. In the spirit of co-operation.'

Sanderson's eyes widened in a mixture of shock and fear as he stared at the little black casing. He looked up at Pete.

'You can tell us or the tech guys at HQ can work on it for a couple of hours. Up to you. But if they have to crack it, then you get no brownie points when the time comes.' Pete grimaced. 'Excuse the pun.'

Sanderson stayed silent, looking at him for several long seconds. Finally, he seemed to slump in his chair. 'All right. It's rebeccaJane, all one word, lower case except for the J.'

'Thank you.' Pete drew the little hard drive towards him. 'And you're sure we're not going to find anything on there that links to any of these missing girls that we're looking into?'

'Any of? I thought there was just Rosie?'

Pete shook his head. 'We've got two bodies that we've pulled out of the Exe in the past few weeks – one of them only about thirty-six hours ago. After Rosie was taken.'

Sanderson paled. 'I don't know anything about that. I swear.'

'So, neither of them are going to feature on this hard drive then?' He nodded at the little drive on the desk in front of him.

'No. No way.'

'Or the girl from Bath. Alison Stretton.'

Sanderson eyes closed for a moment. He swallowed. 'Look, I had nothing to do with her disappearance, all right? Or her death. I've got an alibi.' He looked up from the desktop. 'You've checked it.'

'We have.'

'So, you know I'm not guilty of anything there.'

Pete smiled briefly. 'I wouldn't go that far.'

'You know what I mean.'

Pete shrugged. 'OK. But you may be aware of someone else who was taking an interest in her.'

Fear showed in Sanderson's eyes again. 'I can't . . . I don't know anything.'

'But you suspect, don't you?' Pete leaned forward, covering the hard drive with his arms. 'You can give us a name, someone who might be worth looking at for it.'

'If I do, he'll know it came from me. And he's an evil bastard. Even if you lock him up, he'll send his friends after me. I can't risk people like that coming around my wife, my daughter.'

Pete held his gaze, forcing himself not to shake his head in disbelief. 'They won't,' he said. 'We can make sure of that.'

'How?' Sanderson sat back in his chair. 'Witness protection? This isn't America. And anyway, what about all of Becky's friends? At her age, she won't be able to start afresh like that.'

'She's going to have to, Neil. After this, she won't be able to stay where she is. And as for your wife – she can pick up anywhere with a job like hers.'

Sanderson seemed to crumple in on himself. He dropped his head into his hands and his shoulders slumped. 'Oh, God. What have I done? What have I done?'

Pete waited as the enormity of the situation sank into Sanderson's mind. He sobbed once, then coughed, took a deep breath and lifted his head. 'I believe you're looking for a guy called Steve Southam. He's a black belt in judo, on the competition circuit. Big, broad, hulk of a bloke, a bully and a braggart, with friends in all sorts of unsavoury places. Criminal types.'

Pete smiled. 'Steven Southam is already in prison, Neil. Up in Northumberland. But what makes you think he's involved in Alison Stretton's murder?'

'He was there, in Bath, at the time. He'd been into the club that night, while she was there. I saw him looking at her. And I knew his tastes . . . He left a little while before she did, but he knew when she'd be leaving and that she'd be walking home.'

'But you never said any of this to the police at the time?'

'How could I? He always said that anyone who crossed him would be paying for it for the rest of their lives, and so would their family.'

'Nice bloke, then. We will be following up on this; you know that, don't you? But we'll do everything we can to keep your wife and daughter safe. And you, if needs be. Now, are you certain you can't tell me anything useful about Rosie Whitlock? Who she might have been in contact with? Who might have seen her? Talked to her? Exchanged messages with her? Anything like that?'

Sanderson shook his head. 'There's no one I know of that you don't already. Boys at school or through her swimming and tennis. Teachers. Family friends. I don't know. I don't know anyone, other than Southam, who's into . . . girls of that age. And I only met him through judo.'

Pete pressed his lips together as he studied the man before him. Every indication seemed to suggest he was telling the truth. 'Alright.'

Boys at school or through her swimming or tennis. Pete couldn't help but think of Tommy. He imagined them together, talking and laughing. Smoking. Hell, he may even have seen Rosie himself when he went to pick Tommy up from the pool.

He switched off the recording equipment, picked up the hard drive and stuck his head out of the door. 'Brian. We're done in here, thanks.'

Chapter 29

'Any good, boss?' Jane asked as Pete got back to his desk.

'He gave me the password for that little hard drive you found in his study – rebeccaJane with a small r and a capital J. And he reckons Southam might have killed the girl in Bath, though he's got no proof. But, as far as Rosie Whitlock . . . Did we look at any swimming or tennis coaches she might have had dealings with? Or anyone else at those venues?'

'No, we've been concentrating on family links and her school.' She pushed aside some papers on her desk. 'I'll get on to it.'

'It's all right, I'll do it. You carry on with what you're doing.'

'OK.'

'I'll start with the mother. See if she can give me any names. But first . . .' He picked up the phone and dialled zero.

It was picked up on the second ring. 'Front desk.'

'Hello. Can you put me through to the main station in Bath?'

'Hold on.'

There was a brief pause, then a ringing tone.

'Avon and Somerset police. How can I help?'

'Hello. This is DS Gayle from Devon and Cornwall, Exeter. Can you put me through to your major crimes office?'

Another pause.

'DI Truman, CID.'

'Hello. DS Gayle, Exeter CID. I need to speak to someone regarding a case of yours from 2011. Young girl that went missing. Alison Stretton.'

'That'd be me, DS Gayle. What can I do for you?'

'It's more what I can do for you, sir. I've just had a tip on who was responsible. From her judo teacher, Neil Sanderson. He puts a Steven Arnold Southam of Swindon, currently residing in Morpeth prison, firmly in the frame. Apparently, Southam saw her that evening at the club and preceded her out, knowing that she'd be walking home.'

'Does your man have any evidence against this Southam?'

'Nothing substantive. Just knowledge of his sexual proclivities. But it's a lead you didn't have before. It could take you somewhere, if you can follow it up.'

The man in Bath grunted. 'What are the circumstances with your man down there?'

'We've got him in custody on unrelated child sex charges.'

'Uh-huh. All right if I come down and have a word with him, then?'

'Be my guest. But, we've only got him for another twenty hours.'

'Right. I'll see you soon then.'

'Bye.' Pete ended the call and stood up, hooked his jacket off the back of his chair and headed out, pausing at the custody desk to let Brian know that DI Truman was on his way from Bath.

The traffic was light at this time of day, the press long gone from the front of the station and it took him just minutes to drive to the Whitlocks' home. A small group of reporters stood outside. They surged forward as he got out of the car to open the gates.

'Sergeant Gayle, Sergeant Gayle. Any news? What can you tell us of the latest developments in the case? Have you got any new suspects? What have you come here for today, Sergeant?' He ignored them, opened the gates and drove in. Parking in front of the garage, he rang the bell.

Jessica looked confused when she opened the door and peered around it. Unsure. 'Sergeant.'

'Mrs Whitlock. I've got a few questions, if that's all right.'

She looked past him, saw the reporters clustered by the gates and gulped. Stepping back, she opened the door wider. 'Of course. Come in. Please.'

She headed for the sitting room. She was dressed in a dark red satin gown over what looked like a cream silk nightie. Her hair was dishevelled from the pillow. Pete glanced at his watch as he pushed the door closed. It was almost eleven. Surely, she hadn't just got up?

She went into the lounge, sat down and waved him to the sofa opposite. With her large eyes wide and vulnerable, she looked almost childlike. 'I'm sorry. I'm afraid I couldn't face work this morning, even without the press out there.'

Pete nodded, unfastened his coat and sat forward on the sofa. 'First, I have to tell you that we've arrested Neil Sanderson this morning.'

'Yes, Claire rang. The family liaison. But surely he didn't have anything to do with this?'

'No. That was a different matter. I just thought you should know, that's all. Now, I need to ask you about Rosie's life outside school and your friends. Her tennis. Her swimming. Anything else she might get up to. I need to know about any boys or men she may have had dealings with: coaches, friends, people she commented on, or who you noticed when you dropped her off or picked her up. Anyone who stood out for any reason, positive or negative.'

'I don't . . .' She shook her head. 'There are her coaches, of course. For tennis, she has Derek Tomlinson and for swimming, Mr Dalziel, from the school. There was a boy she talked to after swimming sometimes, but I don't know his name. I just saw her with him a few times.'

'What did he look like?'

'Small. Shorter than Rosie by three or four inches. Slim, with brown hair. I don't know any more than that about him.'

Her description could have been of Tommy, but it could equally have been any of hundreds of boys. 'Anyone else? Anyone you saw hanging around? Or that Rosie did?'

She shook her head slowly. 'No. I'm sorry, there's no one, Sergeant.'

'That's OK, Mrs Whitlock. It's just something we have to check.'

'So . . .' She paused, looking down at her hands then returned her gaze to his. 'Are you any closer to finding Rosie?'

'We're pursuing a number of lines of inquiry. But, we have to leave no stone unturned in cases like this.'

'Which is another way of saying you have no idea who took her. Isn't it?' Her eyes were focused now, almost fierce, with a strange light in them as she stared at him.

Pete tucked his notebook away. 'Mrs Whitlock, the reason I've come here this morning is because a random abduction is very, very unusual. In almost all of these cases, the victim is known to the perpetrator in some way. A relation, a student, someone they see regularly at work or in the street. There's nearly always some kind of link. It's just a question of finding it. Which is why we had to start by investigating your husband, your friends and family. We've also been to Risingbrook School, checked out the teachers and Rosie's school mates. We have made some significant discoveries, but we don't have the full picture yet, and part of that might come from one of the men you've told me about this morning.'

She frowned. 'How? They'd have been checked out thoroughly before they were allowed to work in places like that, surely?'

'Of course. But they may have seen something that you didn't. Or Rosie may have said something to them that she didn't to you.'

She suddenly moved to the edge of the sofa and reached across the coffee table to clasp his hands in hers. 'You will find her, won't you, Sergeant? You must find her. Please. You have to.'

Pete held her desperate gaze. 'I'll do everything I possibly can to find Rosie and bring her back to you, Mrs Whitlock. That's a promise.'

She sighed. 'Thank you, Sergeant.' She held on to his hands for a moment longer, then sat back.

'I'd better get moving.' Pete stood up 'We'll keep you informed, of course.' He wanted to say more, but it would have been platitudes and she was too brittle for those right now. She sat still and watched him leave.

*

King's Tennis Club was a small, exclusive club on the north side of the city. Pete had heard of it, but never been there before. The narrow drive went up the side of the courts, between them and a nursing home. As he drove in, he saw that all but one were occupied, despite it being late morning on a weekday.

The car park told him why. Range Rovers jostled with Jaguars and expensive sports cars. The nearest to a normal person's car, he thought, was the bright red Golf GTI parked two spaces away from the solidly built wooden clubhouse with its tinted windows and wooden planters, bright with flowers despite the season. He found a parking space and went in.

Inside, the place was all expensive, modern wood and glass with big sliding doors looking over a wide balcony to the tennis courts beyond.

The receptionist looked up at the sound of the door and closed the ledger in front of her. Her smooth dark hair was pulled back in a ponytail, her make-up immaculate.

'Can I help you?'

'I hope so.' Pete showed her his warrant card. 'I'm hoping to speak to a Derek Tomlinson.'

'He's with a client at the moment. Court two.' She raised a hand towards the patio doors. 'He won't be long, if you'd like to wait?'

'How long?'

'Just a few minutes.'

'OK. Meantime, perhaps you can tell me if you know this girl?' He brought out the picture of Rosie and put it on the counter in front of her.

She studied it, then met his gaze. 'She's a member, isn't she? Father's a lawyer, mother's a teacher or something?'

Pete nodded.

'Rosie,' she recalled. Then her eyes narrowed. 'Is she the girl that's missing, that's been on the news?'

'That's right.'

She shook her head. 'Awful.'

'You don't recall seeing her with anyone in particular, other than her parents and her coach?'

'No. I, uh . . . try not to take too much notice of what the members do, as long as they don't cause any trouble or embarrassment. And she's never done that. She's too young, and yet too old to run around yelling like a brat.' She gave a small smile. 'The perfect client, from my point of view, I suppose.'

'Do you get much trouble and embarrassment here?' Pete asked.

'Not so much trouble. Occasionally some embarrassment when a member gets a little too involved in the training process.'

Or the trainer, Pete thought. 'And what can you tell me about Mr Tomlinson? Has he ever been the cause of any embarrassment?'

'Derek? No. Most of his clients are either young, like Rosie, or older ladies trying to stay fit.'

'I see. Alright, thanks for your time.' Pete picked up Rosie's picture and headed for the deserted bar area. A man in a white shirt and black trousers was wiping his hands on a tea towel behind the bar. 'What can I get you?'

'A coffee would do nicely, thanks.'

'How do you like it?'

Pete looked at the complicated-looking chromed apparatus on

the back bar and shuddered inwardly. 'Nothing fancy. Just black with a couple of sugars.'

'Coming up.'

The man reached for a cup and saucer from the shelf above the coffee maker. Moments later, there was an explosive, roaring hiss. He spooned two portions of brown sugar into the cup, placed a clean spoon in the saucer and turned back to Pete. 'There you are, sir.'

'Thanks.' Pete showed him his warrant card and the photo of Rosie. 'Do you recognise this girl?' He picked up the spoon and stirred slowly.

The man nodded. 'Tuesday evenings. Usually has a Coke. Why?'

'Have you ever seen her with anyone other than her parents and her coach?' He took a sip of coffee, keeping his eyes on the man in front of him.

He thought for a moment. 'She sometimes has a friend with her. Brown-haired girl, about the same age but smaller. Other than that, she normally sits on her own, over by the window, until her mum or dad turns up for her.'

'OK. Thanks.' Pete took another sip. The coffee was strong and tasty. A completely different animal to what he normally survived on at the station. 'I dare say you overhear quite a bit of chatter in here, eh?'

'Some.'

'Have you ever heard anything about Derek Tomlinson?'

The man's expression shifted. Neutrality gave way to disapproval. 'Something like that would be bad for the club, Detective.'

'Like what?'

'Telling tales on the staff. Not that there's anything to tell in Derek's case.'

'Sure?'

'Positive. Anyway, he doesn't spend that much time here. About a third of the week, probably.'

'Oh? Where else does he work, then?'

'The country club on Topsham Road.'

'Ah.' The country club included a golf course and tennis club, he knew, with some top local coaches. And Pete knew that Tony Chambers was a member there. He made a mental note to have a word.

Footsteps sounded from reception. He heard the receptionist speaking quietly as he took another sip of his coffee. 'Thanks for that, Mr . . .?'

'Paul Fellows.'

Pete nodded and set the coffee cup on the bar as a lean, clean-cut man in his mid-twenties with thick, sandy hair came around the corner from the reception desk.

'DS Gayle?'

'That's me.'

'I understand you're looking for me?'

'Derek Tomlinson, is it?'

'That's right.' He extended a large hand. His grip was powerful but not oppressive.

'Shall we sit?' Pete picked up his coffee and headed for a table towards the windows. 'It won't take long.'

Tomlinson eased back in his chair. 'What do you need to know?'

Pete finished his coffee, using the pause to study his man. The relaxed attitude could be a front but, if so, he was a good actor. He set the cup down. 'Rosie Whitlock,' he said bluntly. 'She's missing. I'm investigating.'

'Yes, I've heard about it on the news. Terrible. What can I do to help?'

'I need to know about anyone she's been seen with, anyone she's spent time with other than her parents.'

'Including me.'

Pete inclined his head. 'Naturally. But, for now, I'm seeing you as a potential witness rather than a suspect.'

'That's good of you, Detective.'

Pete returned his smile. 'So, have you seen anyone talking to her? Anyone watching her?'

'That's creepy.'

Pete shrugged and Tomlinson dropped his gaze in thought. Then he shook his head. 'No one I can think of. She comes here with a girlfriend sometimes, but that's it, I think. That and her parents, of course.'

'And you've never noticed anyone hanging around here, maybe a member doing more watching than playing?'

Tomlinson grinned. 'All these short skirts, you mean?' He shook his head. 'No, I don't recall anyone like that.'

'OK. Thank you.' Pete stood up.

'I hope you find her, Detective. She's a nice kid.' Tomlinson stood and they shook hands again.

Pete followed him out. He would run a check on the coach, of course, but he doubted it would throw up anything. Which left the pool. *Pools*, he corrected himself. Unlike Tommy, Rosie had used both Exeter indoor pool and the outdoor one in Topsham.

He was walking back towards his car when his phone rang. He took it out and saw the number was withheld. 'Hello?'

'Boss? It's Jane. I've just had a call from a Ronald Greenway. Apparently, you left a card in his letterbox?'

'Ah. Yes. Hang on.' He fished out his notebook and pen. 'What's his number?'

Resting the notebook on the bonnet of a black Range Rover, Pete wrote it down as she read it out. 'OK. I'll go and see him next.'

'You getting anywhere, boss?'

'Not yet. You could do a check for me on a Derek Tomlinson. Tennis coach at both King's and the country club. I don't think it'll come to anything, but you never know.'

*

'Ronald Greenway?' Pete asked when the man opened the front door.

'Yes?' He was in his late forties, Pete guessed. Brown hair, neatly cut. Dressed in chinos and an Oxford shirt with expensive-looking brogues.

Pete showed his badge. 'DS Gayle. You called the station a little while ago. I was out, but they contacted me so I thought I'd pop round. Not a problem if it's not convenient. I can come back later or you can come to the station.'

'No, it's fine. What's this about?'

'I gather you went out of the country on Tuesday?'

'That's right. Stockholm on business. Why?'

'What time did you leave here?'

'Nine-fifteen. I caught the train up to London, tube to Heathrow.'

'Before you left, did you happen to notice anything unusual or out of place on the street? A vehicle that struck you as odd maybe? Or a person hanging around that you hadn't seen before?'

Greenway frowned, thinking. Then he blinked. 'Yes. An hour or so before I left there was a white van out there. Transit-type. I'm not sure of the make. I remember thinking I hadn't seen it before, but maybe it was someone working at one of the neighbours' or a father bringing a kid to school when the mother usually does it, perhaps running late for work or something. I noticed it when I went to open the gate. It saves having some fool park across the front of it, thinking a few minutes won't hurt. You'd be surprised how often that happens along here. And the abuse you get, if you tell them to move! Anyway, I don't suppose I'd have taken any notice of it, except I noticed the number plate. It ended in WAJ – the initials of a favourite singer of mine.' He shrugged.

'Oh, yes?' Pete felt a spark of excitement but he wanted to keep the conversation flowing.

'Waylon Jennings. American country star.'

'I've heard of him. Did *The Dukes of Hazard*, didn't he?'

'That's right.' Greenway smiled.

'Yeah, he's quite good. So, this van – was there anything else about it that you noticed? The numbers on the plate? Or the driver, maybe?'

Greenway shook his head. 'I couldn't see if anyone was in it. It was facing away from me. But the number had a seven in it, I think at the end.'

Pete nodded. 'And you didn't see anything else that stuck in your mind that morning?'

'No.'

'OK. Well, thank you. You've been very helpful.' Pete shook the man's hand and walked back to his car. Sitting inside, he drew a deep, calming breath.

This had to be something important. It was the first solid lead they'd got on the van they knew was at the scene when Rosie was taken. He took out his smartphone and brought up the DVLA search site. He tapped in what he had of the registration, narrowed the search criteria by colour and location and hit Search.

The system in Swansea churned away for what seemed like ages until, finally, the little screen changed. Two white vans with a seven and WAJ in the plates came up in the area. One of which had been stolen two weeks before.

Pete felt a grin spreading across his face as he put the phone away and started the engine. The swimming pools could wait. He was going back to the station to follow this up.

Chapter 30

Pete dropped his coat over the back of his chair, put his phone beside his keyboard and sat down, reaching for the power button on his computer.

'Got anything, boss?' Jane asked, looking over the top of her screen.

'Maybe.' He logged on and brought up the NCD search screen. Glancing across at his phone, he typed in the full registration of the stolen van and hit Return.

'Care to share?' Jane asked, still looking at him.

Pete concentrated on the screen in front of him. 'Give me a second and we'll see if there's anything to share.'

The data came up. The stolen van was a Toyota HiAce belonging to a carpenter and joiner from the south side of the city. It had been stolen from outside a job site in broad daylight, eight days ago. There had been no witnesses, according to the report, and the man himself had heard nothing as he had been at the back of the property, using an electric plane.

Pete scrolled down.

There was a new entry, made this morning. The van had been found yesterday afternoon in Plymouth, minus an estimated £2000 worth of tools and sundries.

'Bugger.'

He looked up at Jane, but she had dropped her gaze to her own screen and was concentrating on whatever was there.

'I got a partial plate from Ron Greenway,' he said. 'The bloke you and Dave couldn't get hold of, across the road from the school. There are two local matches of the right colour, one of which was nicked a couple of weeks ago. It was found yesterday in Plymouth, minus a load of tools and stuff.'

'Ah. Still, if they were going to use it to transport a person in, they'd have to make room, wouldn't they? Has there been any sign of the tools turning up?'

'Early days yet, but I doubt there will be. They'll be spread about all over the place – eBay, cash-converters, junk shops, car boots.'

'*If* they were the point of the exercise. If not, they'll have been dumped somewhere. And the van might have been left in Plymouth to throw us off.'

'Maybe.'

Picking up the landline, he tapped in a number.

'Police. How can I help?'

'This is Exeter CID. DS Gayle. I'm looking for information on a stolen van that turned up yesterday on your patch. Toyota HiAce.' He read out the registration.

'Hold on, Sergeant, I'll see what I can find for you.'

There was a click followed by the standard music as he was put on hold. He waited. And waited. Then: 'Hello?'

'Yes.'

'Sorry to keep you. Yes, the van's in the compound here. What do you need to know?'

Pete winced. 'Driven or towed in?'

'Towed.'

'Ah. That's something, at least. I need it checked for fingerprints and forensics. It may have been used in a child abduction here, three days ago.'

There was a hiss on the line. 'Afraid you're out of luck, mate.

The bloke who reported it said it had been there for three days as of yesterday.'

'Damn.'

*

Pete was too impatient to bother with lunch. Jane brought him a sandwich and a Mars bar, but by the time the results of his search came back on the other white van that matched his criteria, he had eaten only half of one of the sandwiches.

The van in question was another Toyota, a ProAce, registered to an Edward Burton, aged eighty-three, of High Acres Farm, Holcomb Burnell. Pete looked up the address on Google maps. It was five or six miles out to the west of the city, in an area dotted with isolated farms and little else except woods and fields. He wondered what Mr Burton would have to say about his van coming up in an abduction inquiry. He finished his first half-sandwich in two bites. He would pay him a visit and find out. Always best to talk to someone face to face, he thought. And if they had no warning, then they had no preparation time.

He grabbed the second half of his sandwich in its triangular plastic packet, shoved the Mars bar in with it and stood up.

'Off out again, boss?' Jane asked.

'Got to see a man about a van. At eighty-three, I don't suppose he's our man, but he hasn't reported it stolen, so he should be able to tell us who would have been driving it at the time.'

'Hope it goes better than the other one.'

Pete grimaced. 'Don't rub it in.'

Her eyes widened innocently. 'I was just saying.'

'Less chatter and more work, DC Bennett.'

'Yes, sir, boss.' She saluted smartly.

Pete suppressed a grin. 'And just you remember it,' he said, heading for the door.

*

Pete turned left at the bottom of Heavitree Road and drove down towards the river. He crossed the bridge and headed out through the western fringes of the city, up the steep, wooded hill to the junction at the top, where he turned onto the Dunsford Road.

The day was bright and crisp, the bare outlines of the trees stark like black filigree overhead. From the edge of the city, the map function on his phone took him along five or six miles of tiny lanes, some with streams running alongside, past dark, oppressive woods and tiny, valley-slope fields.

High Acres Farm was a large, stone-built Georgian farmhouse with a square, formal lawn in front and farm buildings to one side, behind a high stone wall. Pete parked in front of the house and went through the iron gate. There was a bell push on the door frame as well as the heavy knocker in the middle. He pressed the bell. The chime came faintly back to him. Moments later, the lock was turned and the door opened.

A woman in her forties stood before him. Tall, almost rangy, she had dark hair that was pulled up behind her head and dark eyes. Her face was long, with a strong jaw and a mouth that was slightly too big.

'Yes?' she said, wiping her hands on the front of her jeans.

Pete raised his warrant card. 'I'm DS Gayle, Exeter CID. I'm looking for Edward Burton.'

'Ah. Then, you've had a wasted journey, I'm afraid. He's been dead nearly a year. What's it about?'

Pete's eyebrows rose. This was a morning for surprises. 'Dead? Then can I ask who you are?'

'Sarah Knox. My husband and I moved here a couple of months ago.'

'I see. So, can you tell me who the agent was that you bought the place through?'

'Oh, we didn't buy it. We're renting. The agent is Berry's in Exeter.'

'OK. Thanks for that. I'll check with them. What I was actually here about, though, was Mr Burton's van. A Toyota ProAce.'

She was shaking her head again. 'I don't know anything about that. Sorry.'

'Would I be able to speak to your husband?'

'Be my guest. He'll be in the yard, I expect. He's cleaning the sheds out this morning, ready to bring the cattle in.'

As if on cue, the sound of a tractor came from beyond the high wall to Pete's right. He had noticed a door where the wall turned along the road-front. 'Well, thanks for your help, Mrs Knox.'

He went back down the path and along to the wooden door in the wall. Barns and sheds surrounded the yard, with a couple of old-fashioned pigsties in the corner. He could see a tractor just disappearing into one of the sheds at the far side, across a wide expanse of concrete strewn here and there with straw and strands of silage.

When he got closer, he saw that the tractor had a wide bucket on the front, which the driver was using to scrape up a thick layer of old muck and straw. He stood and waited beside the doorway until the man reversed out.

When he saw Pete standing there, he stopped the tractor and shut the engine down to a throaty idle. Pete stepped forward, raising his warrant card, and the man pushed the cab door open and climbed down.

Probably in his fifties, he was greying at the temples under a flat cap, which he wore with green overalls and wellington boots. He was a couple of inches taller than Pete, with hands that swallowed Pete's whole when they shook.

'DS Gayle, Exeter CID,' Pete told him.

'Bill Knox. What can I do for you?'

'What kind of vehicle do you drive, Mr Knox?'

'A Mitsubishi pickup. Why?'

'Have you seen a white Toyota panel van around here? Belonged to the previous owner of this place, I understand.'

Knox shook his head. 'Don't know about that. Never met the old boy. He died, end of last year. That's why we've got the place.'

'And you don't know who owns it now?'

'We just deal with the agents, over in Exeter. Berry's, on Fore Street.'

'I know them.' Pete nodded. 'OK. Well, I'll let you get on, then. Thanks for your help.'

'No trouble.'

Pete walked back across the yard, disappointment flooding his mind. Another dead end. The place had been done up and rented out, so the contents had probably been sold off, including the Toyota van. Why it hadn't been re-registered, he couldn't imagine. Maybe it had gone to a dealer. He would have to track down Edward Burton's beneficiaries and check. He climbed into his car and stared at the sandwich on the passenger seat.

With a shrug, he picked it up, took a large bite and began to chew.

*

'Berry and Co., Danielle speaking. How can I help?'

Pete sat forward in his chair, one elbow resting on his desk. 'My name's Detective Sergeant Gayle, Heavitree Road CID. I'm looking for some information on one of the properties you rent out. High Acres Farm, out near Dunsford. I gather the previous owner died about a year ago, so I'm wondering who owns it now.'

'High Acres Farm? It's not one I'm familiar with. Hold on a sec.' Pete heard her talking to someone in the background, but couldn't hear what was said over Dick Feeney's voice at his side, also on the phone. There was a pause, then she was back. 'Hello? High Acres Farm, Holcomb Burnell?'

'That's the one. You're renting it to the Knoxes.'

'Yes, I've got the file here. The owner is . . . a Mr Burton.'

Pete felt the slump of disappointment.

'Malcolm Burton.'

'Ah.' He smiled, relieved. 'Have you got his address there and maybe a daytime phone number?'

'One second. Here it is. Address is 49 Lathbury Road, Exeter. And the phone number...' She paused a moment then read it out.

'Thank you.' Pete's mind was churning as he ended the call. He recognised that number, but where from? Where the hell had he seen it before? He looked over his computer screen. 'Jane. Telephone number 270789. Where do I know it from?'

'It's the school. The one where Jessica Whitlock works.'

A wave of cold swept through Pete's whole body as he nodded slowly. 'I think we might have something.'

Chapter 31

'What?' Jane demanded.

'The second of those two possible vans. It was registered to an Edward Burton, aged eighty-three, of High Acres Farm, Holcomb Burnell. But Mr Burton died last year. The farm is now owned by a Malcolm Burton, who gives his daytime phone number as that of St Margaret's Primary School.'

'Yes.' She punched the air. 'The force is with you again, boss.'

'Let's not jump the gun. It could be a coincidence.'

'And I could have a dick that I haven't told anyone about,' she said sarcastically. 'You don't believe that any more than I do.'

'But it's possible,' Dave argued from beside her. 'I think we need proof.'

'In your dreams, matey. You going to go see him, boss?'

'First, I'll make sure he's there.' He picked the phone up and dialled.

'St Margaret's Primary. Can I help?'

'Hello, yes. This is DS Gayle, Exeter CID. I'm trying to trace a Malcolm Burton. Is he in today?'

'Mr Burton? Yes. He's in class at the moment though.'

'That's OK. Thanks for your help.'

He put the phone down and grinned. 'He's in.' *Malcolm*. He

recalled the obnoxious man in the staffroom when he'd gone to see Jessica. Was it the same man?

He hoped so.

'You want a hand?' Jane asked. 'I could do with a break from this screen.'

'Come on then.' He stood up and grabbed his jacket.

*

The corridors echoed hollowly as the school secretary led Pete and Jane towards the staffroom, their shoes clacking steadily on the lino floor. The walls were lined with posters, kids' pictures and wooden lockers. They had arrived at break-time, the school playground a noisy mass of running, laughing and shouting kids.

The secretary led them in and indicated a group of teachers near the sink in the left corner.

'Mr Burton.'

Pete recognised the man instantly. Small and slim, he had centrally parted blond hair and a receding chin with a narrow-lipped overbite.

'Zoe?'

'These are detectives Gayle and Bennett. They'd like a word with you before you go back to class.'

'Yes, I remember DS Gayle.' He stepped forward, his head dipping slightly. He was about the same height and weight as Jane, Pete guessed. 'What can I help you with? Shall we sit? I haven't got long.' He raised a hand towards the far side of the room where a square of blue chairs sat unoccupied around a battered-looking coffee table. They headed over and sat down.

Ease in gently, Pete thought. 'I gather your father died last year, Mr Burton. I'm sorry for your loss.'

'Thank you.' He nodded, his blue-grey eyes meeting Pete's.

'I understand he had a Toyota van. A white ProAce. Can you tell me what happened to it? It hasn't been re-registered.'

Burton's eyes widened. 'It hasn't . . . Oh God. I must have forgotten, with everything else to sort out. I'm so sorry. But, really—' he smiled '—is that all this is about? Two detectives need to come out and question me about a missing van? It's OK, I've got it. Not that I use it much. Hardly at all, in fact. It's stuck away in my garage at home. I haven't got round to selling it yet, that's all.'

'I see.' Pete was nodding sagely. He took out his phone and started the audio recording function, just in case Burton said something he wanted to remember word for word. 'That's all right then. Only, we have a possible sighting of it on Tuesday morning, just before eight thirty. You wouldn't have been driving it then?'

Burton swallowed then shook his head. 'No. I'd have been . . . Tuesday? I was going to say, on my way here, but not that day. I was on a course in the city centre. But, either way, I'd have been in my car.'

'Which is?'

'A Citroën C4. Dark blue. It's in the car park.' He nodded towards the front of the building.

'And when did you last check that the van was still in your garage?' Jane asked.

He frowned. 'Not for a while. Last week maybe. Why? What's this about?'

'A missing girl, Mr Burton,' Pete told him bluntly.

'A m—Hang on. Tuesday? That's when Jessica's daughter was taken, wasn't it? You don't think . . .?' He shook his head vigorously. 'No, no, no. Sorry, detectives, but you're barking up the wrong tree entirely there. Now, I must get back to my class. If you'll excuse me . . .' He stood up.

'So, just to confirm, the van's in your garage at home, Mr Burton?' Jane said.

'Yes.'

'And home is . . .?'

'Whipton. Lathbury Road.'

'OK. Thank you.'

They stood up. Pete put his phone away and held out a hand. Burton hesitated but took it. His palm was slightly damp, Pete noticed and applied a little more pressure. 'Good day, sir.'

Burton turned away quickly, heading for the door.

'Good day?' Jane asked quietly. 'I've never heard you say that before.'

'Well, it wasn't goodbye, was it? I'm sure we're going to see more of Mr Malcolm Burton.' He gave her a wink and started for the door, leaving her to follow.

In the car, with his seat belt fastened, Pete paused to glance at Jane.

'What?' she asked.

'His palms are damp. He swallows too much.'

'He's nervous.'

'But why?'

Jane tilted her head. 'That's the big question, isn't it? Do you think he's guilty?'

'Of something, yes.'

'Best we go check on that van then.'

Pete started the engine and slipped the car into gear. 'Meantime, give that head teacher a call, see if she can confirm that he was on that course he mentioned on Tuesday. And when.'

Jane took out her phone and dialled. 'Hello. DC Bennett here, Exeter CID,' she said. 'Can I speak to the head, please?' There was a brief pause. 'Hello. Yes, sorry to trouble you again, but there's just one tiny point we'd like to clear up. Mr Burton told us he was on a course on Tuesday. Is that correct?

'It is . . . OK. Thanks. And can you get confirmation of his actual attendance?'

Another pause.

'No, no. Just routine. To make sure we can discount him . . . Yes, that would be perfect. Thanks again for your help. Goodbye.

'She's getting back to me later on.'

*

Burton's home was no more than half a mile from the school. It was in a street of big, old detached properties. His had a high conifer hedge surrounding it. The lawn was ragged, patchy and unkempt. The gravel drive was weed-choked, mossy and dirty-looking, leading to a tatty-looking wooden garage beside the bay-windowed two-storey house.

Pete parked in front of the garage and climbed out. There were windows across the top sections of the doors. They were filthy with dirt and cobwebs on the inside. Pete stepped up to the doors and shaded his eyes to peer in.

Sure enough, there stood a white Toyota van. He could not see the model or the registration plate – it was too close to the doors and the glass was too filthy. He stepped back and looked at the padlock on the doors. 'Shame that. Let's have a look around, shall we? While we're here.'

'Negligent not to, boss.'

He started up the narrow pathway between the garage and the house. There was a small door near the far end. After pulling on a glove, he tried the handle.

It was unlocked.

'Careless. Invites thieves and burglars, that does.'

The door scraped against the old concrete pathway as it opened.

Along the back wall of the garage was a line of windows, just as dirty as those at the front. A long workbench was scattered with tools, most of them brown with rust and age. Pete stepped in far enough to read the registration plate on the van.

'This is it,' he said. 'Best get that warrant.'

*

'It was my idea, I should do it.'

They had just sat down at their desks when Jane spoke.

'It's my responsibility, either way.'

'Yes, but I've got a sweeter smile than you.'

Jane flashed him an example as he glanced up at her.

'Just don't flutter your eyelashes. You do that and he's bound to suspect something.'

She opened a drawer in her desk and pulled out a thick file. 'Here. While I'm gone, have a shufti at this. Simon's bunch aren't using it at the moment.'

Instantly, her comment put him on his guard. 'What is it?' he asked as he took it from her.

'Just thought you had a right to be in the picture. That should catch you up. Not that I'll be gone long.'

Pete glanced from the folder to her and back again. 'Don't push it. Pride comes before a fall.'

'Yeah, but we're talking Fast-track. He doesn't stand a chance.' She flashed him a pleading look and headed for the DCI's office.

Pete looked down at the file in front of him, his stomach fluttering. He almost didn't want to open it. It wasn't his to open. He could get in all kinds of shit for just reading this stuff – and so could Jane, if it ever came out that she'd got hold of it for him. But, in the end, he had no choice. He took a breath and flipped it open. A picture of his son looked back at him. Staring at the photo, taken at school the previous year, he didn't realise that he was holding his breath until his chest began to ache. He let the stale air slip from his lungs and flipped over the first page, then the second. Basic data that he knew already. Then the interviews began, starting with his own and Louise's. He flipped past them. When he came to Annie's, he started to read. Standard questions and answers.

The first surprise was when she admitted knowing that he smoked in the playground with his mates, before he moved up to senior school. A little further down the page, she said that she had heard him called a bully, but she didn't believe it. Pete shook his head, agreeing with her. He hadn't brought the boy up to be like that.

He read on.

School reports, all of which he'd seen before, were followed by interviews with his teachers. As Tommy had only moved up to senior school a few months before he disappeared, Simon's team had interviewed the teachers from his junior school, too. Pete read through what they had to say about his son with a mounting sense of disbelief. He flipped back and forth through the interviews, comparing what each person had to say, his mind reluctantly building a picture of a boy who he did not recognise as his own son.

Their consensus was that, since the age of eight, Tommy had been increasingly sly, manipulative and cruel. Not a bully – he was too subtle for that – but quietly and deliberately abusive. He had undermined teachers. He had got into fights. He had played tricks on the other children. He had increasingly alienated his friends, but not before making sure they were thoroughly frightened of him. Even the older kids avoided him, it seemed, but there was never anything provable so there was nothing to take to the parents and say, 'This needs to be addressed.' He was too clever for that.

'Jesus,' Pete muttered. Did he really know so little about his own son? What kind of father was he? He couldn't associate the child he was reading about with the small-for-his-age boy that he knew and loved. Tommy couldn't be like this . . .

He flipped the page and began to read another report. It described how a boy, a year older than Tommy, who had fought with him in the playground, had taken a fall down a flight of stairs two days later, breaking his arm. There were no witnesses and the boy claimed it was an accident, but no one had been able to account for Tommy's whereabouts at the time.

But, if Tommy pushed the kid, how the hell did he persuade him not to tell?

He turned the page again and his eye was caught by the phrase, 'Just two weeks ago . . .'

He read on.

Tommy had got into another fight. Pete remembered the bruises on his face and the blood on his shirt when he came home one night, a couple of weeks before he disappeared. He had asked what happened and Tommy had told him he'd been beaten up by one of the big kids. When he had said he would go to the school and put a stop to it, Tommy was adamant that he shouldn't.

The report went on to say that, a week later, an older boy, who they had suspected of being the other party in the fight with Tommy, had opened his locker and been blown backwards by an explosion.

'Jesus,' Pete muttered. *An explosion?*

It turned out that three matches had been stapled to the inside of the locker door, sandpaper stuck to the floor of the locker for them to strike against, and a plastic container of water had been placed in the back of the locker with a nine-volt battery, whose terminals had been connected to wires going into the water.

The victim was unhurt but very shaken.

'I bet he bloody was,' Pete muttered. 'Christ!' Horror at what his son had done was tempered with pride at his ingenuity and resourcefulness. Something like that would certainly put a stop to any bullying.

'Boss?'

Pete blinked and slapped the file shut. Jane was standing at the end of his desk. 'Sorry, Jane. Miles away.'

'I could see. Are you all right?'

Pete put the file in a drawer of his desk. 'What have you got?'

She grinned and waved a piece of paper at him. 'A warrant to search the Toyota and its immediate location – i.e. the garage.'

Pete pushed his chair back. 'Right. What are we waiting for?' He locked his desk, stood up and grabbed his coat. 'Let's do it.'

Chapter 32

'We won't have long before he gets home,' Pete said, checking his watch as he pulled the car off the road outside Burton's property.

'If he comes straight home,' said Jane.

'He will. He'll want to check on the van. He tried not to show it, but I think we put the wind up him.' He reached for the latch and opened the gate.

'Well, wouldn't that be a shame?' she said dryly.

Pete grunted. 'Depending on how he reacts. I just hope we didn't scare him into doing something drastic before we can track down Rosie.'

'Maybe he'll check on the van and then lead us to her, if we let him.'

'Best get a move on then.' He closed and latched the gate, pulled his torch from his pocket and headed up the side of the garage. Pulling the side door open, he nodded for Jane to precede him inside.

She headed for the back of the van while Pete checked the cab, peering through a side window.

'Nothing inside except a toolbox behind the driver's seat,' she called.

'Right. Gloves on and in we go.'

He set the torch on the workbench and followed his own instruction, opening the passenger door carefully to avoid disturbing any latent fingerprints. He looked under the seat, in the door pocket, then opened the glovebox. Nothing. He backed out, shut the door and went around to the other side while Jane crawled into the rear compartment and unlatched the toolbox. She was rummaging through its contents when he opened the driver's door and began a swift search of that side of the cab.

'Anything?' he asked.

'Just tools, apart from these. You?' She held up a packet of foot-long white zip-ties.

'Nothing. It's clean.'

She replaced everything as she'd found it. 'Best drag Harry Pointer out again then, had we?'

Pete had hoped to be in and gone by the time Burton got home. Bringing in forensics would take hours and, in the process, might scare the guy off. But there was no choice. It had to be done. He closed the van door and stepped outside to make the call.

*

The door of the squad room opened and the DI from Bath stepped in. Pete stood up as the man approached, hand outstretched. 'Thanks for that.'

Truman's grip was firm and sure. Small and broad, he was in his early fifties with short grey hair that was thinning on top, and an honest, open face.

'No problem,' Pete said. 'Did you get anything useful out of him?'

'Possibly. He recalled where Southam stayed in Bath and an associate of his that we can follow up on.'

'Not a completely wasted trip then.'

'No.'

Pete's phone rang and he reached for it, hoping it was Harry

Pointer, to tell him they were finished. It was about bloody time. He glanced at his watch. The forensics team had been at Burton's place for over an hour.

'DS Gayle, Exeter CID.'

'Hello. This is Danielle at Berry's, land agents. We spoke earlier about High Acres Farm?'

'Ah. Yes.' He felt the slump of disappointment. 'What can I do for you?'

'There was something about the farm at the back of my mind when we spoke earlier, that I couldn't quite put a finger on. I just found out what it was and thought I'd better tell you. I don't know if it'll be useful or not, but . . .'

'What was it you found, Danielle?'

'Mr and Mrs Knox don't rent the whole farm. There is a piece of land that had already been let to the local wildlife trust when they took it on. It's a meadow and some woodland with a barn, off the road up to the village.'

'I see.'

A barn. Isolated location. Perfect for holding a young girl whose welfare you weren't particularly concerned about.

'Thanks, Danielle. Do you happen to have the file on this meadow there with you?'

'It's here in front of me.'

'Is there a plan in it?'

'Yes. A copy of the OS field plan.'

'Perfect. Any chance you could send that over to me by fax or email?'

'Uh . . . I don't know. It's A3 size, so . . .'

'Could you maybe take a picture of it with your phone and send that?'

'Yes. Of course.' She brightened. 'What number should I send it to?'

Pete gave her the number of his smartphone.

'Right. I'll do it now.'

He thanked her again and ended the call.

'I'll let you get on, then,' said Truman. 'Go see what I can drag up on what Sanderson's given us. Thanks again for the lead.'

'Good to have met you,' Pete said, as his mobile pinged with an incoming message.

The man from Bath headed out and Pete picked up his mobile to check the message.

'What you got, boss?' Jane asked

Pete looked across, the corners of his mouth twitching towards a smile as something in his chest fluttered with excitement. 'A possible location.'

'For?'

'Rosie Whitlock. Our man's got a barn out at Holcomb Burnell that didn't get let out with the rest of the farm.' *Jesus! If she was there, how close had he been to her, earlier in the day?*

'Brilliant.' Jane pushed her chair back. 'So, are we going, or what?' As she grabbed her bag with one hand she punched the air with the other. 'Yes! The Gayle force is back on track.'

Pete grinned. 'Steady on. We haven't found her yet.'

'No, but we're going to. I can feel it in my water.' Jane grabbed her coat off the hook. 'And, at the back of my mind, I'd thought she was probably already dead.'

Pete glanced across at Dave. 'Give FTP a heads-up, will you? And get the chopper up and a full search team out there pronto. If he's not home yet, he's gone somewhere and this sounds like a good possibility.'

'Right, boss.'

*

'Here.'

Pete tossed his phone to Jane and started the car. 'Latest message. There's a map that'll take us to the barn. Figure it out, will you, while I drive?'

'OK.'

He hit the lights and sirens at the same time as the accelerator, shot down the drive beside the station and out into the rush-hour traffic. Heavitree Road was queued up, as usual. He drove down the outside of the queue as quickly as safety would allow, turned left across the front of the car waiting to get onto the roundabout and headed for the bridge over the river. Traffic here was much less dense and he put his foot down hard, keeping the lights and sirens on until they reached the edge of the city. Then, with little or no traffic on the road, the noise and flashing blue lights felt over the top, so he switched them off.

As they crested the top of the hill he glanced at Jane. 'So?'

She looked up from the phone. 'I've got it. Looks like there's woodland along the roadside before the village. There's a lane or track or something going through it. The barn's in a field out the back. Looks like the lane becomes a bridleway beyond the barn, which carries on through more woodland at the other side of the field.'

'OK. I know the woodland you mean. Didn't notice the lane.'

'It might be just a dirt track,' she said. 'You wouldn't necessarily notice it without some reason to.'

He turned off the main road, onto the narrow lanes that wove through the countryside towards the little village of Holcomb Burnell. Up ahead, he caught a glimpse of red tail lights, so flicked the blues and twos back on.

It was best to give the other driver plenty of warning that he was coming. The trouble was, he didn't want to give Malcolm Burton any more warning than he could help, so he would have to turn them off again ASAP. He rounded a left-hand bend, then an even sharper one to the right and there was the car, just ahead. Pete saw the brake lights glow briefly as the driver acknowledged his presence. He powered past the car, let the sirens give a final whoop, then turned them off.

Now, where was that junction?

He recalled the narrow lanes, grass and cow parsley growing high and close at either side, the little Hansel-and-Gretel cottage on the corner, right by the junction. Then it was there, in front of him. He slowed, made the turn. Now they had to find the entrance to the lane or bridleway or whatever it was. 'How far along is it?' he asked.

'Don't know. The junction's not on here.'

'Damn. OK, how far through to the barn, once we turn off?'

Jane checked the scale of the map. 'Um . . . looks like about four, maybe five hundred yards.'

Pete sucked air through his teeth and kept his foot light on the throttle. He couldn't afford to overshoot. If the guy heard him reversing, he'd know something was up. 'Get hold of Dave, will you? Find out how far out that chopper is, and the ground backup.'

'Right.' She put down his phone and took out her own to make the call. 'It's Jane. Where's that chopper? OK. And the search team?' Another pause. 'What! You're joking. Well, taking the piss then. Get them bloody moving, for Christ's sake. We're nearly there.'

'There it is,' Pete said, spotting the dark entrance to the woods on the right, up ahead. 'What's up?'

'All right, bye.' Jane ended the call. 'The chopper's ten minutes out. The backup crew are leaving HQ in fifteen.'

Pete stopped the car abruptly. 'What bloody use do they expect that to be?' He drew a long, slow breath. 'Alright. We'll see what we find and take it from there.'

He put the car back into gear and eased it forward, turning into the end of a dirt track with grass up the middle that led into the inky darkness of the woods. He switched from headlights to sidelights and the night closed in even more oppressively. But, again, he didn't want to give Burton any more warning of his approach than he absolutely had to. Putting Rosie's life at risk, by being careless right at the last minute, was certainly not in his playbook. He let the car crawl forward, foot barely touching the throttle. This was one time when he could have used one of those hybrid cars that made no noise at all in electric mode. But, there was no telling what they would find at the far end of this lane, so he wasn't going to take the chance of not taking the car in.

Tall shuttlecock ferns glowed ghostlike at the sides of the track, long grass brushing the sides of the car as they crept along. The track curved gradually right then left. A huge old oak tree stood to one side, its deeply ridged bark and gnarled appearance like something out of a fantasy film that Pete vaguely remembered watching with Annie. *Harry Potter* or *Lord of the Rings*. He wasn't sure which. Then he saw a dim vertical line of light some distance beyond it.

'There, look.'

'I see it.'

He stopped the car in the middle of the track at the edge of the woods, switched off the lights and the engine. 'Torch is in the glovebox.'

They stepped out, eased the doors softly closed and headed towards the barn. Pete saw its shape vaguely against the sky, black and hulking. Then he sensed a low wall to his left, tall weeds along its near side and the faint shine of barbed wire along the top. They came to a gap in the wall and Pete stepped through towards the big doors, which stood barely ajar, the faint glow of light showing between them. He felt rough cobbles beneath his feet, combining with the wall to form some kind of holding yard.

All was quiet and still. Too still, he thought. Like the world was waiting for him to reach those doors.

He glanced back at Jane. 'Careful with the light,' he murmured.

She shone it forward briefly over the dirt-coated and weed-choked cobbles then switched it off. 'OK?'

'Yep.'

With the picture of the ground in front of him fresh in his mind, he stepped forward, right hand raised, holding the still-collapsed baton like a primitive weapon. *And not even a bloody stab-vest for protection*, he thought. But there had been no time for anything like that. He would find what he would find and react accordingly.

He stepped up close to the doors and crouched to peer through. Could make out no movement at all. There were two torches resting on stacked hay bales, both aimed at a point to his right. He stepped carefully across and squinted through the gap, trying to get a view of what – or who – was over there.

Nothing.

Then someone moaned.

The voice was female. Young.

Rosie.

In one swift move he tugged the door wider with one hand, snapped the baton out to its full length with the other and stepped inside. A sweeping glance took in the shadowy interior – or as much of it as he could see in the low light – then he focused on the source of the moan. Bales had been stacked in a U-shape. As he came closer, he saw her lying within the enclosed space. Long, curly blonde hair. Dark green school uniform, the cardigan discarded. She was lying on her face in the loose hay. She moaned again and struggled to her elbows and knees.

'Rosie?'

She gasped.

Her head snapped around to stare towards him through a tangle of hair.

'It's OK. I'm a police officer.' He glanced away. 'Jane, get in here. Now.' As he looked back at the girl, who now swept her hair back with one hand so that she could see him, despite one eye being swollen almost shut. Blood was leaking from her nose and a cut on her lip, he saw, then heard the roar of an engine from the far side of the barn.

'Shit.'

'Bastard's getting away,' Jane snarled from the doorway behind him.

Pete looked over his shoulder. The engine was heading away, further from the road instead of towards it. 'We won't catch him now. But, we've got Rosie.'

Chapter 33

As Jane helped Rosie up and seated her on the bales, she cast her gaze frantically around the shadowy interior. 'Where's TJ? Is he all right?'

Pete was heading for the door, intent on making a call to Dave, to tell him that Burton, if it was him, was on the move. He stopped and turned. 'TJ?'

'The boy who was here. You have to find him. He was . . . The man knocked him out. They were fighting. He was trying to . . .' She dropped her head into her hands and sobbed. 'We promised. Whichever of us got out, we had to run, regardless. At least one of us would have a chance to escape. But then the man hit him and . . .' She looked up, her eyes pleading for him to understand. 'Is he OK?'

'There's no one else here, Rosie.' Pete could see the vibrations running through her body as her left leg began to bob up and down. 'Just us.'

'You have to find him. Please.'

'We will. What can you tell me about him?'

'He's my age, but he doesn't go to my school. Local comprehensive, I think. I know him from swimming, but just by his nickname. He's a bit smaller than me, brown hair and eyes.' She shook her head, at a loss as to what to add.

Jane put an arm around her. 'It's all right, darling. It's all right now. Ssh.'

She looked up at Pete, saying nothing, though her eyes spoke volumes.

He nodded and headed out to fetch the car.

The other vehicle was long gone. He could no longer even hear it.

TJ, he thought as he hurried through the darkness. *Thomas James. Could it be? Small for his age, brown hair and eyes. The description could easily be of Tommy. It would be a hell of a coincidence, wouldn't it? But, if it was him, what was he doing with Burton?* She had made him sound like another victim. Had Burton been holding him all this time? It seemed incredible. But then he remembered other cases where people had been held captive for years. It was perfectly possible.

Had he really stumbled on a lead to his son?

Butterflies seethed in his stomach. Then anger took over.

If Burton had hurt him . . .

His jaw clamped tight as he struggled to stay calm. He reached the car, climbed in and drove up to the barn, leaving the engine running and lights on as he headed inside. Before he reached the doors, Jane led the girl out carefully, one hand around her shoulders. Pete turned back and opened the back door of the car for them. This wasn't the time to wait for an ambulance. They would take the girl to hospital themselves.

As he swung the car around in the short-mown meadow, he heard the first faint flutter of helicopter blades and saw a light shining bright in the sky to the north-east. *The chopper.*

With the car back on the track, he stopped and took out his phone, using a speed-dial number.

'DC Miles, Exeter CID.'

'Dave, it's Pete. Get forensics out here to the barn ASAP. Rosie and at least one other victim were held here. And the chopper's about to arrive, but Burton and his other victim are in a car, heading along a bridleway from here. We do not have eyes on. What we do have is the girl. We're taking her to the RDE. Get Jill to call her parents, get them to meet us there, will you?'

'Will do. Oh, and I heard back from Harry at Burton's place. They've got hairs and fibres in the back of the van that match Rosie and her school uniform. Plenty of others, too.'

'Good. Get a warrant for the house then.'

'Already in process. DI Underhill's on it.'

'Right. Two more things we need. An arrest team at the house, in case he comes back there and an alert out on his car. It's a dark blue Citroën C4. I don't know the number. You'll have to check with Swansea. You can head up the arrest team at Burton's house. Get the warrants and get over there quick. If he does come back there, it'll be just briefly, to grab some essentials and clear out, I'd imagine.'

'OK, boss.'

Pete ended the call, put away his phone and put the car into gear. Glancing in the mirror, he caught Jane's eye. Rosie was lying across the seat, wrapped in a space blanket that Pete had fetched from the boot of the car, her knees against the back of the passenger seat while her head rested in Jane's lap.

'How's she doing?'

Jane gave him a quick tilt of the head. *As well as can be expected.* 'Won't be long,' he said. 'We'll soon be at the hospital, then you can see your mum and dad.'

*

Annie opened the front door before Pete had a chance to touch his key to the lock.

'Dad! You're early.'

He swept her up into his arms and planted a kiss on her forehead. 'I'm not stopping, Button. Just come to pick something up, then I'm off to the hospital. Got a witness to interview, I hope.'

'You seem happy. It must be an important witness,' she said, as he put her down and they went indoors.

'The main one,' he told her. 'The victim herself.'

'Rosie Whitlock? You found her? Wow! Dad, that's brilliant!'

'What's going on?' asked Louise from the lounge.

Pete's eyes widened. 'Your mum's getting better.' He went through. Louise was sitting in her usual place, the TV on in front of her. He leaned down and kissed her. 'Hello, love. Just popped in to fetch something. I won't be too long. We've recovered the girl. I'm on the way to see her, with a few questions that should help us catch the bloke that took her.'

'Shame Simon Phillips couldn't be as quick about his job as you. Does this mean we'll start to see you before bedtime again?'

He felt a flash of irritation. 'I can't help what cases I get, Lou. But, yes, that's the plan. I'll be back as soon as I can.'

He headed upstairs to his office, closed the door and lifted down his personal file on Tommy's disappearance. Procedure didn't allow him to be involved professionally in the investigation of his own son's case, but no-one could prevent him following leads on his own time. Not that it had done any good, but there were plenty of photographs in here and no questions would be asked about why he'd taken one. He tucked a picture into his jacket pocket and replaced the file on the shelf. Sticking his head into Annie's room, he saw she was at her desk, doing homework. 'See you in a bit, Button. Love you.'

She looked up. 'Love you, too, Dad. Don't be late.'

He laughed. 'I won't.'

Her little face turned serious. 'Be gentle with her, Dad.'

'Who?'

'Rosie Whitlock, of course.'

He felt a swell of pride at her concern. 'Of course I will. And I won't stay with her any longer than I have to, all right?'

She nodded. 'Bye.'

*

Pete drew a long, shuddering breath as he walked into the A & E department. He was nervous, he realised with a shock. He needed to know if the boy Rosie knew as TJ was, in fact, Tommy, but the consequences of that knowledge were . . . frightening. If it was Tommy, then the question became, why was he there? Was he a victim or a part of the plot? And if it wasn't him, then where was he? Was this the last chance he had of finding his son alive?

He stepped up to the desk, lifting his warrant card. 'DS Gayle. My colleague, DC Bennett came in a short time ago with a victim, Rosie Whitlock.'

'Ah, yes.' The nurse pointed around a corner. 'Down there, third bay. I think the doctor's with them now.'

'OK, thanks.'

The third bay had the curtains drawn all around it. Pete stopped outside. 'Jane,' he called gently.

'Boss.' He heard her say something quietly, then the curtains wafted this way and that, like a *Morecambe and Wise* sketch.

Finally, she emerged at one corner. 'The doc's with her at the minute. Doing the exam and the . . . kit. I sent her mum and dad to the canteen for a while.'

He nodded. 'How is she?'

'Considering what she's been through, not too bad, physically. It's going to take some time for her to recover mentally, though.'

'Has she given you any sort of description of the suspect?'

'Not much. He generally wore a black ski mask, so all she knew for sure until tonight was that he was white. Apparently, tonight, he wasn't prepared. Came in a different vehicle. No mask. She still didn't see much of him because it was so dark in the barn and the only light was pointed at her most of the time. But she thinks he had blond or sandy hair. She'd recognise the boy, though. She said he wore a mask, too, until she managed to get it off him earlier. She got the shock of her life when she recognised him.'

'She got it off him?'

'With his help. His idea, she said.'

Pete grimaced. 'No name on the perp?'

'Apparently, the boy called him Mel.'

'Which could be short for Malcolm. By the way, thanks for that file you gave me earlier.'

'No problem.'

The perp had to be Malcolm Burton. It all pointed to him. The van. The barn. The nickname. His knowledge of Rosie's mother. His career choice, even. But the boy . . .

TJ.

Rosie's description of him was vague enough to fit almost half the kids in the city, but it could be Tommy. And, as Jane had said, she could ID him.

If it was Tommy . . .

My God, he thought. Had he been with Burton all this time? Rosie had said he was another victim but, if so, why was he masked? It made no sense. A couple of hours ago, Pete wouldn't have entertained the concept of his son being willingly involved in something like this, but the file Jane had given him – the comments from his school mates and teachers, even from Annie – had shown him a side of his son that he had been completely unaware of. A side that pointed to a disturbed and potentially dangerous mind.

No, he thought. It couldn't be true. But then the small voice at the back of his mind replied: *What if it is?*

But, how could we – I – have gone so wrong? How did I not see that things were so far out of kilter? He sighed heavily. The answer was all too easy. *I was never bloody there, was I? Always out on a job, tracking down some suspect or other, making the city a safer place. But who for?* Who had he been doing it all for? The population in general? His family? Or himself – his own satisfaction and sense of self-worth?

What was he going to tell Lou? He shook his head and refocused on Jane, who was watching him with a worried expression on her face. 'Is she going to be comfortable with me going in there after the exam, do you think? Just for a couple of minutes.'

Jane shrugged. 'She was OK in the car.'

The doctor emerged from between the curtains, tucked a stray strand of dark hair behind her ear and looked from Pete to Jane and back again. 'You can go in now, Detectives, but don't be too long and don't stress her, please.'

'We won't. Thanks, Doc.'

Pete nodded for Jane to go ahead of him. 'Rosie,' she said, 'you remember my boss, Detective Sergeant Gayle?'

Rosie was lying in bed, sheets tucked up to her neck. Her eyes looked huge and somehow hollow, her face pale. She nodded.

He gave her a smile. 'Never mind Detective Sergeant. I'm Peter,' he said. 'I've just got a couple of things I want to ask you about, then I'll leave you with Jane and go fetch your mum and dad, all right?'

She nodded again.

'I'm not going to ask you about what happened to you. There's people a lot more suitable than me for that. What I want to ask about first is the boy, TJ.'

She gasped. 'Have you found him? Is he safe?'

Pete reached into his jacket for the photo. 'Is this him?'

Her eyes got even bigger. 'Yes,' she whispered. 'Is he all right?'

Pete's chest churned. He could barely breathe. An icy feeling spread down the back of his neck, his fingers and legs tingling. He tried to keep a calm exterior. 'You're sure?'

'Of course I'm sure.'

'OK. It's all right. We haven't found him yet, no. But, we will.'

'But the man – Mel – was beating him up. He hurt him last night, but tonight, he was really . . . It was as if he wanted to kill him. And then, when I tried to help, he hit me and . . . the next thing I knew, you were there.'

Pete put the picture away with a hollow feeling in his chest. He gave Jane a brief glance. He could see the question in her eyes, but this was not the moment to answer it. He turned back to the girl. 'We're doing everything we can to find him, Rosie. There's one other thing I need to ask you. I've got a voice recording here.' He brought out his phone. 'Would it be OK for me to play it and see if it's the man who took you? Mel?'

Nervousness flashed in her eyes, followed by doubt and finally resolve. She nodded.

'OK. This is part of an interview Jane and I did earlier today with a man that some evidence led us to.' He found the recording on his phone. 'Here it is.'

He pressed play.

His own voice began: *'That's all right then. Only, we have a possible sighting of it on Tuesday morning, just before eight thirty. You wouldn't have been driving it then?'*

'No. I'd have been . . . Tuesday? I was going to say on my way here, but not that day. I was on a course in the city centre. But, either way, I'd have been in my car.'

Rosie gasped and hugged her knees to her chest, trembling, her eyes huge.

'Which is?'

'A Citroën C4. Dark blue. It's in the car park.'

Pete touched the pause button. 'Is that him?'

Rosie looked up at him and dipped her head slowly.

'You're sure? Do you want to hear a bit more, to be certain?'

She shook her head. 'No. No more. I'm sure.'

'OK then.' He gently squeezed her shoulder. 'That's all I need for now.'

Her eyes were big and haunted. 'He killed Lauren.'

Pete hesitated, in the act of putting his phone away. 'You saw that?'

'No, but he came and took her away and I could tell he was going to. You will catch him, won't you? And put him in prison?'

Pete's throat clogged. He swallowed heavily and reached out

to give her shoulder a squeeze. 'We will. I promise.' He glanced at Jane and stepped out through the curtain.

Jane emerged behind him. 'Boss?'

He paused and turned back to face her.

'The picture. Tommy?'

Pete nodded.

'She told me before you got here that he fought with Burton. Twice. Last night and then again tonight. He told her to run if she got the chance. Not to worry about him. She knew him before, from the swimming pool.'

Something shifted in Pete's gut. It was inevitable now. It was going to come out that Rosie knew Tommy before. What the hell was he going to do about those emails? He grimaced. At this point, he had no idea, but whatever it was, it would not reflect well on him that he had known about it and said nothing. But that was for later. 'I'll go fetch the parents,' he said, and walked away before Jane could ask any more.

*

Dave stepped away from the back of the police van, a new supply of evidence bags in his hand as a car slowed beyond the gates of Malcolm Burton's house, and he saw the blinking glow of indicator lights. Headlights swept across the overgrown garden as it turned in. He heard the handbrake ratchet up in the dark-coloured saloon at the same instant as he recognised the badge on the front.

Citroën.

It was Burton.

He stepped forward. Saw the man's face, pale in the darkness, eyes widening as recognition and fear registered. The Citroën roared and shot backwards through the gateway.

Shit. He was running.

Tyres squealed on the tarmac outside as the Citroën swung

sharply to the right. Headlights flared behind it, a horn blasted and there was a dull crunch of impact. Dave ran forward, the evidence bags falling from his hand. Officers were streaming out around him, aiming to box the fleeing man in, but the car's engine roared again as it surged forward like a wild beast. Burton wasn't stopping for anything. Men scattered, yelling, as Dave went up the road at a run.

He heard a second impact and a shout of pain as a man was hit, but he didn't pause.

His black Norton was parked just twenty yards away, between two cars. He had the key in his hand by the time he reached the motorbike. Shoved it into the ignition and swung his leg over the seat in a single move. One kick and the low, throaty rumble told him it was ready. He kicked away the stand and tapped the gear shift, pulling out of the little gap thirty yards behind the Citroën.

He didn't bother with lights or the helmet that was hooked by its strap over the left handlebar. No time. He opened the throttle, the bike leaping forward like a living thing. He swung it around the Toyota 4 x 4 that was stopped in the middle of the road, having been hit by the Citroën, saw the fleeing schoolteacher turn at the end of the road, the car swinging wildly into the wider cross-street, one brake light shining silver where the impact with the other car had smashed the casing.

Dave made the turn and opened the bike up again. Just the Citroën showed ahead. He saw it brake hard. No indicator, but it turned right into a side road. Dave had to catch up. He couldn't lose Burton now. No way. He left it late to brake, leaning hard into the turn, back tyre sliding, then accelerated hard again up the narrow side street, the roar of the big engine echoing off the tall Georgian houses to his left. Ahead of him, the Citroën turned right again.

Good move, he thought. Whoever had seen Burton driving away would know he was heading west. With no lights behind him, he could turn back on himself and have everyone looking in completely the wrong direction, leaving him free to get away.

Dave kicked down through the gears and leaned into the turn. He saw the French car moving sedately now, a single tail light glowing red.

Moments later, shock jolted through him as brake lights flared, one red, the other bright white, and the Citroën swung into a parking space.

What the hell was he doing?

Had he spotted Dave, despite the black bike and leathers and his lack of lights? Was he setting up to knock him off the bike and make his getaway?

Dave frowned, slowing the bike as he thought he saw a light shine dimly inside the car. Then the driver's door opened. With no defence or hiding place, all Dave had left was attack. He twisted the throttle. The engine growled as the bike accelerated hard towards the man emerging from the car with something shiny in his right hand.

Dave flipped on the bike's headlight. Burton was caught rabbit-like, frozen in the beam, some kind of narrow blade in his hand. Then, leaving the car door open, he started forward. The distance between them was down to feet. Dave lined the bike up, twisted the throttle further and jerked up the handlebars, lifting the front wheel off the tarmac, aiming straight for the man in front of him.

Fear and shock were etched on Burton's face as he yelled out, the bike coming at him like a mechanical battle horse.

Dave turned the wheel at the last moment so that it hit him at an angle across his thighs, slamming him backwards into the open car door. He went down hard and the back wheel of the bike went over his outstretched legs. He screamed. Dave rode the bucking bike clear then slammed on the brakes, pulling it around into a spinning halt in the road. He killed the engine.

'You stupid bastard, you could have killed me,' Burton yelled in the sudden silence. He sat against the open car door, his legs outstretched on the tarmac, the left one twisted at an odd angle.

Dave pushed down the bike stand and swung his leg clear. 'I reckon that's broke, mate.'

Burton looked up at him. 'Of course it's bloody broken. Look at it! I need an ambulance.'

'Dare say you do, but there's something else you need first.' He lifted out his handcuffs, leaned down and attached one end to Burton's right wrist. 'Arresting. You're nicked, matey.' He saw that what Burton had been holding was a screwdriver. It had rolled a couple of feet away, almost under the car. He lifted Burton's arm and clipped the other end of the cuffs to the handle of the car door. 'You do not have to say anything, but it may harm your defence if you fail to mention, when questioned, something that you later rely on in court. Anything you do say may be used in evidence. Do you understand?'

Chapter 34

The night air was crisp as Pete wove his way briskly through the maze of hospital buildings, heading for the central block.

He was almost there when his phone rang in his pocket. He took it out and checked the caller ID. Colin Underhill.

'Already?' he muttered. He had only called the DI a few minutes ago, as he left the A & E block, to request warrants for Malcolm Burton's arrest and a search of his home. Surely, they couldn't be through yet?

'Guv'nor?'

'Pete. Just calling to let you know, the warrant for Burton's arrest isn't going to be necessary.'

'Why the hell not?'

'Because he's just been arrested. Leaving the scene of a road traffic accident, injuring a police officer and evading arrest. For now. Dave Miles nabbed him. He turned up at his house, but spotted the guys before they could arrest him and tried to do a runner.'

Pete laughed. 'Brilliant. Nice one, Dave.'

'He's on his way to the hospital, as soon as an ambulance arrives to fetch him. Broken leg. Dave ran over him with that bloody great bike of his.'

'Ouch. Great news, Guv. Thanks for letting me know.'

'No problem. Goodnight, Pete. And well done.'

'Thanks.'

Pete ended the call and slipped his phone back into his pocket. Warm air enveloped him like a blanket as he pulled open the glass door in front of him.

Now, he really had some news for the Whitlocks. He couldn't help grinning as he checked the colour-coded signs and headed down the corridor.

The café in the main concourse was almost deserted. The Whitlocks were the only customers and they were sitting like strangers, quietly concentrating on the cups on the table in front of them.

After the admission she'd had to make the day before, though, Pete was surprised that they were even sitting at the same table. That was not going to be a happy household for Rosie to go back to, he imagined.

Alistair looked up expectantly as he approached.

'Mr Whitlock.'

Jessica's head rose at the sound of his voice.

'I came to tell you the doctors have finished with Rosie for now. You can go and see her. And I can also tell you that we've made an arrest. The man we suspect of abducting your daughter.'

'My God,' Jessica stood up quickly to face him. 'Who is he? Do we know him?'

Pete pressed his lips together. 'Yes, I'm afraid you do, Mrs Whitlock. It's a colleague of yours. Malcolm Burton.'

'What?' She looked, horror-struck, from Pete to her husband and back. 'Oh my God! I can't believe it. I spent time with him in the staffroom yesterday. He was so sympathetic and . . . and all the time, he . . . I feel sick.' She leaned on the edge of the table as Alistair got up quickly and Pete stepped aside.

'There are toilets just round the corner there.'

Jessica heaved, but managed not to puke. She took a deep

breath and looked up. Her skin was pale and shining. As Alistair caught her elbow, she looked around for her chair and sat back down again, fixing her gaze on Pete. 'Malcolm? Really?'

'I'm afraid so. We're still investigating, of course, but there is evidence.'

'Well, at least if you've got him, no other girls will have to go through what Rosie did or worse,' Alistair said firmly.

Pete nodded. 'I'll walk back with you, when you're ready. No hurry, Mrs Whitlock. Get yourself steady first.'

'I think a bit of fresh air might do me good, if I can stop my legs from shaking.' She pushed herself upright and walked slowly between Alistair and Pete.

Back in A & E, having taken a call from Dave Miles on the way across to tell him of Burton's arrest, Pete led Alistair and Jessica to the bay where Rosie waited for them with Jane, the curtains still drawn along the sides of the bed, but now open at the foot. Rosie was sitting up, dressed in a white T-shirt and pale green scrubs. The clothes she'd had on when she arrived would have gone for forensic examination, he knew.

Jessica rushed in, arms stretched wide. 'Rosie! Oh, darling, I'm so glad you're all right.' She clamped her into a crushing hug.

Rosie responded almost reluctantly, but she closed her eyes and submitted as Alistair followed his wife in and bent to embrace her from the other side.

Pete looked away and found Jane looking at him.

'You know Dave just brought Malcolm Burton in?'

'Yeah. Where?' he asked.

She stayed quiet for a moment. 'You need to stay away, boss. You know that. If Tommy's involved, anything he says in your presence is potentially contaminated. Inadmissible.'

'Where is he?' Pete said, low and firm.

'He could walk if you go after him now.' She thrust her chin at the reunited family behind him. 'Look at her. Could you honestly jeopardise her chance of justice for the sake of something that could well turn out to be a lie anyway? And those two dead girls – what about them?'

'They're dead. Tommy's alive. Or, he was a few hours ago. And if Burton's in here, then he's potentially out there, somewhere, alone. What do you think is more important to me right now, Jane?'

She looked up at him. 'Right now? Tommy. You wouldn't be a father if he wasn't. But an hour ago and a few hours from now, it would be justice. For Rosie, for Lauren Carter and for Amanda Kernick. And for all those potential victims that letting Burton loose again will put at risk.'

'Aah!' Pete felt the frustration twisting his features into a grimace. He spun away before he hit out at something, or yelled at Jane in a way that he knew he would regret later.

She was right, of course, yet he couldn't let go of the possibility of finding Tommy alive and well, after all these months.

'Talk to Dave then. Tell him what we know. And tell him to get whatever there is to get out of the bastard or I'll do it myself.'

Jane knew perfectly well what he meant. She held his gaze until she saw that he was beginning to calm down. 'I'll tell him,' she said at last. 'In the meantime, you need to call the DI and fill him in. Fully. He'll tell you to stay away from Burton, but you're already doing that. Right?' Her eyes searched his for confirmation. He didn't give it, but nor did he deny the fact. 'So, no loss there. And any lead is better than none on Tommy. He'll pass it on to DS Phillips and kick-start their investigation. With any luck you'll have Tommy home in a few days.'

Pete pursed his lips, staring at Jane as he struggled not to bite the hand that he knew was feeding him. 'All right,' he said at last. 'Give my best to Rosie and her family before they leave. And get what you can from her about Tommy.'

'I already have, boss.' She patted him on the arm and jerked her head towards the door. 'Off you go, now, before you get yourself in trouble.'

Pete grunted. 'I'm already in trouble,' he said, as he stalked away grumpily.

*

The squad room was dark and deserted when Pete walked in a few minutes later. All the lights were off, all the computer screens dark. The only source of light was Colin Underhill's office, in the corner to his left, the door of which was half open.

Pete had called Colin as he walked back to his car, catching him as he was about to leave. He had asked him to stay. 'I'm on the way in. I need to talk to you. Face to face.'

Colin had asked what about, but Pete was adamant. It had to be in person. It was the only way.

He crossed to his desk, unlocked it and reached into the middle drawer for the file on his son. Then he headed for the DI's office. He could see Colin, head down, concentrating.

That was Colin all over. If he was here, he'd be working. But Pete had neither knocked nor spoken when Underhill said, 'Pete. I hear you've been spreading your influence up to Bath. Had a phone call from a DI Truman. He said that Steven Southam came from Swindon – well, just outside of it, actually. He had a farm there. Bred dogs. Mostly breeds that aren't legal any more. Anyway, they got on to the Wiltshire force and they've still got the evidence in storage from when Southam was charged and convicted, some of which they'd never identified. But amongst it was a pair of girl's underwear that turned out to match what Alison Stretton was known to have been wearing when she disappeared. They'll do DNA to confirm it, but they said it was pretty distinctive. It hadn't been picked up on because Avon and Somerset never publicised it.'

'Well, you wouldn't, would you?'

Colin tipped his head and put down his pen. 'So, what's up? What did you want to talk about?'

Pete put the file down in front of him. 'I expect you've read this?'

The DI lifted the cover for confirmation then let it drop closed again. 'Of course.'

'Somebody put it on my desk earlier. I don't know who. I haven't read all of it, but I don't much like what I have.'

Colin grimaced. He waved Pete to a chair and leaned back in his own.

'Thing is, talking to Rosie Whitlock, there was a boy there with her. It was Tommy.'

Underhill sat forward abruptly. 'You're sure?'

Pete nodded. 'She knows him as TJ, but it's him. I showed her a photo and she confirmed it. Jane's spoken to her in more depth. I don't know what she's told her though.'

'You'll have to stay clear of Burton, or anything to do with him, from now on then.'

'So, what am I supposed to do?'

'Go home. Be with your wife. Your daughter. You've got good people here. Jane or Dave can head the tidying-up operation. They'll have to liaise with Simon, get him up to date on Tommy's whereabouts and so on. Dave arrested Burton, so he can question him. He's perfectly competent. And Jane can do the search of Burton's house. If there's another potential victim somewhere, that'll have to be sooner, rather than later. We'll have to get a search team out to the barn, come morning, but, in the meantime, there might be clues in the house to another likely location. I'll talk to Jane about that.' He rested his hand on the file. 'And to Simon about this.'

Pete grimaced. He didn't want Jane to get into trouble over the file. 'Thing is, my team will need it now, with Tommy being another potential victim of Burton's.'

'Maybe. But they didn't until now. It was specifically not your case or theirs.'

'I know, but it's not like it left the squad room, is it? It didn't get into the public's hands. Or the press.'

'Not this time, but what about next? If I let it lie, you never know. Start of a slippery slope.'

God, what could he say to put Colin off this? 'That's a bit of a leap, isn't it? I'd have thought morale was low enough already, without banging on about data protection rules.' He wanted to say more, but didn't want to over-egg it. With difficulty, he left it at that.

Colin looked at him. 'Maybe.'

What the hell did that mean? But he had to drop it or risk making the DI suspicious. 'Well, I'm off home then.' He looked up at the clock on the wall of Underhill's office. It was 7.17. 'Blimey. I didn't realise it was that late.'

'Early for you, the last few days.'

Pete shrugged. 'True. Lou and Annie'll be shocked.' His shoulders slumped 'But, what am I going to tell them about Tommy?'

'There's nothing to tell until tomorrow, at least. We know he was still alive this afternoon. He was involved in Rosie Whitlock's abduction. But we don't know enough yet to understand the circumstances. And they'll want facts. To know what's going on with him.'

Pete nodded.

'So, keep schtum for now, until you've got something concrete to say.'

'Yeah.'

'Just tell them that the case is almost closed. We've got the girl and the bloke responsible. Leave it at that.'

Standard operating procedure, Pete thought. Same old, same old. Except this wasn't. One way or another, it involved his son.

'Have a beer and an early night,' Underhill told him. 'You've earned it. And tomorrow, you've got a whole pile of paperwork to do.'

Pete grunted. 'Thanks.'

'Goodnight, Pete.'

''Night, Guv.'

*

Darkness enveloped him, inky and oppressive. Ever since the clocks changed, the street lights had gone off at eleven instead of midnight. It was now as dark here in the city, as it would have been in a remote village like Holcomb Burnell.

Bloody council and their bloody cutbacks, he thought. Turning the street lights off might save a bit of cash, but it didn't add to public safety. Did they think about that when they came up with these damn fool ideas?

He turned onto his right side and tried to relax enough to sleep. But sleep wouldn't come.

He had been tossing and turning ever since they came to bed. Beside him, Louise was quiet. He wasn't sure if she was asleep. He thought not and he desperately wanted to talk to her, needed to talk to her. Staying silent was eating him up. Much longer, and he'd lose his marbles entirely, and what good would that be to anyone? He'd be forced to have more time off, this time on sick leave.

But what could he say? What could he tell her?

Nothing, with any degree of certainty.

He punched his pillow, then reached down and scratched yet another tiny itch. They had been springing up here and there, all over his body, ever since he got into bed. He knew they were psychosomatic, but it didn't help stop them any more than ignoring them would.

His phone buzzed softly on the bedside cabinet; he pushed himself up on one elbow and reached for it.

Caller ID said it was Jane Bennett. He pressed the green icon to accept the call. 'Hello,' he said softly.

'Hi, boss. It's Jane.'

'Hold on a sec,' he said and climbed carefully out of bed. He went out to the hallway and headed for the stairs. As he stepped gently down them, he said, 'OK, what's up?'

'We just finished the search of Burton's house. Two things of significance. One: he has had a boy staying with him for some time. Don't know who for sure. Forensics will have to confirm that with DNA. But records show Burton as an only child and a bachelor, which is suggestive.'

Pete stepped carefully over the squeaky stair. 'Yes,' he said dryly.

'Sorry. Pun not intended. The other thing was a secret room in the loft. He's got a darkroom up there. It's not been used for a while. Everything's digital, these days, isn't it? But behind a set of shelves there is a hidden door into another room. No windows. It's set up as a projection room – 35mm, digital and 8mm. And there are stacks of pictures and films in there. I had a quick scan through some of the recent stuff, the digital files. Some of it looks like security-type film from the barn. All stored on a hard drive, linked up to a laptop and a digital projector. There's some pretty sick stuff on there, boss. And some of it includes a boy molesting the girls. You only ever see his back, plus he's always wearing one of those full head masks, like the Mexican wrestlers. No way to identify him. But the girls he's with include Lauren Carter and Rosie.'

Pete reached the kitchen and took a glass from the cupboard to get himself a drink of water. 'OK. Thanks for letting me know, Jane. I'll see you in the morning.'

'Goodnight, boss.'

'Goodnight.' He ended the call, poured himself a glass of water and called Dave.

'Boss?'

'Is he talking yet?'

'No. Still out for the count. He's in recovery. They finished the operation about ten minutes ago.'

Pete sighed and took a mouthful of water. 'Alright. Thanks, Dave. And good job tonight.'

'Cheers.'

'Goodnight.'

''Night, boss.'

Pete ended the call, finished his drink and headed back upstairs. He climbed gently back into bed and settled down.

'So, what's happening?' Louise asked in the darkness.

He blinked. 'Jane's just finished searching the suspect's house. Found plenty of incriminating evidence. And the man himself is still unconscious after the operation to repair his leg, where Dave ran him over with his bike.'

'And?'

'What?'

'I'm not stupid, Pete. There's something more going on. What is it?'

Pete grimaced. She was recovering quickly, if she was noticing things like that. It was disconcerting that she could read him so easily, even in the dark. But then, they had lived together for fifteen years.

'There is more going on,' he admitted, 'but it's not something I can talk about. Not yet. It's still up in the air.'

'Then forget about it until it's settled,' she said. 'Get some sleep.'

Pete couldn't help the chuckle that shook his belly. He wished to God it was as easy as that. He leaned over and kissed her hair. 'I do love you,' he said.

'You hate it when I'm right, though, don't you?'

This time he laughed out loud. 'And there you go being right again.'

Chapter 35

'Morning, Malcolm. How's your pins?' Dave asked brightly, as he walked into the private room at the end of the surgical ward. He gave Burton's knee beneath the blankets a friendly tap, making him wince as he went to the chair beside the bed and sat down.

'You had breakfast yet?' he continued. 'I know they wake you up early in these places. I tell you what, they do a bloody good fry-up in the restaurant here. Had one before I came in. Bacon, sausage, fried egg, hash browns, mushrooms and beans with a slice of toast on the side and a mug of tea.' He smacked his lips. 'Beautiful. Sets you up for the day, it does. And you and me, we've got a long old day ahead of us, eh?'

'Why?' Burton frowned, confused.

'A lot of talking to get done. What d'you reckon? Should I send Mickey, out there, for some tea? Bit of lubrication?'

Burton's confusion turned to doubt.

'Oh, you're safe enough with me,' Dave assured him. 'Only problem is, he won't be there to hear the screams, eh?' He laughed. 'That's the advantage of us talking here, instead of at the station. There's no recorders. Unless I decide to use my phone instead of taking notes. And being a hospital, and a surgical ward, you're expected to holler and wail a bit now and then.'

Burton shifted in the bed. The doubt on his face had turned now to fear. 'You can't do that. I want my lawyer.'

'Your lawyer? What for? I don't need to ask you about what you've done. Between the van, the barn, your attic and the boy's room in your house, we've got all the evidence we need. We hardly even need the girl's testimony. Twenty-five to life is your next stop, matey. Guaranteed. In fact, if I was to rough you up a bit, it would be doing you a favour. Get you accustomed to what your life's about to become. One long round of fear and pain.' He stood up and tapped Burton's plastered leg again, harder this time, then leaned over him. 'No, Malcolm, I'm not here to hear your confession or your excuses. I'm not interested, frankly. The only thing I want from you is to tell me about the boy. What did you do with him? We know he was in the barn yesterday afternoon. The girl told us that much. But he wasn't with you when you got home, so where is he now? What did you do with him?'

'This is where I say I want a deal, isn't it? Then you get my lawyer and your boss and they agree on something between them.'

Dave shook his head slowly. 'You really don't want to see my boss, Malcy. I let him in here, your next stop won't be twenty-five to life, it'll be the mortuary. No way he'd make any deals with you. You tell me or you don't. The only deal you get is, if you don't, you'll find yourself in general population after an accidental leak of what you're in there for. And, by Christ, you'll know what it is to suffer then, believe me. I've seen it and it ain't pretty.' He shook his head again. 'Not pretty at all. So, do you want to tell me or not? Final answer, no conferring.' He stood back, hands in his pockets. 'No?' He shrugged and started for the door. 'OK. We know about your auntie in the village. Have you got any other relatives that we ought to invite to the funeral?'

Burton's eyes widened. 'You wouldn't dare. There'd be an outcry. Police brutality gone amok.'

'What brutality? We won't even be there. Inmates fight amongst themselves all the time. Probably get reported as an accident.

Nobody will ever go to court over it, that's for sure. Anyway, your choice, you live with it. Or not. Bye.'

He headed for the door again and was turning the handle before Burton stopped him again.

'All right. What do you want to know?'

Dave stopped. He turned back to face Burton. The man looked reluctant, still, but he knew he had to give up what he knew. 'I told you. The boy. Who is he? When and where did you abduct him? How have you managed to keep him all this time? And where is he now?' He walked back as far as the foot of Burton's bed and leaned both hands on the metal frame, staring into Burton's pale eyes. 'And the bodies. We've recovered two. How many more are there, who and when?'

Burton was shaking his head. 'I didn't abduct the boy. He took up with me. He spotted me one day, at the park. I was taking pictures. Long lens, sitting in the van under the trees. He saw me and saw what I was doing. Somehow, he recognised me, said if I didn't do what he wanted, he'd go to the authorities and tell them all about me. Next thing I knew, he was in the van, wanting to come back to my house and, once he was there, that was it. He was in. Then, a few days later, he found my files. What could I do? I'm not a killer.'

'So, what are we doing with two bodies in the mortuary, one of which we can certainly tie to you through a witness?'

'I didn't kill them. He did. I'm telling you, he's a vicious little sod. I know you think I'm a pervert, but you haven't seen anything. He's far worse than me. Utterly sick. He came up with scenarios that I'd never have dreamed of, never mind indulged in. I was just a simple voyeur until he came along. I took my pictures, a few videos, and that was it. Girls playing in the park or down on the beach. But he had these ideas, and once he got them in his head, there was no stopping him. It was like he thought he was invincible, could do whatever he liked and get away with it. I had to go along with him. I had my career to think of. He'd have ruined me. He didn't care. He was like some sort of parasite. This wasn't a partnership. It was a user-ship. And not in the direction you think. *He* was using *me*. I'm glad it's over, in some ways. It was getting to be more than I could cope with.'

Dave pushed himself upright and took a deep breath. His whole body was squirming with disgust and contempt, but he couldn't let it show. Not yet. 'So, where is he? You were all set to kill him and the girl. You left her behind, but what have you done with him?'

'You've got it wrong. Him being in the barn – that was his idea. Suffering for his art, he called it. Getting into her good graces so that he could abuse her and she'd go along with it. Leaving her behind was a mistake, yes. There just wasn't time, by the time we spotted the car coming through the trees. But I never set out to kill them.'

'Where is he, Malcolm?'

'I don't know. When it all went belly-up, he cleared off. Said I was no use to him anymore and just went.'

'On foot, from the back of bloody beyond? Come on, Malcolm. Be serious. Where is he?'

'I don't know. I told you: he's gone. You're right – he didn't leave from the barn. I had to give him a lift back into the city. I dropped him off at the Co-op on the Dunsford Road. He took all the cash I had in my pocket and just went. The last I saw of him, he was walking into the Co-op. I swear.'

'You know we can check on that, don't you? And we will.'

Burton dropped his gaze, nodding slowly.

'And the bodies. The girls. How many are there? And when did they die?'

'You've got them. There were just the two.'

Dave already knew the results of the two autopsies. There was no need to pursue the question of who had killed them. 'Just the two? Like just the two drinks, Officer?' He felt his lip curl. 'You know, I don't think I've ever come across anything or anyone that disgusts me as much as you do, Burton. I'll be glad to see you go down, when it happens. And it will. Even if I have to take the day off, I'll be in that court to see you sentenced.' He spun away and walked out of the room, lifting his phone from his pocket as he went. He had to call Pete Gayle and report what Burton had said.

He leaned his back against the wall a few yards along from the entrance to the ward and hit the speed-dial number.

'Dave?'

'Yeah. Don't shoot the messenger, boss. I've just been talking to Malcolm Burton.'

*

'Thanks, Dave.'

Pete put the phone down feeling sick to his stomach.

Burton was a consummate liar and manipulator — it was a common trait among paedophiles — and he was up to his neck in the proverbial. He would say anything to get himself out of the mire. But Rosie was firm in her opinion that Tommy was nothing more than another victim in the whole situation.

Of course, at least part of her story had come from Tommy himself, and Pete could not help but recall Simon Phillips' file on the boy and what interview after interview had said about him — even one with his own sister — but still . . . He could not believe that he had raised the kind of monster that Burton was suggesting. He just couldn't.

He let his head drop forward into his hands.

The only answer was in the evidence. He had to find all there was to find, in order to exonerate his son.

But until he did, what was he going to tell Louise? He had to tell her something. If she found out that Tommy was tied up in all this through the newspapers or the TV, it would devastate her and their marriage. And yet, Lauren Carter's body told an irrefutable story. Tommy had at least partially strangled her. That was a forensic fact. Buton's hands were simply too big to have left the marks on her neck. So, as hard as it was for Pete to stomach, Tommy had to have been complicit in, if not actually guilty of, her murder.

For Louise to find that out now could destroy her.

Pete wiped his hands down his face and glanced around the squad room. His team were studiously ignoring him, getting on with a variety of tasks. He sighed. Then an idea struck him.

He got up and walked quickly down the length of the squad room to knock on the glass of Colin Underhill's door.

Colin looked up from his desk and beckoned.

Pete stepped in. Closing the door carefully behind him, he faced the older man.

'What is it, Pete?'

'We need a watch put on Burton's place.'

'Why?'

'I just talked to Dave Miles. Burton puts all the blame on Tommy. He would, of course. The type of person he is. But, either way, Tommy hasn't come out of the woodwork yet. It's been over twelve hours. If he was going to, he would have by now. So, if he's alive and well, as Burton claims, then he's on the run for whatever reason. And he'll need food, clothes and cash. He could go on a nicking spree or try to sneak home, but he'd see Burton's place as an easier option.'

Colin was nodding in agreement. 'I see what you mean. We haven't got the manpower to do that at the same time as searching the woods around that barn, though.'

'Then I'll assign a member of my team in the meantime. We're wrapping up on Haynes, Enstone and Sanderson, anyway. All that stuff we found at Enstone's and Sanderson's will have to go to CEOP, won't it? We haven't got the resources for an investigation like that.'

'True. We'll make damn sure your team gets the credit for uncovering it all though.'

'There's no need to go stepping on toes for that. As long as it gets dealt with effectively, that's all that matters.'

Underhill pursed his lips. 'Very magnanimous of you, I'm sure. But it's not just you that's involved, is it? Jane, Dave and the rest of them could use the recognition. I've already spoken to DCI Silverstone about it and he's adamant. He wants the team to be recognised.'

Pete nodded. 'Of course he does.'

Fast-track wanted the team recognised, because they'd achieved what they had under his command, albeit without his input. It would reflect well on him.

Underhill looked up at him sternly. 'If I didn't know better, I might think that was a cynical comment, Sergeant.'

'Guv'nor.'

'As for Burton's house, you're right. Put someone there until the search is done, then the uniform branch can take over.'

'OK. Then, if it's all right with you, I'll go and talk to Louise. Tell her what we know before she finds it out on the news or something.'

'Yes.' Colin stood up and came around his desk to clap Pete on the back. 'You do that. I know she's still delicate, emotionally. Take as much time as you need. The paperwork can wait for a day or two.'

'Thanks, Colin.' Pete shook his hand and turned away. 'I won't be any longer than I need to.'

'I know.'

*

'What are you doing here?'

Louise looked up from the TV as he came into the sitting room. 'It's not even lunchtime yet.'

'I know. I need to talk to you, Lou.' He sat down on the sofa beside her, took her hand in his and waited until she met his gaze.

'What is it? It's Tommy, isn't it? What's happened? You've found him? Where is he?' She stiffened, shifting in her seat, her other hand finding his, clutching it like a lifeline.

'Slow down, Lou. Yes, it's Tommy. He's been seen. He . . . We know he was alive, as of yesterday afternoon. But he's disappeared again. We're not sure if he's run away from the man he was with or if he's . . . if he's been killed. The last reported location we have for him, from the man he was with, is the Co-op on the Dunsford Road. They'll have CCTV. It's being checked. If he went in there, we'll know soon and we'll know if he was on his own.'

'Then where is he? Why hasn't he come home?' Her eyes had grown large and brimmed with unshed tears.

'We don't know,' Pete admitted. 'He could just be frightened. He's been with this man for some time. We don't know the details yet. We've got the man in custody, but he's telling a very different story to the one Rosie Whitlock gave us.'

'He was with the Whitlock girl? How?'

'He . . . He was involved in her abduction. Under duress, according to what he told her, but nevertheless, he was there.'

'What do you mean, "according to what he told her"? Of course he was forced into it. Tommy wouldn't hurt anyone.'

Pete grimaced. 'Well, that's the other thing, Lou. I shouldn't have, but I've read Simon Phillips' file on Tommy. He uncovered evidence – and a lot of it – that Tommy's not entirely who we thought he was. There are reports in that file from teachers, other kids, even from Annie, that he was not a nice kid sometimes. He could be cruel. Vicious. You know he was bullied in his last school. He wasn't at the new one. Apparently, he changed. Got wilder, more reckless. Like he had no fear of consequences. No boundaries. It's like there were two sides of him. He could be really nice, especially to girls, although, apparently, some of them thought he was creepy, whatever than means. But if he was confronted, he could turn on a sixpence and be completely remorseless.'

'So, you're saying our son turned into some kind of psycho?

And we didn't see it? I don't believe this.' She was shaking her head repeatedly, like a metronome, unaware that she was doing it. 'How could you even listen to this crap? He's your son, for God's sake! Your own flesh and blood and you sit there condemning him? What kind of father could even do that?' She snatched her hands away and pushed herself back on the sofa, fear and loathing filling her eyes.

Something twisted in Pete's stomach. This wasn't going as he'd hoped – not at all. 'I'm not condemning him. I'm not even accusing him of anything. If you listened to what I said, Lou, I said that he was there. Willingly or not. I'm a police officer. It's just a figure of speech. I want as much as you do, as much as Rosie Whitlock does, to see him proved innocent. Another victim of this bloke he was with. All I'm saying is, there are people out there who'll paint a different picture. And that may be why Tommy's not come home. If he's aware of that, it might scare him into thinking he'll be arrested, accused of being a willing participant in what happened to Rosie and those other girls. And there is evidence, Lou. Forensics. The bloke could twist things around to accuse Tommy instead of himself. These paedophiles do that kind of thing. They're often master manipulators. It's how they get what they want in life. How they get to abuse their victims and get away with it.'

'And this man's going to accuse our son, our Tommy, of being part of what he was clearly a victim of? Can't you disprove it? Can't you fight him?'

'As I said, there is forensic evidence on his side. There's a lot of work still to do, but the surface impression isn't good. That's all I know, at the moment.'

'Then get it looked into more deeply.' She sat forward, her gaze fixed on his with an almost desperate intensity. 'Get everything done that can be done, Pete. We need the truth. The finest details of it, if they can prove this man's setting Tommy up.'

'I know. And it's in hand. But, what I'm saying is, Tommy

doesn't know that. If he's out there, alive and free as I hope he is, then he's probably running scared. Who knows what the man told him? Probably put the fear of God into him with all kinds of nightmare scenarios.'

Behind him, in the hall, the phone rang. Louise jumped violently. Pete stood up and went to answer it.

'Yes?'

'Boss, it's Dave. We've looked through the CCTV from the Co-op on the Dunsford Road, for when Burton claimed to have dropped Tommy off there.'

Fear swooped in Pete's stomach. 'And?'

'Nothing. No sign of him. There's a peripheral view of what could be Burton's Citroën driving past at the right time, but we can't get a registration off it and it doesn't stop. Tommy wasn't there, boss. Burton was lying.'

Pete sagged against the wall, eyes closing, but it wasn't enough. He sat down heavily on the stairs.

'Boss?'

'Yes. Sorry, Dave. I'm still here. Thanks for letting me know. You'll have to have another go at Burton, then.'

'My pleasure, boss.'

'Don't enjoy it too much, Dave. We want to be able to convict the bastard afterwards.'

'True. But priority one's got to be finding Tommy. If he's back to being a misper, then we can pull out all the stops. No stone unturned and no quarter given.'

Pete squeezed his eyes shut as tight as he could, then snapped them open and shook his head. 'You'd best talk that through with Colin. He's my son, so that's me back on the sidelines, isn't it? I've already had orders to that effect.'

Dave went quiet. Pete could almost feel him fighting with himself on the other end of the line. 'I'll keep you posted, boss.'

'Thanks, Dave.' He put the phone down and sat for a moment.

If Tommy wasn't at the Co-op, what else was Burton lying

about? Surely, that deception would discount the rest of his testimony. And, with the victim herself onside, that would mean that Tommy had no case to answer. He'd be considered as another victim.

Pete drew a deep breath and stood up to go back into the sitting room.

Louise looked up as he entered. 'Work?'

'Dave. He's got proof that Burton's lying about Tommy – at least about part of his story.'

She slumped in her seat. 'Thank God! Then . . .' She stood up, took his hands in hers. 'We can reach out to him. Put out a press appeal. Let him know that everything will be all right and he can come home!' She broke off with a sob.

'Nothing's set in stone yet, Lou. We need to finish interrogating Burton. Or Dave does. And how's Tommy going to get to see something like that, if he's on the run? He won't be looking at newspapers and how's he going to see a TV, except in a shop window with no sound? It's not going to be easy to reach him.'

'Then, think!' she shouted. 'Figure it out, because this is our son we're talking about. Our son!' She broke down and cried and Pete leaned in and took her in his arms, trying to comfort her, but she fought him off. 'Don't just sit there,' she sobbed. 'Get out there and fix this.'

'You think I wouldn't, if I could?' He stepped back from her, holding her at arm's length as he stared into her tear-stained face. 'He's my son, too, remember. I know I haven't been the best dad in the world. Christ, if I could go back in time . . .' He shook his head quickly. 'I'll do whatever I can to find him, to bring him back to us. Believe me, I will. I'm just saying, it's not going to be easy or quick. And, in the meantime, I'm going to change my priorities in life. From now on, family comes first, no matter what. The job takes second place.'

'Yeah, I'll believe that when I see it,' she snorted.

'Then believe it. Because you will see it, starting with Tommy.

Somehow – and I don't know how yet – I will get a message to him, to come home. That he's safe. He's loved and needed here.'

He drew her into a hug, stroking her hair with one hand while the other held her close.

They stood like that for a long time, as if in a pause between the steps of a slow dance. He could feel her face buried into his neck, her arms around his body, breasts pressed into his chest. Even their thighs were in contact. God, he had missed this closeness over the past few months! Finally, they were fitting together like they used to – like two halves of the same being. Yin and yang. It was like the part of him that had been missing all this time was suddenly back in place. He was whole again. The hollow space, that he had barely been aware of in a conscious sense, was filled – perfectly and completely.

He moved his hand down from her hair to her back, pulling her in even tighter, squeezing with not just his arms but his whole body in an intense but gentle reaffirmation of their one-ness together. He kissed her hair.

'I'm sorry,' he breathed.

'What for?' she murmured.

'For not being here for you, or for Tommy and Annie as much as I should have been.'

Her arms tightened around him and she clung to him. 'It's not just you. I haven't been the best, lately. And even before . . .'

He stroked her hair again. 'You're the best mother I know. The only one our kids have got and the only one they want. We will get through this together. I promise.'

He felt her stiffen for the briefest moment, then she relaxed into him once again. 'I know.'

No Place to Hide

**A house fire. A suspicious death.
A serial killer to catch.**

When a body is found in a house fire DS Peter Gayle is called to the scene. It looks like an accidental death, but the evidence just doesn't add up.

With only one murder victim they can't make any calls, but it looks like a serial killer is operating in Exeter and it's up to Pete to track him down.

But with his wife still desperate for news on their missing son and his boss watching his every move, the pressure is on for Pete to bring the murderer to justice before it is too late.

No Way Home

**A dead body. A mysterious murder.
A serial killer on the loose.**

A taxi driver is found murdered in a remote part of Exeter. He is a family man with no enemies to be found.

The only physical evidence is dozens of fingerprints inside the cab. How will DS Peter Gayle ever track down his killer?

Then another cab driver is found dead. Now this isn't just a case of one murder, but a serial killer on the loose . . .

Acknowledgements

Thanks once again to former Thames Valley Police Officer Rick Ell and his wife Christine for their invaluable advice on technical matters, and to my wife Pru for . . . too much to list here.

Also to Charlotte Mursell and everyone else at HQ Digital for their hard work and insight. And to Kathy Gale, who suggested I step onto this road in the first place. Although it's a detour from the direction I was going in, it has been a joy getting to know Pete Gayle and his team and sharing their adventures and adversities.

Which brings me to you – the readers who have come along for the ride. Without you, there would be no point to this journey, so thank you for the interest you have taken in my work and all the messages of support I've received. I really appreciate you all. This last year has been a hell of a ride – long may it continue.

Dear Reader,

We hope you enjoyed reading this book. If you did, we'd be so appreciative if you left a review. It really helps us and the author to bring more books like this to you.

Here at HQ Digital we are dedicated to publishing fiction that will keep you turning the pages into the early hours. Don't want to miss a thing? To find out more about our books, promotions, discover exclusive content and enter competitions you can keep in touch in the following ways:

JOIN OUR COMMUNITY:

Sign up to our new email newsletter:
http://smarturl.it/SignUpHQ

Read our new blog www.hqstories.co.uk

X https://twitter.com/HQStories

f www.facebook.com/HQStories

BUDDING WRITER?

We're also looking for authors to join the HQ Digital family!
Find out more here:

https://www.hqstories.co.uk/want-to-write-for-us/

Thanks for reading, from the HQ Digital team